ROCAMORA RISING

ROCAMORA RISING

BY

DONALD MICHAEL PLATT

www.penmorepress.com

ROCAMORA RISING

Rocamora Rising by Donald Michael Platt

ISBN-13: 978-1-957851-32-7(Paperback)
ISBN -13:978-1-957851-31-0 (e-book)

BISAC Subject Headings:
HIS045000 HISTORY / Europe / Spain &Portugal
FIC032000FICTION / War&Military
FIC031020FICTION / Thrillers / Historical

Editors: Lauren McElroy, Chris Wozney

Front Cover and Back Cover Illustration by
EMILIJA RAKIĆ

Address all correspondence to:
Michael James
Penmore Press LLC
920 N Javelina Pl
Tucson AZ 85748
mjames@penmorepress.com

DEDICATION

Kurt Jakucz, Susie Stephenson Jaeger, and June Mizuki Kingdon. Kurt saved my life after I suffered a UTI attack night of June 27-28, 2022, which rendered me unconscious and hallucinating on my bathroom floor, and with no food and water during four days and nights. Failing to reach me by phone or e-mail, or by knocking on my door, Kurt called the police July 1, 2022.

After I was taken to a hospital, Kurt and Susie protected my possessions, finances, and writing during my six-and-a-half month hospitalization and therapy. They also found a retirement home for me while I was in therapy. Kurt and Susie had much stress going on in their lives while caring for me until my mind cleared and I regained control of my body.

June Mizuki Kingdon, AP European History student at Fairfax High School, class of 1983, at Los Angeles, organized a celebration and honoring of my teaching and writing in May of 2017. My former students from 1970-1987 attended, some with spouses and children.

Also, while I recuperated from my UTI, June alerted many on the Internet about my hospitalization, contacted me regularly, and sent surprises to cheer me.

For all that I am eternally grateful to Kurt, Susie, and June.

Previously

Yo soy un hombre...
I am a man...
Limpio de sangre y jamás
Pure of blood and never
De hebrea o mora manchada
Stained by Hebrew or Moor.

— Lope de Vega, Captain Alonso de Contreras,
and other Spanish Old Christians

ROCAMORA RISING is the third historical novel in the Rocamora saga. My first novel in the series, *Rocamora, Man of Masks*, currently published by Penmore Press, was a finalist in the Historical Fiction Category at the 2013 International Book Awards.

Little-known historical individuals who led exceptional lives arouse my interest. The less documented about them the freer I am to create character motivation and an entertaining story line. Also, I enjoy playing "detective" and unearthing previously unknown facts about them, some contrary to certain established descriptions. That is why I selected Vicente de Rocamora, 1601-1684, to be the protagonist of my two novels *Rocamora* and *House of Rocamora*. He went from Dominican Royal Confessor until 1643 to esteemed Jewish physician in Amsterdam at age 47 to his death at age 83. Several anomalies in his life piqued my curiosity, and the few available facts about him in Spain are unexplained. Rocamora is mentioned in footnotes, sentences, and paragraphs in books about Judaizers and new-Christians who fled Spain and Portugal in the sixteenth, seventeenth, and eighteenth centuries, in others about the Sephardic community of Amsterdam, and in both Jewish and Valencian encyclopedias. Yet, according to my research and that of others on my behalf, no book, monograph, or extended article in any historical journal has been written about, to quote Cecil Roth, "... *this most extraordinary if not the most profound of Manasseh's (ben Israel) physician friends.*"

I first encountered Vicente de Rocamora when I read Roth's *A History of the Marranos* in the late 1950s, and the idea for a novel gestated over decades. In 1990, I initiated intensive research into his life and times and discovered little more about him than what had been repeated in books and encyclopedias mentioned above. I have italicized basic known facts about his life and added my comments.

Rocamora was born in Valencia into a Marrano or new-Christian family. I found no documentation to confirm if he was born in the city or somewhere else in the kingdom, no evidence of his parents, and no proof that he or they Judaized in Spain.

In the 1600s all historic male De Rocamoras were certified as *limpio* old Christians and members of the *caballero* caste or titled *Condes* and *Marqueses*. Some were Knights of Santiago, which required certificates of *limpieza de sangre*.

Rocamora was educated for the Church. I discovered no documentation explaining why he entered the Dominican Order. Did he come from an impoverished family and seek food and shelter within the Church? Did he experience a calling to be a monk? Was he a *segundón*, a second son, forced into the clergy by his family to help advance them socially?

Rocamora would have been sixteen when he matriculated at the College of Confessors of Santo Domingo in the cathedral town of Orihuela at the southern end of Valencia, now part of Alicante, and about twenty-five miles from Murcia.

Orihuela in 1617 was the home of Don Jerónimo de Rocamora y Roda García Lassa, Señor de Rafal, Señor de Benferri, Barón de la Puebla de Rocamora, Knight of Santiago and *maestro de campo de infantería*. Nearby resided his cousin Don Francisco de Rocamora y Maza, another renowned solder and Señor de la Granja de Rocamora, whose brother Tomás was a Dominican lector and polemicist.

Other de Rocamoras of the caballero caste resided in Murcia. Were they and Vicente kin? I did discover they were.

Were any of them descended from conversos? It is possible, on their maternal sides. In 1391, during a great pogrom, all the Jews of Orihuela and most in the Kingdom of Valencia chose conversion over death or exile.

Vicente would have graduated as a Dominican confessor at age twenty in 1621. That year, sixteen-year-old Philip IV was crowned King of Spain, and his tutor, the Count—soon to be Count-Duke—de Olivares, became his chief minister for the following twenty-two years.

Rocamora was the confessor and spiritual director for Infanta María, Philip's younger sister. I did not discover exactly when Vicente arrived in Madrid or who sponsored him at *la Corte*. To be a royal confessor, he would have needed a certificate of *limpieza de sangre*, purity of blood untainted by Jew, Moor, or recent converts.

Vicente and María, b. 1606, were separated in age by only five years. I discovered no direct explanation why so protected an *Infanta* of Spain was allowed to have so young a confessor. Except for her brothers, the *Infanta* had no personal contact with males close to her age. María's *meninas* slept at the foot of her bed. Her only private moments would have been when she retired to her privy, prayed or confessed.

A pawn to be used in a diplomatic marriage, the *Infanta* faced a convent-prison if she did not wed one of three eligible men: her nephew, a dauphin of France not yet born; the Prince of Wales, provided he converted to the True Faith; and her cousin Ferdinand, son of HRE Emperor Ferdinand II.

One clue suggests when and why Rocamora was appointed the *Infanta*'s confessor and spiritual director. Olivares removed Maria's reactionary confessors and replaced them with his "men" in 1621, before the heretic Prince of Wales arrived in Madrid to woo the *Infanta* in 1623.

María honored Rocamora, showered him with gifts, confessed often, and remembered him fondly after she left Spain at age twenty-three to marry her Cousin Ferdinand, King of Hungary and future Holy Roman Emperor.

Can we ever know the true relationship between María and Vicente? Perhaps the answer lies in the old Spanish saying, "No man is closer to a woman than her confessor, not her father, not her brother, not her husband."

A fashionable confessor, Rocamora was renowned for his piety and eloquence. I discovered nothing significant about Vicente's life at Court after María left Spain in December of 1629. Did he harangue victims of the Inquisition in the dungeons while they were tortured, at *autos de fe* where they were scourged and shamed, and at the *quemadero* before they were burned? Was he an Olivarista, a supporter of the Count-Duke's attempts to remove the *limpieza* statutes and end inquisitorial investigations of new-Christians without proof of their Judaizing? Did he alert denounced New-Christians to flee Spain when they were about to be arrested?

Vicente also became a protégé of Grand Inquisitor Fray Antonio Sotomayor who held no *autos de fe* of Jews in Madrid during his tenure.

While Vicente was at Court, Philip IV made Don Francisco de Rocamora hereditary First Conde de la Granja de Rocamora and Knight of Santiago in 1628, and Don Jerónimo de Rocamora hereditary First Marqués de Rafal in 1636 and Knight of Santiago. In 1642, Tomás de Rocamora was appointed Dominican Provincial of Aragon and in 1644 Bishop and Viceroy of Mallorca. Surely, they and Vicente would have interacted over the years.

In 1643, Rocamora disappeared from court and went to Amsterdam where he declared himself a Jew, and took the name Isaac Israel de Rocamora. Why did he leave Spain in 1643 and not before or later? My research confirmed Rocamora was never denounced to the Inquisition, nor was his effigy paraded at an *auto de fe* and burned at the *quemadero* as commonly happened after others fled Spain and identified as Jews.

The most likely reason Rocamora left Spain in 1643 is the Count-Duke de Olivares fell from power, and a reactionary bigot, Diego Arce y Reynoso, replaced the relatively benign Antonio de Sotomayor as Inquisitor General.

The Holy Office and Rocamora's family in Spain may have, wherever possible, destroyed evidence of his existence in Spain because Church and Crown would have been embarrassed to lose so highly placed a friar to the Jews. His kin might have done the same for fear of scandal and denunciation to the Inquisition. One example of such a policy occurred when Olivares was painted over as if he had never existed on Velázquez' *Infante Baltazar Carlos at the Riding Academy.*

In Amsterdam, many in the Jewish Spanish-Portuguese community did not trust or accept Rocamora because he never Judaized in Spain and was still a Dominican of the order controlling the Inquisition. Also it was illegal for Jews to convert a Christian in Amsterdam.

Rocamora Rising

The historical Vicente de Rocamora does something unique upon his arrival in Amsterdam. It is the dramatic conclusion of my novel. Rocamora circumcises himself, declares he is now a Jew, and takes the name Isaac Israel, the latter name added in place of his father's, who never Judaized.

I cover the second half of Rocamora's life in a sequel, *HOUSE OF ROCAMORA*, also published by Penmore Press.

Rocamora did not immediately join the Sephardic community in Amsterdam. His life from 1643 to 1645 is undocumented, with the exception of Rabbi Manasseh ben Israel who became his good friend and introduced him to his Christian scholar acquaintances as a trophy.

In August 1645, as Isaac Israel de Rocamora, Vicente matriculated at the University of Leyden Medical School. There is no evidence that he followed the Law of Moses during his two years there.

Rocamora received his license to practice medicine on the 29th of March, 1647, and in July wed twenty-five-year-old Abigail Moses Toro (Toura). He joined the Sephardic community of Amsterdam, sired nine children over the next eleven years, and established a multi-generational dynasty of physicians.

One may speculate regarding to what degree Rocamora had been celibate in Spain. During his years in Amsterdam, Rocamora practiced medicine and earned a reputation as a philanthropist.

The late Helga Becker Leeser, a genealogist in the Netherlands, found for me a transcript of a lecture about Rocamora by Jack Zwartz given in 1934. It had documentation from the Municipal Archives of Amsterdam which does not appear in any other source I have seen where Rocamora's name appears. That information altered the original course of my novel.

In 1650, after the birth of his second child, Rocamora almost converted to the Dutch Reformed Church because he found the restrictions and prohibitions of the Sephardic community to be as intolerable as those of Spanish Catholicism. Zwartz describes Rocamora as a freethinker.

In 1660, Rocamora received full membership in the Amsterdam Collegium Medicum, and citizenship equal to that of Dutch Christians, one of only three Jewish physicians in seventeenth-century Amsterdam to be so honored.

The Municipal Archives of Amsterdam have no documents showing Rocamora owned taxable property or wealth accrued through imports and exports. Did they exist at one time, or is there another, still unknown, reason why he was so honored?

Known as an Ornament of his Community, Rocamora was mentioned as a philanthropist and a gifted poet in Latin and Spanish, but none of his writing is extant. He appeared prominently in David Levi de Barrios' Aplauso Harmónico, *published in 1683, which outlined his life and accomplishments. He died in April 1684.*

Rocamora and Abigail raised their children in the Sephardic version of Judaism and celebrated its holy days. Through his second son, Salomon, Rocamora seeded a multigenerational line of physicians. His descendants married amongst the following families: Méndez da Costa, da Costa Athias, Valhe del Saldanha, Santcroos, Gaon, Abarbanel, Brandón, de la Penha, Ricardo, Cassuto, Abendena Méndez, and Abendena Belmonte.

In his will of 1676, Vicente-Isaac de Rocamora commanded his second son, Salomon, to take care of his eldest, Moses, "who is slow of wit."

I did not discover if Moses' slowness was caused by a birth defect or a later injury. His fictional grandson Jacob Moses will become the protagonist of *ROCAMORA RISING*.

What follows is the connection I mentioned between Vicente and the de Rocamoras of Orihuela and Murcia.

About 1265 CE, Pierre Román, a second son of the Sieur de Roquemaure on the Rhone River, who was a nephew of Louis VIII of France, joined the army of Jaime of Aragon, aka the Conqueror, who drove the Moors from Valencia and Murcia. As a reward for Pierre Román's heroism, Jaime bestowed upon him entails of land near Orihuela and Murcia. Pierre Román next "Castilianized" his name to Pedro Ramón de Rocamora. The de Rocamoras of Rafal, Benferri, and Granja de Rocamora, and others in Murcia, were his descendants.

Vicente's descendant Rachael David de Rocamora married Judah Cassuto in 1828, and her brother, Isaac David de Rocamora, married Judah's sister Miriam Cassuto in Hamburg. In 1992, the Cassuto family donated documents to the *Bibliotheka Rosenthal* in the Netherlands. Helga Becker-Leeser, a genealogist researching on my behalf, found two items of interest amongst them. One was a legal decision from 1660 confirming Isabella de Rocamora's right to succeed as Condeza de la Granja de Rocamora against a plaintiff kin of "impure" blood.

A second legal document records a dispute over inherited property in Murcia dated 1737. The principal plaintiff was Joseph (not spelled José or Josip) Nicolás de Rocamora. I do not know how or when these documents left Spain or who brought them to Amsterdam or Hamburg.

Also, on 12 July 1740, Bourbon King Felipe V signed a royal *cédulo* for another Francisco de Rocamora, *Deán* of the cathedral in Orihuela, asserting that he was *limpio*, contrary to calumnies.

The name "Rocamora" translates as "Rock of the Moors," and *mora* also is the Latin genus for the mulberry. Both a rock and mulberries appear on the noble de Rocamora heraldry. Two *fleur de lys* show the de Rocamoras' origins in Roquemaure on the Rhone. Thus, according to my research, two common errors have been exposed: the patrilineal de Rocamoras were indeed Old Christians, and Rocamora never Judaized while in Spain. If he had any Jewish blood it would have come from a maternal ancestor, a likely scenario be-

cause, as stated earlier, all Jews of Orihuela and most throughout Spain chose to convert or flee to Portugal rather than die or go into exile during the great pogrom of 1391.

In 2013 I had an interesting exchange of emails with Rick Rocamora, a direct descendant of Vicente-Isaac through his granddaughter, Lea Salomon. He told me family tradition accepts as fact that Vicente-Isaac was an atheist and always sat in the last row of the Amsterdam synagogue. Many pairs of de Rocamora first cousins married each other over generations. He also had access to a copy of a portrait of the aforementioned Tomás de Rocamora from another descendant of Vicente de Rocamora, Alfonso Cassouto, composer and conductor of the Portuguese National Orchestra. No portrait of Vicente-Isaac de Rocamora has been found; Tomás de Rocamora was Vicente's second cousin, the same as his brother Francisco, 1st Conde de la Granja de Rocamora. Philip IV appointed Tomás Bishop and Viceroy of Mallorca. Did he and Vicente resemble each other?

I answered many of the questions posed above from my research, with my imagination, and, I like to believe, with some logic, all entertaining and informative for the reader. Perhaps my novels may encourage scholars to research further Vicente and de Rocamora contemporaries with him. Until then, if, as Napoleon said, "History is a myth men agree upon," let mine be the definitive myth.

My third novel, *ROCAMORA RISING*, follows the life, adventures, and romances of Vicente de Rocamora's fictional grandson Jacob Moses de Rocamora, set during the reigns of the last English Stuarts and Hanoverian George I. He appears first in *HOUSE OF ROCAMORA*.

Part One
Glorious Revolution
1688-1691

"Envious and foule Disease, could there not be
One beauty in an Age, and free from thee?"

— *Ben Johnson, 1616*
"An Epigram to the Smallpox"

"My *Lady* she Complain'd our Love was coarse,
our *Poetry*
Unfit for modest *Ears,* small *Whores,* and *Play'rs*
Were of our Hair-brain'd *Youth,* the only cares;
Who were too wild for any virtuous *League,*
Too rotten to consummate the Intrigue."

— **Satyr**, "Poem on Several Occasions
By the Right Honourable The E.of R—"

CHAPTER ONE
PERSONAL SACRAMENT

Twenty-three-year-old Dutch cavalry captain Jacob Moses de Rocamora awakened several hours before a cold late September dawn, according to a gold-plated clock beneath flickering candlelight from a sconce on a nearby mantel. He moved deeper under scarlet velour covers against Lady Joan Fairfield, asleep in her suite at Prince William of Orange's palace in The Hague.

Lady Joan's toy Spaniel, Milady, a royal gift from Charles II's kennels, licked Jacob's face. He'd been together with Lady Joan for seven months. Never before had he felt true love, which had begun the instant they'd met. Joan, sun-bright, smiled at first sight of Jacob, and soon she ended his self-imposed celibacy.

Prior to Lady Joan, Jacob had experienced remorse, emptiness, and frustration after "playing at rumpscuttle"—as his English soldiers phrased it—with this wench or that doxy. With Joan, Jacob preferred using a more playful description he created, *making moofkie-foofkie.*

With Joan, Jacob experienced true affection and passion. He did not want to be mistaken as an opportunist because he loved Joan as he had no other before her. He accepted as truth Joan's assertion that he was her first lover of choice.

"Jacob."

"Joan, I tried not to awaken you.""So pleased you did.""Joan wrapped her arms and legs around Jacob's six-foot-three-inch body, and they made love as one.

Afterward, Joan rested her head on Jacob's chest. "Never have I said this to any man. Jacob, I want to marry you. And I want to have your children."

"Joan, you are my personal Sacrament. Because you are Princess Mary's lady-in-waiting, we will need her permission."

"I am confident Her Highness will approve. I have spoken often about you to Princess Mary."

Chapter Two

William and Mary

One week later, Jacob obeyed a summons to appear in The Hague Palace throne room. The room was furnished in the French style and William and Mary sat on their thrones, on a dais, attended by his staff and her ladies. Ambassador Dirck Van Noordwijk, Jacob's mentor and second father, and Colonel Randall MacFarlane, his regimental commander, stood among William's staff. Lady Joan stood closest to Mary.

Jacob genuflected before Prince William III of Orange-Nassau and Princess Mary Stuart, getting his first close look at the royal first cousins. Mary was the Protestant daughter of William's Catholic uncle, James II of England, and the niece of their deceased uncle Charles II. They could not have been more mismatched in appearance and manner. William was no more than five feet six in height, slight of build, and dour of personality, while Mary was close to six feet tall and had the handsome looks of the Stuarts along with a facial expression of one ready for merriment.

Jacob stood tall again. William addressed him between asthmatic coughs. "Captain Jacobus de Rocamora, the number and quality of your partisans along with your success as a cavalry officer impress us."

William's commanding deep voice, Roman nose, and forceful personality all impressed Jacob. He realized that William must never be underestimated.

"As a result of Colonel MacFarlane's Recommendations and Ambassador Van Noordwijk's confirmation, we add you to our staff with the rank of Major," William continued.

Before Jacob found his voice Mary approached him carrying a scarlet sash decorated with three gold rosettes. She attached it to his doublet. "Congratulations, Major."

Damn! Mary is most desirable. Fortunately, I still prefer Lady Joan, but not by much.

Mary returned to her ladies, and William spoke again to Jacob. "Major, we shall be removing King James from his throne, and England shall be our new home. The English do not welcome foreigners easily, so we believe it best to Anglicize our names. We have replaced our Dutch given name Willem with William. Your given name Jacob suggests Jacobites, followers of King James. We have learned that many of your English soldiers refer to you as Captain Jack, and that de Rocamora is a Spanish surname. Consider also changing your surname to Rockmore."

Jacob did not protest, although he took great pride in his surname and all it represented. Mary prevented Jacob from offending William when she announced her support for a marriage between Lady Joan and Jacob to take place before the Army sailed to England.

After applause and cheering abated, William stood. "Major Jack Rockmore, your wedding will take place according to the Established Church of England. You may no longer be a Collegian, the least Christian Protestant sect of all."

And Anglican Christianity is but one step away from Rome.

Lady Joan kissed Jacob to much applause.

William gestured for Colonel MacFarlane to approach. "Have you decided upon a replacement for Major Rockmore? We pray it is not that vexatious nuisance Lord Lyndby."

"Your Highness, Major Rockmore and I have agreed upon his replacement."

"Inform us when your decision is announced."

APTER THREE

VEXATIOUS NUISANCE

The cavalry regiment assembled on a vast grassy field near The Hague Palace. Jacob sat on his black Frisian Hannibal beside his mounted regimental colonel, Sir Randall MacFarlane, a martinet but a fair-minded Presbyterian and capable soldier. His Scots burr confounded Jacob at times, but not today.

"Congratulations again, Major Rockmore. Are you ready to announce your replacement, the captain of your former squadron?"

"Yes, Sir. Lieutenant Henry Lambert. The men would follow him anywhere."

"But Lord Lyndby will assert his right to lead by title and birth. How shall we prevent that vexatious nuisance from doing that?" McFarlane asked.

"We cannot. Only His Highness has sufficient authority. Most likely Lyndby will petition Prince William, who despises him."

Jacob had been told Lyndby's father and an older brother had supported the failed Monmouth revolt against papist James II in 1685. After they surrendered, King James's chief justice, Jeffries, had condemned them and other prominent rebels to be hanged, drawn, quartered, and beheaded.

Lyndby had been too young to fight, and he and his mother resided safely at their Barbados plantation whilst King James gave their entailed lands in England to one of his supporters. Lyndby had petitioned Prince William to restore his title and lands once he'd defeated James II.

Jacob faced his cavalry squadron, who'd received three months' pay in advance of the invasion. He advised them not to spend it foolishly on women and gambling. Jacob next announced his transfer to Prince William's staff and promotion to major.

Arrogant twenty-one year old Edmund Wilmot, putative 3rd Earl of Lyndby, accompanied by his manservant slave, Ramses, confronted Jacob and MacFarlane. "By breeding and title I should be made captain of this cavalry squadron."

MacFarlane deferred to Jacob. Ramses, who shadowed his master everywhere, interested Jacob. Although a slave, Ramses had near identical features to Lyndby except for more of a saddle nose and thicker lips. His eyes were the same color blue, his skin more golden, and his reddish hair was curly.

Jacob guessed they were half-brothers. Most likely Ramses' maternal grandparents had been a typical pairing of an Irish slave and a black African to create mulattos, and their mulatta daughter must have been raped by Lyndby's father. Ramses received relentless verbal abuse from Lyndby, and resentment clouded his eyes; the scar across his left cheek indicated much physical mistreatment.

Jacob glared at Lyndby. "My decision has been approved by our regimental commander," he said. Jacob beckoned a lieutenant to approach. "Henry Lambert, you are promoted to captain. You shall take immediate command of this cavalry squadron."

The men cheered and congratulated Lambert.

"Impossible," Lyndby grumbled. His face reddened, his eyes bulged, and the veins on his temples enlarged. "I shall speak to their Highnesses of your foul and insulting decision."

"Do as you wish. If you prefer, 'Your Lordship,' I can also allow the men to vote between you and Captain Lambert."

Lyndby prepared to draw his sword. "Vote? This rabble cannot vote in England. Are you deliberately insulting me?"

"If you want satisfaction, I shall be happy to oblige. Your choice of weapons."

Lyndby released his hand from the hilt. "You are too far beneath me, Dutchman, to condescend to a duel. In England, I'd have my lackeys deal with you."

"We're not in England, and I can trace my paternal lineage well beyond yours, to the houses of Arnulf and King David."

Lyndby slapped Ramses' face. "Why are you loitering here? And you, Dutchman, one day we'll meet again, and then I shall have satisfaction."

A hollow threat. Jacob watched them set out toward the palace. He'd observed Ramses' murderous expression before and after Lyndby's slap.

How much more abuse can this mulatto tolerate??

*****

Jacob awakened drenched in perspiration. Lady Joan slept undisturbed. He set Milady aside and slid from under their well-covered bed.

Behind a floral tapestry screen, Jacob peed into his personal "looking glass," as the English called their chamber pots. He sponged his face and torso with rose-scented water from a porcelain bowl atop a table. A curvilinear gilt-framed wall mirror above reflected Lady Joan still asleep in bed, despite repeated licking by Milady.

Daughter of an ambitious squire, thirty-three year old Lady Joan continued to be renowned as one of England's great beauties. At age fifteen she'd caught the connoisseurs' eyes of both Sir John Ridgely of Fairfield, whom she'd wed, and Charles II. Court painter Lely had immortalized Lady Joan in several dazzling portraits. The king had made Joan's husband Duke of Fairfield, just as he had bestowed titles on the spouses of other favorite mistresses.

Jacob added kindling on smoking embers for more heat in Lady Joan's suite. She awakened and beckoned Jacob to return to bed. "Must you leave me bereft of your company so soon, my inexhaustible lover?"

"Because you are irresistible, I shall linger until the final moment possible."

Jacob had enjoyed yet another night with widowed Lady Joan, the aggressor in their relationship.

Their first night together, Jacob had learned that Lady Joan had skills in lovemaking he'd never imagined possible.

"Come here."

"Your Grace..."

"Can you not address me as 'Joan'?"

"I fear I might commit a gaffe in public were I to become too comfortable using your given name."

Jacob sat beside the voluptuous blonde and held her hand, concerned. She used her other hand to pet Milady. He'd assumed her sweat had been the result of their intense lovemaking, but now no cause existed for it to continue.

"When we wed, you will have a title of your own after my good friend Mary Stuart is queen of England. You know I have her ear as lady-in-waiting."

Jacob well understood that playing stud for an amorous titled mare could make a man's career in England. "I cannot think of marriage until William and Mary rule England."

"When will that be? I shall be a gap-tooth old hag by the time Prince William overthrows our Catholic tyrant, King James."

"You will always glow with the fresh loveliness of an adolescent, and your beauty is far greater than its fame."

"Flatterer."

"No flattery, 'Tis but an objective appreciation of your charms."

A long minute of silence followed.

"For shame. You have deserted me already for your thoughts."

"I apologize for that, Joan."

"That is better. I find names to be important, more so than titles. I do not approve your allowing the men in your cavalry squadron to address you as 'Captain Jack.' It is a low class, common, vulgar name."

"Protestant soldiers hate the name 'James,' the English equivalent of Jacob, and the Catholic king's adherents are known as Jacobites. Thus my given name is awkward for them. Some of my fellow Dutchmen call me 'Jacobus.'"

"Then you must assume another given name."

"Have you a preference?"

"Any good English name will do. William, Edward, Henry."

"Perhaps we should try Saxon names. Aethelred De Rocamora? Or Arthur, Lancelot, Gawain... Gareth?"

"Oh, Jacob..."

He silenced Lady Joan with a kiss. Her face tasted of salt; her body was still sweat-soaked.

Lady Joan screamed, startling Milady, and touched her temples. "My head."

Jacob felt Joan's hot, moist forehead. *Fever.* He hurried to a window and parted the heavy drapes. Clear dawn illuminated Joan's bedroom. Jacob saw rashes now visible on Lady Joan's face. He recognized them as the first symptoms of *de vreselijkste aller harpije*, smallpox, the worst of all harpies, a metaphor for the vicious beasts of Greek mythology who came with the west wind and brought unbearable suffering and death.

"Joan, you are not well. I must leave you now to summon a physician."

*****

Jacob hurried through the palace corridors toward the apartments of the palace physicians. He feared for Lady Joan's life. Jacob doubted any had the knowledge of his grandfather, Vicente-Isaac de Rocamora, who had prevented further smallpox contagion amongst his patients' families, but not by the common treatment of bloodletting and purges inducing vomit.

Whilst a boy, Jacob had watched his grandfather apply remedies proven efficacious by Indian and Chinese physicians: rubbing pus from a smallpox victim into healthy family members' skin lesions, or blowing powdered smallpox scabs into their noses. If that treatment brought on a mild case of the disease, a patient might become immune to its worst effects. Most families Isaac de Rocamora treated had given their consent, so great was their trust in his skills and knowledge.

Jacob believed he would not be infected by Lady Joan. His grandfather had applied those remedies to his wife and children during a smallpox outbreak.

Smallpox had become a greater scourge throughout England and Europe than plague, leprosy, and the French sickness also known as the Great Pox. The foul-smelling disease could be fatal or leave survivors disfigured. During epidemics, it afflicted all classes and brought down royal dynasties. Prince William III's father had died of the pox a week before William was born, in 1650, and his mother had died from it a decade later. He himself had barely survived the plague.

Jacob hoped his diagnosis was wrong and Lady Joan had, at worst, measles. If indeed he was correct, he prayed Lady Joan did not have hemorrhagic smallpox, sometimes called "bloody pox" or "black pox," which was more likely to lead to death. As with all types of pox, early signs included fever, headache, chills, nausea, vomiting and severe muscle aches. Uneven rashes covered the face, identical to the symptoms of measles. Next, small blisters appeared, similar to the lesions of chickenpox and those seen in measles.

When Jacob had visited patients with his grandfather, he'd seen worsened symptoms. The skin took on a deep purple color. The mucous membranes in the nose and mouth bled, and more blood appeared in patients' stools and urine.

Vain Lady Joan might well prefer death to disfigurement, he thought.

*****

Jacob sent a palace physician to Lady Joan and hastened to the royal apartments to keep his appointment with the elderly Dirck van Noordwijk. The ambassador awaited him in a crowded antechamber decorated in the French style.

"You are almost late, Jacob. Lady Joan delayed you?"

"Yes, and I believe she has smallpox."

Van Noordwijk paled. "Then we must have an immediate audience with Their Highnesses."

At the gilded carved doors of the royal suites, Van Noordwijk whispered to an officer guarding them. The soldier opened a door and relayed the ambassador's message to the chamberlain.

Moments later, Jacob and van Noordwijk genuflected before Prince William III of Orange-Nassau and his first-cousin-and-wife, Princess Mary Stuart.

Jacob described Lady Joan's symptoms. William frowned, concerned. "We must prevent an epidemic. It will delay our invasion. And you, my wife, must quarantine yourself and all others who have not yet had that deadly scourge."

Mary rose. "Yesterday, Lady Joan complained her chambermaid was ill with fever, and we ordered her quarantined. With your permission, Sire, we shall withdraw and see to the condition of all women and men in the palace. We shall demand more quarantines if necessary."

William consented and confronted Jacob. "There is likelihood you have been infected."

"No, Your Highness, for I have been inoculated against smallpox by my grandfather, whom you knew, the physician Isaac de Rocamora."

"Yes, we remember your grandfather well. But, first, apprise your regimental colonel of our decision. And, Ambassador, we have a mission for you." William handed van Noordwijk a sealed scroll. "You must leave again for Amsterdam, this very day, with these instructions."

Jacob returned to Lady Joan's bedroom. She greeted him with tears, and lamented, "The physicians say I have smallpox but do not know if it will be the black scourge."

"Perhaps it is not."

"'Perhaps' you say, but you do not know. I was at Court when King Charles II suffered a stroke in the winter of 1665. His physicians applied cures worse than the affliction."

Jacob listened, horrified, to what physicians had done to their king. They assumed he had apoplexy. They bled him daily, up to sixteen ounces, and again each night. They also shaved his head, blistered him with irons, and applied enemas.

"Jacob, those physicians tortured poor Charles until his death in February 1685. Had I access to a poison, I would have given it to Charles and brought him peace." Lady Joan reached for Jacob's hand. "Promise me, promise me—if I do have the black pox and my pustules do not break outside but inside, to mix with my blood, I beg you... give me a poison that will hasten my death, to spare further pain and disfigurement."

Unprepared for Lady Joan's request, Jacob calmed her with false assurances. He faced a moral dilemma. In his collection of efficacious medicines and balms, which he'd inherited from his grandfather, he also had lethal reptile, spider, and blue frog venom. Jacob had enough affection for Lady Joan to oblige her.

But do I have courage to play God, hasten Joan's inevitable death and spare her more pain and suffering?

CHAPTER THREE

WEARING THE WILLOW

Jacob stood amongst hordes of soldiers and sailors at the embarkation Port of Hellevoetsluis where the Haring Vliet emptied into the North Sea. He saluted his former cavalry squadron, led by Lambert, as they boarded their ship. Grooms herded neighing horses up planks to other vessels.

As Jacob expected, William and Mary had rejected Lord Lyndby's demand that he be raised in rank to captain and replace Lambert as commander of Jacob's former cavalry squadron. The disgruntled aristocrat resigned his commission and left with Ramses for Amsterdam where he intended to set sail for his plantation in Barbados.

In advance of William's invasion, his supporters in England distributed more than 60,000 copies of a pamphlet entitled *Declaration of The Hague*. It reassured the populace that the Prince of Orange was a true Stuart and a devout Protestant, free from the family's usual vices of absolutism, debauchery, and crypto-Catholicism. The pamphlet also emphasized that William sought to protect the Protestant religion, install a free parliament, and investigate the legitimacy of the infant Prince of Wales, while continuing to respect his uncle James as king of England.

Jacob heard otherwise from van Noordwijk. William intended to replace James II with himself and Mary as king and queen of England.

Brisk winds continued to favor the Protestants under a gray sky matching Jacob's bleak mood. He did not hear men shouting, officers commanding, feet trudging on planks, and squeaky wheels of caissons bearing cannon, ammunition, food and drink.

Lady Joan died from the Black pox whilst he was away with the Army. A regimental musician seated on a barrel plucked the strings of his lute and sang of disappointed love, which suited Jacob's state of mind.

> *"How now, shepherd, what means that?*
> *Why that willow in thy cap?*
> *Why thy scarfs of red and yellow,*
> *Turned to branches of green willow?*
> *They are changed, and so am I;*
> *Sorrows live, but pleasures die:*
> *Phyllis hath forsaken me,*
> *Which makes me wear the willow-tree."*

Jacob lamented, *His Phyllis, my Joan.*

Ambassador Dirck van Noordwijk, who'd returned this day from his mission to Amsterdam, approached Jacob near Prince William's flagship. "I might never have found you amidst this throng were it not for your height. The winds favor our Protestant fleet."

During those years in Jacob's *yesibót*, religious school, whilst preparing for his *berit milah,* blond, fair, and blue-eyed, he'd stood taller than his swarthy classmates, and now towered over most men at six feet three inches of height without boots.

"She that long true love profest,
She hath robbed my heart of rest."

"I am cursed. Shall I ever know the love of a woman? My mother's family let her bleed to death when I was born. My aunt Sara Isaac, who raised me, died when I was twelve. That same year, my Uncle Salomon Isaac told me I could never wed his daughter Sara Salomon nor anyone else from the Sephardic community because I was not born of a Jewish woman. Now my true love, Lady Joan, has been taken by the black pox."

"Yet, Phyllis, shall I pine for thee,
And still must wear the willow-tree?"

Van Noordwijk patted Jacob's shoulder. "Then always remember the examples and standards your grandfather, Don Vicente-Isaac de Rocamora, set for you to follow."

"There are so many. I would like nothing more than to be as he."

"Your grandfather lived a most unique life. First, as Vicente de Rocamora of the Spanish *caballero* caste and as a Dominican royal confessor. Of necessity, he had to leave his beloved Spain and make a new life, which he did with great success. He found true love with your grandmother and, as you know, became an esteemed physician. Jacob, as he did with Spain, so must you turn your back on Amsterdam and face the future, for which you have been so well prepared. Our prince will soon be king of England, and your future best lies there, where you must become more English than the English."

"It seems I have already made a start. My English comrades prefer to call me 'Jack Rockmore.'"

"Rockmore is the name by which you must be known."

"But I take great pride in my patrilineal name. We de Rocamoras are descended from the Sieur de Roquemaure, nephew of King Charles VIII of France, and, farther back, to the Houses of Arnulf, Roman Consuls, and King David."

Cheering, joyous shouting and horn fanfares interrupted their conversation. Preceded by heralds in orange, white and blue livery, Prince William on horseback led a parade of gilded carriages followed by the Stadholder's elite blue and white uniformed *Blauwe Garde,* Blue Guard, and a company of black Africans in native garb. Princess Mary, Princess Anne, and their ladies alighted from their carriages, followed by court notables and advisors. Mary had Lady Joan's dog on a leash.

Van Noordwijk placed his hand on Jacob's shoulder. "Now that Prince William has arrived, we shall be setting sail for *Het Glorieuze Overtocht*, the Glorious Crossing."

To Jacob the ruby ring the Infanta of Spain had gifted his grandfather, who'd bequeathed it to him, weighed as a boulder in his pouch. *To whom shall I bestow it one day?*

Jacob decided his future with new resolve as the musician concluded his lament:

> *"Henceforth I will do as they,*
> *And love a new love every day."*

Not I, Jacob vowed. *No woman can replace Lady Joan in my heart and mind.*

Chapter Four

Glorious Crossing

Prince William boarded his frigate *Den Briel*, the Brill. Jacob and van Noordwijk, with their horses, followed, amongst other members of his entourage. William's wife, Princess Mary, and her younger sister, Princess Anne, were to follow and arrive in England by Christmas after William had defeated their father, James II.

Drums and horns sounded. Sailors raised the Stadholder's standard. It bore the arms of Orange-Nassau quartered with those of England and the motto of his great-great grandfather, William the Silent, who'd led a Protestant Dutch Revolt against Catholic Spain: *Pro Religione et Libertate*, "For Liberty and Religion." A second banner proclaimed the House of Orange's motto, *Je maintiendrai*, "I will maintain."

Jacob further scrutinized William, whose parents had died of smallpox and who had himself also suffered a severe attack from *that murderer of dynasties* in early manhood, which had left him frail. His persistent deep cough resulted from chronic asthma. Despite William's physical ailments, his aquiline Roman nose, deep voice, and cold blue eyes left no doubt he was in command.

William's invasion fleet provided by the Admiralty of Amsterdam impressed both Jacob and van Noordwijk who stood near their prince on the bridge when he addressed his staff and proclaimed:

"Look around you. Our fleet is double the size of the Spanish Armada and was assembled in a tenth of the time the Spaniards took. No need for you to count. We have 20,000 sailors and 40,000 men aboard 463 vessels. They include 40 warships with at least 20 cannon each. Nine are frigates, 28 long narrow sail and oar galliots, nine fire ships, 76 transports to carry our soldiers, 100 smaller transports for 5,000 horses, about 70 supply vessels and 60 fishing vessels serving as landing craft."

*****

29 October. William's fleet departed from Hellevoetsluis. Made aware by van Noordwijk that the Prince of Orange suffered from sea sickness, Jacob had added chamomile and peppermint tea leaves to his bag of balms, salves, and remedies.

About halfway to England the Protestant wind changed to a Papist gale and scattered all ships. On the bridge, two aides tried to support William, who was seasick.

Jacob gripped the portside railing. Better to be on the bridge than below and tossed between walls. Elderly Van Noordwijk clung to the starboard railing as roiling waves splashed everyone on deck. Jacob worried the flagship might capsize if it listed to either side another two degrees.

William and his aides fell when a powerful gust assailed *The Brill*. The Prince of Orange slid toward Jacob as his ship came close to capsizing. Jacob held William and prevented him from falling overboard as waves splashed over them.

"Sire, allow me to take you to your quarters."

"No. we shall remain on the bridge, with your assistance."

*****

After the gale passed, Jacob brought his medicine bag to William's spacious cabin. Van Noordwijk and other advisors were in attendance, all in fresh dry clothes.

Jacob had a servant bring him a mug of steaming hot water and dropped into it dried petals from a flower. He offered the brew to William.

"Sire, please drink this. It is a chamomile tea, and will help settle your stomach. I suggest you also take dried crackers with it."

William did as told and gestured toward Jacob's bag. "Are you also a physician?"

"No, Sire, but whilst a child I accompanied my grandfather on his rounds and acquired more knowledge and experience about the practice of medicine than any school could teach. He bequeathed me this bag and its contents."

"But you prefer soldiering?"

"Yes."

William drank his tea. "Our innards are soothed." He motioned to a servant. "Martin, bring us a beer. Tell us, Major, of our many Protestant faiths do you still profess Collegian?"

"Yes, Sire."

"Hah! Close to atheism. We are Dutch Reformed, a Calvinist, as you well know. We regret we may have to convert to the Church of England so we may rule, depending upon Dame Fortuna. And then so must you."

William's utterance confirmed for Jacob what van Noordwijk had told him earlier. William intended to replace his uncle James as king of England.

William coughed and faced his staff. "Now, signal all ships we must return to home port."

*****

31 October. William's fleet returned to Hellevoetsluis. He refused to go ashore whilst he supervised the reassembling of his fleet. Losses included only one grounded ship, but about 1,000 horses crippled by the gale had to be tossed overboard. Hannibal survived on *The Brill*, and Jacob rode him each day for exercise and to raise his horse's spirit.

William ignored bulletins and broadsides asserting the invasion would have to be postponed until spring. He sent aides to requisition new horses and supplies. He drank heavily and needed amusement to pass the time. Jacob entertained him with card tricks his grandfather Isaac de Rocamora had taught him, and how to deal seconds and bottoms from any deck.

"Sire, I have also shown my men these tricks so they may identify a card cheat if they are foolish enough to gamble."

CHAPTER FIVE

ANOTHER ATTEMPT TO CROSS THE CHANNEL

11 November, 1688. East winds became Protestant again. William's invasion fleet departed a second time and sailed toward Harwich, where his chief advisor and confidant, Hans Willem Bentinck, had prepared a landing site.

A sudden north wind forced his fleet to change its course southward, passing twice in sight of King James's navy. The English could not engage in battle because of adverse winds and an unfavorable tide.

13 November. William's fleet entered the English Channel through the Strait of Dover in a square formation, 25 ships deep, the right and left flanks off Dover and Calais to show the enemy its size. Full colors waved in the wind. Soldiers in formation on deck fired musket volley salutes, and military bands played rousing tunes.

On the bridge near William, van Noordwijk pointed in all directions. "Jacob, has anyone ever seen so grand a spectacle?"

"It may not be visible for long. A dense fog approaches."

Soon, thick fog caused William's fleet to sail past Torbay by mistake. Winds prevented a return to that chosen landing site, and the nearest port at Plymouth had a garrison loyal to King James.

The English navy approached in pursuit but winds changed yet again. Fog lifted, enabling William's fleet to sail into Torbay, near Brixham in Devon.

15-17 November. William's army disembarked in calm weather. He announced to his staff, "We have 11,212 horse and foot, including 3,660 cavalry and dragoons. Our artillery train contains twenty-one 24-pounder cannon. Including the supply train, we have in total an army of 15,000 men. We have reports saying that James's army totals about 30,000, but we can equip our local English Protestant supporters with 20,000 stands of arms."

Jacob concluded that William had every right to express confidence. The Dutch had pioneered the development of platoon fire, which allowed infantry formations to shoot continuously, giving them an advantage in firepower over armies not using that system.

During a heavy rainstorm, William met with his staff in his spacious headquarters tent. Servants supplied them with beer and gin. Jacob listened to new reports of enemy strength. Louis XIV sent James 300,000 livres, which enabled him to raise five new regiments of foot and five of horse, augmented by veteran Scottish and Irish soldiers. Louis hoped a protracted English civil war would prevent the Dutch from interfering with his German campaign.

Van Noordwijk pointed to the Mediterranean on a large map of Europe spread on a nearby table. "We are fortunate Louis XIV has concentrated his fleet here to assist an attack on the Papal State."

William drank a second beer. "Our veteran army is sufficient in size to defeat any inexperienced force James has raised. We shall not attack him yet. It is best to avoid hazards of battle and maintain a defensive posture. James's position might collapse by itself. That is why we landed far away from his army in the expectation our English allies will take the initiative against him whilst we ensure our own protection against potential attacks."

William drank again and spoke to his commanders. "Have you given every man strict orders not ever to forage, for fear this would degenerate into plundering and alienate the population?"

All confirmed they had. Toasts to victory followed.

Jacob understood why William chose to be patient. He had paid his troops for a three-month campaign. A slow advance necessitated by heavy rains added a benefit of not overextending his supply lines.

*****

Van Noordwijk met with Jacob in his tent where they smoked their clay pipes and shared glasses of Port. "Jacob, there may be less warfare ahead and more politics to decide who shall rule England."

"Politics does not interest me."

"Ah, the folly of youth. Trust me, Jacob. You must understand that politics embraces all—wealth, power, and a man's pride in self."

"What is it you wish to tell me?"

"Two political parties dominate the English Parliament, Tories and Whigs."

"You mean one side wears periwigs and the other does not? Most absurd."

Van Noordwijk smiled at his protégé's ignorance. "It is spelled W-H I G. Whig and Tory were terms of abuse common in 1679 during a heated struggle over a bill to exclude James, then Duke of York, from succeeding his heirless brother Charles II. Whigs had been a party in the Parliaments of England, Scotland, and Ireland for several decades.

Scot Covenanter opponents of the established Church of England called them an insulting name—*whiggamaire or whiggamores,* cattle drivers, shortened to Whig—during a march against royalists at Edinburgh in 1648. They later supported the exclusion of James, Duke of York, from succession to the thrones of Scotland and England and Ireland. Whig also was a term applied to horse thieves and, later, to Scottish Presbyterians. It connoted nonconformity and rebellion and applied to those in Parliament who wanted to prevent Catholic James from becoming King of England."

"And the Whigs invited William and Mary to take the throne."

"Exactly."

"What is the origin of 'Tory'?"

"Whigs called their opponents Tories, derived from an old Irish word, *tóraidhe*, meaning outlaw. 'Tory' is applied to those who support the hereditary rights of James despite his Roman Catholic faith. Both parties started as loose groupings with similar beliefs and goals. They were founded by wealthy politicians more than by popular votes. These elites control voters in the House of Commons.

Jacob raised his glass to van Noordwijk. "Then I must be a Whig."

"Or, whichever way political winds blow. In the end, patronage, nepotism, and money dominate all politics."

Jacob determined to be politically circumspect until he understood more.

Van Noordwijk next told Jacob all he knew about Mary. She wanted children more than anything else in her life. Soon after her marriage to William, Mary was pregnant. Wanting to be with her husband, she traveled to Breda, near where he was encamped with his army, and there she suffered a terrible miscarriage. Their relationship deteriorated after a second miscarriage and, later, Mary's false pregnancy.

William then initiated an affair with Mary's erstwhile best friend and lady-in-waiting, Elizabeth "Betty" Villiers."

"Did Mary take on lovers for revenge?"

"No, Jacob. But know this about her: at first, Mary had misgivings about usurping her father's throne. James was a loving father to her, but she was torn between duty to her father and to her husband ... and to her Protestant religion."

"What changed her mind?"

"James's extreme cruelty toward her Protestant royal bastard cousin, Monmouth, and to all rebels who supported him, including many innocents as well. Love of her Protestant faith and for William triumphed over any devotion toward her father. Mary believes that, once married, a woman must support her husband first and foremost."

Van Noordwijk refilled their glasses. "Jacob, I am aware that Lady Joan spoke well of you to Princess Mary. Find a way to use it to your advantage."

Jacob's expression and tone became those of contempt. "And be a courtier?"

"Yes. Ingratiate yourself and you may advance in rank sooner rather than later. Once William is king, he may well knight you for saving his life."

CHAPTER SIX

FAMILY AFFAIR

Early January, 1689. Jacob reflected upon the swift success of the Williamites during November and December. To his surprise, James had chosen not to attack Prince William, even though he'd had successes in battle during previous decades and a larger army. His great victory years earlier had led to New Amsterdam becoming New York. Reports revealed James regarded William as family and knew how much his beloved eldest daughter Mary loved her husband. James continued to be distressed by the previous year's outbreak of anti-Catholic riots throughout northern England, and he did not want to initiate a new civil war.

William's swift conquest of England had commenced on 9 November, 1688, after Exeter's magistrates fled. He'd entered the city on a white palfrey with 200 Africans as guards of honor, dressed in white with turbans and colorful feathers.

12 November. Many nobles declared for William, influenced by public readings of the *Declaration*.

James rejected a French offer to send an expeditionary force. He feared it would cost him domestic support.

19 November. James's army totaled about 19,000. Defectors informed William that James had discovered a conspiracy within his army as early as September, but for unknown reasons he'd refused to arrest any officers involved.

Amidst anti-Catholic rioting in London, James's troops were not eager to fight, In Salisbury, after some of his officers deserted, James suffered a serious nose-bleed he interpreted as an evil omen indicating he should order his army to retreat.

24 November. More deserters told William that James had wept when his greatest military commander, John Churchill, 1st Duke of Marlborough, who defeated Monmouth, deserted to William.

Two days later, James's younger daughter, Princess Anne, doubting the authenticity of her new Catholic half-brother and influenced by Churchill's wife, Sarah, did the same. Both were serious losses. So was the English navy's defection to William.

James returned to London that same day. Beginning in late November and into early December, William's army rolled through Sherborne, Hindon, Amesbury, Salisbury, and Hungerford, where he met with James's commissioners.

Jacob conceded that Van Noordwijk had been prescient. Politics and negotiations took precedence over battle. Playing for time, James offered free elections and a general amnesty for the surviving Monmouth rebels he'd enslaved.

More spies and defectors reported King James had decided to flee England. He feared his enemies would demand he be executed and that William might assent to their demands.

Jacob continued to be amazed he had seen no fighting. *Could there be a peaceful end after all?*

That evening a stray one-eyed feral cat attached himself to Jacob in his tent. This furry feline was a magnificent beast, with an estimated weight of 30 pounds and a length of three feet. Van Noordwijk identified it as a Norwegian Forest cat. Jacob had been raised amongst cats in his grandfather's home. He named the cat Buccaneer.

8 December. William met with James's representatives. He agreed to James's proposals but demanded all Catholics be dismissed from state functions and that England pay for all Dutch military expenses. He received no reply.

9 December. A fateful day, the two armies engaged, and the Williamites defeated the Jacobites. Attached to William's staff, Jacob did not participate but watched the rout through a telescope.

*****

Convinced his army was unreliable, James disbanded it as anti-Catholic rioting broke out in Bristol, Bury St. Edmunds, Hereford, York, Cambridge, and Shropshire. That same day a Protestant mob stormed Dover Castle, which had a Catholic governor, and seized it.

On the night of the 9th to the 10th of December, James' Catholic Queen Mary of Modena fled to France with her infant Prince of Wales. James threw The Great Seal into the Thames along his escape route, because no lawful Parliament could be summoned without it.

Fishermen captured James, and the Whig party formed a provisional government. They asked William to restore order and invited James to return to London to reach an agreement with his nephew-son-in-law.

Unaware of happenings in London, William accepted an invitation from Oxford University. He left Newbury for Abingdon.

On the night of 11 December, false rumors of an impending Irish army attack on London circulated in the capital. A mob of over 100,000 assembled, ready to defend the city. Protestants rioted and looted homes of Papists and several foreign embassies of Catholic countries.

Hearing of James's flight, William turned and headed down the Thames valley through Wallingford and Henley, accepting the surrender of Jacobite soldiers he encountered along the way. He arrived at Windsor on 14 December, 1688.

16 December. Cheering Jacobite crowds welcomed James's return to London. He presided over a meeting of the Privy Council and sent Louis de Duras, Second Earl of Feversham, to William. He requested a personal meeting to resume negotiations.

William told his advisors, Jacob and Van Noordwijk amongst them, that he no longer desired to keep James in power in England. Lord Feversham's arrival angered him. He refused the earl's suggestion he simply arrest James because it violated his declarations and would affect his relationship with Mary.

Jacob was present when William conferred with Bentinck, van Noordwijk, and others on his staff. All agreed they should exploit James's fears. William sent a message to his uncle saying he could no longer guarantee the king's wellbeing and that for his own safety he must leave London.

17 December. Unsure of the English troops' complete loyalty, William next ordered all of them to depart the capital, whilst his Dutch army entered the city. That same day, James, by his own choice, went under Dutch protective guard to Rochester in Kent.

18 December. William entered London, cheered by crowds festooned in orange ribbons, and waving distributed oranges. He issued a command to his army:

"If James flees, do not prevent him, but allow him to gently slip through."

Although James's followers urged him to stay, he left for France on 23 December. By then, Princess Mary and her entourage had arrived in England.

William celebrated amongst his closest advisors. "I pray a successful flight will avoid the difficulty of deciding what to do with James. The memory of Charles I's execution is still vivid amongst the English."

Jacob agreed. By fleeing, James helped resolve the awkward question of whether he was still legally king or not, having created, according to Whig politicians, a situation of interregnum.

28 December. William took over the provisional government by appointment of Peers of the Realm, as was their legal right in circumstances when the King was incapacitated, and, on advice of his Whig allies He summoned an assembly of all surviving members of Parliament from Charles II's reign, thus sidelining the Tories of James' Loyal Parliament of 1685.

5 January, 1689. This assembly called for a chosen English Convention Parliament, to be elected. William did not intervene in the following election.

22 January. This new body consisted of 513 members, 341 of whom had been elected before, 238 having been members of at least one Exclusion Bill Parliament, but only 193 having been elected in 1685.

Van Noordwijk clarified for Jacob, "The name *Convention* has been chosen because only a king may call for a parliament. Although William has been appointed *de facto* regent by the peers, a Convention can be argued to be, strictly speaking, a lawful parliament."

HAPTER EIGHT

MARY COMMANDS

Early in January, 1689, Jacob received a summons to attend Princess Mary in the sere gardens of a property she was considering purchasing. Six ladies, some pages, and architect Sir Christopher Wren with a sketchbook accompanied her. So did a trio of toy Spaniels.

This was the first time Jacob had personal contact with the putative queen of England, who would be twenty-seven in April. Five feet eleven inches in height, Mary was covered with heavy fur to buffer against chill winds and her boots had heels high enough to bring her eye level with Jacob. She dispensed with court formality and beckoned him to sit beside her on a stone bench.

"Major Rockmore, tell us in full detail how you saved our husband's life."

Jacob related all that happened during the gale and why it had forced William's invasion fleet to return to port. He added the story of how, whilst in his cabin, he had helped amuse the Prince of Orange with card tricks and the art of cheating by dealing seconds and thirds.

"Major, you did more than save our beloved husband's life. You made it possible for us to become king and queen of

England. We do not yet have our thrones, but after we do have them, we shall acquire authority to reward you as you so well deserve."

Jacob had no idea what Mary meant or if it would come to pass. All rulers could be fickle or of short memory.

A chill wind knifed through their clothes, and Mary rose. So did Jacob.

"Come, walk with us, Major." Mary gestured for her entourage not to follow. "Lady Joan spoke often about you. She hoped to wed you."

"I adored her, Your Highness, and it might well have happened, were it not for the pox."

"You should find another to marry, but do not confine your choices to great beauties. Women's inner souls matter most."

By now, Jacob found Mary to be attractive, too much so. She was desirable as well. Whilst advising him in matters of the heart she expressed a natural irresistible sweetness and charm. She also stopped using her Royal *we* and *us*.

"When I was fifteen, for reasons of State, I was forced to wed my much older first cousin, the Prince of Orange. At first sight, I wept when I met my intended husband. He was so unlike many of the handsome and attentive English courtiers I had known."

Jacob hid his discomfort whilst Mary spoke of personal matters.

"Prince William was dour, taciturn, much shorter than me, and not physically attractive. Yet, within a short period of time, I fell in love with my husband because of his basic kindness of heart, intelligence, and brilliance in diplomacy. And so, Major, heed my advice and when you meet an eligible woman, look beyond the superficial and deeply into the essential."

"I promise I shall, Your Highness."

"Also. we suggest you convert to the Church of England and Anglicize your name. How does Jack Rockmore appeal to you?"

"I had considered that very name."

"Excellent. Prince William and I, we both want you to make England your permanent home and you will always be welcome at our court. Perhaps you shall one day show me your skill at cards that amazed His Highness. Playing card games is one of our sweetest pleasures."

"That would be my pleasure, as well, Your Highness."

Dismissed, Jacob left the garden deep in thought. Away from Mary's presence, he recalled his grandfather's story. As Dominican royal confessor and spiritual director for the *Infanta* of Spain, who'd been a mere five years younger than he, he'd shared an unspoken love with her.

Best to be practical rather than waste time thinking about the unattainable.

*****

That afternoon, Jacob attended a staff meeting. He would see no military action in Scotland. William decided to let loyal Presbyterian and Covenanter Scots deal with recalcitrant Highlander Jacobites. He next sent the Duke of Schomberg to take charge of the Irish campaign. Schomberg, a seventy-five -year-old professional soldier born in Heidelberg, had been a Marshal of France. A Huguenot, he'd fled France in 1685 after Louis XIV revoked the Edict of Nantes, which guaranteed tolerance for Protestants.

William expected Schomberg to make a swift conquest of Ireland, thus saving his main army for a return to the Continent, and that the duke would lead his Grand Alliance against Louis XIV.

Aside from drilling and staff meetings with William, Jacob had free time and looked forward to acclimating himself to London.

Chapter Seven

London

Despite extended political haggling in both houses of Parliament, Jacob expected William and Mary to become king and queen of England. He set about familiarizing himself with London, a growing city of about 600,000 inhabitants. He spent his free daytime hours and many evenings exploring neighborhoods and the attractions the metropolis had to offer, on occasion with Van Noordwijk, but more often with Henry Lambert who had been born and raised inside the city.

A cluster of small communities, London offered access to diverse public spaces, contact with a mixture of people, participation in urban spectacles, and freedom of movement. Inns, taverns, coffee-houses, baths, and brothels appeared in each neighborhood. When not at court, exercising Hannibal, or training with the regiments, Jacob mingled with all classes—in streets and plazas, in shops and marts, in parks, walks, and pleasure gardens, in coffee-houses, taverns, playhouses, and masquerades; but he avoided bagnios and brothels.

Noise and congestion accompanied Jacob's every step. Shops of all kinds tempted him with well displayed goods.

Executed criminals' quarters impaled on city gates disgusted Jacob, and his speed of walking increased when he encountered crowds enjoying cockfighting, bear and bull baiting.

Jacob enjoyed entertainments, exhibitions, and political dramas. He frequented coffee-houses with Lambert but did not collect his mail at a favorite as a typical lodger might. He chose to use his banking house for receiving and sending all correspondence.

At coffee-houses Jacob socialized, purchased lottery tickets, listened to men conducting business, and read newspapers. He often walked to Lombard Street where scriveners and goldsmiths plied their trades, then detoured into Exchange Alley. There he rested at Jonathan's coffee-house, or Garraway's. Next, he followed an alleyway to the Royal Exchange.

Continuing along Cornhill to Cheapside, Jacob and Lambert passed goldsmiths, drapers, and sundry artisan retailers. This street took them to bookstalls in St. Paul's Churchyard and to the booksellers and silk mercers of Paternoster Row.

Along his walks, Jacob acquired information relating to trade, ships, and speculations.

Lambert explained how within each neighborhood inhabitants developed networks marked by kinship, friendship, and reciprocity. Multiple roles were played by neighbors as creditors, investors, patrons, executors, witnesses, godparents, and pallbearers.

Covent Garden contained theatrical, artistic and entertainment communities, and London's largest market.

Drury Lane Theatre attracted writers, artists, prostitutes, criminals, and other lowlifes. But on its Piazza large four-storied residences rose above a common arcade. Minor nobility, admirals, and bishops lodged amongst the middling sort.

Adjacent to Russell and James Streets were second-tier genteel streets, but in back lanes the mix was more spurious. A rising population forced even the best buildings to be subdivided and crammed with lodgers, whilst shops encroached at ground level.

Van Noordwijk described merchants as rich men with great credit and repute, their equipage noble, many honored with knighthood. He divided urban merchants into three groups, distinguishing them from craftsmen and common laborers: those skilled in navigation, by which merchandise was brought in and out by sea; a second group imported commodities into the city and kept retailing shops. A third group was known as overseas traders. Fear of debt produced unique merchant practices, he said: time management, self-discipline, and thrift.

Pamphlets credited merchants' improved standing to their giving and lending money and allowing their daughters to wed impoverished titled gentlemen. Conduct books such as *The Gentleman Instructed* advised:

"Nobility stript of means makes no gentile figure. It can't stand without golden supporters."

*****

Attached to William's staff, Jacob faced challenges to his free time, and he needed lodging outside Whitehall. What was the cost of living in an unfamiliar country? What were his 5,000 guilders, also called florins, in Amsterdam's Wisselbank, worth in England? What were England's customs and manners?

Van Noordwijk found Jacob a spacious room in Lady Barbara Corning's four-story, twenty-four-room brick and stone mansion in Covent Garden. Its luxurious interior had wainscoted walls filled with paintings, floors covered with

Dutch tiles and Turkish carpets, and was also adorned with Greco-Roman sculptures and colorful vases from Asia.

The ambassador's deceased wife came from the powerful Howard family of dukes, earls, and viscounts. Lady Barbara Corning, fortyish, was one of her widowed cousins, and avoided penury by renting out space in her home. Van Noordwijk chose one suite, and Jacob took another at an expensive £50 for a year.

Van Noordwijk informed Jacob about Lady Barbara's background. A woman of high intelligence with charm, wit, and beauty, she was a former mistress of Charles II. Her unrivaled salon attracted former mistresses of King Charles, other aristocrats, and women of intelligence. She held it in a comfortable parlor where women met to discuss current plays, books, and music, sometimes listening to authors reciting their creations and musicians playing their compositions. They also discussed politics, diplomacy, science, and theology, often contradicting church and Bible dicta, just as men were doing in coffee houses.

Lady Barbara also hosted gambling in a former ballroom where her guests played card games and Hazard, from which she collected a percentage of the winnings. In gambling women were equal to men, a financial anomaly in England.

When Lady Barbara took command of a table, Jacob observed her skill in dealing seconds and bottoms. He chose not to reveal the aristocrat as a cheat and sever a useful connection.

Jacob and van Noordwijk dined often with Lady Barbara and other lodgers, mostly nobility, gentry, ranking military, a magistrate, and one Whig parliamentarian. Several amongst them shared rooms.

Lady Barbara never allowed anyone to see her without heavy powder or lead-based ceruse that masked a fine-featured face damaged by smallpox. Her attractive female servants let Jacob know they were available for companionship. Her handsome male servants also serviced lady patrons.

Conversations at meals and afterward over Port, sherry, or claret kept Jacob well informed about politics. Although exiled in France, James II still had many followers throughout England, Scotland, and Wales, and in the House of Lords.

One evening van Noordwijk dominated the conversation after they supped. "If James returns, as more than a few wish, they would make William Regent. Were that to transpire, our Prince of Orange has promised he will return to the Netherlands."

That much Jacob knew and more. Radical Whigs in Commons wanted to elect William King, thus ensuring his reign would be derived from the people. Moderates wanted both William and Mary acclaimed King and Queen by assent of Parliament. Some Tories wanted William to be Regent or Mary as Queen alone.

*****

Buccaneer the Cat joined Jacob each night in his room, content to sleep at his feet, facing the fireplace.

Jacob stayed away from Lady Barbara's card tables and instead preferred Hazard, a game of dice. It suited his skill figuring odds. Some players fixated on certain numbers for their main and lost more often than winning. Jacob won nearly each time at Hazard.

A physician checked Lady Barbara's female servants each week to certify them free from Cupid's diseases. Jacob was not yet ready to avail himself of their charms and other pleasures of the flesh in London. Henry Lambert also avoided prostitutes, saving himself for a lady he loved and hoped to wed.

*****

Accompanied by Van Noordwijk during daylight and by Lambert at night, Jacob familiarized himself with London's districts, including information on which offered potential profitable investments and the best places in which to reside. The city had developed from an amalgam of villages, and most neighborhoods embraced all classes with scant residential segregation. Tradesmen, laborers, and the poor jammed together amongst the rich in squares, places, rows, streets, lanes, courts, alleys and yards.

Yet many grand houses were built west of London, whilst working class houses were constructed east of the city, creating a division between wealthy and poor. London's streets were narrow, dark and dangerous at night.

Certain improvements had come to London before Jacob arrived. Piped water from a reservoir traveled along elm-covered conduits through the streets, and through lead pipes to individual houses, at great cost. In the 1680s, an oil lamp was hung outside every tenth house and lit during the darkest months.

At many bookstalls and stores, Jacob read or purchased newspapers, pamphlets, and skimmed books on many relevant topics. Weekly, *Bills of Mortality* listed causes of death: murder, *Lunatick* or frenzy, and of aged elderly. Gaping in the guts, bloody flux, diarrhea, malaria, smallpox and worms were typical killers.

Physician Thomas Cogan recommended: *Wash your face and hands with clean cold water, and especially bathe and plunge the eyes therein: For that not only cleanseth away the filth, but also comforteth, and greatly preserveth the sight."*

Quality soap was too expensive for most. Many believed it unhealthy to immerse the entire body in water, and in winter, with no hot water, bathing in cold water had no appeal.

Men and women cleaned hands and faces daily when possible. In such circumstances, pleasant scents and aromas were welcome. In his popular seventeenth-century work *The English Housewife*, Gervase Markham wrote of how to make pomanders to carry and sniff if near a particularly foul stench. Pomanders included:

> *two pennyworth of labdanum, two pennyworth of storax liquid, one pennyworth of calamus aromaticus, as much balm, half a quarter of a pound of fine wax, of cloves and mace two pennyworth, of liquid aloes three pennyworth, of nutmegs eight pennyworth, and of musk four grains. Beat all together till they come to a perfect substance, then mould it in any fashion you please and dry it.*

Hannah Wooley advised, *"For stench under arm-holes, first pluck away the hairs of the armhole and wash them well with white wine and rosewater wherein you have boiled Cassia lignum."*

Plague broke out in London in the years 1603, 1636 and 1665, killing a significant part of the population, but each time London recovered, having been replenished by large numbers of country poor eager to work in the city.

At first Hatton Garden in St. Andrew Holborn Parish impressed Jacob. Speculators erected dwellings according to Lord Hatton's standards. Each home had a twenty-two-foot frontage, two rooms each on three main floors, a basement, an attic, a back closet, an oak staircase, casement windows, and a doorway carved to personal taste with street balusters and window glass. Interiors included ten hearths. Van Noordwijk told Jacob that in Hatton Garden's premium section resided wealthy merchants, fifteen titled residents, one bishop, two generals, nineteen esquires, six doctors and six lawyers.

During one tour with Lambert, Jacob's friend gestured toward a four-story house across the street. "That is my family's home. I'd invite you to meet them, but my father pressures me each time I visit to leave the army and join him in his business."

"Which is?"

"Importer of porcelain. My father has a warehouse on the Thames and a factory in Delft. He also imports from China. I shall wait for the best moment to introduce you."

Jacob rejected Hatton Garden because Lord Hatton could not prevent leaseholders from subletting to shopkeepers, braziers, pewterers, butchers, fishmongers and tallow chandlers. The parish also included Ely Rents and Saffron Hill, populated by meaner sorts of people. Modest dwellers resided in adjacent Little Kirby and Cross Streets, and nearby Leather Lane and Hatton Wall led to alleys, brew houses, and workshops. Jacob still favored Covent Garden and the area adjacent to Lady Barbara's residence.

Chapter Eight

Sex and the City

One late afternoon, Jacob shared a laugh with Henry Lambert at one of several booksellers they toured. He read a couplet aloud from a book of poems by John Wilmot, late Earl of Rochester and kinsman of Edmund Wilmot.

*Fair nasty nymph be clean and kind, and all my joys
    restore,*
By using paper still behind, and spunges still before.

Later, relaxing in one of London's numerous coffee-houses, Jacob lit his long clay pipe and savored a cup of Turkish brew. "Henry, I can understand why Puritans and those living outside of London view our capital as a corrupting influence for male and female similar to Sodom and Gomorrah. I am still amazed by the amount of pornography available from those booksellers we visited today."

"True, Major. Educated men like ourselves have read and own editions written by great classical masters of erotica, obscene pornography, and bawdy tales. Who indeed amongst the literate has not read Ovid, Catullus, Propertius, Boccaccio, Martial, Petronius, Apuleius, Terence, and Plautus?"

Like most students who studied Latin and Greek, Jacob read the great teacher of extra-marital seduction, Ovid. Vivid translations into English of *The Elegies, The Art of Love,* and *The Remedies of Love* were available from all booksellers. They influenced past and current authors, poets, and playwrights.

"Henry, I have observed a commonality of story and character in contemporary publications," Jacob remarked.

"Yes, female characters are written as either temptresses or victims, Messalinas or Lucretias, sexually ravenous or ravished. I have been told instructional manuals of sexual techniques provide a popular medium for pornographic and obscene writers and bring the most profit."

Jacob concluded Lambert had read more than a few of those books and pamphlets of sexual instruction, which would horrify his Calvinist family if they ever knew. Several titles also amused him:

The School of Venus, A Dialogue between a Married Lady and a Maid, Tullia and Octavia, originally *Aloisiae Sigeae Toletanae Satyra Sotadica de Arcanis Amoris et Veneris,* and *The Whores' Rhetoric Calculated to the Meridian of London,* a translation of Ferrante Pallavicino's *La Retorica delle Puttane.*

Lambert ordered another round of coffee. "Jack, all three titles have been condemned by many as primers for teaching and practicing a diversity of lewdness."

Jacob had perused several outdated publications still available: *The Wandering Whore* had lists of whores and abettors working in London appended at the end of each part. Part Five, published early in 1661, listed 138 bawds who ran houses of prostitution, 269 common whores, and sundry male foyers/hunters, kidnappers, decoys, pimps, hectors bullies, and trapanners/ensnarers.

The Ladies Champion, a rival publication to *The Wandering Whore*, estimated the 49 jaculates "of this type of caterpillars and poisonous vermine" as 1,500. *The Practical Part of Love*, published in the same year, stated a full list would cover thirty pages, which at a rough computation based on lists in *The Wandering Whore* totaled 3,600.

To quote Gusman, a pimping hector, in the sixth part of *The Wandering Whore*:

> *If you step aside into Coven Garden, Long Acre, and Drury Lane, where those Doves of Venus, those birds of youth and beauty, (the wanton Ladies), this town swarms with alehouses, and every one of them they tell is also a bawdy house. Now the privat Whores have got the knack on to knock in corners, so that all our Cattel in Dog and Bitch Yard, Drury-Lane, Luterners-Lane Parkhurst-Lane, Bloomsbury, Hatten-Wall, &c. cannot with all their painting, perfuming, clean linen or sweetest Oratory or loudest calling, persuade a Gallant to enter their Forts, notwithstanding there hangs out white Colors to draw on to a treaty all weathers, Ergo, Publick trading is destroy'd by privat correspondencies and actings, which was not formerly when our lists of whores were printed.*

Certain women maintained outward respectability and thus were more difficult to identify and count than employees of brothels dond street-walkers whose livelihood depended on their calling attention to themselves.

"Some others also cannot be counted," Lambert commented, sipping his coffee. "How easy it is for bawds and their male employees each day to lure, contract, or even abduct country girls newly arrived in London... and all of them afflicted with *the green sickness*."

"*Green sickness?* Pray tell me, Henry, what is that?"

"A common complaint of *dells*, adolescent girls burdened with unwanted maidenheads, ripe for whoredom but not yet inducted into its arts. In London, we cure, and cure them again and again. Any young man proficient with his geometric staff can fill the longitude, latitude and profundity of any cavity."

Jacob smiled at Lambert's metaphor. "*Green sickness*—it seems I must acquire a new vocabulary of London cant and jargon."

"Well and good, Major, but 'tis best to avoid loathsome superannuated whores, riddled with pox, teeth fallen out, breath like a bear, nose and chin meeting, their wares well-worn."

"Disgusting, and even more so child prostitution and pornography," Jacob replied. "Henry, I consider child prostitution worse than the use of child labor in mines, factories, and businesses, which I also oppose..."

"Major, I share your sentiments."

*****

Another evening, Jacob encountered his former valet, Corporal Hugh Tinker and accompanied him to an ale house. Jacob drank and observed whilst Tinker wenched, smoked, and added to Jacob's vocabulary.

"There are several words and phrases commonly used for *ejaculation praecox*. 'Play at rumpscuttle,' 'clapperdepouch,' 'lerriecompoop,' 'rides a dragon upon St. George,' and 'houghmagandy.' I have no knowledge of their origins."

Jacob drank his ale. "I am learning that English is a most creative language."

"Back to jargon and cant, 'French Marbles' refers to venereal diseases. 'Adam's Ale' is drinkable water. We call a witless, stupid fellow a blunderbuss."

"I've heard that used often."

"Cackling farts are eggs laid by hens."

"Corporal Tinker, that might cause me to lose my taste for eggs."

"'Dumbfounded' means you beat someone to a bloody pulp. To 'mill' means to kill. Your sword is a porker. A pig is a grunter. 'English Cane' is a common term for an oak tree. An oak is a rich man. A hussy is a housewife. 'Rum glaziers' means one has excellent eyesight. Breeches are called 'farting-crackers' or 'a pair of kicks.' Bum fodder is used to wipe the tail. A chamber pot is a looking glass. 'Jakes' is a privy. 'Stew' is a brothel, 'traffic' a whore. So is 'Winchester goose.' 'Nipper' is a cut- purse. 'Trull' is someone of low character."

Jacob dabbed his wet eyes with a handkerchief after a laughing fit. "I cannot remember having lost so much control. Please continue."

"An implacable enemy is cruel and relentless. A grumbletonian is a malcontent politician who fails to achieve a place or has lost one. 'Brabble' is to quarrel. 'Cuttle' is a knife. 'Nutcracker' refers to a pillory used for punishment. 'Quad' is debtor's prison. 'A garnish' is a bribe given to a prison officer. 'Vampers' are stockings. Am I going too fast for you?"

"Not at all."

"'Water-pads' are boats rowed by thieves on the Thames to attack other boats and ferries. 'Argent' means coins. An artificer is a skilled workman. A popinjay is a vain, overdressed, strutting ...."

"Lord Lyndby," Jacob interrupted. "May he remain in Barbados until death."

Chapter Nine

Declaration of Rights

Jacob's political leanings solidified when the Whig-dominated House of Commons decided by acclamation that James II had broken the original contract between king and Parliament when he'd abdicated, thus leaving the throne vacant.

Jacob despised Tories when the House of Lords by a slim majority remained loyal to James. They rejected a proposal for regency in James's name by 51 to 48 on February 2nd. The Lords also substituted the word "abdicated" for "deserted" and removed the vacancy clause. In addition, the Lords voted against proclaiming William and Mary king and queen by 52 to 47.

Jacob was present when William in private conversation with his supporters in the Lords gave an ultimatum: "Accept me as king or I shall return to the Netherlands with my army. Mary shall be queen in name, and preference in any succession shall be given to Princess Anne's children over any of mine if, God forbid, I must wed again."

Anne waived her right to immediate succession should Mary die before William. If William did not become king, Jacob intended to return with the Prince of Orange to the Netherlands.

Mary impressed Jacob when she refused to be made queen without William as king. Fearing another civil war, on February 6th the Lords accepted "abdication" and "vacancy" and appointed William and Mary as joint monarchs. On the 13th of February, the clerk of the House of Lords read the Declaration of Rights and Lord Halifax, in the name of all estates of the realm, asked William and Mary to accept the throne. William replied for his wife and himself, "We thankfully accept what you have offered us."

*****

At their coronation, William and Mary swore an oath to uphold the laws made by Parliament and The Coronation Oath Act of 1688, by which the monarchs were to "solemnly promise and swear to govern the people of this kingdom of England, and the dominions thereunto belonging, according to the statutes in parliament agreed on, and the laws and customs of the same." They also swore to maintain the laws of God, the true profession of the Gospel, and the Protestant Reformed faith established by law. That oath and The Declaration ended any possibility of an absolutist Catholic king or queen ever recapturing the English throne. Parliament also listed infractions committed by King James II:

Whereas the late King James II, by the assistance of evil counselors, judges and ministers employed by him, did endeavor to subvert and extirpate the Protestant religion and the laws and liberties of this kingdom. All of which are utterly and directly contrary to the known laws and statutes and freedom of this realm by assuming and exercising a power of dispensing with and suspending of laws and the execution of laws without consent of Parliament.

1. By committing and prosecuting divers worthy prelates for humbly petitioning to be excused from concurring to the said assumed power.
2. By issuing and causing to be executed a commission under the great seal for erecting a court called the Court of Commissioners for Ecclesiastical Causes.
3. By levying money for and to the use of the Crown by the pretense of prerogative for other time and in another manner than the same was granted by Parliament.
4. By raising and keeping a standing army within this kingdom in time of peace without consent of Parliament, and quartering soldiers contrary to law.
5. By causing several good subjects being Protestants to be disarmed at the same time when papists were both armed and employed contrary to law.
6. By violating the freedom of election of members to serve in Parliament.
7. By prosecutions in the Court of King's Bench for matters and causes cognizable only in Parliament, and by divers other arbitrary and illegal courses.
8. And whereas of late years partial corrupt and unqualified persons have been returned and served on juries in trials, and particularly divers jurors in trials for high treason which were not freeholders.
9. And excessive bail hath been required of persons committed in criminal cases to elude the benefit of the laws made for the liberty of the subjects.
10. And excessive fines have been imposed.

11. And illegal and cruel punishments inflicted.

12. And several grants and promises made of fines and forfeitures before any conviction or judgment against the persons upon whom the same were to be levied.

*****

The clauses limiting the powers of the Crown excited Jacob most: The suspension and execution of laws belonged to Parliament. The suspension of laws or execution of laws by regal authority without the consent of Parliament was illegal. Mary's charm and suggestions influenced Jacob's decision to reside in England, and the policies that Parliament's promulgated next intensified his conviction that England was the best of all nations, where one had the most freedoms:

That the commission for erecting the late Court of Commissioners for Ecclesiastical Causes, and all other commissions and courts of like nature, are illegal and pernicious.

That the levying of money for or to the use of the Crown by pretense of prerogative, without grant of Parliament, for longer time, or in other manner than the same is or shall be granted, is illegal.

That it is the right of the subjects to petition the king, and all commitments and prosecutions for such petitioning are illegal.

13. That the raising or keeping a standing army within the kingdom in time of peace, unless it is with consent of Parliament, is against law.

14. These the subjects which are Protestants may have arms for their defense suitable to their conditions and as allowed by law.

15.   That election of members of Parliament ought to be free.

16.   That the freedom of speech and debates or proceedings in Parliament ought not to be impeached or questioned in any court or place out of Parliament.

17.   That excessive bail ought not to be required, nor excessive fines imposed, nor cruel and unusual punishments inflicted.

18.   That jurors ought to be duly impaneled and returned, and jurors which pass upon men in trials for high treason ought to be freeholders.

19.   That all grants and promises of fines and forfeitures of particular persons before conviction are illegal and void.

And that for redress of all grievances, and for the amending, strengthening and preserving of the laws, Parliaments ought to be held frequently.

Those rights within a king's reign limited by Parliament cemented Jacob's commitment to a life in England. Still, he had one concern:

But what shall my place be?

Chapter Ten

A Surprise

On the 11th of April, Jacob and Van Noordwijk walked amongst a great procession to the Great Gate at Whitehall where the Garter King at Arms proclaimed William and Mary King and Queen of England, France, and Ireland, following which, they gathered in the Chapel Royal for prayers and a sermon.

Afterward, William and Mary awarded their favorites titles and honors at Whitehall Palace. They granted confiscated earldoms to William's aristocratic young Dutch favorites to increase loyalist votes in the Lords. Jacobites later spread word that those favored handsome men were thus William's catamites.

The Royal Chamberlain interrupted Jacob's musings when he called his name to approach Their Majesties. Mary smiled before Jacob kneeled, whilst William's mien continued inscrutable.

The king spoke without emotion between asthmatic coughing. "Major Jack Rockmore, we are forever in your debt for saving our life at sea. We are well aware of your loyalty and other accomplishments. For these reasons"—

William tapped both Jacob's shoulders with a ceremonial sword—"arise, Colonel Sir Jack Rockmore."

Jacob rose, stunned. William had bestowed knighthood and a double promotion in rank upon him.

That evening and into the night, Jacob celebrated with van Noordwijk, Lambert, and other friends at Lady Barbara's establishment. When all addressed him as "Sir Jack," he surprised himself by how much he enjoyed hearing it.

Lambert congratulated Jacob and offered him an invitation from his father to sup with his family in Hatton Gardens. "My father is an ambitious man, and I have risen in his estimation because I am friends with a knight and colonel."

"You may drop the 'sir' when we are alone. What does your father want from me?"

"Access to the Court. I do agree—what he wishes for does have merit."

*****

The following morning, Jacob sat on a bench in the gardens of Hampton Court, still under construction, to clear his head after a night of celebrating his knighthood and promotion to Colonel. The moment had come to assess his place in England and decide upon which road he should travel after King William pacified Scotland and Ireland.

William and Mary held England and Wales, but Scotland's divided and recalcitrant Jacobite Highlanders needed to be defeated. Ireland presented a more difficult challenge. The Catholic population continued to support James with aid from the deposed king's cousin Louis XIV.

That William did not lead the Blue Guards and cavalry to fight in Scotland disappointed Jacob. Unlike the English and Scottish Presbyterians, Highlanders and Episcopalians continued to support James after the Protestant majority of the Scottish Privy Council asked William on the 7th of January to govern Scotland. They mustered on May 14th, 1689,

56

on the banks of Douglas Water in South Lanarkshire. Eight hundred Covenanters deployed north to the town of Dunkeld to confront 5,000 Highlanders.

Jacob had reports of the battle along with William and his staff. Fighting started at dawn and ended at last light, sixteen hours later. The Covenanters fought with great zeal, and the Jacobites withdrew.

Highlanders were heard to describe Covenanters, saying, "They could fight against men, not fit to fight any more against devils." It was said that "the Covenanters prayed as they fought and fought as they prayed."

Support for James in Scotland continued with a contingent of Irish troops. Viscount Dundee raised an army in the Highlands and won a convincing victory at Killiecrankie but suffered heavy losses. Dundee was fatally wounded, and the rebellion ended.

Command of the Jacobites was passed to Colonel Alexander Cannon, leader of the recruits from Ireland, instead of veteran sixty-year-old Sir Ewen Cameron of Lochiel, one of the most formidable Highland chiefs. Cameron was so insulted he left, taking with him most of his clan.

The Privy Council of Scotland ordered a new regiment, under command of Lieutenant Colonel William Cleland, to move north from Perth and to hold Dunkeld at all costs.

Whilst everyone awaited news from Scotland throughout the summer, William and Mary purchased two palaces for the asthmatic king's comfort. Whitehall Palace was too near the Thames River's dense, foul fog and floods.

William and Mary bought Nottingham House in Kensington from Secretary of State Daniel Finch, 2nd Earl of Nottingham, for £20,000, a figure Jacob intended to keep in mind should he decide to invest in property. They renamed it Kensington Palace and expected a thorough remodeling to be completed by Christmas.

William and Mary gave instructions to Sir Christopher Wren, Surveyor of the King's Works, to begin an expansion of the house. Mary allowed Jacob to see the plans. To save time and money, Wren kept the original structure intact and added three-story pavilions at each corner to accommodate the king and queen, and their attendants.

The queen's apartments were in the northwest pavilion and the king's in the south-east. Wren reoriented the palace to face west, building north and south wings to flank the approach, made into a proper *cour d'honneur* entered through an archway surmounted by a clock tower. Straight-cut solitary lawns, formal stately gardens with paths and flower beds at right angles, in the Dutch style, surrounded the palace.

Mary convinced Wren to alter his original plans and add an extension of her apartments with a gallery. William later had Wren change a wood staircase to marble and added a Guard Chamber facing the foot of the stairs.

William and Mary's second palace was more ambitious. Hampton Court was twelve miles away from Kensington, in the London Borough of Richmond upon Thames, Greater London, in Middlesex County.

William showed his plans, drawn by Wren, to Jacob and others he trusted. He intended his massive rebuilding and expansion project to rival Versailles. His intention was to demolish the Tudor palace one section at a time, whilst replacing it with a huge modern palace, retaining only Henry VIII's Great Hall. The vast palace was to be constructed around two courtyards at right angles to each other. Wren's design for a domed palace resembled works of architects employed by Louis XIV at Versailles.

Chapter Eleven

To Be a Courtier?

After leaving a daily staff meeting with King William in Whitehall Palace, Jacob strode looking neither right nor left. Well known as a favorite of Their Majesties, he asked himself, *What is it to be this time? Courtiers offering cash bribes to arrange access to William and Mary? Or will it be the gift of a daughter, sister or wife in payment for some favor?*

The Declaration of Rights might have promised more freedoms than in any other nation, but Jacob viewed William and Mary's court as a gilded prison and agreed with Lord Halifax's assessment: "The Court may be said to be a company of well-bred fashionable Beggars. A Man who will rise at Court must begin by creeping on all Fours; a Place at Court, like a Place in Heaven, is to be got by being much upon one's knees."

Court rankings below William and Mary included, first, the Lord Chancellor, Keeper of the Great Seal; the Lord Treasurer, custodian of royal revenue; the Lord President, who proposed business for the King's Council and presided during His Majesty's absence; the Lord Privy Seal; and two Secretaries of State, who prepared business for the Council, and through whose hands passed grants and warrants for royal signature, and all detailed workings of the administration.

The Lord Chamberlain received livery and lodging at court. At each coronation, he received forty ells of crimson velvet for his own robes. He bore the ceremonial sword, gold oblation, and crown, before the new king at the ceremony, and he governed Westminster Palace. When Parliament opened, he sat at the king's right hand. He supervised all officers of the King's Chamber—comedians, physicians, trumpeters, and chaplains.

Other great officials in descending rank included the Lord Constable and the Earl Marshal, who held power to order, judge, and appoint officers to fill vacancies in the College of Arms, and to punish and correct Officers of Arms for misbehavior. He also held power over Marshalsea debtor prison. They were followed by the Lord High Admiral, who controlled all maritime affairs and held the entire patronage of the Navy in his hands.

Next came the Master of the King's Horse; the Lord High Almoner, who dispensed the royal alms; the Master of the Ceremonies; the Gentlemen of the Bedchamber; the Dean of the Chapel Royal, who acknowledged no episcopal jurisdiction; and a group of officials, presided over by the Treasurer of the Household, who constituted the "Board of Green Cloth," which examined the household accounts and dealt with minor disturbances in the court, within a twelve-mile radius of the palace.

Below those great officials came the Keeper of the King's Wardrobe, the Master of the Revels, physicians, surgeons, numerous chaplains, and the Library Keeper, down to trumpeters, heralds, the Master of the King's Barges, musicians, cooks, the Keeper of Ice and Snow, the Keeper of the Cormorants, and the Master of the Bears.

Jacob viewed with contempt the daily spectacle of every sort of courtier, each seeking to advance his prosperity at the Crown's expense.

Lord Halifax wrote about those annoyances the king endured from the hangers-on at Court: "There being galled with Importunities, pursued from one Room to another with asking Faces, dismal sound of unreasonable Complaints and ill-grounded Pretences, the Deformity of Fraud, ill-disguised, all these would make any Man run away from them, and I used to think it was the Motive for making him walk so fast."

From what Jacob observed, William and Mary's court never relapsed into the licensed disorder of that of Charles II, and from it public morality took its tone. If it sometimes condoned certain vices, it also performed a valuable service to the nation in its steady encouragement of art and learning.

On the negative side, Jacob agreed with van Noordwijk's comment regarding many courtiers and "ladies": "Our gallants being every way so Frenchified that they are become mere cock-sparrows. Never did men wear greater breeches or carry less in them of any mettle whatsoever."

Dress became colorful and elaborate. Women wore towering lace head-dresses above stiff curls of powdered hair or wigs. They kilted up their full skirts to show brocaded petticoats, and applied small black patches in the shape of crescent moons or stars to their cheeks and chins.

Jacob appreciated women who had a genuine pleasure in learning, many educated at home. Other families sent their daughters to Mr. Josiah Priest's school where they were taught to play musical instruments, some excelling because of innate talent.

*****

Jacob's plan to distance himself from court life ended after King William summoned him for a private audience at Hampton Court. He invited Jacob to sit opposite him at a small table in an antechamber and shared a bottle of French brandy from Cognac.

"As you know, Sir Jack, Her Majesty enjoys balls and dancing. We do not. Our queen has remarked you are her favorite partner, and she looks upon you with favor, not only for saving our life but also for your kind treatment of Lady Joan Fairfield."

"Yes, Sire, and we would have wed were it not for the black pox."

"Our opinion is that balls and dancing are a waste of valuable time, so we have a request. Attend all balls with Her Majesty. Cheer her, for she received a vicious letter from her father excoriating her for treason against him and violating the biblical Commandment of honoring one's father. Be her favorite partner and amuse her, so I may be free to attend to other, more important matters."

Such as your mistress Betty Villiers, Jacob thought. "I shall do as you request, Your Majesty."

"Then you shall attend Her Majesty's ball this evening at Kensington Palace."

*****

Queen Mary preferred Jacob as her partner that evening during pavannes, sarabands, gavottes, passagaglias, and chaconnes. He saw no signs of grief or anger over her father's letter of rebuke. Mary stood with him whilst fanning herself after an intense chaconne. "Sir Jack, we cannot adequately express how delighted we are to have so accomplished a partner whose eyes are close to our level."

"I am honored to have pleased Your Majesty."

"You have proven truth to court gossip. It is said you are the greatest leaper since the Duke of Buckingham, who was a favorite of James I. You must also partner us at cards afterward."

Thus, Queen Mary took a portion of Jacob's time and, resist as he might, he succumbed to Mary's charm, wit, beauty and desirability.

Jacob prayed William would soon lead his army to Ireland. He had to be away from Mary before he gave in to a temptation that could end his life in the Tower of London.

Chapter Twelve

Choices

Jacob considered his options for a future career and life once King William conquered Ireland. Should he continue to soldier or join his mentor van Noordwijk in the diplomatic service? Become a merchant or a banker? Or invest in trade, stocks, factories, or land?

Jacob's inheritance from his grandfather, the esteemed physician and philanthropist Vicente-Isaac de Rocamora, made him wealthier than many great English ducal landowners. Those 5,000 gold florins, not silver as he had first assumed, secure in the Amsterdam Wisselbank, were worth fifteen to twenty times the same figure in English pounds sterling.

Not even his Uncle Salomon Isaac de Rocamora knew the extent of Jacob's wealth; it was known only by the wealthy merchant and banker Abraham Santcroos. He had increased it by twenty percent over the previous five years since The passing of Jacob's grandfather on April 5th, 1684.

Jacob's 5,000 florins, worth £90,000 to £120,000 sterling, were enough to allow him a life of leisure. Although he enjoyed drinking, gambling, and wenching no less than any other twenty-four year-old, he knew he needed to choose a stable career once William and Mary secured their reign.

Also, everyone advised Jacob to wed an English heiress or a titled wealthy widow and become a squire eligible for a seat in Parliament. Several suggested he emulate the career of John Churchill. His sister Arabella was James II's mistress, which had enabled him to become a page at James' court. Churchill's cousin Barbara, Lady Castlemaine, had been a favored mistress of Charles II. His wife, Sarah Jennings, had been inseparable from Princess Anne.

In England, as Colonel Sir Jack Rockmore, his bronze-blond hair, fair skin, and blue eyes, meant Jacob blended with the general population despite his paternal Spanish origins. Jacob's grandfather had loved him as a favorite son. So did van Noordwijk, who had lost his only son to smallpox.

Jacob considered his place in England's hierarchy based on his own observations at Court and as explained in detail by van Noordwijk. At the top of seventeenth-century English society were the royals, hereditary nobility, and highest-ranking clergy from the established Church of England. Landowning squirearchy and gentry came next. Some were not rich but well off.

Wealth and nobility ensured one could be of the governing classes. Jacob had much wealth, but owned neither land nor any property in London. Nor would he, until the military campaign in Ireland ended. Perhaps he might invest in city property. He preferred a residence in lively London to an isolated estate in the provinces.

Status gradations existed laterally along streets, and vertically within individual houses—shopkeepers below, servants at the top, and household and lodgers in between. Gentry leased houses in fashionable terraces. Lesser families rented furnished houses, and a floating mass of lodgers crowded into rooms. Servants and apprentices slept in basements and attics.

Yeomen, farmers who owned their own land, could be financially secure, but often worked alongside their laborers and tenants. Below them came the masses: craftsmen, tenant farmers and laborers. In London Jacob observed a middle class growing and doing well financially. They included scientists, journalists, accountants, bookkeepers, teachers, attorneys, solicitors, physicians, surgeons, dealers in money, and merchants. Careers in the army, navy, and clergy had become attractive to younger sons of gentlemen.

Van Noordwijk estimated half the population could afford to eat meat every day. In other words, about 50% of the people were wealthy or at least reasonably well off. Below them about 30% of the population could afford to eat meat between two and six times a week. The bottom 20% might eat meat once a week. They were near destitute, and part of the time they relied on poor relief.

The poor ate food that was plain and monotonous, subsisting on bread, cheese, and onions. Each day ordinary people ate pottage, a stew made by boiling grain in water to make porridge. They added vegetables, and, if they could afford it, pieces of chicken, mutton, pigeon, or fish.

Jacob afforded and indulged in all London offered. His favorite dish was the Florentine, made of minced meat, eggs, currants, and spices.

He compared his wealth with wages and costs of living. A gentleman did not work with his hands. Van Noordwijk estimated there were about 15,000 landed gentlemen separate from freeholders with incomes of £55 per year; farmers had £42.10s; those in the liberal arts had £60, and shopkeepers and tradesmen had £45. Agricultural laborers earned £17, 15s. 7d. on average yearly, day laborers 16 to 18 pence a day, and general laborers £19, 4s. 5d., provided one had steady work.

For a young boy chopping wood the going rate was 1½ pence per hour, whilst a porter could expect a penny for shifting a bushel of coal. A waterman charged six pence from Westminster to London Bridge. A barber's shave and dressing one's wig also cost six pence.

Wages for female domestic servants ran from £2 to between £6 and £8 a year for a housemaid, and up to £15 per year for a skilled housekeeper. A footman cost £8 per year, and a coachman between £12 and £26. All wages included uniforms, food, and lodging. Domestics often received two to four shillings for their services to visitors.

Independent artisans needed to earn substantially more than domestic servants. They paid for their own food, lodging, and clothes. A low wage was £15 to £20 per year, and about £40 was needed to keep a family.

To live comfortably, a family required an income of at least £100 per year, whilst the boundary between the increasing middle class and the wealthy reached £500. By way of comparison, the First Lord of the Treasury received an annual salary of £4,000.

Jacob calculated costs of living in London aside from wages. A man's suit cost a minimum of £8. Rent affected most budgets. A shared bed in a cheap lodging house cost 2d. per night; and an unfurnished room cost 1s. 4d. per week. To be more secure, one needed £10 or more to rent a house for a year.

No profligate, Jacob added to his wealth by winning at Hazard and through investments by his Jewish merchant and banking contacts. On his first free day in London, Jacob had contacted his former *yesibót* classmates as well as friends of his grandfather now residing in the city.

*****

Back in the 1650s, Oliver Cromwell had given the wealthy Jews of Amsterdam permission to come to London and transfer their vital trade interests with the Spanish Main from Holland to England. Thus, several hundred Spanish and Portuguese Jews settled in London. The first Sephardic synagogue was established in 1656 at Creechurch Lane, and a burial ground was leased at Mile End, farther to the east.

Free to practice their religion and to be buried according to their rites and customs, Jews flourished in London. In the 1650s, they brought with them £1,500,000 in capital, which, by the time Jacob arrived in London, had increased to more than £7,000,000.

At various times, Parliamentary coalitions of aristocrats, Christian zealots and businessmen voted to expel all Jews. They failed to obtain a majority because the merchants were too useful to Cromwell and, after the Restoration, to the Crown.

Jacob calculated about 400 Jews resided in England. Not all were great merchants. Sephardic Jews also worked as physicians, jewelers, engravers, confectioners and street traders. All were likeminded regarding their daughters, the same as his Uncle Salomon.

This day, Abraham Santcroos had some advice for Jacob. "King William's wars on the Continent will eventually drain the Dutch treasury. London, not Amsterdam, will become Europe's diamond capital and financial center of trade."

His younger partner and Jacob's former classmate, Joseph Salvador, agreed. "Before it is too late, you should move your wealth from the Wisselbank to London."

"I have given that much thought," Jacob replied and ordered another coffee. "King William wants to create a Bank of England. Whatever I learn, I shall share with you."

"And I am pleased to share this with you. Our partners in *la Cofradía de los Judíos de Holanda*, the Jewish Brotherhood of Holland, captured two Spanish ships laden with gold and silver and sunk them."

Jacob had invested before with Santcroos and other merchants who supplied Jewish pirates of the Caribbean operating out of Port Royal, Jamaica, with ships, guns, powder, and provisions.

Santcroos handed Jacob a receipt for a profit of 8,500 gold florins added to his account. "London or the Wisselbank?" he asked.

Jacob raised his cup of coffee to Santcroos. "Let the sum rest here in London."

Chapter Thirteen

Coffee Houses

Jacob did not deny his addiction to coffee, which had begun in Amsterdam, and accompanied sociability in houses all over London and environs. Literate London males started their days in coffee rooms to read and hear the latest news. Watching shoeblacks and other riffraff poring over papers and discussing political affairs with their betters amused Jacob. He marveled at how strangers, whatever their social background or political allegiances, were welcomed into lively, convivial company.

According to Lambert, London's coffee craze commenced in 1652 when Pasqua Rosée, a Greek servant of a coffee-loving British Levant merchant, opened London's first coffee shack against a stone wall of St Michael's churchyard near The Royal Exchange. Within a few years, Pasqua was selling over 600 dishes of coffee each day, and other shops proliferated, to the horror of local tavern keepers.

Jacob and Lambert conceded that coffee, which both took to at first drink, was an acquired taste for many. They liked an old Turkish proverb, which called it: "A brew black as hell, strong as death, sweet as love."

Yet many contemporaries found coffee disgusting and gritty. Jacob and Lambert shared a laugh over one negative description of the brew: "a syrup of soot and essence of old shoes." Coffee reminded other dissenters of oil, ink, mud, damp, and shit. Partisans loved how the "bitter Mohammedan gruel" livened conversations, fired debates, sparked ideas and, as Pasqua wrote in his handbill of 1652, *The Virtue Drink,* "made one fit for business."

Another handbill published in 1652 to promote the launch of Pasqua Rosée's coffeehouse instructed people on how to drink coffee and promoted it as a miracle cure for dropsy, scurvy, gout, scrofula and miscarrying in childbearing women.

Lambert also explained why tavern owners hated coffeehouses. "Jack, my grandfather and father told me that until Oliver Cromwell's rule, most people in England were slightly to very drunk all the time. One still drinks London's fetid river water at one's own peril. Most people favored watered-down ale or beer. Coffee's arrival created sobriety, laying foundations for our spectacular economic growth because people thought clearly for the first time. Our stock exchange, insurance industry, and auctioneering all exploded into life in our coffeehouses. Credit, security, and markets facilitated a rapid expansion of England's network of global trade in Asia, Africa and the Americas. The coffeehouse's formula of maximized sociability, critical judgment, and relative sobriety proved to be a catalyst for creativity, and capitalist and journalistic innovations."

Lambert paused to sip his brew. "No respectable woman enters a coffeehouse. As Richard Steele wrote in the *Tatler,* "Wives become frustrated at the amount of time their husbands idle drinking coffee from the comfort of a fireside, deposing princes, settling the bounds of kingdoms, and balancing the powers of Europe with great justice and impartiality."

Jacob read *The Women's Petition Against Coffee*, which lambasted "excessive use of that Newfangled, Abominable, Heathenish Liquor called COFFEE, which reduced their virile industrious men into effeminate, babbling, French layabouts."

The author added:

On the occasion of this insufferable disaster, after a serious enquiry and discussion of the point by the learned of the faculty, we can attribute to nothing more than the excessive use of that newfangled, abominable, heathenish liquor called coffee, which rifling Nature of her choicest treasures, and drying up the radical moisture, has so eunuched our husbands and crippled our more kind gallants that they are become as impotent, as aged, as those deserts whence that unhappy berry is said to be brought. For the continual sipping of this pitiful drink is enough to bewitch men of two and twenty and tie up the codpiece point without a charm.

Certainly our countrymen's palates are become as fanatical as their brains; how else is it possible they should apostatize from the good old way of ale drinking, to run a whoring after such variety of destructive foreign liquors, to trifle away their time, scald their chops, and spend their money—all for a little base, black, thick, nasty, bitter, stinking, nauseous puddle water. Yet, as all witches have their charms, so this ugly Turkish enchantress by certain invisible wires attracts both rich and poor, so that those that have scarce two pence to buy their children bread must spend a penny each evening on this insipid stuff; nor can we send one of our husbands to call a midwife or borrow a clyster [enema] pipe, but he

*must stay an hour by the way drinking his two dishes
and two pipes.*

A swift reply appeared in *Men's Answer to the Women's
Petition Against Coffee*, which claimed coffee made "the
erection more vigorous, the ejaculation more full, and added
a spiritual ascendency to the sperm." Their response ended
further Women's Petitions.

Informed political debate had been a preserve of the social elite, but in the coffeehouse it was anyone's business who
could afford a one-penny entrance fee. An intrinsic feature of
urban life, early coffeehouses all followed the same blueprint,
maximizing interaction between customers and forging a
creative, convivial environment. They emerged as smoky,
candlelit forums for commercial transactions, spirited debate, and the exchange of information, ideas, gossip and lies.
The West End and Exchange Alley coffeehouses had Spartan,
wooden interiors. Customers sat on long communal tables
strewn with pamphlets, broadsides, newspapers, and maga-
zines, listening in to each other's conversations, interjecting
and opining whenever they pleased.

As each new customer entered, they'd be assailed by cries
of "What news have you?" Or, more formally, "Your servant,
sir. What news from Tripoli?" And, if you were in the Latin
Coffeehouse, "*Quid Novi?*"

Coffeehouses functioned as post-boxes for many customers, which added to this newsgathering function. Yet, Jacob observed, far from co-existing in perfect harmony on the
fireside bench, people in coffeehouses sat in relentless judgment of one another. At one of his favorites, Bedford Coffeehouse in Covent Garden, hung a "theatrical thermometer"
with temperatures ranging from "excellent" to "execrable,"
thus tormenting playwrights and actors.

Lambert estimated more than one hundred companies traded shares at Jonathan's Coffeehouse. The owner posted news behind his bar. Traders employed runners to bring information from returning ships.

Waghorn's and the Parliament Coffee House in Westminster were other favorites where customers shamed politicians for making tedious or ineffectual speeches, and at the Grecian they judged scientists' experiments.

Jacob most often drank coffee at Canela's near the Sephardic Synagogue where gathered merchants, brokers, and traders in gold, silver, diamonds, and other precious gems. He sat amongst his friends and trusted merchant bankers Abraham Santcroos, Francis Salvador, and Isaac Mocatta, whom he'd known from his *yesibót* school days in Amsterdam. His free-thinking grandfather had raised him a Jew, both circumcised and bar mitzvahed, but nurtured his natural proclivity for critical thinking. That he might serve in the Dutch army, Jacob had converted to the least orthodox Protestant Christianity, the Collegians. Having decided to make his life in England, he reasoned it to be most advantageous if he converted to the Anglican Church, despite it being one step away from Rome.

King William III of England faced a similar dilemma. He was a member of the Dutch Reformed Church, identical to Calvinists and Presbyterians. As king, he became head of the Church of England, while a Nonconformist.

William promised legal toleration for Catholics in his *Declaration* of October, 1688, but opposition in the new Parliament prevented it. The Glorious Revolution led to the Act of Toleration of 1689, which granted freedom of worship for Nonconformist Protestants, but not to Catholics.

CHAPTER FOURTEEN

IRELAND, STATUS QUO

In the first week of January 1690, Jacob and van Noordwijk were walking toward William's suite in Hampton Court Palace. Sir Christopher Wren had replaced half the original Tudor palace, including Henry VIII's state rooms and private apartments. New wings around the Fountain Court contained state apartments and private rooms of equal size and furnishings, one for William and another for Mary, to reflect their status as joint sovereigns.

The king's apartments faced south over the Privy Garden, the queen's, east, above the Fountain Garden. A gallery length of the east façade linked their suites with frescos. Delicate ironwork decorated William's staircase. Artists and artisans embellished and furnished their rooms in styles similar to those at Versailles.

Jacob and van Noordwijk arrived in William's suite with other staff. Wearing furs, His Majesty stood at the end of a rectangular table closest to a blazing fireplace. A detailed map of Ireland covered its top. Jacob observed only Dutch, Danish, and German commanders and advisors in attendance, no English or Scots.

William summarized a lack of progress in Ireland. His army there was led by seventy-five-year-old Frederick, 1st Duke of Schomberg. He poked Ulster with his forefinger. "I do not trust our English and Scottish troops, with the exception of Ulster's Protestant irregulars. I believe them to be unreliable, since James was their legitimate monarch only a year ago. Moreover, they are recently recruited and have yet to be tested in battle."

William paused during a coughing attack. "Our English troops are unaccustomed to Ireland's climate, and too many suffer from fever. Our army has lost men from both disease and from wounds ending in death. Corruption is rife. Here is one complaint amongst many from one soldier."

William read to his staff. "'We soldiers are so much neglected that lions in Africa are not more barbarous than some of your officers are to their sick men. Though Chelsea Hospital now exists for the disabled, it is inadequate to cope with so much widespread suffering.'"

Jacob also had complained more than once about the contempt and unnecessary cruelty noble and gentry officers displayed toward their common-born troops.

William continued, "Whilst we pacified England and Scotland, my Uncle James Stuart left France and returned to Ireland with 6,000 French soldiers, and raised an army to restore him to his throne. Now the Catholics control all of Ireland except for the province of Ulster. Schomberg is too old and his health is too poor to be effective. We need a permanent victory in Ireland to end Catholic rule and threats to all Protestants there. Our victory will enable us to acquire more allies who will join our Grand Alliance to thwart Louis XIV's ambitions to dominate all of Europe."

Jacob didn't need to be told the Irish wanted sovereignty, religious toleration for Catholicism, and land ownership. After Cromwell's conquest of Ireland in the 1650s, Catholic upper classes had lost most of their lands, and the rights to hold public office, to practice their religion, and to sit in the Irish Parliament. In 1685, they expected Catholic King James II to redress their grievances and restore Ireland's independence from England.

William concluded, "It is imperative we reestablish and maintain Protestant English rule in Ireland. If James and his Catholic supporters were to rule Ireland, they would decree Catholicism as the sole State religion. And, they would make Ireland a staging area for a French invasion of England to restore James to the throne. Our diplomacy has created The League of Augsburg to resist French aggression in Europe. Even Pope Alexander VIII and the Papal States have joined our Grand Alliance. He shares our hostility toward Catholic Louis XIV of France, who seeks dominance in Europe, and toward James his ally. Ireland is another battlefield in our war against Louis XIV."

Jacob compared both royal commanders. James had proved his bravery when fighting for his brother Charles II, but he had often panicked under pressure and made rash decisions. William, also an experienced soldier, had yet to win a major battle. Many ended in stalemates because he lacked the ability to manage armies in the thick of conflict. William's success against the French had been reliant upon tactical maneuvers and wise diplomacy rather than force.

William faced van Noordwijk. "Sir Dirck, you will leave for the Germanys and encourage more of those states to join our cause. We know they shall, after we lead a new and larger army to invade that pestilential island by June. One more thing, we need someone capable to lead our Huguenot cavalry into battle. Have any amongst you a recommendation?"

Jacob raised his hand. "Sire..."

"No, not you, Sir Jack. I need you amongst my staff."

"Your Majesty, I was going to recommend Captain Henry Lambert. He is both a Huguenot and a most capable cavalry officer. If you remember, we chose him over Lord Lyndby."

"Ah, yes, that popinjay who skulked away to Barbados. Sir Jack, send Captain Lambert to us. If we approve, he will be raised in rank to lt. colonel and lead a Huguenot cavalry regiment."

Action at last.

Jacob's pulse raced. He looked forward to sharing all he heard with Lambert.

*****

Jacob brought Lambert from the drill field to Hampton Court Palace, his friend still in Cavalry combat dress, front and back metal plates, metal helmet, sabre, and a brace of flintlock pistols. He waited in an anteroom whilst Lambert had a private audience with William III.

After fifteen minutes passed, Lambert emerged, faced flushed. He embraced Jacob. "You have helped make my career in the army. His Majesty has bestowed upon me the rank of lt. colonel and command of a Huguenot cavalry regiment to help liberate Ireland from its Catholic scourge."

"Then we must celebrate in style at Lady Barbara's."

Chapter Fifteen

To the Boyne and Dublin

William disembarked at Carrickfergus, a port town in County Antrim situated on the north shore of Belfast Lough, eleven miles from the city in Ulster. His army totaled 36,000 troops from many Protestant countries. Twenty thousand more soldiers had been in Ireland since 1689, commanded by Schomberg. They also included an effective Protestant irregular cavalry from Ulster, who called themselves *Inniskillingers* and were referred to as Scots-Irish. Jacob believed the best Williamite infantry came from Denmark and the Netherlands, professional soldiers all, equipped with the latest flintlock muskets.

William addressed his staff. "We shall encounter James' subordinate commander and Lord Deputy of Ireland, and French General Lauzun. We calculate the Jacobite army totals about 23,500. James has several regiments of French troops, but Irish Catholics provide the bulk of his infantry. The Jacobite cavalry recruited from dispossessed gentry has proven to be formidable in battle."

Jacob read reports from Schomberg confirming that the Irish infantry included a majority of inexperienced peasants who had been pressed into service. They received little training and many carried farm implements such as scythes, pitchforks, or a club known as a *shillelagh*, a knotty wooden walking stick with a large knob at the top, used as a cudgel.

Williamite tactical use of platoon fire added to Jacob's expectations of victory. Earlier in the century firearms had been either matchlocks or wheel locks. A matchlock held a slow-burning match, which was touched to the powder when the trigger was pulled. A wheel lock's metal wheel spun against iron pyrites, making sparks.

By 1690, William had replaced all matchlocks and wheel locks with flintlocks, which worked by hitting a piece of flint and steel, making sparks. Furthermore, the cartridge was invented. The musket ball was placed in a container, which held the right amount of gunpowder to fire it. The soldier no longer had to measure powder from a powder horn into his gun, which slowed reloading.

William armed his cavalry with wheel lock pistols, flintlock carbines, and sabers; they were protected by metal back and breast plates, and helmets.

Infantry had once consisted of men armed with muskets and others armed with pikes. A musket took a long time to reload and soldiers were vulnerable while they did so. They were protected by pike men with long spears. In theory there were two musketeers to each pike man. The pike men had steel helmets, but musketeers did not wear armor.

A decade earlier, the bayonet had been invented. A long blade attached to a musket could be used as a weapon, even if the musket had been fired and not reloaded. The bayonet did away with any need for pike men.

*****

William marched his army south to take Dublin. James placed his line of defense along the River Boyne, thirty miles from Ireland's capital. Buccaneer accompanied Jacob and killed many rats along the way to the Boyne.

With his staff, William surveyed the best crossings. He pointed at a black box attached to Jacob's saddle. "Sir Jack, what is in that box you always carry?"

"Some powders, salves, and bandages, Sire, should I need to attend to wounds and disinfect them. My grandfather taught me much. But, Sire, why are you not wearing armor?"

"Those breast and back metal plates interfere with my breathing."

Jacobite artillery fired in their direction, and William was hit in the shoulder by shrapnel. Jacob prevented him from falling off his horse.

"You again, Rockmore. You must ride at my side until our war is won."

"Sire, let me tend your wound before it is infected."

They rode out of range from more cannon fire and Jacob helped William dismount and remove his doublet and shirt.

"Sire, your wound is only of the flesh and not bone or vein. Let me tend to it."

Jacob opened his box and staunched the bleeding. He applied disinfecting balms and bandaged William's wound. "No cauterizing or stiches necessary, Sire."

William thanked Jacob and donned both shirt and doublet. He mounted his horse without help and rode with Jacob to his tent for a staff meeting. They decided where to cross the Boyne soon after.

*****

On July 1st, William denied Jacob's request to participate in active combat because he wanted him at his side. He sent a quarter of his troops, led by the Duke of Schomberg's son, Meinhardt, to cross the Boyne at Rough Grange, six miles southwest of Oldbridge hamlet, where they overwhelmed Irish dragoon pickets.

Defectors revealed James had assumed he might be out-flanked and sent half his army, along with most of his artillery, to counter Meinhardt's attack.

At a main ford near Oldbridge, William's infantry, led by his elite Dutch Blue Guards, forced their way across the river, using superior firepower to drive back James' foot soldiers.

Having secured the village of Oldbridge, Williamite infantry resisted successive Jacobite cavalry attacks with disciplined volley fire until they were scattered and driven into the river, except for the Blue Guards. Lambert's Huguenot cavalry crossed the Boyne. After taking heavy casualties, they forced the Jacobites to retreat and regroup at Donore, where they again put up stiff resistance before James ordered them to retire from battle. Other Jacobite infantry also retreated in good order.

William had an opportunity to trap James' army as it withdrew across the River Nanny at Duleek, but a successful Jacobite rearguard action slowed their advance. William's tactics did not surprise Jacob, who knew his king was disinclined to endanger James, since he was both his uncle and father-in-law.

William called for a staff meeting to assess his victory. Lambert received a promotion to full colonel for his turning the tide of battle, but no knighthood. All agreed casualties were low for combat on such a scale. Of 50,000 or so participants on both sides, no more than 2,000 died, three-quarters of them Jacobites. Yet Jacob assumed William's army had far more wounded, who were likely to die later because of infections, fever, and incompetent physicians and surgeons.

Reports arrived describing how James' order for a premature retreat had demoralized his army. His men believed it cost them a battle they should have won. Many Irish infantry deserted.

Back in Dublin, James abandoned Ireland's capital with a small escort and hurried toward Duncannon Port. From there, he boarded a sloop and set sail for France and a return to exile, even though his army had left the field relatively unscathed. His loss of nerve and speedy exit from the battlefield enraged his Irish supporters, who nicknamed him "*Seamus a' chaca*," James the Shit.

The Jacobite army abandoned Dublin and retreated toward Limerick across the River Shannon. William marched into Dublin two days after the battle.

*****

While William prepared his army for a march to Limerick, Jacob and Lambert discussed the results of their victory as reports arrived from the Continent. Crossing the Boyne and taking Dublin strengthened the League of Augsburg and led to a first-ever alliance between the Vatican and Protestant countries. As William had expected, it motivated more Protestant Germans to join the alliance, and ended fear of an imminent French conquest of Europe.

Pope Alexander VIII hailed William's victory at the Boyne. He ordered Vatican bells to be rung in celebration.

Jacob and Lambert agreed William's victory had strategic significance for both England and Ireland. It ended James' hope of regaining his throne by military means and assured the triumph of the Glorious Revolution. In Scotland, news of James' defeat stalled Highlanders' support for a Jacobite rising.

A complete conquest of Ireland was now a necessity, A large Jacobite army held an enclave behind the River Shannon and wanted to surrender whilst they could still negotiate good terms, but other Irish officers, such as Cavalry commander Patrick Sarsfield, objected, with good reason.

Many Jacobite officers were reluctant to surrender because William had published harsh terms whilst in Dublin. He offered a pardon only to Jacobite rank and file, but not to officers and the landowning class.

The French commander, Lauzun, also wanted to surrender. He expressed his dismay at the state of Limerick's fortifications, saying "they could be knocked down by roasted apples."

Jacob calculated 14,500 Jacobite infantry were stationed in Limerick, and another 2,500 cavalry in Clare under Sarsfield. The morale of ordinary soldiers was high due to circulation of an ancient prophecy the Irish would win a great victory over the English outside Limerick and drive them out of Ireland. Such prophecies were an important part of Irish popular culture.

*****

On August 7th, 1690, William, with 25,000 men, approached Limerick. They occupied Ireton's and Cromwell's forts outside the city. He had with him only his field artillery, as his siege cannon were making slower progress from Dublin with a light escort.

Stansfield's 600-man cavalry unit led by "Galloping" Hogan intercepted the siege train at Bully Net in county Limerick and destroyed all siege guns and ammunition. William had to wait another ten days before he could bombard Limerick in earnest after another siege train arrived from Waterford.

William summoned his commanders. "It is late in August. Winter approaches. Now that our siege cannon have arrived, we must complete our conquest of Ireland so I can return to the Netherlands dand get on with our war against France. I now order a full assault on Limerick."

On August 27th, William's siege guns blasted a breach in the walls of the *Irish Town* section of the city, launching his assault. At William's side, Jacob watched Danish grenadiers attempt to break through the breach, but the Jacobite French officer Boisseleau had built an earthwork inside the walls and barricades in the streets.

The Danish grenadiers and the eight regiments who followed them into the breach suffered from musket and cannon fire at point blank range. Jacobite soldiers without arms and civilians, including women, lined walls and threw stones and bottles at the attackers.

From outside Limerick, a regiment of Jacobite dragoons attacked William's soldiers in the breach. After three and a half hours of fighting, William called off the assault.

Jacob calculated William's men suffered about 3,000 casualties, including many of their best Dutch, Danish, German and Huguenot troops. The Jacobites lost 400 men.

Due to worsening weather, William called off the siege and put his troops into winter quarters, where another 2,000 died of disease.

Chapter Sixteen

Hazard

Jacob returned with William to Carrickfergus where they prepared to embark for England. Lambert stayed behind with his Huguenot cavalry.

After a staff meeting, Jacob and Buccaneer walked past hundreds of Irish Catholic prisoners tortured by victorious Protestants until they converted. He ignored their screams. How many would be no different from the *anusim*, Jews who converted to the Catholic faith in Spain and Portugal yet continued to practice the Law of Moses in secret?

At a plateau on a bluff above Carrickfergus Port, Jacob entered a spacious, noisy sutler's tent filled with soldiers waiting to embark for England. At long tables they drank ale, smoked pipes, and wenched with camp followers. Jacob purchased a brew and sat on a bench between two drunks sleeping faces down on the table board across from a pair of hardened men speaking Dutch. Buccaneer settled in his lap and slept.

*****

Jacob attended a staff meeting called by William on his flagship before it reached England. The king decided not to leave for the Continent until Limerick fell and its Jacobite army surrendered, which he expected by the summer of 1691.

Back in London, Jacob returned to his lodging at Lady Barbara's home in Covent Garden. Gamblers and spectators filled her gaming room, many of whom had gathered at a Hazard table. Lady Barbara controlled the game as its "setter."

Jacob had mastered Hazard's terminologies, wagering, and best odds. The "main" was any number from 5 to 9. Jacob understood all odds and outcomes in Hazard, which was why he always selected 7 as his main. If the first roll was his main, he won the "nick." If the first roll was a 2 or 3, known as "crabs," he'd be nicked out. If the first roll was an 11 or 12, then with a main of 5 or 9 both 11 and 12 lost. With a main of 6 or 8, 11 lost and 12 won. With a main of 7, 11 won and 12 lost.

Other numbers were "chances." If the main was 5, chances were 4, 6, 7, 8, 9, and 10. If the caster rolled one of those numbers, it became the chance. The caster threw dice from a small box until he rolled either his main or a chance. If the chance appeared first, the caster won; if his main came first, he lost his wager.

Jacob was surprised to see arrogant Lord Lyndby, resplendent in effete French style garments and oversized periwig, casting dice.

When did he return from Barbados?

Lyndby's English estate must have been restored to him by William's decrees.

"Five again. My nick." Lyndby poked his sullen liveried mulatto slave Ramses with a riding crop to sweep a pile of bank notes to his master. Lady Barbara collected her percentage.

Two men and a woman who'd lost left the table. Lyndby gloated as he gathered his winnings. "What? No one left to challenge me?"

Jacob recognized Sir Douglas Greenway, Baron Dumbrille from the House of Lords, urging Lyndby to quit while so successful. Lyndby addressed him as "Uncle."

"Listen to your uncle, young man."

Also advising Lyndby to cash in was Jacob's neighbor from across the hall, Sir Simon Monrose, a magistrate.

Jacob carried five one-thousand-pound banknotes and loose coins on his person. He estimated Lyndby had at least 10,000 guineas on the table, possibly more in his pockets. Lady Barbara stared at Jacob in expectation of a challenge to Lyndby.

How pleasurable it will be for me to pluck that popinjay's feathers.

"I accept your challenge man to ... man."

Lyndby scowled when he recognized Jacob. "You, Dutchman—it will be my pleasure to take revenge at this table."

Jacob sat opposite Lyndby. Lady Barbara took control of the dice. "Your Grace, Sir Jack, high roll shall determine the caster."

Lyndby threw first. "Eleven."

Jacob took the dice. He tested their balance and dropped them on the table to be certain they were not shaved. He shook the dice in the casting box and tossed the pair across the table.

Lady Barbara announced, "Sir Jack has cast twelve."

"*Sir* Jack?"

"Yes, Sir Jack was raised in rank to colonel and knighted by King William whilst you were away in Barbados." Lady Barbara gestured at Lyndby. "Select your wager."

"One thousand guineas."

More spectators gathered around the table and made side wagers. Jacob placed a banknote plus a shilling beside Lyndby's bet. Hazard's pace was fast. One needed a clear head to play well. Lyndby continued to drink Port and paid much attention to several ladies standing behind, the type who clustered around winners, hoping for spontaneous gifts. Lyndby should not have continued gambling. His slave Ramses poured more Port for him, to the rim.

Jacob announced his main as 7 and cast the dice; 7 came up. Lyndby doubled his wager for the next casting. Jacob continued to win until Lyndby had to reach into his doublet pockets for more banknotes to cover his last loss. He paid the guineas he owed. Lady Barbara counted the winnings and took her percentage.

Despite Dumbrille's objections, Lyndby demanded more Port and slurred, "Your luck has to end, Dutchman. I have 10,000 guineas left. That is my wager."

"As you wish."

"But I want fresh dice."

Lady Barbara accommodated Lyndby's request. He took the dice as if to place his imprimatur upon them. Jacob also verified the dice were not unbalanced. He dropped them in the casting box and cast a 6, which became the chance.

Lyndby gloated, "Now your luck has turned at last."

"But not yours."

Jacob cast another 6. Lady Barbara swept all the banknotes and shillings toward her station, counted them for her percentage and pushed the rest to Jacob.

"Wait!" Lyndby shouted. "I have more to wager." He whispered in Ramses' ear, and when his slave did not react he slashed his cheek with his crop. "As you know, Lady Barbara, my home is two houses away from yours. I have more to wager. Ramses, hurry there." Lyndby ignored Dumbrille's remonstrations.

Lady Barbara nodded at Jacob. "That is true. It was completed before Monmouth's rebellion, and it is grander than mine."

Jacob did not waste time speculating how many more guineas the fool intended to wager. By now, more ladies had moved to his side of the table. He lit his pipe and prepared himself for Lyndby's wager.

Ten minutes passed before Ramses returned with a metal box. Lyndby unlocked it and showed a document to Lady Barbara and Jacob. "Here is the deed to my home, which I shall wager against your winnings."

Jacob made eye contact with Ramses, who shrugged. He intended to show no mercy. "If all furnishings and servants are included."

"Yes, yes, the whole damned lot."

Spectators gasped. Lady Barbara held Lyndby's deed and gestured for Jacob to cast the dice. He paused, snuffed his pipe, and watched Lyndby empty and refill another glass of Port. Jacob called his main as 7 and cast an 11, to win the nick.

Lyndby cursed as he signed over the deed to his home.

"Sir Jack."

"Lady Barbara?"

"We shall appraise the worth of your new home and its belongings on the morrow so you may pay me my percentage of its value."

"Wait. I have more to wager." All stared aghast at Lyndby who removed another document from the box and pushed it to Lady Barbara, ignoring Dumbrille's protests.

"Sir Jack, he is offering his plantation in Barbados, all furnishings and chattel with it."

Lyndby swilled more Port and slurred, "An income of around 20,000 guineas and about two hundred slaves."

Jacob again made eye contact with Ramses. "Including this man here?"

"Yes, yes, so let us get on with it."

Jacob held the box and hesitated. "I believe you'd wager your estate were it not entailed. Lyndby grunted. "Who runs the plantation when you are away?"

"My widowed mother, but she is a most capable woman."

"My sister." Dumbrille lamented.

Jacob rattled dice in the box. "My main is seven."

Jacob ended the game with a roll of eleven. While the enormity of Jacob's wins sunk in, Lyndby sat in a stupor.

Ramses came to Jacob's chair. "You are my master now."

Lyndby giggled, took out a pistol, and aimed it at Jacob's heart. Spectators gasped. Some shouted at Lyndby to put away his weapon.

Jacob raised his right hand. "Lyndby, don't be rash. Get a night's sleep. Be sober on the morrow, and I shall meet you to settle differences with pistols as men of honor."

Lyndby giggled again and placed the pistol's barrel in his mouth. Jacob watched Ramses stand still even though the slave could have seized his master's weapon. Lyndby fired his pistol. Nearby spectators recoiled from blood and flesh on their persons. Others screamed, horrified.

Dumbrille tried to wipe blood and flesh off his doublet. "Rockmore, you'll pay dearly for this, taking advantage of my nephew's drinking."

Lady Barbara summoned servants to remove Lyndby's body and clean the area. She arranged for those men and women splattered with blood and flesh to be taken to another area to be cleaned as best possible. Magistrate Sir Simon

Montrose assured Lady Barbara the matter of Lord Lyndby's suicide would be disposed of with little or no scandal.

Jacob had another matter to discuss with the judge and made an appointment for the morrow. He took Ramses aside. "You were close enough to have taken his pistol."

"I believed you would be a kinder master."

Jacob listened to Ramses' well-spoken patterns of speech. Wilmot's slave had an Irish brogue he must have inherited from his mother, and a tendency to place wrong accents on certain syllables. *Is that Barbadian slave patois?*

*****

Jacob brought Ramses with him to the Santcroos-Salvador banking house. He deposited most of his winnings of almost 30,000 guineas and kept £5,000 in smaller banknotes and coins. He also gave Ramses £1,000 for pocket money.

The bankers again advised Jacob to transfer his wealth from the Wisselbank in Amsterdam to theirs. "The center of banking will be here in England. The Dutch will soon go into decline because of King William's spending on war."

Jacob appreciated their advice and said he would give it much thought.

Next, they visited the magistrate who arranged for Ramses' freedom. Now a freeman, Ramses asked to have his name changed to Sean Wilmot.

The magistrate raised his eyebrows. "Are you claiming a relationship to Earl Lyndby?"

"Sire, Earl Lyndby's father raped my Irish grandmother and my Irish mother after each arrived as slaves at his plantation in Barbados. My mother was given to an African slave who became my father, and bred my brothers and sisters. She secretly named me Sean."

"A pity you are not legitimate. Otherwise, you would be the next Earl Lyndby."

CHAPTER SEVENTEEN

RELUCTANT

"Is it true Earl Lyndby took his life last night at Lady Barbara's gaming table?"

Jacob stood before William and Mary in an anteroom at Kensington Palace. "Yes, Sire. I won all his money, his home in Covent Garden, and his plantation and town home in Barbados. He might have wagered his title and estate in York were it not entailed, so drunk and desperate he was."

"And now those revert to the Crown, unless a legitimate claimant comes forward within the next two years. Do you intend to visit your plantation in Barbados? We prefer you at our side on the Continent, but there are serious problems in Barbados. It is run by Planters as an independent country. They have not yet honored our pardon of all Monmouth rebels, who still live as indentured slaves there. Earlier today, we met a most amazing man, Henry Pitman. Have you heard of him?"

"No, Sire."

William told Jacob about this surgeon who, in 1685, had been falsely accused and convicted by King James' Court of Assizes of being a Monmouth supporter. They'd sentenced

Pitman to ten years of indentured slavery on a sugar planta-tion in Barbados. Despite being brutalized, Pitman escaped and made it back to England, where he published details of his life on Barbados.

"We summoned him for an audience, and he described how those planters disobeyed our pardon of the Monmouth rebels. And more. A delegation of Jews brought evidence from Barbados showing they are taxed higher than Chris-tians and not allowed to own plantations. We need someone in Barbados to bring those planters to heel and submit to our authority. You are well suited to be that man."

"When do I leave, Sire?"

"Early in March, that you may arrive before the rainy sea-son."

Mary spoke for the first time. "We must not place Sir Jack in a position of responsibility but with no ability to enforce our wishes."

"Agreed. We have until March to think on it."

*****

Jacob had to deal first with the servants who'd worked for Lyndby. He gave them a choice of quitting or continuing in service under Sean in his role as *major domo*. None mourned Lyndby, and all agreed to stay after Jacob im-proved their wages.

During the following months, Jacob organized his home. Lyndby had an extensive wardrobe, which fit Sean as if they had been twins. He also gave Sean Lyndby's swords, daggers, and pistols.

When Sean dressed in his new clothes, he exposed his bare back, crisscrossed with scars from past floggings.

"Did Lyndby do all that?"

"Some, but not all. His overseer Hobart did the most damage. He's a villainous bigot who hates all Irish more than the Africans because he believes we are Papists."

Jacob rid his home of all Wilmot family portraits, which he sent to the Lyndby entailed estate in York. Jacob replaced the Lyndby coats-of-arms with that of de Rocamora; he changed the Wilmot colors of servants' livery to de Rocamora blue and white.

97

Part Two

Barbados

1691-1693

".... thus we may see the buying
and selling of free men into slavery."

—Henry Pitman,
Surgeon and convicted Monmouth rebel, ca.1685-1689

Chapter Eighteen

Paradise,
or Irish and African Hell on Earth,
or Both?

Whilst Buccaneer adjusted to his new home, Jacob read all he could find about Barbados. He also encountered rare survivors of their servitude there and some who'd escaped their bondage. Sean also provided valuable information.

Barbados had a tropical monsoon climate, with mild breezes throughout the year, and suffered heavy rains of long duration during its wet season, which began in June and lasted through November. The dry season started in December and ended May 31st.

Sean assured Jacob that Barbados was spared the worst effects of tropical storms and hurricanes because its location in the south-east Caribbean region was outside most typical hurricane strike zones. On average, a major hurricane hit Barbados about once every twenty-six years. Other infrequent natural hazards included earthquakes and landslips.

From the beginning of colonization and sugar cultivation, few European settlers arrived in the Caribbean and the Americas to labor on plantations. Spanish and Portuguese *conquistadores* and colonists from Holland, England, and France enslaved indigenous populations to work on their first plantations. Many indigenous slaves escaped, but large numbers died from lack of immunity to European diseases of smallpox and scarlet fever, and from the harsh working conditions.

A Catholic priest, Bartolomé de las Casas, asked King Ferdinand of Spain to protect the Taino Indians of the Caribbean by importing African slaves instead. Beginning in 1505, slaves of African origin provided much of the labor for sugar plantations.

At first most English arrivals were indentured volunteers. Laws required prospective indentured servants to appear before, and be examined by, a justice of the peace, to ensure all who signed indentures were "voluntary, free and willing at their own Liberties," rather than "those whose labor and bodies had been stolen by Sinistery means."

Jacob found an original, decades-old indenture form describing young Englishmen who "Voluntarily Covenanteth, Promiseth and Granteth" their labor for a period of four years, in return for passage. Also, they were to "receive Meat, Drink, Apparel, Lodging and Washing." Moreover, at "the end of said Term" the planter would be bound by local practice, "to give, pay and allow unto the bound laborer no more than what was allowed to him or her according to the Custom of the Country."

After five years of labor, they received freedom dues of £10, usually in goods, and also five to ten acres of land, until the mid-1630s, when Barbados' population had grown so large free land no longer existed.

Jacob also read about the Irish slave trade, which had begun when James I issued his Proclamation requiring that 30,000 Irish Catholic political prisoners be sold to English settlers in the West Indies.

During the English civil war between Parliament and Charles I, the Irish rebelled against England's oppressive rule and recaptured all but Dublin and Derry. After Parliament defeated and executed King Charles in 1649, Oliver Cromwell led a brutal reconquest of Ireland. He and his Protestant armies claimed that all Irish were savage, barbarous Papists unworthy of the rights accorded English and Scottish convicts and other prisoners of war.

In September of 1649, Irish defenders of Drogheda refused to surrender, and Cromwell instructed his army to give no quarter. They massacred thousands of men, women, and children. Cromwell wrote, "This was a righteous judgment of God upon these barbarous wretches."

With bloody efficiency, English armies reconquered Ireland. Men not killed were sent to Barbados, Jamaica, and other colonies. One contemporary estimated that 34,000 Irishmen were sent to the Americas, close to one-sixth of Ireland's adult male population, and more went to Barbados than to any other English colony.

In December of 1649, in the Clonmacnoise Decrees, Ireland's Catholic hierarchy condemned "England's attempt to destroy Catholicism, uproot the common people and dispatch them to the Tobacco Island, as Barbados was known, and then replace them in Ireland with English soldiers and settlers."

English merchants petitioned Cromwell for permission to transport Irish prisoners "out of Ireland for planting in the Caribbee Islands before returning with cargoes of tobacco, sugar, and other crops."

Jacob was horrified to learn that from 1641 to 1652, 500,000 Irish were killed by the English and another 300,000 sold as bonded or indentured servants for a ten-year sentence, to be treated as slaves without English rights. Ireland's population fell from about 1,500,000 to 600,000 during Cromwell's reign as Lord Protector in the 1650s. *Servants, a euphemism for white slavery.*

Irish fathers, husbands, and male siblings having been sent to the Caribbean, a significant number of homeless women and children roamed the Irish countryside. The English auctioned those they caught during Cromwell's reign. Also, more than 100,000 Irish children between the ages of ten and fourteen were taken from their parents and sold as slaves in the West Indies and New England. Eighty-two thousand more Irish, mostly women and children, were shipped to Barbados and Virginia, all treated as human cattle. In 1656, Cromwell sent 2,000 Irish children to Jamaica and sold them as slaves to English settlers.

Jacob pitied the Irish and compared their travails to what his Jewish forebears had suffered in Spain under the Inquisition, until brutal reality reminded him Catholics were bigots who tolerated no rival religions and believed in Divine Right, absolute monarchies with power and authority derived from God.

A decade later, many Irish volunteers joined James II's Royalist cause, and when captured those Catholics faced brutal treatment from Protestants. Sir William Bereton hanged all Irish prisoners he captured.

*****

The African slave trade intensified at the same time. Because they were not hated Catholics and were more costly to purchase, some Africans were treated better than their Irish counterparts. A typical cost for an African was £50 Sterling, whilst indentured Irish were sold for no more than £5 Sterling. If a planter whipped, branded or beat an Irish slave to death, it was never a crime, merely a minor monetary setback, and far cheaper than killing a more expensive African.

During Oliver Cromwell's reign as Lord Protector between 1641 and 1658, 50,000 Irish were sent to West Indies plantations. By 1669, around 8,000 slaved on Barbados, while another 4,000 could be found on other Caribbean plantations.

English planters and overseers raped Irish women for both their pleasure and for greater profit. Children of slaves were slaves at no cost, which increased the size of a planter's free workforce. If an Irish woman obtained her freedom after ten years, her children continued as slaves of her master. Thus, Irish mothers, even with newfound emancipation, seldom abandoned their children and chose to remain in servitude.

English settlers also mated Irish women and girls with African males as soon as they were nubile, thus creating mulatto slaves of varying colors. They brought a higher price than Irish livestock and, likewise, enabled the settlers to save money rather than purchase new African slaves.

Mating Irish females with African men went on for several decades and became so widespread it lessened the profits of African slave transport companies. In 1681, legislation forbade the practice of mating Irish bonded women to African males for the purpose of producing mulatto slaves.

*****

Sean found a map of Barbados that Wilmot had owned, printed twenty years earlier. It showed in detail more than eight hundred plantations, watermills, windmills, cattle mills, and a thousand sugar mills. An extensive network of roads connected parishes, towns, ports, mills and plantations. Annually, 200 ships carried refined and clayed *muscovado* sugar to England and to Europe.

Irish, and later Scottish, rebels did not adapt well to Barbados' climate. Many died as bound laborers while working in sugarcane fields or sugar works.

Sean's said in a bitter tone, "One did not dare raise the possibility of achieving freedom with one's master, for to follow this course might incur a planter's wrath and extend one's bondage. Most men assumed they were likely to die as slaves. The hopelessness of a life and death in servitude was the norm for many Catholic English, Irish, and Scots as well as others taken as convicts, rebels, and vagrants and transported to brutal conditions working long days in boiling hot weather. They also suffered from disease, malnutrition, and cruel planters whose overseers used lash, torture, and chained deprivation to enforce discipline and extract labor that lasted for life."

Jacob was surprised to learn Barbados had more white and black slaves than any other English colony. Currently, Africans were employed either in hoeing, dunging, and planting in the wet season or cutting, carrying, grinding, and boiling sugar during the dry season. As white slaves grew scarce, enslaved Africans replaced them as the main source of plantation skilled labor.

Jacob did not look forward to being the master of almost two hundred slaves whom he could not free. He'd wait and see for himself how best he might make their treatment less brutal.

Chapter Nineteen

Henry Pitman

Jacob added to his knowledge about Barbados by reading surgeon Henry Pitman's misadventures during and after Monmouth's failed rebellion against James II in *A Relation of the Great Sufferings and Strange Adventures of Henry Pitman*, published in 1689.

During Monmouth's rebellion, the two armies fought at Sedgemoor after midnight on July 6th, 1685. The Earl of Feversham, Louis Duras, commanded the Royalist troops. The battle raged until dawn, when Monmouth's rebellion ended.

At that time, Henry Pitman and his younger brother were visiting relatives in Sandford, a nearby town in Somersetshire. Friends convinced him to watch the Duke of Monmouth and his army. As he later wrote:

> *After some stay there, having fully satisfied my curiosity, by a full view both of his person and his army, I resolved to return home: and in order thereunto, I took the direct road...but...if we went forward, we should be certainly intercepted by the Lord of Ox-*

ford's Troop, then in our way; we found ourselves, of necessity, obliged to retire back again to the Duke's forces, till we could meet with a more safe and convenient opportunity.

Pitman lost his horse and, unable to secure another:

I was prevailed upon to stay and take care of the sick and wounded men. I saw many sick and wounded men miserably lamenting the want of chirurgeons to dress their wounds. So that pity and compassion on my fellow creatures, more especially being my brothers in Christianity, obliged me to perform the duty of my calling among them, and to assist my brother chirurgeons toward those that, otherwise, would have languished in misery, though, indeed, there were many who did not, withstanding our utmost care and diligence.

Royalists arrested Pitman and his brother and took them with other prisoners to the Assizes in Wells. Imprisonment did not guarantee a rebel the right to a trial. Feversham condemned a number of prisoners for execution, innocent or not.

Pitman and his brother stood in the dock before Lord Chief Justice Jeffreys at what became known as the Bloody Assizes. They and others were coerced into confessing, "which acquainted Jeffreys with our crimes and provide d the True Bill against us, by the Grand Jury, rather than proving us guilty of treason."

Jeffreys made it certain no one would recant his confession and prolong the trials.

He caused about twenty-eight persons at the As-sizes at Dorchester, to be chosen from among the rest, against whom he knew he could procure evidence, and brought them first to their trial. Anyone who dared to say "Not Guilty" was shown evidence to contradict such a plea. Then Jeffreys immediately condemned them, and a warrant signed for their execution that same afternoon.

That singular mass execution convinced most of the remaining prisoners to plead guilty and throw themselves on the mercy of the court. All traitors, the Pitmans included, were "condemned to be hanged, drawn, and quartered. And by his order, there were two hundred and thirty executed; besides a great number hanged immediately after the Fight. The rest of us were ordered to be transported to the Caribbee Islands."

While the Pitmans appeared at the Autumn Assizes in Wells, they faced Lord Jeffreys, appointed Lord Chief Justice of England two years before the Monmouth Rebellion and also Lord Chancellor in 1685. His brutal judgments and penchant for taunting defendants with elaborate details of their impending punishments earned him the unflattering nickname "Hanging Judge" Jeffreys.

The Pitmans' death sentences were not carried out because Secretary of State Sir Robert Spencer, Earl of Sunderland, ordered that "rebels should be furnished for transportation to some of His Majesty's southern plantations, Jamaica, Barbados, or any of the Leeward Islands."

Transportation by ship across the Atlantic added to prisoners' misery and chances of survival. Jacob read about life on a typical wooden sailing ship. Ordinary seamen lived in damp, cramped, and filthy quarters. Cockroaches, fleas, and rats infested those vessels. The latter gnawed through anything, including a ship's hull, while sea creatures and plants worked on the hull from the outside. Food was spoiled or infested with maggots. Drinking water became rancid. Lower decks reeked of bilge water, human excrement, and body odor due to poor ventilation.

Bathroom facilities were primitive. Their equivalent of toilet paper was a rope dangling in the water. When stormy weather prevented using the head, sailors urinated and defecated into the hold. They rinsed their clothes by towing them in the sea, and on rare occasions bathed using a bucket of fresh water shared by many men. Soap was useless in salt water.

Although conditions were worse for transported treasonous convicts, Pitman and his brother survived their five-week voyage, which he referred to as "a sickly passage, insomuch as nine of my fellow prisoners were buried at sea."

Jacob was surprised Pitman made no mention of their being sold at auction. He wrote that he was consigned to Charles Thomas and his company, who in turn commanded him to serve Robert Bishop. Pitman's brother went to a different master.

Our diet was very mean. 5lbs of salt Irish beef. Or salt fish a week for each man, and Indian or Guinea corn ground on a stone, and made into dumplings instead of bread. Pitman described Bishop as a tyrant who grew more and more unkind unto us, and would not give us any clothes, nor me any benefits of practice,

My angry master, when I complained about his harsh treatment, was greatly enraged ... he could not content himself with the bare execution of his cane upon my head, arms and back. Although he played so long thereon, like a furious fencer, until he had split it in pieces; but he also confined me close prisoner in the Stocks which stood in an open place exposed to the scorching heat of the sun; where I remained about twelve hours.

Bishop eventually owed so much money all his property, including Pitman, was confiscated and resold.

Although convicted rebels were welcome labor for plantations, Barbados' government kept tight reins on those dangerous men. Pitman included in his account a copy of *An Act for Governing and Retaining Within this Island,* which named "All such rebel convicts, as by His most sacred Majesty' Order or Permit, have been or shall be transported ..." Pitman considered what followed to be unchristian. The Act included rules and regulations for governing rebels during their period of servitude, and regulations to prevent citizens from abetting them in any escape attempt.

*That is one or more of the aforesaid Servants or rebels convict[ed], shall attempt, and endevour, or contrive to make his or their escape from off this island before the said Term of Ten Years be fully complete[d] and ended; such Servant or Servants, for his or their so attempting or endeavouring to make escape, shall, upon proof thereof made to the Governor, receive, by his warrant, Thirty-nine lashes on his bare body, on some public day, in the next market town to his Master's town, be set in the pillory, by the space of one hour; and be burnt in the forehead with the letters **F. T.** signifying Fugitive Traitor, so as the letters may plainly appear in his forehead.*

Branding a criminal in the courtroom after conviction was common practice: 'T' for thief; 'F' for felon; 'M' for manslaughter, and so on. Authorities burned letters on thumb, hand. or wrist.

Pitman referred to another section of the Act:

> *... every Owner or Keeper of any small vessel... shall, within twenty days after publication thereof, give into the Secretary's Office...[security] in the sum of Two Hundred Pounds sterling...that he will not convey or carry off...any of the aforesaid rebels convict.......if any Owner or Keeper of such small vessel... hereafter make sale...thereof, without first giving notice in the Secretary's Office...such vessel...shall be forfeited to His Majesty his heirs and successors....*

Henry Pitman resolved to flee Barbados after learning his brother had died in servitude. He also gave up the hope he'd receive a pardon, which his relatives back in England had attempted to secure for him. Nor could he endure the abuse.

Around this time he made the acquaintance of John Nuthall:

> *...a carver; whose condition was somewhat mean, and therefore one that wanted money to carry me off the island: I imparted my design unto him, and employed him to buy a boat of a Guiney Man that lay in the road; promising him for his reward, not only his passage free, and money for his present expenses, but to give him the boat also, when we arrived at our port.*

The supplies Nuthall and Henry purchased for their escape impressed Jacob. They included:

...one hundredweight of bread, a convenient quantity of cheese, a cask of water, some few bottles of Canary and Madeira wine and beer, a compass, quadrant, chart, half-hour glass, half-minute glass, log and line, large tarpaulin, a hatchet, hammer, saw and nails, some spare boards, a lantern and candles.

Henry's group departed late on the evening of May 9th, 1685, while Governor Edward Steed entertained a fellow governor from another island. Although Steed put his militia on alert:

...reveling, drinking, and feasting to excess resulted in drowsy security and carelessness. We embarked in our small vessel; being in number eight, viz., John Whicker, Peter Bagwell, William Woodcock, John Cooke, Jeremiah Atkins, and myself, which were Sufferers on the account of the Duke of Monmouth: the other two were John Nuthall, who bought the boat for me, and Thomas Waker.

Pitman and his comrades departed Barbados in a small leaking boat:

...but having the conveniency of a tub and a large wooden bowl, we now fell to work, and in a little time we pretty well emptied our boat, and then we set our mast, and hoisted our sail, steered our course southwest as near as I could judge ... for although we endevoured all we could do to stop her gaping seams with our linen and all the rags we had ... yet she was so thin, so feeble, so heavily ladened, and wrought, so exceedingly by reason of the great motion of the sea, that we could not possibly make her tight, but were

forced to keep one person almost continually day and night to throw out the water, during our whole voyage.

Jacob was impressed by Pitman's resiliency regarding turning turtles after they beached on an island:

....we walked along the sea shore to watch for tortoises or turtle: which when they came up out of the sea... we turned on their backs. And they being incapable of turning themselves again, we let them remain so till the day following, or until we had conveniency of killing them: for if they were sufficiently defended from the heat of the sun by shade... they would live several days out of the water.... in the night-time, to turn turtle; and in the day-time, we were employed in killing them: whose flesh was the chiefest of our diet, being roasted by the fire on wooden spits.

Pitman wrote much about them and how they prepared the food turtles provided. Rather than eat bread, which they no longer had, they beat the yolks of turtle eggs "in calabashes with some salt, and fried them with the fat of the tortoise, like to pancakes, in an earthen jar found by the seaside..."

Privateers they encountered on the island attempted to dissuade Henry and his comrades from repairing their boat, instead suggesting they become privateers like themselves and accompany them in their piraguas. Failing to convince the rebel convicts of this idea, the privateers burned the leaky boat, expecting Henry and company would go with them rather than remain on the island until a ship passed in "eight or nine months," or risk capture by Spaniards who would accuse them of being pirates:

But this contrivance answered not their expectations. For notwithstanding they burnt our boat and took our sails and other utensils from us, I continued my resolution, and chose rather to trust Divine Providence on that desolate and uninhabitable island than to partake or be any ways concerned with them in their piracy: having confidence in myself, that GOD, who had so wonderfully and miraculously preserved us on the sea and brought us to this island, would, in like manner, deliver us hence, if we continued faithful to Him.

Four of the privateers opted to remain with Pitman and the others. After three months, a ship manned by privateers ventured near the island. Its captain invited Pitman alone to board his ship:

... where I was not only feasted with wine and choice provisions, but had given me by the Doctor a pair of silk stockings, a pair of shoes, and a great deal of linen cloths to make me shirts, &c.

Since the privateers were bound for port with a recently captured prize, I requested that I and my comrades accompany them. As was the custom on pirate ships, however, the captain could not make that decision without the consent of the Company, having but two votes and as many shares in the ship and cargo....

The Privateers agreed to take Pitman, but not his companions. They didn't, however, leave those men empty handed: "...they sent them a cask of wine, some bread and cheese, a gammon of bacon, some linen cloth, thread and needles to make them shirts, &c. And the next day, they permitted them to come on board, and entertained them very courteously."

After two days, Pitman and the privateers sailed to Providence in the Bahamas. "The English had built a town by the seaside and elected a Governor from among themselves, who with the consent of twelve more of the chief men on the island, made and enacted divers laws for the good of their little commonwealth, being as yet under the protection of no prince."

Pitman stayed for about two weeks before departing aboard a ketch bound for Carolina and New York. One morning he went for a walk and encountered an acquaintance from Barbados. This man told him:

...of the different resentments people had at our departure, and how after we were gone, our Masters had hired a sloop to send after us; but thinking it in vain, they did not pursue us. However, they sent our names and the description of our persons to the Leeward Islands, that so, if any of us came thither, we might be taken prisoners and sent up again. Most believed we had perished at sea.

Pitman sailed to Amsterdam. Five weeks later, the ship stopped first at the Isle of Wight, and he headed for Southampton incognito, only to learn upon his arrival that this disguise was unnecessary. "My relatives had procured my Pardon; and joyfully received me, as one risen from the dead."

Pitman ended his account with a devout prayer to the Almighty for seeing him through his trials, and completed his misadventures while residing at the sign of the Ship, in Paul's Churchyard, London on June 10th, 1689.

Jacob resolved to meet Pitman before he left for Barbados.

CHAPTER TWENTY

RETURN TO AMSTERDAM

Before Jacob departed for Amsterdam, he received a message to attend William and Mary at Hampton Court Palace. No one else appeared at his audience in the king's antechamber.

William beckoned Jacob to join him and Mary at a map of Europe spread on a large table. "Now that the Scots and Irish are pacified, we can return to putting all our efforts to thwarting Louis XIV on the continent and at sea. I shall be leaving for The Hague to take command of my army. Queen Mary shall reign here whilst I am away. Shortly, we shall be sending a flotilla to the Caribbean. Although we expected you to serve on our staff, we think it best you go to Barbados and report to us regarding their planters' disobedience and the maritime situation there. I shall prepare the proper documents for you to deliver to Governor Kendall."

Mary intervened. "It seems we are sending Sir Jack to Barbados on a fool's errand. He will have responsibilities. He requires authority as well. I suggest we make him Viceroy to act in our names."

William squinted at Jacob. "We suspect you are anti-slavery."

"I am, Sire, but I am also a realist. I promise I will not attempt to free all slaves on Barbados in your names."

"We believe you, Sir Jack. We shall make you Viceroy, with all our authority to act in our names. For how long do you intend to stay on Barbados?"

"Until I settle matters that concern the Crown and sell the plantation I won from Lord Lyndby at Hazard. Hopefully no longer than a year. When do I sail?"

"In two weeks, from Rotterdam."

"Then I have enough time to visit my father in Amsterdam."

*****

Later, in an ale house, Jacob met Henry Pitman, a handsome, weathered man of charm and wit, who attracted many women in the establishment. Jacob introduced himself with his new title of Viceroy and praised Pitman's account of his unjust sentencing and time in Barbados.

"An adventure I could have done without, which cost my brother's life," Pitman replied. "Do you plan to stay in Barbados and run your plantation, Sir Jack?"

"I have a specific mission on behalf of Their Majestys, but I intend to sell the plantation as soon it is practical. I wish I could free all slaves. I am an abolitionist."

"Then keep those opinions to yourself, if you can, or you will make powerful enemies on Barbados."

"Your story has made me well aware of that likelihood. Dr. Pitman, I must tell you, as I read your account, I expected you to include how a fair lady helped you escape."

Pitman laughed at Jacob's fantasy. "Would that it could have been possible, Sir James. Beware of Barbadian planter women. Some can be more cruel and vicious than their men. I pray we meet again after your return."

"If all goes according to plan, it should be no more than a year."

*****

Jacob shared Port with Sean in the room he intended to make his library. "I shall be leaving soon for Barbados as their Majesties' Viceroy, with the intention to sell Wilmot Plantation. You are free to travel with me or to stay here. Barbadians may not take kindly to your freedom."

"I prefer to accompany you, Sir Jack. You may need my advice about Plantation management and how best to survive the climate there."

"As you prefer."

Sean's decision caused Jacob to change his mind about keeping staff in London. He closed his house in Covent Garden, paid off all servants, and added new locks.

"Sean, I have family matters to deal with in Amsterdam. Meet me in Rotterdam. From there we sail to Barbados."

"Are you taking Buccaneer with you?"

"No. He is best suited to cooler climates. I must leave Hannibal behind at a grooming stable as well."

*****

Jacob had last been in Amsterdam more than three years earlier. He first visited Ouderkirk Sephardic cemetery. He passed the graves of his uncles Joseph, Daniel, and David. As was the Jewish custom, he placed stones on the graves of his Aunt Sarah, who'd raised him like a mother until her early death, his Grandmother Abigail, whom he'd never met, and his beloved grandfather, Don Vicente-Isaac Israel de Rocamora.

From Ouderkirk, Jacob walked through Amsterdam to the great Sephardic synagogue and arrived during morning prayers. He chose not to enter and instead sat on a bench in a park across the street.

Jacob stood when, amongst the congregation leaving the synagogue, his Uncle Salomon appeared with his two sons, fifteen-year-old Isaac and nine year-old-Abraham. He rushed across the street.

"*Tío.*"

Salomon Isaac de Rocamora stared, surprised. "Jacob? Is it really you? You are clothed as an aristocrat. Of course, you remember my sons. Isaac is attending medical school in Utrecht and Abraham also will become a physician. Come, walk with us and share our midday meal. Why have you come to Amsterdam?"

"To visit my father and you. How is his health?"

"Strong as always, as you shall see. Moses will outlive us all. Tell me about your exploits. I heard from Santcroos you fought in Ireland."

Jacob recounted his adventures from the day he sailed with Prince William in the "Glorious Crossing" to his becoming a baronet and winning a plantation on Barbados. "I sail from Rotterdam in ten days."

They reached the home Jacob knew from first memory until he joined the Dutch army. Salomon's wife Abigail greeted him with cold formality. He'd never win her over. Salomon's fourteen-year-old daughter Ester remembered him with a warm welcome. Six-year-old Hanna, who did not recognize Jacob, and two-year-old Debra stared at him with curiosity.

Salomon removed his plumed, wide-brimmed hat and replaced it with a skullcap. Bald on top, his long graying hair fell from the edges of his head to his shoulders. Jacob also noted his uncle's glasses were thicker than before.

Salomon led Jacob upstairs to where his father sat by the window in an attic, physically sturdy, but still childlike. Forty-two-year-old Moses Isaac de Rocamora did not recognize his son. Jacob had expected as much. Whilst Ester combed Moses' full head of white hair and beard, Salomon described his brother's daily routine. The daughters played with him and Lea took him to the park every afternoon after his midday meal.

"I should like to do that today, *Tío*. I know Sara wed last year ...."

"And she is with child."

"You will soon be a grandfather. My congratulations. But where is Lea?"

"Of course you would not have heard. Last month she wed Isaac da Costa Athias."

"From a good and well respected family, as I recall. *Tío*, I have something to tell you that at first may distress you. You call me Jacob, but I am known by another name in England. Colonel Sir Jack Rockmore, Their Majesties' Viceroy to Barbados."

"Rocamora to Rockmore. Most interesting. And your religion?"

"Anglican, so far, but I conform without believing. It will, in the end, depend upon whom I wed."

"There is someone?"

"Not yet."

Salomon frowned. "Sara is happily wed."

Point taken.

Ester finished grooming Moses, and Jacob said, "I would like to take my father to the park."

*****

Jacob sat on a bench with his slow-witted father and reflected on what might have been had Moses not been assaulted by the Schiffers. A life with Cordelia in New Amsterdam, now New York, would have included brothers and sisters. Moses' good physical health and natural strength continued to amaze Jacob until his thoughts turned to another what-might-have-been.

Had he and Cousin Sara wed, his life would have been one of predictable routine, the same as that of all Sephardim: daily and evening prayers at the synagogue, many children, and extended family obligations, which had no appeal for Jacob. He no longer regretted not marrying Sara or another woman from any Spanish-Portuguese Jewish community. More appealing to Jacob, a great adventure lay before him filled with unanticipated friends, foes, women, and unpredictable occurrences.

When Jacob said his farewell to Salomon and Ester, he gave his uncle a draft from the Wisselbank of five thousand Florins. "*Tío*, this is to ensure my father continues to be well cared for by you and my cousins. If you need more, please contact me through Santcroos."

Chapter Twenty-One

To Barbados

King William arrived at Hellevoetsluis. He inspected all three ships of a small flotilla he was sending to augment his Caribbean fleet. He introduced Jacob to Flotilla Admiral Sir John Pierce. The austere veteran sailor acknowledged Jacob with respect but ignored Sean when they boarded *The Endurance*, his flagship and first-rate ship-of-the-line.

First- and second-rate warships were three-deckers with 120 cannon on the, lower, middle, and upper decks, and smaller weapons on the quarterdeck, forecastle and poop. Two third-deckers accompanied *The Endurance*, with 80 cannon plus smaller weapons on their quarterdecks, forecastles and poops.

After William wished Pierce a successful crossing and Jacob a successful mission, Pierce continued to ignore Sean and faced Jacob. "Sir Jack, your slave will not have a private room or dine at my table."

"Sean is no slave."

When Sean showed Pierce his certificate of freedom, it mattered not to the admiral. "Is it not presumptuous for an

African to take the name of Wilmot, that of a most distinguished family?"

Jacob intervened. "His grandfather and great-grandfather were Wilmots, and his mother and grandmother were Irish and born free. Only his father ...."

"Sir Jack, those women were bonded Irish slaves ...."

"But born free, as I said."

"And he was born a bastard slave. Sir Jack, I will not break protocol and allow any disruption to the natural order on my ships... nor will my fellow planters on Barbados and every other island in the Caribbean do so. If he chooses to protest, I will remove him from my ship."

Jacob observed Sean's sullen expression and took him aside, saying loud enough for Pierce to hear, "I will ensure you are not mistreated."

*****

Once at sea during an evening spent conversing over fine Port in his cabinet, Pierce asked Jacob, "Why did you free the slave you call Sean? Are you an abolitionist?"

"If had my way, yes—I have no wish to own another person."

"I am familiar with Wilmot Plantation. You now own close to two hundred slaves. Do you intend to free them in the king's and queen's names?"

"I gave my word to Their Majesties I would not. But I shall sell the plantation as soon as I discharge my duties on behalf of Their Majesties."

*****

At dawn six weeks out from Rotterdam, during the end of the dry season, Barbados came into view, a lush island amidst azure waters.

In the early morning, Pierce's flotilla anchored a mile off Bridgetown Harbor, a noisy teeming port and the impressive capital of Barbados. Longboats from each ship rowed toward its docks carrying officers and crew.

Jacob and Sean disembarked with Admiral Pierce on a steaming day. At the docks they watched sweating African slaves load and unload cargo from other ships under a scorching sun and the snapping whips of brutal overseers. Planters and their women with slaves carrying parasols for them gathered at an auction block selling Africans.

Jacob had read a critique of Bridgetown back in London. It had developed into a center of commerce on Barbados after a land bridge was erected over bog land to link the harbor with the settlement.

The author described it as:

A Town ill scituate; for if they had considered health, as they did conveniency, they would never have set it there; or, if they had any intention at first, to have built a Town there, they could not have been so improvident, as not to forsee the main inconveniences that must ensue, by making choice of so unhealthy a place to live in. But the main oversight was, to build their Town upon so unwholsome a place. For, the ground being somewhat lower within the Land, than the Sea-banks are, the spring-Tides flow over, and there remains, making a great part of that flat, a kinde of Bog or Morasse, which vents out so loathsome a savour, as cannot but breed ill blood, and is (no doubt) the occasion of much sicknesse to those that live there.

Pierce gestured toward numerous storehouses built close to the waterfront. "Sir Jack, Bridgetown is a busy harbor with numerous storehouses built close to the waterfront. They store most of the island's sugar. An equally important settlement is Speightstown, situated to the north-west. It is also called Little Bristol in honor of the regular trade it enjoys with its namesake in England. Goods flow by ship between our two harbors of Bridgetown and Speightstown, which is a more efficient method of transport than maneuvering the roads."

Jacob dispatched Sean with their baggage to find an inn where they might refresh and stay the night. He preferred to meet Wilmot's mother before occupying his town home.

Carrying a carved Jacandra box, Jacob accompanied Admiral Pierce toward Governor Kendall, a lean hard man in a periwig standing by a four-horse carriage under a parasol held by a slave boy.

Jacob had sought information from Van Noordwijk about forty-five-year-old Sir James Kendall, who had been a soldier and politician before William and Mary appointed him Governor of Barbados in 1689. His family for many generations had been active in the politics of Cornwall and England. Kendall had served in the Coldstream Guards until 1685, when he became a Member of Parliament and Commissioner for the Office of Lords High Admiral. Wealthier than many dukes, most of his property was at Kendall Plantation on Barbados.

Kendall admired Pierce's flotilla. "Delighted to add more cannon and men to our fleet based around Barbados. And who is this gentleman accompanying you, Admiral Pierce?"

Jacob stepped forward. "I am Colonel Sir Jack Rockmore. I have journeyed to Barbados for reasons I prefer to discuss with you in private immediately."

Jacob opened his box. He handed Governor Kendall a scroll from William and Mary introducing him as their Viceroy due all cooperation, courtesies, and respect.

"Yes, we must discuss your mission in more comfortable quarters. This heat is unbearable, and, Sir Jack, Admiral Pierce, I see you are sweating like horses. My office is nearby at the Assembly Hall."

Jacob replaced the scroll in his box. "I also must speak to Sir Arthur Greenway. It is a matter that has much to do with my journey to Barbados."

"Sir Arthur and his sons are at their plantation. Why do you wish to speak with him?"

"I will explain when we settle in your office."

Kendall beckoned his carriage to come closer. After they settled inside, he asked Pierce about recent naval battles.

"Have you seen naval action, Sir Jack?"

"I sailed with King William to England in 1688, and fought in some battles before James Stuart fled to France. I also participated in the Irish campaign on King William's staff."

"You must have done a great service for His Majesty to earn your rank and knighthood."

Jacob described how he had saved William's life during The Glorious Crossing and again helped him keep his seat when a minor wound almost caused him to fall from his saddle.

"Then His Majesty may want you at his side in land battles against Louis XIV. For how long will you stay in Barbados?"

Jacob noted a tone of hope in Kendall's voice. "I cannot yet say."

Chapter Twenty-Two

Barbadian History and Government

Kendall's spacious office impressed Jacob. Cool white marble floor and columns, a high ceiling, mahogany shutters, and two large ceiling fans controlled by slave boys no older than ten cooled the room. Fresh water, beer, and fruit carried in by female slaves refreshed them. Kendall sat at his mahogany desk on a well-cushioned chair higher than those facing him. He removed his hat and periwig revealing a shaved head.

Jacob also removed his hat, scratched his head and wiped his damp face with a handkerchief.

"Sir Jack, I suggest you cut your hair, at the least, or shave your head. Otherwise, you will have an attractive nest for assorted parasites on our island."

"Thank you for the suggestion."

Jacob relished his first taste of a delicious fruit called mango. "Their Majesties have charged me with enforcing this decree." He handed Kendall a second scroll, which reddened the governor's face. "This royal command is for all Protestant Monmouth rebels to be freed from servitude immediately," Jacob stated.

Kendall snorted. "Too late for them. Most died from disease and punishments, a small number escaped, and only five have survived on Barbados. I cannot speak for any other island or our colonies in North America."

Jacob showed Kendall a third scroll certifying himself as the new owner of Wilmot Plantation and town house in Bridgetown. "Has this news reached Barbados?"

Kendall stared at the deed in shock. "Not yet."

Then Baron Dumbrille's letter has yet to arrive.

"Sir Jack, how did you persuade young Wilmot to sell his plantation? And why?"

Jacob told Kendall in detail of their duel at Hazard. "I also have the deed to his home in Covent Garden."

"Sir Arthur Greenway and his widowed sister, who is young Wilmot's mother, have not yet received this dreadful news. So where is Edmund Wilmot? Is he ashamed to return to Barbados?"

"No, he took his life after I won."

"Coward. Fool."

Sean appeared, and Kendall recoiled. "Ramses? What are you doing here pretending to be of the gentry by the cut of your clothes? Why did you not stop Wilmot from gambling away his plantation?"

Jacob intervened and showed Kendall a copy of Sean's emancipation.

The governor ignored Sean. "Fortunately for him it was signed by a prominent magistrate in England. That could never happen here. Be assured he can never inherit Wilmot Plantation. Sir Jack, if you are an abolitionist and plan to free all your slaves, disabuse yourself of that notion. That is also something that cannot happen here. This is not England. We have our own laws."

Kendall paused and told Sean to wait outside. Jacob nodded for Sean to obey.

"Sir Jack, now that you own Wilmot's plantation, you are amongst a select elite, more exclusive and powerful than the great dukes and earls in England."

Jacob settled deeper in his chair whilst Kendall lectured about the realities of power on Barbados. "Sir Jack, you should know that our Barbados census of 1680 revealed that here on Barbados 159 families own 175 great plantations, between 50 and 60 percent of the island's property, including slaves and bonded servants, I amongst them. And now, you. We land owners are less than one percent of Barbados' white population and only one-third of one percent of the island's population. Many of us are second- or third-generation settlers, including Admiral Pierce, the Allyns, the Codringtons, the Draxes, the Freres, the Guys, the Hothersalls, the Greenways, the Pears, and the Yeamans, who have owned plantations on the island since the 1630s. You'll meet them all eventually."

"And they, I presume, control all aspects of government."

"That is true, Sir Jack. Those great planter families serve on the Governor's Council or sit in the Assembly. They hold the highest political, military, and judicial positions. Many have held up to four offices concurrently."

Kendall paused to withdraw from his desk drawer several sheets of paper. "One hundred and nine of 175 great planters have held office. Twenty-five of the remainder are women, Jews, or Quakers, who are ineligible. We great planters enjoy unrestrained political and judicial power on Barbados. We have shaped the island to protect our interests."

Kendall lectured Jacob about Barbadian laws and customs. Much of it Jacob had learned before through research and questioning Sean and Admiral Pierce during their voyage. Kendall's stern demeanor whilst he spoke made Barbados seem more hellish to Jacob.

Over decades, planters had defined the terms of bound laborers' service by legislation and government policy on Barbados. As early as the 1640s they faced a dwindling supply of voluntary laborers and became dependent upon involuntary workers from English and Scottish prisons, or captives from wars and rebellions. Mixed in were an unknown number of boys and youths kidnapped to work on the island, and African slaves.

Kendall paused to drink more beer, and continued his lecture. The terms and nature of labor were defined not by English custom or law but by Barbadian necessities. Indentured servants in Barbados served longer sentences than English laborers. For a period varying between three and ten years they were bought, sold, and traded in a way unknown in Britain.

Servants in Barbados had no enforceable rights in planter-dominated local courts, and they were controlled by a planter class whose members used violence to control and punish their workforce.

"Servant" is a euphemism for slave.

Kendall beckoned a slave to bring him a soft-upholstered ottoman on which he rested a gouty foot. "Planters' domination of the courts, Council, and Assembly guarantee servants have little or no redress in our legal system. Disputes between planters and their bound servants are heard before one of the island's courts of common pleas, presided over by a judge, and four assistants appointed by the governor. Any servant judged to have brought a frivolous suit against his or her master receives thirteen lashes or has his term of bound labor increased by our planter-dominated court. Few clauses of Barbadian law refer to the rights of bound servants, while many list the authority planters hold over their laborers."

A tall standing clock behind Kendall chimed eleven. Jacob searched for an excuse to leave for the inn Sean had found, where he could wash and change into clothes more suitable to Barbados' climate.

"Sir Jack, it must be obvious to you that sugar is the most valuable staple crop grown in Barbados, Jamaica, and the Leeward Islands. We supply half of all sugar consumed in Europe. Bridgetown is now the finest and largest city in all the islands and English colonies abroad. It is a nexus for one of the richest trades in agricultural output in the world. Sugar and commercial success—together with political and social stability—has made Barbados an attractive venue for investment. Land prices have soared throughout the decades. If you run your plantation efficiently, you shall become a wealthy man, a very wealthy man."

Kendall will never know how wealthy I already am.

Jacob was not surprised a small, powerful planter elite controlled Barbadian government, justice, and military power. Their bound British laborers' lives were forfeit beyond all the legal and customary protections of England, Scotland, and Wales.

As Jacob had learned from William and Mary, when they considered pardoning all Monmouth rebels, Kendall and his Barbados Council protested. They argued it would unfairly harm planters who had taught them to be boilers, distillers, and refiners.

Jacob reminded Kendall, "Still William and Mary freed all former Monmouth rebels in March of 1691."

"Too late for most, as I said. Many have perished."

Whilst Jacob had still been in England, Pitman had told him how their masters denied them basic rights of liberty and adequate food and clothing, which never happened in England. Barbadian planters punished their indentured slaves for the slightest infraction, real or imagined, with the lash, canings, and stocks in boiling weather.

Sean had added more information about the Monmouth rebels on Barbados. A few were hired as overseers. Some continued as wage laborers or served as militia men on plantations. Others wandered the island, dependent upon vestry poor relief.

Kendall offered Jacob more beer. "Sir Jack, by now nearly all white indentured servants in Barbados have been displaced by African slaves on most plantations. Fishing, dock work, boating, and plantation management remain for whites. Demand for white servants is strong, in part because many of these servants were prisoners of war and rebels with few rights. Planters may benefit from their labor for a decade, placing them in skilled and supervisory positions over the growing enslaved workforce at little cost."

Kendall told Jacob that in 1686 the Barbados Assembly had passed a law detailing the conditions of service of political and military prisoners: their decade-long indentures could not be sold off the island. They were prohibited from marrying white servants. They could not be freed before their terms expired; and those who attempted to escape would be whipped and branded with "FT" to mark them as fugitive traitors.

Kendall confirmed everything Pitman described. Planters enjoyed absolute control over white servants. A cruel master ensured a wearisome and miserable life. Verbal and physical resistance brought brutal punishment and extension of servitude. Masters dealt with impudent, saucy and provoking servants by reporting them to a local justice of the peace, who was required by law "to inflict such corporal punishment as he shall judge the crime to deserve".

Of more significance was the total control Barbadian planters had of a servant's time, not only the hours of labor contracted for. Planters restricted and controlled all aspects of a servant's life. Laborers were the most valued commodities purchased by planters. Local laws and custom allowed planters to exploit those investments. Because of lengthy bondage,, these servants resembled pauper or vagrant apprentices bound to a master for a decade.

Ethnic and religious differences amongst white servants, along with the brutal control exercised by the planter class, prevented them from uniting and organizing any significant resistance.

The Planters hated Irish servants for their Catholicism. Those religious and cultural differences divided the white servant class. Discrimination persisted against those who survived their period of bound labor, possessing skills of value on Barbadian plantations. Still, they could expect to enjoy better conditions during their four-year terms than would have been enjoyed by unskilled bound vagrants, convicts, and prisoners. In addition to practicing their crafts, these skilled men trained Africans in craftsmanship, so by the late seventeenth century they had rendered white skilled labor unnecessary.

The need for skilled carpenters, joiners, and potters for making kilns on Barbados was such that free men set the terms of their employment. Potters used local clay for the kilns to manufacture the large pots required to process *Muscovado* sugar, a word derived from the Portuguese *açúcar mascavado*, unrefined sugar, with a strong molasses content and flavor. The main uses of *Muscovado* were in food, confectionery, and the manufacture of rum and other forms of alcohol.

Jacob fantasized over freeing all the slaves he'd won from Lyndby, but knew it would never be allowed on Barbados. Kendall had reinforced his gloomy conclusion. At least he might be able to improve their miserable conditions of servitude.

"Think on this, Sir Jack. Barbadian planters are the wealthiest men, by far, in British America, and our sugar shipped to the British Isles is more valuable than tobacco and all the other crops and products shipped from the mainland North American colonies combined."

Jacob was not surprised white indentured servants were more susceptible to tropical diseases, including yellow fever, dropsy, and yaws, than the African slaves who eventually replaced them. Instead of protecting their white servants, masters extracted as much labor as quickly as possible, for the smallest outlay of expense to maximize profits.

During the years between 1650 and 1690 at least 40 to 50 percent of the Barbadian servant population was Irish. It was common for Irish servants to be worked alongside early African slaves, and Irish prisoners were treated with exceptional brutality by Barbadian planters. They held great hatred and contempt for them as illiterate Catholic savages, whom they feared were likely to join with African slaves in bloody rebellion. Given the brutal treatment Irish prisoners received, such fears were well founded. A multiracial group of thirty Irish and African slaves and servants took shelter in forested land in St. Philip Parish during the mid-1650s. Rebellion by bonded servants was a constant threat. Cruel masters provoked their servants by extreme ill usage, and often with vicious beatings. They grew desperate, and joined together to revenge themselves upon the Planters.

In 1649 the sufferings of bound laborers were so great that some amongst them, whose spirits were unable to endure such slavery, resolved to end it or die. Convinced a majority of Barbados' bound white work force were supportive, they planned a rebellion, which was betrayed. Eighteen of their leaders were executed.

As numbers of enslaved African laborers grew, fear of rebellion intensified, and planters dreaded any alliance between Irish and Africans. They formed militia groups of English and Scots, separating them from runaway enslaved Africans but also from the Irish.

"Sir Jack, I will concede we planters are so terrified of potential alliances between Irish Catholics and black slaves that in March 1689 our Council ordered that blacks believed to be Catholic must be transported off Barbados and sold. A potential rebellious combination of slaves, Irish, and other Catholics created nightmares."

"But why did you treat your Scots so harshly? They were your fellow Protestants and Monmouth rebels. Is Barbados a nest of Jacobites?"

"Definitely not. Our religion is the established Church of England. True, there are Quakers and Jews residing here as well, but they are not likely to be violent. Not all Scots transported from jails were vagrants and common criminals. Dissenters were sent here after rebellions in 1666 and 1679 in which Presbyterian Covenanters rose against restoration of the episcopacy in Scotland. Following the rebellion in 1666, the Scottish Privy Council appointed a committee to examine imprisoned religious rebels to establish their various creeds and willingness to renounce their beliefs and pledge allegiance to Charles II and the new religious order. Those deemed most incorrigible, guilty of rebellion, or who refused allegiance and Episcopacy, on the order of King Charles II and his Privy Council, were sent to Barbados at first opportunity."

Kendall described how frequent wars and rebellions provided more prisoners, in addition to vagrants and criminals. European laws of war sanctioned extreme measures against soldiers and civilians alike. The list included pirates, rebels, robbers, and traitors, and the Law of Armies was not to be observed and kept for them. Expensive to maintain, imprisoned rebels and prisoners of war could usually expect to be executed or, if they were fortunate, pardoned and released.

The labor needs of England's New World colonies, such as Barbados and later Jamaica, provided a convenient and profitable alternative for officials, who wanted neither to execute tens of thousands nor to release them without penalty. Instead, capital sentences were commuted to banishment to plantations for ten years.

Before Jacob had left England, he'd read a shocking petition describing how victims experienced transport, sale, and labor in Barbados. Having been taken prisoner in 1654, two authors arrived on Barbados in May 1656 and were sold to planters:

> *Suffering the most insupportable Captivity, generally grinding at the Mills attending the Furnaces or digging in this scorching island, having nothing to feed on but Potato Roots, nor to drink but water... These men found themselves being bought and sold still from one planter to another, and any infraction led to their being whipt at whipping-posts, as Rogues, for their masters' pleasure.*

Chapter Twenty-Three

Toward Wilmot Plantation

In pain from his gout, Governor Kendal chose not to accompany Jacob to Wilmot Plantation. He left it for Jacob to inform Lady Mary Wilmot, Lyndby's widowed mother, of her son's folly and demise.

Sean had found an inn on Swan Street, also known as Jew Street, one block away from a Synagogue. There Barbadians patronized Sephardic traders, merchants, and vendors who sold clothing, jewelry, and housewares. Of interest, one Isaac Pereira owned the inn. Jacob introduced himself as Colonel Sir Jack Rockmore. He'd reveal his origins to the Sephardic community another time.

Jacob's room was spacious and cool. He showered on the veranda while Sean poured buckets of water over his hair and body. Afterward, Jacob donned a white linen shirt and trousers and black boots. He attached two loaded pistols and sabre to a black sash around his waist, and wore a broad brimmed straw hat. He added a loaded carbine to his horse's saddle. Jacob did not know what resistance if any he might face at Wilmot plantation. He advised Sean to arm himself.

Jacob rented a cart for their baggage and two horses. Sean took the reins because he was familiar with the route. They passed plantations with sprawling sugar cane fields and slaves planting in the brutal heat.

Barbadian roads were rutted and broken by tree stumps from land clearing. They passed carriages and wagons carrying goods in the opposite direction to Bridgetown by horse, oxen, and camel. Oil skin tarps covered the sugar to protect it from sudden rain showers.

Sean volunteered, "One camel alone can carry about sixteen hundred pounds of sugar. Beware if you must seek shelter during sudden shower not to sit under those Manchineel trees. They are poisonous and rain runoff causes severe blistering."

"I'll have much to learn about you flora and fauna."

Sean continued his introduction to Barbados for Jacob's benefit. "Concerns over tropical storms requires houses be designed with north/south facing windows rather than east/west. Unfortunately, that construction didn't allow for cooling breezes to circulate throughout the house.

"A large plantation like Wilmot's is about 500 acres, although numerous smaller plantations can be found across the island. Out of 500 acres, 200 are used to grow sugar cane, 30 acres to growing tobacco, 120 acres for wood, 5 for ginger or cotton and 70 for other household crops such as plantains, corn, cassava and orchard fruit. Oxen must be imported from England, but they often succumb to disease. Pigs, goats, and wild turkeys do well here."

"And free humans?"

"Some adapt, others suffer. As you will see, slave and indentured servants' quarters are thatched huts far from the main house. Slaves sleep on rough pallets on dirt floors, while indentured servants and Christian African slaves are spared discomfort from creepy-crawlies; they sleep off the ground on hammocks."

Jacob took out a handkerchief and wiped his brow and face. "What do people eat, and what are hours of work for slaves?"

"Plantation owners and their families dine and drink well. For workers, the first meal of the day is around eleven in the morning and the last one after six in the evening. During the heat of the day, indentured servants and slaves are given a two hour break to cook, eat and rest before heading back to the fields and continue their work. Their main staple is gruel of cornmeal called loblolly. No wheat, but a flatbread made from a root vegetable called cassava is another staple; boiled and ground into meal. At the end of the work week on Saturday, servants and slaves are given extra food allotments of two mackerels for the men and one for the women. Bone meat might be given perhaps a couple of times a week. Dead animals, even if diseased, are given to servants and slaves to eat, although slaves generally receive head and entrails."

"And drink?

"The most common grog is called *mobbie*, made of sweet potatoes. It has the strength of a German white wine and can be colored red if red potato skins are used in the fermentation process. As a by-product of sugar production, rum or kill-devil is distilled and given to servants and slaves. Excess rum is sold in Bridgetown to the ships. Of course the best imported brandies and spirits are reserved for the master's table."

"Governor Kendall told me sugar is king on Barbados."

"Yes, there is little hard currency on the island so people rely on bartering and currency of sugar for every major purchase, including payment of fines. A large plantation with 200 acres of sugarcane yields one million pounds of sugar over a twenty month cycle. Ah, we have arrived."

Chapter Twenty-Four

Greenways

Wilmot Plantation came into view, built of coral limestone rock with mahogany porticos, verandas, and shutters, typical of other great houses they'd passed.

"Sir Jack, our Caribbean climate of high winds, heavy rain and extreme heat has affected Barbadian architecture. Most homes have gabled roofs, wide and open verandas, low, hurricane-resistant rectangular shapes, and sturdy shutters protecting sash and jalousie windows."

"I shall decide if I approve of the interior after I see it."

Curious African and mulatto house slaves gathered around their cart. Some stared at Sean with puzzlement or shock when they recognized him.

An elderly mulatto butler Sean addressed as Agamemnon led them through a majestic carved mahogany pair of doors into a home filled with well-designed upholstered and cane furniture. Tray ceilings above led into a study with high windows.

Lady Mary Wilmot sat at a desk about to sign a document. Her bookkeeper, a Sephardic Jew Jacob guessed, sat opposite. An older man and two younger, probably his sons, stood behind her. Their faces were those of snarling dogs with feral mouths like that of their kinsman Baron Dumbrille.

A sullen, handsome white overseer stood at one side of the desk and glared at Sean and Jacob while gripping both shoulders of a trembling young mulatta.

Sean whispered, "She is Matty, the girl I wish to wed."

"Be calm, Sean, and I will take my property." Jacob had never seen so beautiful a face: golden skin, white features, and aqua blue eyes. Her hair was covered by a red bandana, with a loose blue blouse and billowing yellow skirt hiding her form. Sean did not take his eyes away from her, except to sneer at Hobart.

Lady Mary Wilmot, a lean, fading beauty, stopped writing and scowled at Jacob. "Who are you? What is the meaning of this intrusion? Ramses, what are you doing here? Where is Edmund?"

Jacob strode to her desk. "Lady Mary, I have met with Governor Kendall to inform him I am Colonel Sir Jack Rockmore, and I have come to Barbados as Viceroy of their Majesties to represent them here."

The older man said, "I am Sir Arthur Greenway, Lady Mary's brother ... and these are my two sons Henry and Richard." He frowned at Sean. "Why is this slave dressed as a gentleman—well-armed, too? And where is Edmund?"

Jacob placed his box on Lady Mary's desk. "Lady Mary, Sir Arthur, I have here the deeds to this plantation, as well as those of your former homes in Bridgetown and Covent Garden. And I would have had the Lyndby estate in York as well, were it not entailed." He paused while they absorbed all he said. "Edmund hated me. He believed I ruined his military career, and he tried to destroy me at Hazard."

Greenway pointed a finger at Lady Mary. "That damned fool. You spoiled and ruined him. He was probably too ashamed to come home and face us."

"Lady Mary, I regret to inform you, your son Edmund shot himself in front of all in attendance."

Lady Mary screamed and Hobart rushed to her side and supported her. The mulatta moved to Agamemnon for protection.

Greenway faced Jacob. "So you, Sir Jack, now you are the presumptive owner of Wilmot plantation and all chattel?"

"Not presumptive. I am the actual owner."

Greenway shouted at Lady Mary, "Edmund always was a spoiled fool!"

Lady Mary screamed at Sean, "Ramses, why did you not stop him?"

"I tried, but he struck me."

"Hobart, take Ramses away and give him fifty lashes."

"Hobart will not lash Ramses or anyone else on *my* plantation." Jacob declared. He showed all in attendance the document certifying Ramses' freedom. "He is no longer a slave, and he has taken the name his mother gave him... Sean... Sean Wilmot."

Lady Mary's face reddened. "How dare ....?" She wept, frustrated.

"Who are these other men?" Jacob asked.

Greenway answered for his sister, "Plantation bookkeeper, Abraham Mendes. And overseer John Hobart."

More than overseer, Jacob suspected of the handsome mustachioed Englishman. "A Monmouth rebel?"

"Aye, and proud of it."

"Protestant?"

"What if I am?"

Jacob showed Hobart the royal decree freeing all Protestant Monmouth rebels from bonded servitude throughout the colonies. "If you wish passage back to England I shall arrange and pay for it."

Lady Mary panicked. "John, you mustn't abandon me. Sir Jack, are you throwing me out of my home today?"

"I give you a few hours to pack your necessities." Jacob saw the overseer move to regain control of the mulatta. "Hobart, do not touch that girl."

"But I sold Matty to my brother. Here is the bill of sale."

Jacob swept the paper from her desk. *Five hundred guineas for a slave?* He observed one of the Greenway sons nudge his father.

Sir Arthur cleared his throat. "We concluded this bill of sale for the slave before you arrived."

Why is she so valuable?

Jacob tore the bill of sale into confetti. "My acquisition of this plantation and all chattels predates Matty's sale. She will remain here. Sir Arthur, we have no further business to discuss at this time. You and your sons are free to leave now. And you as well, Hobart. You are dismissed as overseer."

Jacob turned to the bookkeeper and spoke in Portuguese. "*Senhor* Mendes, I shall retain you in your capacity as bookkeeper, and I want you to stay here for further instructions."

Greenway restrained his angry sons and lit his pipe. "Colonel Rockmore, many English find the climate here unbearable. Some die from local diseases. Should you decide to leave Barbados, there are many planters who covet this plantation and might pay you a small fortune for it."

"You'd purchase it for Lady Mary?"

"Yes, at a fair market price."

"We shall discuss prices another time. Now, Lady Mary, I will take the room upstairs that belonged to your husband, and Sean will be given Edmund's room."

"He cannot live in this house!"

"Lady Mary, understand this: I am master here now, not you. Sean will have that room." Jacob turned again to book-keeper Mendes. "Don Abraham, on the morrow, I will go over all accounts with you."

Jacob noted Mendes' surprise at being addressed as "Don" according to Sephardic tradition. He beckoned Agamemnon and told him to find some men to take their baggage to his and Sean's rooms. "Also, notify the cook that and Sean and I will dine at each meal."

Lady Mary snapped at Matty. "You will help me pack."

Jacob intervened. "Matty is no longer your servant. I give you two hours. Hobart and your nephews may help you."

Sean looked toward the door. "Agamemnon, I wish to see my father and sister."

"Of course."

*****

They supped that evening in an atmosphere of tension. Sean did not speak. Servants who brought food and drink to their table regarded him with contempt or hostility.

Afterward, when they drank rum together on the veranda, Sean complained how his father, sister, and other slaves scorned him. Some were consumed with envy. Pure Africans accused him of trying to be white.

"Sean, you might be better off if you return to England, where laws are more equitable. As a free man there, you can select a trade, an education for a profession, and find a good woman for a wife."

"When do we sail?"

Jacob did not reveal his intention to leave at the start of the next dry season in January. "I have not yet decided, but you may depart at any time. I believe you will be treated best in London."

Strange creatures startled Jacob when one leaped onto his shoulder and another swiped a mango from a bowl on the table between him and Sean. More joined their fellows on the veranda, the younger ones chasing each other and chattering.

"Who are these lively fellows, Sean?"

"Green monkeys. Their families were brought from West Africa about a decade or so ago. Now they behave as if they own the island. Harmless, but can be a nuisance."

"Indeed, an entire family has taken over our veranda." Jacob studied the nearest monkey on the table munching on the mango. It had long black fingers and toes, and a black face, thick body fur and a long tail. "I don't see any green color."

"That's because it's twilight, Sir Jack. The adults develop a thick brownish-grey fur with specks of yellow and olive green. In some lights, they look green." Sean brushed away a flying insect and stood. "Best we go inside now. Mosquitos are about to swarm."

Jacob did not argue. He'd have to become more familiar with the fauna and flora of Barbados.

*****

That night Jacob found Matty preparing his bed. Her golden skin, vivid azure eyes, and flirtatious lingering aroused him. He hadn't been with a woman since Lady Joan.

"What are you doing here?"

"I am a house slave, here to ensure your room has all necessities. My grandfather, Agamemnon the butler, told me to be sure you have everything for your comfort. That wash bowl on the table is filled with fresh water and scented flower petals. Your chamber pot is so clean you may see your reflection in it. This net around your bed is well secured. No insect can penetrate it. And, I thank you, Master."

"For what?"

"You prevented my being sold to the Greenways. They wanted me to be their sex slave. I am grateful to you."

Jacob enjoyed listening to her voice, deep toned and musical, and occasional wrong accents on certain syllables, as Sean had, which he thought charming.

"May I help you remove your boots, Master?"

"Yes." Jacob sat on his bed. "So you are called Matty?"

"I am called Juba by my family because I was born on a Monday. My masters named me Matty."

"I am the only master here now. Which name do you prefer?"

She placed Jacob's boots on the floor at the foot of his bed. "Whichever name you choose, Master."

Jacob stood barefoot. Matty's tone when she addressed him as *Master* sounded as an invitation. "I prefer Matty."

Matty's smile revealed healthy, even teeth. She moved closer, and their bodies almost touched. "Is there anything else I can do for you, Master?"

Her breath was sweet. "How old are you, Matty?"

"I am fifteen, sixteen next month."

Matty's fresh floral scent with hints of spice indicated she'd washed before entering his room. She removed her bandana and revealed lustrous ash-blonde hair. She unbuttoned her blouse and dropped her skirt. Matty stood naked before Jacob, her figure more perfect than that of any woman or statue, her body hair fine as silk. She could pass for white except here on Barbados. His desire for Matty increased, yet Jacob's conscience caused him to hesitate. As her master she had no ability or legal standing to resist.

"Master...."

"I prefer you address me as 'Sir Jack.'"

"Sir Jack, if not you, one day, someone will take me by force. I prefer to choose the man who shall be my first. I come to you willingly because I see kindness in your eyes."

Tempted by Matty's offer, Jacob's conscience caused him to hesitate. Part child, part desirable woman, she was a slave and he her master. If he bedded Matty, he'd be the same as a typical Barbadian planter.

"Tell me, Matty, why did the Greenways offer so high a price for you?"

"Lady Mary knew I was desired by many men, even when I was a child. She protected me to increase my value as I matured. She even forbade her son Edmund to come near me. When he did not return with money, she needed to sell me. The Greenways offered the highest bid."

Matty's eyes teared, and she kneeled before Jacob, clutching her hands as if praying. "Please, Sir James, please, I beg you. Do not sell me."

Jacob lifted Matty to her feet. He continued to hold her hands. "I promise. I'll never sell you. Do you love Sean ... Ramses?

"Yes, Mast..."

"Then go to him now. Go now."

Chapter Twenty-Five

Lay of the Land

Early in the morning, Sean took Jacob on an overview tour of the property. He had not exaggerated about his welcome. Africans reacted with envy, disdain, and hostility toward Sean.

Jacob, accompanied by Sean, toured his property from sugar cane fields to sugar works producing rum and molasses. With much sorrow he understood the necessity for slavery. A large agricultural labor force was required for planting the cane, tending it, and harvesting, hauling, grinding, and boiling it.

Bookkeeper Mendes gave Jacob Wilmot Plantation's inventory of Negroes, horses, cattle, and Barbadian Black belly sheep.

Jacob now owned 191 male and female slaves of all ages and conditions, and three female white bonded servants, followed by lists of real estate and other chattel.

In answer to Jacob's question, Mendes estimated about 45,000 African and mulatto slaves and 15,000 whites populated Barbados. Mendes showed Jacob a list of his slaves' names, many of which amused him, some had been born

Christian on Barbados and others were of West African origin. Their most common day names were Cuffey (Friday) and Quashy (Sunday) for males, and Phibah (Friday) and Juba (Monday) for females. Of interest to Jacob, Cubenah, a male name in West Africa, occurred several times as a female and never as a male name in Barbados, and Quashy, though mainly a male name, also appeared as a female second name. A few like Agamemnon and Ramses were given Greek, Roman, or Egyptian names.

With vast cane fields, Wilmot plantation included a dwelling mansion, an *engenho* sugar works in a 500-square-foot building, a boiling house, filling room cisterns, a still house with a carding house for wool, 150 feet long and 45 feet wide.

Jacob visited the stables with Sean. "Sir Jack, we have fourteen stallions and as many mares. Most are out in the cane fields."

Sean took Jacob to an adjacent forge and rooms containing provisions of corn and Bonavist beans transplanted from India. The houses for African slaves and their children seemed adequate at first inspection. He counted fifty-one cattle used for working and ten milk cows.

Jacob confirmed all he'd been told about sugar planting, harvesting, and processing, which was tiring, hot, and dangerous work. He pitied his slaves' hopeless existence and decided to sell his plantation as soon as possible and leave Barbados for good, frustrated he could not free them. Time passed for slaves with dreary regularity. He'd heard about conditions on other plantations, which drove some to suicide and infanticide. Others fought back with insubordination, malingering and feigned illnesses.

That must never happen here.

Sean swept an arm across Wilmot plantation's vast sugar fields. "The sugar cycle begins in August or September, and you can see slaves preparing the fields for planting."

Jacob watched men and women wielding hoes under a merciless hot sun. They dug five or six inches deep into the soil and five feet square, and into this plot they placed cane cuttings, covered them with a layer of mold, and prayed for rain.

"Sir Jack, they will tend new cane shoots as they grow. The crop will be harvested, one field at a time, fifteen months later. Workdays in the fields last from dawn to dusk, with a noon break. During harvest, field slaves work longer hours. A healthy, adult slave is expected to plow, plant, and harvest five acres of sugar. Sugar planting is back-breaking work. Slaves—men, women and children—move across the fields, row by row, hand-planting thousands of seed-cane stems. Between 5,000 and 8,000 pieces must be planted to produce one acre of sugar cane. The cane's tough exterior requires slaves to cut through the stem with sabers or machetes. They also must stoop at ground level because the lower stems contain the most sugar."

*****

At day's end, flanked by Sean and bookkeeper Mendes, Jacob summoned those Sean recommended as natural leaders amongst his slave population and introduced himself as the new master of the plantation. "Sean, formerly known as Ramses, will act in my name as manager of this plantation," he added.

Jacob raised his hand and voice to quiet grumbling. "We are making many changes, which Sean will enforce. Sundays will be days of rest so you may attend church. Those amongst you who wish to marry may do so, provided you wed according to rituals of the Established Church of England. Hobart no longer works and lives at this plantation."

Jacob paused during murmurs of approval, and pointed at several stocks. "No one on this plantation will ever be punished with these again." He nodded to Sean, who torched them, and few slaves dared to to cheer, and were not sdilenced.

Then Jacob called for quiet. "Sean will replace those overseers he deems to be unnecessarily cruel. Overseers will no longer carry whips, and lashings are now ended. Sean will explain certain improvements in living quarters, diets, and new rules for working."

Sean read from a list. "You will organize yourselves into teams. If you reach your quotas early or surpass them, your team will receive extra meat, and six pence each, recorded by our bookkeeper, to be withdrawn as needed. Any who wish to be literate will have opportunities to learn to read and write English."

"All that sounds too good to be true!" one slave shouted. "What punishments are there if we malinger or do not reach quotas?"

Jacob stepped forward. "Your team will withhold what meat or coins they earn from such malingerers."

"And if we escape?"

"If you are caught you shall be sold to another, more unforgiving planter at a cheap price. Save your money, and your teams may be made up of any number, or complete families."

Despite Barbadian laws, Jacob ended terms of indenture for his bonded servants, three Irish women, who begged to stay so they could be close to their mulatto children. He arranged wages for the women, and no slavery for their boys and girls on the planation.

Jacob hired Matty and her grandfather Agamemnon to reside in Bridgetown at his home, which was larger than his narrower house in Covent Garden. He allowed them to select the other servants and cook.

*****

When June arrived with strong winds and rain, Sean familiarized Jacob with new insects and animals common to Barbados. On the veranda before sunset, whilst he and Sean drank rum, rain birds and velvet-tailed bats caught flying termites and rain ants mid-flight.

Sean identified two- to six-inch cane toads emerging from flower beds, plant pots and burrows in the grass. "They're waiting for the sun to set and a night of hunting and mating. They've survived months of drought unaffected by the lack of moisture. Ah, those high-pitched sounds come from small whistling frogs to attract a mate."

Green cock-lizards on his veranda amused Jacob. They puffed yellow throats as threats before engaging in vicious battles for supremacy to attract females. Competitors locked together, rolling across his veranda deck, legs and tails entwined, making it difficult to tell one from the other, until the weaker broke free and retreated.

Over the following days, with Sean's help, Jacob encountered nesting turtles, green turtles, loggerheads, hawksbills, and leatherbacks.

Decades earlier, settlers had introduced to Barbados the Norway rat, house mice, the European hare, green monkeys from Africa, and feral dogs and cats.

Blackbirds, yellow canaries, ramier pigeons, green parrots, and doves flocked across Jacob's plantation. At sunset, they returned to favorite trees and roosted for the night.

Parrots favored the seed pods of the tamarind tree. Delicate pale yellow flowers that developed into little green berries on the lower branches of palm trees attracted honeybees for their nectar, whilst sparrows consumed the fruit. Lady bugs devoured aphids feeding on the flower buds of purple and yellow allamandas. Honeybees also fed on the nectar of basil flowers.

Sean alerted Jacob to the frangipani trees on his property. Many insects avoided their poisonous sap, except hawk moth caterpillars.

"Sir Jack, hundreds of these large caterpillars can cover each tree and devour every leaf in a few days. Although the adult hawk moth is striking, with coral-colored stripes, birds and other predators will not go near it, as it is poisonous from feeding on the frangipani's leaves."

Another day, Sean took Jacob to a small but dense and valuable mahogany grove at the far end of his plantation. "When Europeans first settled Barbados in 1624, abundant groves of these trees provided construction materials, firewood and materials to build furniture. Barbadian mahogany furniture is well known for its quality, strength and beauty. Many homes on the island are furnished entirely with these valuable antiques. The mahogany has small papery leaves with large seed pods that split open when they are dry, releasing the seeds to be distributed by the wind. The bark of the mahogany tree is thick and rough. Mahogany trees do not lose all of their leaves at the same time, but they do shed a lot just prior to the emergence of their feathery new light green leaves."

"Sean, you are so knowledgeable about all the creatures and plants of Barbados, you should write a book about them."

"Perhaps I shall one day, after we return to England."

Chapter Twenty-Six

Jews of Barbados

Jacob left Sean to run his plantation. He spent most of his time in Bridgetown familiarizing himself with government policies and the Sephardic population.

Holland, and later England, had allowed "New Christians" who had wealth, international trade connections, and a shared hatred of Spain to settle in all the colonies they wrested from the Spanish and Portuguese. In Dutch Brazil and Surinam, practicing Jews dominated the sugar trade, and a few ventured to British-controlled Barbados, which also had a climate and soil suited to growing sugar. They called Barbados "Land of Coconut Milk and Sugar Cane," and they decided to stay.

Barbados' Jewish community dated from 1628, with an added influx of 254 Jews arriving in 1654 from Recife, Brazil, after Portugal took it from the Dutch. The Portuguese expelled all the Jewish residents from Recife, considering them to be heretics, and targeted them for torture and death by the Inquisition.

Oliver Cromwell allowed more Jews to settle in Barbados in 1655 because they had expertise in trade and commerce, which strengthened the island's economy. The Jews built a synagogue, *Bet Knesset Nide Yisrael*, the "Synagogue of the Scattered of Israel," and a *mikvah*, their ritual cleansing bath.

This Jewish presence rejuvenated Barbados' economy. The Jews who fled Recife were experts in the cultivation of sugar. A Sephardic Jew, David de Mercado introduced the windmill, which was crucial for sugar cane production, and within twenty years an economic phenomenon known as the sugar revolution transformed Barbados forever. Jewish expertise in the cultivation of sugar acted as an engine driving this economic miracle.

By the time Jacob arrived on Barbados, discriminatory laws had been promulgated against all Jews. They faced discrimination when they first came to Barbados in terms of employment and through the extra taxes levied on them. Given Barbados' small size, Christians owned all arable land by the 1660s, and laws restricted Jewish ownership of both land and people.

Sephardic Orthodox Jews who came to Barbados in the 1600s wanted to establish their cemetery on a plot of land well away from their synagogue, in accordance with Jewish law. The British colonial authorities refused them permission to do so, saying they should do as Christians and locate their cemetery next to their place of worship. The authorities also restricted Jews to one slave per person to prevent them from establishing plantations.

Consequently, Jews settled in Bridgetown as merchants, with a smaller community in northern Speightstown. Skilled in the sugar industry, they passed on their skills in cultivation and production to Barbadian landowners. By the 1660s, Barbados was England's wealthiest colony.

Barbados' early planters observed the successes of Jewish planters in Brazil, and borrowed their technology. In 1640,

James Drax, an elite Barbadian planter who owned more than 700 acres in Barbados, visited the Sephardic colony in Brazil. He brought back with him two key innovations: a triple-roller sugar mill for crushing sugar cane, and copper cauldrons for boiling cane juice to form crystals.

Just as the Christians did, certain Sephardic men had relationships with enslaved Africans, mulattas, or free colored women, many of whom were in effect their mistresses and whose children took their masters' surnames, such as Abiah, Val Verde, de Mercado, Lindo and Depeiza.

Jacob observed that, as in Amsterdam and London, these Sephardim practiced an extreme orthodoxy. Because they assumed he was a *goy*, a pejorative word for a non-Jew, they were friendly to him only in matters of business. Jacob was not surprised to encounter a cousin from the da Costa family of his cousin Lea Salomon's husband. Also, he established business relations with Don Samuel de Abarbanel, a factor representing his Santcroos-Salvador merchant bankers in London and Amsterdam. Don Samuel told Jacob several Sephardim invested in Barbadian plantations and traded in sugar after it was harvested, bypassing laws preventing them from direct ownership.

During a first-time business meeting, amongst themselves they spoke Ladino, a medieval Spanish-Hebrew tongue mixed with current Iberian languages, discussing how much of a fee they intended to charge Jacob beyond the norm.

After Jacob had heard enough, he addressed them in fluent Ladino. "My Sephardic name is Jacob Moses de Rocamora, and I am the grandson of the esteemed physician Vicente-Isaac Israel de Rocamora, may he rest in peace. I attended the *Yesibót*, our school that prepared us for bar mitzvah in Amsterdam, with the Santcroos and Salvador boys. I know your true fee schedule, so now let us talk serious business."

Jacob negotiated an acceptable fee with the stunned businessmen. He understood their relationship would be limited to business. Because he was not born of a Jewish woman and had converted to the Anglican High Church, they made it clear he could never wed any of their daughters, share a Sabbath meal, or be welcome at any synagogue.

A committed abolitionist, Jacob could not resist asking how slave-owning Jews dealt with Passover without being hypocrites. How could Spanish and Portuguese Jews seek their own religious liberty at the same time they enslaved Africans in the plantation economies of the Caribbean and Guyana coast?

Mercado conceded that Jews shared with Dutch and English Christians an entrepreneurial desire for profit. "We Jews regard our own biblical exodus out of slavery as different from the destiny of African captives. As you know, Sephardic inhabitants of Holland became involved in Dutch trade, especially with Spanish South America. We also contributed to the Dutch West Indies Company, the Company that expanded the established slave trade of Africa to the colonies in the Americas. Our African slaves cannot be ruled by Jewish law, *halacha*, but by Dutch or English legislation. That is why we cannot free them."

Abarbanel added, "In 1677, Christian merchants complained to the Barbados Assembly that Jews controlled more than their fair share of trade. The Assembly then passed an Act restraining Jews from keeping or trading in African slaves. At that time, Jews, 54 of whom were adults, owned 163 Negroes and white indentured servants."

Mercado informed Jacob, "On August 9th, 1688, the Assembly granted the Jews of Barbados use of the courts for their protection as traders, as well as the right to trade. But in 1688 those Jews who were not denizens residing in seaport towns or islands were restricted to the holding of one slave apiece, under penalty of forfeiture of their slaves."

Jacob might have evaluated Mercado's and Abarbanel's explanations as flimsy justifications for owning slaves, but under Barbadian laws, he could not free his slaves, either. He changed the subject to avoid creating animosity. "I want to assure you that, as Their Majesties' Viceroy, I shall make a report favorable to ridding Barbados of discriminatory taxes and restrictions on Jews and on your businesses."

Mercado told Jacob that Jews never went into the African interior to hunt for slaves, nor was it necessary for other Europeans to do so. African warrior tribes captured men, women, and children, and brought their prisoners in chains to the coast to be sold as slaves.

"Don Jack, slavery has existed since the times of the Egyptian, Assyrian, Babylonian, Persian, Greek, and Roman kingdoms and empires. It is also a necessary part of Islam."

Jacob chose not to tell them of his resolve to rid himself of investments in the East and West India Companies upon his return to England because they profited from the Atlantic slave trade.

No hypocrite, I.

"One more thing, *Senhores,* do ships of *la Cofradía de los Judios de Holanda* ever anchor here in Barbados?"

A hearty laugh shook Santcroos' belly. "Of course you would be well informed about the Jewish Brotherhood of Holland. Your grandfather partnered with mine in investing in their pirating against the Spanish throughout the Caribbean."

"Yes, I have been investing with them through Santcroos Salvador in London."

Mercado lowered his voice. "There is a cove beyond Speightstown. We shall alert you when their ships arrive from Port Royal, Jamaica. May I ask what business you intend to have with them?"

"I shall inform you, depending upon their destination."

Chapter Twenty-Seven

Planter Society

Barbadian planters and their families had great curiosity about Jacob. Who was this viceroy? Why did William and Mary send him here? How did he gain control over the Wilmot plantation? Was it true he'd abolished the stocks and flogging?

Jacob described for Governor Kendall how production had increased by fifteen percent during the first month of his experiment.

Kendall asked, "What if you have a malingerer?"

"Each team reports any malingerer who receives pay or bonuses the first time. All know that if the recalcitrant persists in idleness, I will sell him or her. So far, that has not been necessary."

Their speculations led to many invitations to dinners and fetes at the planters' great estates, but they excluded Sean. Because Jacob held the rank of Colonel on King William's staff, Kendall invited him to join his militia. They toured Barbados together, inspecting fortifications against a French attack and posts established to alert any sighting of ships. Together with ship captains, they planned an eventual attack against the French colony of Guadalupe, to be carried out before the next dry season ended in June.

Women asked questions about Queen Mary and Princess Anne, their latest fashions, and the estrangement between the royal sisters. Jacob avoided gossip but humored their requests to play whist.

Well aware of human behavior, Jacob sensed envy amongst certain planters who resented the attention he received from desirable heiresses. Several eligible unwed younger women, Kendall's attractive niece amongst them, made no secret of the fact that they desired to marry in the expectation they'd live in England. He did not find any of them attractive enough to consider as a wife.

Henry and Richard Greenway, Sir Arthur's sons, in their early twenties, were the most hostile amongst the planters. They resented Jacob for winning Wilmot Plantation, the attention he received from eligible planter women, and, most of all, his canceling their purchase of Matty.

At those planters' homes after lavish meals, with their women in separate rooms, Jacob kept abreast of politics on the island. One evening at the Drax plantation, Governor Kendall took Jacob and Drax aside and they sat on the veranda smoking pipes and drinking rum.

Kendall began an interrogation. "Sir Jack, is it true you will sell your plantation, your home in Bridgetown, and all chattel?"

"Yes."

"And return to England?"

"Yes."

"May I inquire what you will be reporting to Their Majesties about Barbados?"

Jacob guessed one answer the governor hoped to hear. "You once told me that all laws on this island are made for the benefit of planters. As much as I wish for it, I cannot recommend abolishing slavery on Barbados. Were that to happen, your plantation economy would end."

Kendall and Drax exhaled, pleased. "Anything else you wish to share with us?"

"Yes. I will recommend you end laws punishing Jewish merchants with higher taxes and other limiting restrictions."

"Why do you care about the Jews?"

"My surname, Rockmore, is an Anglicization of my birth surname. I was born Jacob Moses de Rocamora in Amsterdam and was raised by my grandfather as a Jew. My mother was Christian but died the day I was born. I have since converted to the Anglican faith."

Drax gaped at Jacob. "Most astonishing."

*****

Back inside Drax's gaming room, where both genders mixed, Jacob sat for a round of whist with three ladies. He observed Governor Kendall speaking with several planters. Soon all stared at Jacob, shocked, some with hostility.

The burly brothers Henry and Richard Greenway approached Jacob at his whist table. A sneer snaked across Richard's lips. "Ladies, you will not have heard what Governor Kendall said about Sir Jack. He is half Dutch and half Jew."

The ladies stared, speechless, at Jacob.

"Yes, half Jew, and a questionable Christian," Henry added. "You Jews are as treacherous in religion as you are in business dealings. It seems you are a mulatto like Ramses when it comes to religion, black on the inside."

Jacob left the table and boxed Henry's ear. "Apologize now or choose your weapon for a duel."

Sir Arthur intervened. "Sir Jack, my son has had too much to drink and doesn't know what he's saying."

Henry rubbed his ear. "I will never condescend to duel with a Jew."

"A coward's way out."

Henry turned his back to Jacob, who took hold of Henry's collar and the seat of his pants. "Then I shall give you a thrashing anyway," Jacob said.

He forced Henry outside and threw him down the veranda steps. He followed and struck blows to Henry face, breaking his nose and hitting his mouth so hard, teeth fell out.

Governor Kendall fired his pistol in the air. "Enough, Sir Jack. You have had your satisfaction. Sir Arthur, take your son to the nearest physician."

Jacob calmed himself. The Greenways' enmity had been exposed for all to see. He promised himself to prevent their purchasing Wilmot plantation at his eventual auction.

Chapter Twenty-Eight

Sugar Harvest and Planting

August 1691 arrived, and Barbados' sugar cycle continued. Jacob watched his slaves wield hoes under a mercilessly hot sun. He ensured water was plentiful for each man and woman. The slaves dug the holes into which they placed cane cuttings. They covered them with a layer of mold and tended the new cane shoots as they grew, to be harvested, one field at a time, fifteen months later.

In early November, slaves harvested the sugarcane planted fifteen months earlier. The hours of labor increased. Each day at four in the morning a bell summoned all slaves to the field. At nine o'clock they had half an hour for breakfast in the field. They returned to work until eleven or noon, when bells rang. Slaves left to pick up natural grass and weeds for horses, cattle and sheep before preparing and eating their own lunch.

At two in the afternoon, a bell summoned the slaves to deliver their grass and return to the fields. Half an hour before sunset, they were required to collect more grass and deliver it until seven in the evening or later .

Overseers dismissed all the slaves to return to their huts, picking up brushwood or dry cow dung along the way to prepare supper and breakfast. All were asleep by midnight.

Timing was essential during harvest. As soon as sugar cane ripened, it had to be cut and ground, often within 24 hours, to keep it from spoiling. African overseers, called drivers, stood behind a line of slaves and gave the order to start cutting. From break of dawn until after dusk, the slaves toiled in hot, sticky fields cutting cane, gathering stalks, stripping off the leaves and loading 100-pound bundles onto ox carts bound for the mill. The pace was so frenzied that pregnant women sometimes gave birth in the field and continued working.

For the slaves who fed the mill, work was less physically demanding but posed different dangers. When exhausted they might get their fingers caught between the vertical rollers crushing the cane. A watchman stood ready with a hatchet or cachet to sever an arm before it could be drawn into the machine. The alternative was worse. The rollers could not be stopped by flipping a switch. If the limb was not chopped off in time, the slave would be crushed to death.

The boiler men had a less exacting but hotter and heavier task. Juice from the sugar cane entered the boiling house through a pipe that ran from the mill. Slaves would siphon it into a great copper basin. After several hours of boiling and skimming, slaves ladled the steamy liquid into a number of successively smaller coppers until it was ready to crystallize. The sugar was then cooled and packed into barrels rolled into the curing room.

Laboring in unbearably hot temperatures, boiler men often worked through the night. Darkness increased the likelihood of serious burns from scalding, sugary liquid. Because their job required a high degree of knowledge and skill, boiler men were amongst the most valued slaves on each plantation.

Slaves used molasses and skimmings from the boiling house to make rum. Water, molasses, yeast and lees combined in a fermenting cistern for a week to ten days. They then distilled the fermented liquid into rum. Slaves decanted rum into wooden barrels and stored it with sugar and molasses inside warehouses at the docks until a ship arrived to carry it either to Europe or to one of the North American colonies.

*****

In sugar mills, slaves fed sugar stalks between giant rollers. Up to a dozen boys and men worked around the clock to process sugar, working with the stench of rotting cane in intense heat.

As machinery grew more complex, with conveyor belts, sugar processing evaporators and centrifuges, slaves working in the sugar houses developed into skilled mechanics. Yet it was not unusual for them to be injured or crushed when trapped and pulled into the rollers as they fed stalks into the mill or tried to untangle stalks from flywheels and gears.

Slaves boiled cane juice, ladling scum from the surface of the scalding liquid and transferring it from kettle to kettle, reducing the syrup to crystals. They routinely suffered burns during this process, often referred to as "the Jamaica Train," and heat in the sugar houses was so intense overseers rotated slaves after four hours, their limbs swollen from heat and humidity.

Once crystals formed, slaves used shovels, picks, and crowbars to break up solid cakes of sugar. Next, they packed them in hogsheads, plugging barrel holes with sugar cane. The sugarcane plug helped to siphon out the remaining molasses from the sugar in the hogshead; the molasses dripped onto a floor angled so it would drain into a trough or cistern.

Next, slaves scooped molasses into barrels by hand. The expected yield from each slave's labor was five hogsheads of sugar and 250 gallons of molasses.

During harvest, slaves worked day and night, in mills and sugarhouses, to prevent bottlenecks in production. Shifts lasted up to eighteen hours. Sugar production paused only when slaves cleaned out fireboxes or other equipment. Although some intelligent planters like Jacob provided extra food and drink during harvest, and some encouraged competitions to boost production, sugar production on other plantations came with coercion. Threats and the lash controlled slaves in the sugar fields and mills.

A hogshead of raw sugar was worth about £11 and a cask of molasses was worth £3. The wealth that came from sugar was extraordinary. Annual income from the 500-acre Wilmot cane Plantation and its processing factory was sufficient to support the lifestyle of a duke in England. Feeling both pity and guilt for his slaves, Jacob left Sean in charge of field and mill workers. He preferred residing in Bridgetown and visited his plantation once each week.

Bookkeeper Mendes assured Jacob his rewarding of teams and improved living conditions had increased production by fifteen percent over previous years.

*****

During fall planting and harvesting, Barbadians celebrated news about Ireland. In September 1691, word arrived by boat that William's army had defeated the Jacobites at Augh rim in July, killing 4,000 men—including the French commander the Marquis de St. Ruth—and that thousands more had been taken prisoner or deserted.

Also in July, another Jacobite army retreated from Galway to Limerick where its defenses had been strengthened since 1690. William's general Godert de Glinkell surrounded the city. His bombardments opened a breach in the walls of

English Town. Ginkell's surprise attack drove the Irish defenders from the earthworks defending Thomond Bridge back toward Limerick.

More news reported how French defenders of the city's main gate refused to open for the fleeing Irish and 800 were killed or drowned in the River Shannon. Patrick Sarsfield removed all French commanders in Limerick and opened negotiations to surrender. He and Glinkel signed a treaty. It respected the civilian population of Limerick, tolerated Catholicism in Ireland, promised landowners they could keep their land if they swore allegiance to William of Orange. He also allowed Sarsfield and his armed Jacobite army to withdraw to France. Limerick capitulated under these favorable terms in October 1691. Sarsfield left Ireland with 10,000 soldiers and 4,000 women and children, all of whom went to France.

Protestants in England were outraged by such generous terms for the hated Catholics. Because of this, Parliament voted for new penal laws. Catholics were forbidden to own weapons, their landholdings were reduced in size, and they were prohibited from working in the legal profession.

Jacob hoped Lambert fought well enough to earn a knighthood.

CHAPTER TWENTY-NINE

JACOB'S GAMBIT

By the advent of spring 1692, Jacob had no offers for his property, and he discovered the reason why. Greenway led a cabal to purchase his plantation and town home by leading a secret auction, which he won. He promised to pay off his rival planters and to make Jacob a low offer, the only offer.

At the same time, Jacob devised a plan to thwart Greenway. First, he researched all laws regarding absentee landlords. What documents needed to be signed? Second, he needed willing allies.

Jacob had made many friends in the Sephardic community after he promised to deliver to William and Mary their petition for redress of unfair taxes and their plea for treatment equal to all British subjects on the island. His bookkeeper Abraham Mendes arranged a meeting in Bridgetown with the wealthiest Jews on Barbados at the home of Don Samuel Abarbanel. Also in attendance were Don Moses da Costa and Don Isaac Mercado, men in their late seventies who had lived in Barbados since 1655 and before, after their families had fled their sugar plantations in Brazil.

After a kosher midday meal, Jacob addressed the men in Portuguese. "*Senhores*, as you may or may not have heard, I plan to leave Barbados for good as soon as I sell my property."

"Then you can present our petition to Their Majesties sooner than we hoped."

"Yes, Don Moses, and I had planned to auction both my plantation and house in Bridgetown."

Mercado hit the table with his fist. "If only Jews were eligible to own land, we would purchase yours."

Jacob took from his doublet several sheets of paper. "So far, there will be no auction. The planters will not make bids except for Sir Arthur Greenway. Thus he will obtain everything for an absurdly low price, and pay off the other landlords for not competing."

Don Samuel stroked his graying beard. "I suspect you have an alternate plan, Sir Jack."

"I have." Jacob related how he had spent many hours looking at legal documents in the Barbados Hall of Records, specifically regarding absentee plantation owners. Governor Kendall himself had signed papers for a trusted employee to handle all legal matters and daily management of sugar planting and harvesting whilst he resided in England.

"I could not find any law or restriction forbidding a Jew to hold a similar position of factor for an absentee landlord," Jacob said.

Mercado nodded agreement. "I know of no legal restriction."

"Nor I," Da Costa said.

Abarbanel leaned forward, excited. "If I understand correctly, you will ask one of us to manage your plantation."

"That is my idea. One of you, or a group, as *de facto* investors at an agreed upon price."

*****

After a storm and rain-drenched night, morning at Bridgetown dawned bright and clear.

"Sir Jack?"

"Yes, Matty."

"When you sell your plantation and this house, will I and my grandfather be included with the other slaves?"

Jacob reprimanded himself. He hadn't considered how much Matty might have been worrying about her future. He cupped her face with his hands. "I should have told you sooner, Matty. I will take you and Sean with me to England, your grandfather, too. There I shall free you; and Sean shall wed you."

"You have made me so happy. I hesitated telling you, but I am with child."

"And he shall be born free."

Now Jacob determined to sell his property at any cost and leave Barbados immediately afterward. Matty promised Sean to give him many children.

Jacob often thought about how Matty might be received in London. She could pass for white at first sight. Her beauty might be admired, but might also cause jealousy amongst certain women. If any suspected the slightest suggestion of partial African origin through her accent, or if she gave birth to a dusky child, he'd deal with that forcefully.

*****

Fresh air further invigorated Jacob, who sauntered along crowded docks toward Governor Kendall's office. Just as on the first day he'd arrived, slaves loaded and unloaded cargo. Overseers snapped whips to move them faster. Slavers prepared a dais under an awning for an auction. Jacob espied off shore a pod of bottlenose dolphins leaping across the azure water. He was the first to arrive at Kendall's office.

The governor gestured for a slave to take away his breakfast tray. "Good morning, Sir Jack. Please sit."

Jacob sat opposite Kendall's desk. "Thank you for seeing me without an advance request for an audience. I shall be brief. I am canceling the auction of my plantation."

Kendall raised his eyebrows. "You have decided to stay on Barbados?"

"No, but I shall be an absentee plantation owner, as you and many others have been when away from the island."

"But you have no kin, as I and the others have had, to run a plantation. Whom have you chosen? It cannot be your former slave, Ramses."

Jacob did not miss the Governor's negative reference to Sean. "No, he shall be leaving with me." Jacob showed Kendall the agreement signed by Mercado, da Costa, and Abarbanel, agreeing to take charge of Wilmot Plantation while he was away from Barbados.

Kendall's face reddened. "You know that Jews are forbidden..."

"Forbidden to own land and therefore a plantation, yes. I have read your edicts and found none prohibiting Jews from acting as factors."

"That subject never came up. I shall call an assembly and request a law be passed to redress that error."

"That may not be necessary. As you can read, I have not yet signed the agreement. I am aware... and I am certain you are as well... those planters who wanted to bid for my plantation held a drawing. The winner, Sir Arthur Greenway, would then offer me a low price with no others bidding higher. After that, he would pay each rival a significant price to compensate."

"What are you suggesting?"

"That you advise the planters to forget their cabal, and if an auction proceeds normally, no Jew will be overseeing Wilmot Plantation after I leave Barbados."

"So clever... Nay... so cunning of you, Sir Jack. Yes, I believe I can suggest those planters forget their cabal, as you have phrased it."

Chapter Thirty

Auction

Jacob sat with Sean on the townhouse veranda in Bridgetown drinking rum and smoking cigars before his auction. "Sean, would you prefer to keep the plantation in your name or share in whatever money the auction brings?"

Sean had trouble finding his voice. "You are offering me a partnership?"

"It's the moral and ethical thing to do. By blood you are an heir."

"Sell it, and I want to be done with this island."

"When we leave, Matty and Agamemnon will sail with us. In England, I can free them and you can wed Matty. There I shall make you co-owner of the townhouse I won from Lyndby and you will be free financially as well."

"Then I can get an education and become a lawyer."

Jacob touched Sean's glass. "To a life of free choice."

*****

Governor Kendall agreed to each request made by Jacob concerning the conduct and place of his auction on Wilmot Plantation, to be held April 2nd, 1692. All the land, slaves, chattel, and the Bridgetown house were to be sold to the highest bidder. Jacob excluded two slaves, Matty and Agamemnon, whom he intended to take with him and Sean to England. Jacob retained all rights of residence in the townhouse until he set sail for England.

Accompanied by overseer Hobart, Greenway voiced disappointment that Matty was unattainable. Jacob was well aware Greenway wanted Wilmot Plantation for his sister Lady Mary.

Jacob supplied a repast and drinks on the veranda. Twenty-six planters, several magistrates, and Governor Kendall attended. Flanked by Sean and bookkeeper Mendes, Jacob conducted his auction. Bidding opened at 500 guineas. Planters dropped out as costs escalated, and bidding soon reached 20,000 guineas.

At 24,500, two competitors were left, Greenway and Colonel Thomas Colleton, Kendall's best friend on Barbados, whose daughter was the governor's mistress. Greenway bid 25,000 guineas. Colleton countered with 25,500. Before Greenway made another bid, Jacob hammered his gavel. "Sold to Colonel Colleton for 25,500 guineas."

Greenway protested to Kendall he hadn't been given an opportunity to bid again. The governor sided with Jacob. Colleton agreed to meet Jacob on the morrow in Bridgetown to sign all necessary documents.

The slaves had already loaded two carts with Jacob's and Sean's personal possessions. As they drove away, Hobart and Greenway glared at them with hatred.

*****

The following morning before noon, Jacob met with Colonel Colleton and Governor Kendall in banker Mercado's office. "Gentlemen, as you know, I abolished stocks, the lash, and chains. I established teams to compete for rewards of meat and wages. Production increased by fifteen percent as a result. I pray you will continue that practice, Colonel Colleton."

Colleton responded with a non-committal grunt.

Kendal studied Jacob's inventory of slaves. "I see you have twenty-seven fewer than when you won the plantation from Wilmot."

"Some died naturally, and others made a successful escape. If you remember, I posted reward notices to find them."

Jacob did not reveal what happened to those slaves, all male. He'd encouraged them to meet with a Sephardic privateer and secret business associate from Jamaica docked at a secluded inlet. He paid its captain to take twenty three men to Surinam where a large number of runaway slaves lived freely and well-armed in their own jungle colony.

They signed, notarized, and witnessed documents. Mercado handed Jacob an exchange note for 25,500 guineas to be deposited at the Santcroos-Salvador bank in London. The men celebrated Colleton's purchase of Wilmot Plantation with Port supplied by Mercado until a servant brought in Agamemnon, covered in blood from wounds.

The elderly slave fell to the floor gasping. "Granddaughter Matty ... Sean ... Hobart ... Greenway's sons abducted..."

Agamemnon died. Jacob hurried outside. He mounted his horse and gave chase. Colleton and Kendall followed.

Jacob took a logical route toward Greenway's plantation. He was well armed as always with two pistols, a sabre, a long knife and a whip. Jacob slowed when riding into a grove of frangipani, hearing a woman screaming. He veered into the woods and took in a horrific sight. Matty struggled on the ground against two captors. Henry Greenway hit her on the head with a stone, pulled her skirt over her face, and held her arms over her head. Richard Greenway, pants down, spread

Matty's legs to penetrate her. Off to one side, Hobart had tied a naked Sean to a frangipani trunk.

Jacob drew his sabre, spurred his horse, and impaled Richard through his anus into his internal organs. He lifted young Greenway high in the air and tossed him aside, freeing his sword. Jacob next rode toward a surprised Henry, decapitated him with one slash from the sabre and charged toward Hobart.

The overseer finished gelding Sean and slit his throat before Jacob rode him down. He dismounted and confronted Hobart, who readied his whip to strike. Jacob dropped his sabre and fired both pistols. Hobart fell dead.

Jacob rushed to Matty. No breath, no pulse, Henry Greenway's blow had killed her. Jacob held Matty in his arms and wept. Kendall and Colleton rode into the grove having heard gun shots. They dismounted and inspected each body.

Colleton cut Sean loose. "A nasty lot, the Greenways."

"I have not finished with the father." Jacob placed Matty's head on the ground. He reloaded his pistols and returned his sabre to its scabbard on the saddle. He went through the Greenways' and Hobart's possessions. They had taken nothing from his home, so eager were they to ravish Matty and torture Sean.

Jacob took the overseer's rope and tied the two Greenway corpses to each side of his saddle. He seized Henry Greenway's head by its long hair and mounted his horse.

Kendall held the reins of Jacob's horse. "Don't be foolish, Sir Jack. We do have a justice system on Barbados."

"You have indeed familiarized me with your planter justice. All I want is the pleasure of delivering his sons to Greenway. Gentlemen, come ride with me and be witness if I must defend myself."

Jacob turned for a last look at Matty and Sean. Now was not the time for mourning. "We can tell Greenway to send his slaves to give them a proper burial."

*****

As they approached Greenway Plantation, Jacob commanded the first slaves he encountered to summon their master. They reacted in a terrified manner to their master's two dead sons and scurried to the main house. Greenway and Lady Mary stood on their veranda, confused. Jacob let Kendall and Colleton advance first.

Greenway smiled, "Governor, Colonel, what a pleasant ... my sons." He gasped.

Jacob cut the ropes. "Here they are, your sons, cowards, rapists, and murderers."

Lady Mary screamed and fainted. Female servants came to her aid.

Greenway recovered and drew his sword. "Viceroy or not, you shall pay..."

Jacob snapped Hobart's whip and gashed Greenway's right cheek. "I could have taken one of your eyes."

Kendall dismounted and confronted Greenway. "Listen to me, Sir Arthur. Colonel Colleton and I are witnesses to the foul acts of your sons and overseer."

Greenway listened to the governor's description. "That damned mulatta witch. She is the cause of all that has happened."

Lady Mary recovered. "Hobart, my handsome Hobart, where is he?"

Jacob dropped Hobart's whip at her feet. "I shot him dead."

Lady Mary screamed and fainted a second time.

Before Jacob rode away, Greenway threatened vengeance.

"Choose your weapon, time, and place, but I suspect you will take the coward's path and avoid facing me man to man!" Jacob shouted.

"There will be no duel," Kendall said. He spoke to several slaves. "Gather your shovels, and Colonel Colleton will lead you to their place of burial. Sir Jack, I suggest you ride with the colonel. No good can come from your lingering here."

*****

Jacob entered an empty townhouse, dark and dreary until he lit candles. Blood splattered the floor where old Agamemnon had been attacked, more where Hobart had abducted Sean. Matty's room brought Jacob to tears. He'd made so many plans for Sean's beautiful, sweet mulatta. He brooded over Sean's and Matty's aborted future in England. Freedom, education, and marriage.

Two weeks before his ship sailed for England, Jacob faced long days and longer nights on Barbados, brooding over his losses, until an unexpected diversion.

Chapter Thirty-One

Naval Excursion

In June of 1693 Rear Admiral Sir Francis Wheeler arrived at Barbados from England with his 68-gun flagship *Resolution* and a large fleet: 52-gun *Dunkirk*; 42-gun ships *Advice, Chester* and *Ruby*; 40-gun *Dragon*; 36-gun frigate *Falcon*; 32-gun frigates *Pembroke, Mermaid,* and *Experiment*; store-ship *Canterbury*; 10-gun ketch *Quaker*; and unnamed bomb vessels. All were there to join the part of the fleet already in Barbados: Admiral Pierce's 84-gun *Endurance*; three fires ships, 24-gun *Diamond,* and *Merchant,* and 28-gun frigate *Guernsey* and 24-gun *Henry Prize*.

Accompanying the flotilla, troop transports arrived with two regiments commanded by General John Foulke and Colonel Godwin. Their mission was to eliminate the last French stronghold in the Lesser Antilles. After driving the French out of Saint Domingue with Spanish assistance, the fleet was to proceed north to New England and assist the colonists there in an invasion of Canada.

Foulke handed Jacob a scroll signed by William and Mary commanding him to observe and participate in planning and in combat if he was still in Barbados.

Governor Kendall raised 900 volunteer Barbadians and sent a sloop to Antigua to advise Governor-General Codrington of the fleet's arrival. The leaders agreed to attack Martinique. The *Chester* and *Mermaid* left Barbados to escort Codrington's contingent toward a rendezvous.

Jacob searched in vain for Greenway amongst the Barbadians.

He must be home grieving with his sister, Lady Mary.

On June 9th, the Wheeler-Foulke expedition departed Barbados augmented by ten island sloops carrying 900 volunteers, bringing total strength to thirty-two vessels of various sizes: nine bark, three brigantines, two ketches, and a galliot.

Jacob reminded Kendall about the effect of deadly insects and extreme heat on Englishmen unused to the sub-tropical climate. "Too many English soldiers and sailors are already weakened from scurvy. I advise we save our 900 men for reserves."

"You think the expedition is doomed?"

Jacob shrugged. "The plans seem sound, but I worry their men may not be fit enough to execute them well."

On June 11th, the formation circled north around Martinique and headed down the western shore, shadowed by French militia cavalry. French Governor Gabaret concentrated his forces at Fort Saint Pierre. The English surprised him when their fleet swept past both Pointe d'Arlet and Pointe Du Diamont and into Cul-de-sac Marin, which had no defenses because sixty French soldiers had fled.

The following day, Colonel Foulke disembarked 2,300 troops and 1,500 sailors at nearby Anse de Sainte-Anne before sunset. The English intended to approach Martinique's defenses from the rear.

The following day, April 13th, General Wheeler and Colonel Foulke sent 30 vessels, supported by a galliot and two barks, to the Rivière-Pilot settlement. They over-whelmed the defenders and ravaged the countryside.

At noon on the 15th of June, the English sent five barks, three brigantines, and twenty-eight boats disembarking sol-diers to leapfrog further west and destroy French planta-tions.

Kendall listened to Jacob's advice and kept his Barbadi-ans in reserve. Snobbish attitudes held by the English com-manders toward the "inferior bloody colonials" reinforced his decision.

On the 19th of June, Governor Codrington arrived from Antigua with four 24-gun ships, four brigantines, and two barks with 1,500 volunteers as Colonel Foulke's regiment had fallen ill from malaria, dysentery, and other tropical ail-ments. The English gave up their land strategy and reem-barked their troops on June 22nd, 1692.

The fleet failed to locate any safe disembarking points af-ter sailing south. French reinforcements checked the English marines at every point, and the English took high casualties. Eight hundred Englishmen were killed, wounded, captured, or were too sick to be of use. On June 30th, defeated on land, the English embarked their surviving marines and aban-doned Martinique.

The Barbadian volunteers returned to Bridgetown having seen no action. Codrington, hoping to salvage a victory, wanted to attack Guadeloupe, but General Wheeler objected after his fleet staggered into Domenica. Barbadian volun-teers dispersed to their homes. Wheeler escorted Codrington to St. Kitts and ended the expedition to take French colonies.

Chapter Thirty-Two

Glittering Serendipity

Jacob boarded a 64-gun merchant brigantine, *HMS Elida*—no connection to Henry Lambert's love. A year earlier, the *Elida* had been captured in a sea battle against a pirate captain, to be refurbished, renamed, and made a ship of the line for the English navy. Jacob didn't look back when he left Bridgetown Harbor.

During early days at sea, Jacob wrote his report on Barbados and the failed conquest of Martinique, with recommendations for William and Mary. He could not avoid brooding over his loss of Matty, Sean, and Agamemnon. As a practical matter, they would have helped staff his home in Covent Garden. Jacob did not look forward to hiring a full, trustworthy staff for his home there: manservant, butler, porter, cook, maids, other servants, and a groom for his Frisian, Hannibal, that he'd left in London.

Ship captain Caleb Fletcher hosted Jacob at each meal, impressed that he was both a Viceroy and a knight.

One day a lookout on the top mast yelled "Ship Ahoy!" and pointed beyond the starboard side.

Jacob followed Fletcher to the deck. The captain peered through his telescope. "It's a 140-gun Spanish galleon, but it has no masts."

Jacob took the telescope. "No damage from cannon on its hulk. It's named *Santa Teresa*. Possibly a treasure ship."

Fletcher took the wheel and turned toward the derelict galleon. Jacob stood beside Fletcher and again peered through his telescope. "No sign of life on deck. Broken masts and some canvas scattered. No bodies. Must have run into a severe storm."

Fletcher turned his ship parallel with the galleon. "There were reports of hurricanes off Brazil and the north coast of Spanish America last November. Yes, Sir Jack, it has to be storm damage. We should board her."

Fletcher shouted to his crew, "Prepare grappling hooks! Make certain the ropes have rat guards!"

Fletcher's crew attached hinged metal disks and cones to hinder rats climbing onto the lines and into his ship. He selected a half dozen of his best men to board the galleon. Jacob joined them. Hooks flew through the air and connected.

Jacob swung onto the galleon deck, and Fletcher told his crew to check the galley.

"Sir Jack, let us go to the captain's quarters. I pray his log book may give us answers to this mystery."

Fetid air greeted them when Fletcher opened the deckside door to the Spanish captain's quarters. Jacob placed a scented handkerchief to his mouth and nose, overwhelmed by familiar stench of rotting corpses. One of them, the Spanish ship's captain, lay on the floor amidst shattered furniture. A dent in the skull provided a clue to his death. An astrolabe nearby had struck him during a ferocious storm.

Fletcher found a log book amongst the debris. "Damn, it's in Spanish."

"I'm fluent in the language." Jacob read and translated the final entries. "Mother of God ... worst storm I have seen ...waves higher than masts ... they are breaking ... men swept overboard ... we are doomed ..."

Jacob next read the opening pages. "Most interesting. It *is* a treasure ship. Several passengers listed, all Cascantes, two of them women, mother and daughter who was a bride to be, with her *duenna*, chaperone, and four servants."

Jacob lowered his voice when he heard men on deck. "If there is treasure aboard this galleon, it must be in one of the other staterooms."

"You look for it, Sir Jack. I'll find you after I order my crew to stay on deck."

Jacob located four trunks in the women's quarters. One contained a bride's trousseau of elegant, jeweled gowns as well as gold and silver ear rings, necklaces, bracelets, and trinkets. *A perfect gift for Queen Mary.*

A second trunk held a fortune in coins, native masks and carved images, all solid gold.

Fletcher entered and shut the door. "My crew is sick from what they encountered in the galley ... rotting corpses of oarsmen chained to their benches and oars, horses and some cattle, all with broken bones. The stench overwhelmed them. Did you find anything of value?"

Jacob showed Fletcher the bride's trunk filled with jewel-encrusted gowns, pearl accessories, and a jacaranda box filled with bracelets, earrings, and necklaces. "This, I shall deliver to Her Majesty."

"A fitting gift."

The contents of a second trunk filled with gold coins and more carved artifacts awed Fletcher. "A fortune for each of us, even if only a portion can be divided amongst my crew."

"As Viceroy, I shall claim both trunks for William and Mary. Do not be disappointed, Captain. Here in an adjacent storage room I found two more treasure-filled trunks." Jacob lowered his voice again. "You and I ... we must decide how much we can take for ourselves."

"And how much of the gold to apportion for my crew along with their regular pay after we dock. Now, let's get these trunks aboard my ship. After we detach the grappling hooks, I believe it best to set fire to this accursed galleon."

Alone in his cabin, Jacob read anew the Spanish captain's log as well as other documents he'd recovered from the women's suite. The bride's putative husband's name startled him: "Tomás de Rocamora y Bustamante Faxardo of Murcia."

How might we be related?

Jacob doubted he'd ever visit Spain. Yet, unanticipated possibilities might decide otherwise. At least his immediate future arrived with no further surprises as the remaining days at sea proved uneventful, winds favorable. Alone in his cabin, Jacob sequestered a significant amount of gold coins and artifacts in his personal luggage. Captain Fletcher did the same in his.

Were they stealing from the Crown? Jacob knew enough about the prices of gold and gems to calculate he'd deliver a prize worth several million pounds sterling to William and Mary.

*****

They docked in Bristol six weeks out of Barbados. Before disembarking, Fletcher took command of one trunk of treasure and apportioned gold coins to his men by rank and years of service, admonishing them not to spend it all drinking, gambling, and wenching. He kept a significant amount for himself as agreed with Jacob.

Whilst Fletcher paid his crew and unloaded his ship's cargo of sugar, molasses, and rum, Jacob met the local garrison commander. Asserting his commission as Viceroy, he obtained a coach and military guard for himself and Fletcher to protect their treasure from highwaymen during the last 260-mile leg of their journey to London.

Chapter Thirty-Three

Royal Welcome

One week after departing Bristol, Jacob went to his home in Covent Garden and sequestered there his luggage filled with the treasure he'd taken for himself. He changed into more acceptable clothes for a Court appearance. Whilst Fletcher did the same at his home, Jacob next reclaimed his Frisian Hannibal from its lodging stable. His steed neighed and licked his face.

"I'll not desert you again, my noble friend."

In late July, 1692, Mary II reigned alone whilst William III led his anti-French coalition on the Continent. She was holding Court when Jacob and Fletcher arrived and she granted them instant access for an audience.

Mary left her throne. Jacob and Fletcher kneeled and kissed her hand. "Your Majesty, Captain Fletcher and I bring you a surprise."

"Captain Fletcher, rise. You also, Sir Jack, and welcome back to Court. We have missed you and ..." Mary paused when Jacob's soldier escort carried in two trunks and placed them before the queen. They genuflected and left.

Jacob observed that Mary had gained weight, revealed in her décolletage, and that she had dark shadows beneath her still vivacious eyes. Neither diminished her beauty and desirability. She also wore small face patches, as her ladies did. They wore them to cover skin blemishes such as pox marks and unsightly moles. Mary had no marks on her face but used her patches to cover part of her shadows and highlight her blue eyes.

"Sir Jack, what are in these trunks? Gifts from Barbados?"

"Nay, Your Majesty, not from Barbados. A greater surprise, from a derelict Spanish treasure galleon." Jacob opened a trunk. "A trousseau from an unfortunate bride."

Mary cried out with pleasure at the sparkling jewels. Her ladies broke decorum and joined their queen. Mary allowed them to remove dresses and undergarments from the trunk, some of woven gold and silver threads on lustrous silk, many adorned with pearls and gems.

Jacob stepped back to evaluate Mary's ladies. In 1690 the queen had commissioned Godfrey Kneller to paint all the principal women attending Her Majesty, the portraits to be exhibited in the Water Gallery at Hampton Court. Each lady was of impeccable pedigree. Most he viewed were attractive and wellborn, but were wed to some earl, duke, or count. None appealed to him.

According to gossip, Lady Dorchester had advised Mary II against having the most beautiful women of her court painted: "Madam, if the King were to ask for portraits of all the wits in his court, would not the rest think he called them fools?"

Jacob observed an unfamiliar Court lady dressed in mourning black, whose eyes fixed on him and did not waver whilst he evaluated her. She continued to stare without blinking. She was younger than the other great ladies. She looked no older than sixteen, Jacob guessed, and had enormous dark eyes, raven black hair, pale skin, and regal bearing.

Mary calmed her ladies. "Now, Sir Jack, pray tell us, what surprise have you in this other trunk?"

Jacob opened it. "Gold, silver, and more jewels, Your Majesty, treasure from Peru and other Spanish colonies."

The young lady in black moved closer. Jacob saw that her eyes were not black, but darkest blue. She stood a few feet away from him now, a force of nature, as if a storm enveloped the palace.

Mary took a golden mask and placed it against her face, to much applause. "What say you, Sir Jack?"

Jacob recovered and made a slight bow. "Although this mask is a wondrous man-made creation, and of pure gold, I prefer the natural, God-given beauty of my sovereign's face."

All present except the young lady applauded Jacob's flattery. Mary removed her mask, her face flushed.

"Your Majesty, when may I submit my report on Barbados?"

"Sir Jack, attend me in my garden at Hampton Court tomorrow morning. Captain Fletcher, we raise you in rank to Admiral. Report to the Admiralty on the morrow."

Fletcher kneeled a second time and kissed Mary's hand.

Dismissed, Jacob glimpsed the young woman still fixing her eyes on him with speculative intensity.

Who is she? What is her status at Court??

Chapter Thirty-Four

Labyrinth and Octagon

Outside Hampton Court, Jacob and Fletcher parted ways. "Again, Admiral, my congratulations."

"Thank you, Sir Jack, but my promotion has created complications. I'd planned to retire and live a life of comfort and leisure with my new wealth."

Before they parted, Jacob and Fletcher exchanged promises never to reveal how much treasure they'd kept for themselves. Jacob rode to Lady Barbara's establishment where she provided his former room. He was not ready to open for habitation the town home he'd won from Lyndby and still dreaded the difficulties of having to hire competent staff.

The following day Jacob met Queen Mary in one of Hampton Court's gardens. Above, summer storm clouds threatened much rain. Covered in blue and gold silk with a daring décolletage, Mary supervised several gardeners to ensure her Dutch-style flower beds were well laid out and ready for spring blooming. She bade Jacob sit with her on a cushioned wooden bench, and gestured for her attending ladies to maintain a distance out of hearing.

Jacob offered Mary a leather folder. "My Barbados report, Ma'am."

Mary set it aside on the bench. "We can discuss that another time." She glanced at her ladies. "It is well known we prefer to be surrounded by attractive people, beautiful women and handsome men. But our Court is not licentious as in the reign of our Uncle King Charles II and our father, King James II."

"So it is known, Ma'am."

"We have missed you at cards and dancing."

"I hope to resume those pleasant pastimes with Your Majesty."

"We are aware you observed our ladies yesterday as a hunter seeking prey. Nay, do not protest, Sir Jack. How old are you?"

"Twenty-seven."

"And we are thirty. Sir Jack, it is time you wed and sired many children. Is there no one here at Court or in London you fancy for a wife?"

"Only one who is happily married and forever unattainable because of rank."

Mary's face flushed.

She understood my meaning but has chosen to ignore it. How far dare I go?

"Do you seek to wed one you *may* love, or for her wealth and position?"

Jacob hesitated. He hadn't yet guessed Mary's end game. "Love or wealth, Ma'am? Hopefully both."

Mary smiled at Jacob. "Then you are unencumbered by chains that bind you to any woman."

"I am still free to choose."

"Pray tell us, do you find Margaret Cecil attractive?"

"She is the fairest amongst your ladies."

"She is widowed and not yet committed to any man. Are you inclined to woo her? I believe she favors you."

"No, Ma'am, nor any other lady at Court, regardless of beauty, charm, or pedigree."

An explosion of thunder punctuated Jacob's last sentence. Lightning split the darkening sky, followed by a heavy downpour. Mary rose, and Jacob covered her with his cloak. She gestured permission for her ladies to seek shelter in the palace.

"Sir Jack, come with me and bring your report with you."

Instead of following her ladies, Mary led Jacob to the far end of her Dutch garden, to a high wall covered with ivy he hadn't seen before.

Unobserved, Mary parted several vines to reveal a door. She took out a key, unlocked the door, and shut it behind them. She led Jacob into a maze toward a domed octagonal Palladian structure enclosed by more vine-covered high walls.

Another downpour drenched them before they went inside. Candles, sconces and a crackling fireplace illuminated the interior.

This is not spontaneous but well-planned.

Thick drapes covered all windows. A large bed with satellites of plush lounges and chairs dominated the room. Paintings of nude classical allegories by famous artists covered the walls: Mars and Venus, Adam and Eve, Venus and Adonis, Rape of the Sabines, and Paris abducting Helen of Troy.

At the fireplace, Jacob helped Mary out of his soaked cloak and her wet silk over garment. He laid them on the floor by the fire to dry. Mary faced him, breathing so heavily her breasts seemed ready to explode from her dress.

Jacob removed his wet hat and doublet and placed them by the fire. "What is this place, Ma'am?

"Our Uncle King Charles II had Sir Christopher Wren design the labyrinth and this pavilion in secret for a trysting place with his mistresses. My father also used it so, and now our husband, with Betty Villiers, our erstwhile closest friend from childhood."

Jacob heard resentment in Mary's voice.

"When Our Father left for the Continent, I found his key, had copies made, and discovered how to solve the maze. I have never taken a lover ... until now. Sir Jack, I fully understood all you have said ... and your meaning. Your eyes do not lie when you look at me. I must confess I have been interested in you since Lady Joan Fairfield confided much about you. She would have wed you."

Mary has replaced her Royal "we" with a personal I. Potential Tower of London or not, I shall do what my grandfather did not dare attempt with the beautiful Infanta of Spain when he was her confessor.

Those paintings and ambiance did not stimulate Jacob. Mary's allure already aroused him beyond any scruples he might have had. Aware he might be sent to the Tower and be drawn and quartered if King William discovered his next move, Jacob placed both hands on Mary's face and kissed her lips. A torrential rain roared outside with more thunder and lightning. Mary responded with ardor and pulled Jacob onto King William's bed. Full breasts plump as partridges burst free from her décolletage. Mary surprised Jacob when she laughed with merriment at her exposure.

"Sir Jack, you are the first and only man with whom we broken our wedding vows with King William. I am a religious woman, yet astonished I feel no shame or guilt. I take pleasure in paying back my husband and Betty Villiers for their philandering. When we followed him and confirmed my suspicions of his philandering, he lied, saying it was a harmless visit. We also broke another commandment when we replaced our father on the throne. Yet we did encourage our husband to spare his life."

"For that you will receive no punishment."

"Would that you are correct, but we cannot confess and seek absolution for our sinning." Mary kissed Jacob and laughed. "Heigh-ho, no one must know."

*****

After Mary and Jacob slaked their lust, she rested her head on his chest. "Sir Jack, our husband may have spies watching us to report any transgressions. We shall have another key made for you, so we can meet and leave here separately."

*****

Word arrived that William had suspended fighting. He intended to return to England in late October or early November and stay through the winter with his mistress.

Mary met Jacob in her Dutch garden. "Because we cannot meet alone, if you find a woman, wed her. It will be easier for both of us."

"You have someone in mind? One of your ladies after all?"

"We have been burdened with a problem that must be solved immediately. We are responsible for a ward, a young lady, who became orphaned the same month you left for Barbados. Her parents and siblings also were felled by smallpox. The young lady survived without serious disfiguring, except for a few pock marks on her face. As her guardians, we are charged with selecting a husband for her."

Jacob tensed, anticipating a command.

"No woman is as desirable as our ward. Her estate is worth more than £3,000,000 sterling and a peer of the realm title comes with it."

"She must have many eligible suitors here at Court."

"And she has rejected each with ridicule and humiliation, regardless of rank, title, or appearance."

"Perhaps she may fancy women?"

Mary forced a laugh. "No, she has the most extreme swings of mood. They occur during each week before her monthly time arrives. Then she becomes shrewish, a termagant. A most innocuous comment can cause her to throw vases or other objects in a room—even unemptied chamber pots—at her suitors for what she perceives as their insolence. No man has a pedigree good enough to equal hers, which traces back to the reigns of William the Conqueror and his successors. She is descended from a child of Fair Rosamund de Clifford of Woodstock, mistress of Henry II, and poisoned by his wife, Queen Eleanor. Henry fathered Rosamund's child. She also has Stuart blood."

"Have I seen her at Court?"

"Yes, she was present when you brought us that Spanish treasure. She could not take her eyes from you. After you left, she demanded to know who you were and your pedigree."

"And she lost interest in me because I am not a peer of the realm?"

"No, to the contrary, which surprised us. She insisted we arrange an audience for you to meet her."

Jacob guessed Mary's ward was the young lady who had fixed her eyes on him—fair, wealthy, and pedigreed beyond any Stuart or Tudor. "What is her name?"

"Rosamund, the same as her ancestor. We pray you shall be the solution to a problem which vexes us and His Majesty. Are you familiar with William Shakespeare's play *The Taming of the Shrew*?"

"Yes. Are you suggesting I play Petruchio to Rosamund's Kate the Cursed?"

Mary's expression hardened. "No suggestion, Sir Jack. Consider it a command. You shall sup with us at a convenient time, and with *Fair* Rosamund."

Chapter Thirty-Five

Personal Wealth

Jacob rode to his bankers, Santcroos and Salvador. He deposited letters of credit from Barbados and was informed his total wealth now accrued to more than £500,000 sterling through other investments.

Jacob took possession of a scroll he'd left with his bankers. He insisted they come to his home in Covent Garden well armed and with weights and measures. There, Jacob showed them what gold he'd kept for himself from the galleon's treasure.

Astonished, Santcroos and Salvador scrutinized and weighed Jacob's gold coins and artifacts. They calculated and showed him their total amount. "Sir Jack, you have here a fortune worth £4,175,000 sterling after we take our commission. You have become one of the wealthiest men in the world, all liquid."

Jacob had expected as much. "I trust you will ensure complete secrecy."

Santcroos produced several sheets of paper. "We shall make you a silent partner in our bank. Later today, we shall sign and our agreements and have them notarized. You will be privy to all loans and investments we make."

Salvador closed and locked Jacob's treasure. "We shall sequester your gold in our secret vaults."

"One more thing. Please sell all my stock in both the East India and West Indies Corporations. My reason for doing so is that they deal in the slave trade."

*****

That evening, Jacob went to an ale house frequented by retired and disabled soldiers. He found one whom he hoped to make his major domo—his former valet in the Army, Corporal Hugh Tinker. Tinker agreed to Jacob's generous offer and helped him select footmen, a porter, and coachmen, each well trained in arms, which guaranteed security at home and on the road.

The following morning, at the barracks, a Colonel told Jacob his friend Henry Lambert was serving with King William's army in Europe with his Huguenot cavalry regiment. And at her establishment, Lady Barbara prepared a room for Ambassador Van Noordwijk, whom she expected to arrive within a day or two.

*****

Portly John Lambert left his desk and welcomed Jacob. "I have heard much about you from my son Henry. You must come and dine with us this evening. I am eager to hear about your adventures in Barbados."

"Thank you, but not this evening. I shall be supping with Queen Mary."

Lambert raised his eyebrows. "Most impressive."

"I've been told Henry is on the Continent."

"Yes, and he's been promoted to full colonel. It seems I was wrong about bringing him into my business. He is best suited, after all, for a successful career in the Army."

Lambert's wealth had increased through his importing of fine Dutch and Chinese porcelain whilst Jacob was in Barbados. "You may be unaware of this, Sir Jack, but before Charles II's Portuguese wife Catherine of Braganza arrived in England, people ate from bowls and trenchers. They slurped liquids from horn cups, tankards, two-handled cups, or dishes made of earthenware, wood, or even tough leather. Porcelain for the general public was not available in England until William and Mary brought it with them when they came to rule. Now it is common to see shiploads of 250,000 porcelain pieces at a time arrive in London."

Lambert added that English taste and manners had become more dignified and refined because of porcelain. "Sir James, I have a favor to ask. I'd be eternally grateful and obliged were you to find a way for me to have my porcelain accepted by Appointment to Their Majesties."

"And a knighthood, too?"

"I have my ambitions, and I would pay well for a title."

Jacob suspected this austere Huguenot viewed money as a means and not for profligacy. "A purchased title not only can cost one a high price, one must spend more money to keep up appearances commensurate with an elevated status."

Lambert showed Jacob his best porcelain. "Let me assure you, Sir Jack, I have accumulated greater wealth than most gentry and knights. I am infinitely pleased you think I have the sort of wisdom as to love money. As the saying goes, 'All persons that love money do preserve themselves and their families from being destroyed. 'Tis a most difficult thing for a man to use money well. Pleasure and riot can be attendants of wealth.'"

Jacob and Lambert discussed how the boundaries between city investors and country squires often blurred. London's rising importance in trade, a financial revolution, changing demographic patterns, a pool of younger sons, and an expansive urban culture had created a window of opportunity for ambitious men like John Lambert and himself. The convergence of trends led to diminishing cultural distinctions between landed and non-landed groups.

Jacob had an inspiration. Lambert listened and agreed. Jacob added, "One more thing you should know—Queen Mary favors blue and white porcelain.

Chapter Thirty-Six

New Identity

In early October, 1692, Queen Mary summoned Jacob to attend her. Before he left for Hampton Court Palace, a barber shaved Jacob, who no longer wore mustache and beard. Washed bronze-blond hair again fell to his shoulders, freed for the moment from lice. He preferred his own hair. Wigs could be uncomfortable and also attracted parasites.

Jacob wore his best waistcoat, frock coat, breeches, stockings, and boots, all in black with thin gold trim. A Peregrine feather topped his black broad-brimmed hat.

At Hampton Court, guards escorted Jacob to Mary II's throne room filled with officials and ladies.

Mary's silk sky-blue bodice had trim the color of copper and revealed much décolletage. She wore two long skirts; a blue outer skirt was cinched to reveal an underskirt of copper, the same color as her bodice trim. Her face patches represented plants and flowers.

When Jacob removed his hat and kneeled, Queen Mary asked for his sword. Jacob obliged, unsure why, until she tapped each shoulder with its blade.

"For your honesty with the Spanish treasure and for your valuable services in Barbados ... rise Colonel Sir Jack, First Count Rockmore."

Surprised, Jacob stood whilst accepting his sword, and all present applauded. He would now be addressed as Lord Rockmore and seated in the House of Lords.

Mary dismissed her Court and approached Jacob. "Lord Rockmore, pray accompany us to our repast."

Jacob offered his arm, and they walked to a room in the Queen's suite. As the sun set, a table set for three had been placed by a window overlooking one of Mary's gardens illuminated by torches.

Rosamund left her position near a fireplace, genuflected before Mary, and faced Jacob.

"Lady Rosamund de Clifford, this is Colonel Lord James, First Count Rockmore. Lord Rockmore, Lady Rosamund de Clifford, Eleventh Duchess of Basingstoke."

Jacob bowed to Rosamund's curtsy. "My Lady." He appraised Rosamund, who was no more than five feet in height. Her hair was raven black and she had even teeth and her face was slightly pock-marked. Her figure was proportionate, her bodice as low as Mary's. Yes, he did find her fair—nay, more than that. She was desirable. Still, he could not read her expression, which was neither of pleasure nor displeasure.

Mary bade them sit with her, and servants materialized with their meal. Rosamund fixed her dark blue eyes on Jacob. "Lord Rockmore, you are made a new Count, so I might be more impressed with you. Tell me the true story of your lineage."

Rosamund's tone held no charm, suggesting an inquisitor. Jacob wasn't sure if he wanted to wed her. He began by revealing his maternal lineage, to discourage Rosamund.

"My mother was Cordelia Schiffer, from a family of bricklayers in Amsterdam. She died giving birth to me. The midwife brought me to my paternal grandfather, the esteemed physician Don Vicente Isaac de Rocamora, who raised me."

Jacob removed a scrolled parchment from his frock coat. "This is a notarized and certified genealogy of my paternal origins." He handed it to the queen, who beckoned Rosamund to move closer so they might read together.

Mary raised her eyebrows, impressed. "Descended from Charlemagne's grandfather Arnulf? Most impressive, is it not, Lady Rosamund?" She first moved her finger from Arnulf to Pepin the Short. "Who is Natronai Bustanai?"

"A descendant of Israel's King David."

Jacob related how Charlemagne's father King Pepin had brought a Persian Jewish prince from the House of David to rule over the Jewish principality of Narbonne in the eighth century, and how his descendants intermarried with Pepin's children,

"Then you are a Jew?"

"Not according to Jewish law, Lady Rosamund, because my mother was Christian. True, I was raised in the Jewish faith, but I have since converted to the established Church of England."

Rosamund nodded and handed Jacob his scroll. "I approve."

Still no change in expression. Jacob sensed Rosamund must be terrified of losing her independence to some male.... and more ... her maidenhead.

Servants brought legs of mutton. Jacob observed how daintily both Mary and Rosamund cut morsels of meat off the bone. "My Queen, Lady Rosamund, you give the lie to a saying I once heard. 'Of course, she is beautiful, until you see her gnawing on a leg of mutton.'"

He'd caught the two women by surprise, and their laughter erased any lingering tension.

Chapter Thirty-Seven

Her Majesty Suggests

Queen Mary finished supping and rose. Jacob and Rosamund also left the table.

"The night is beautiful. Full moon. Constellations glittering like diamonds. Lord Rockmore, Lady Rosamund, you should walk in the gardens and become better acquainted. Lady Rosamund, first thing in the morning, you will attend us and relate all that happened."

Rosamund recovered her cloak and pulled its hood over her head. Jacob put on his broad-brimmed hat, and they took leave from the Queen. Outside in the torch-lit garden, Jacob guided Rosamund to a bench and sat beside her.

"Queen Mary has expectations that we shall wed," Jacob began.

"Yes, she has made that most clear."

"Why have you not accepted a suitor amongst so many at Court?"

"Not one has appealed to me. I need neither their wealth nor any debt-ridden title added to mine. Cock-sparrows, all, in their French-style garb of feminine colors and exaggerated breeches. Tell me, Sir Jack, have you married and sired children?"

"Never wed. No children."

No need for Rosamund to know about his trysts with Mary.

"That pleases me." Rosamund threw back her hood and faced Jacob. "I shall speak plainly. Will you?"

"Yes."

"Court gossip says you almost wed Lady Joan, Duchess of Fairfield."

"Alas, she died of the black pox."

"Have you lain with many other women?"

"I have."

"Have you caught the French sickness?"

"No, nor any other of Cupid's diseases."

"How have you avoided it?"

Jacob told her of advice his physician grandfather had given him. "And you, Lady Rosamund, have you allowed any man to penetrate your defenses?"

"Never. I still have my maidenhead. Nor have I allowed any man to kiss my lips."

"You are sixteen?"

"Almost seventeen. Do you find me attractive?"

"Attractive and desirable."

"Because of my wealth and titles?"

"I have both of my own. My wealth is liquid, not tied up in land and chattel. I am worth more than £250,000 sterling." Rosamund need not know about his treasure, his true wealth, nor his banking partnership. "There is much I find attractive about you. Your symmetrical features, your high spirit and strength of character. Do I attract you?"

"You know I could not take my eyes from you at first sight. You are a magnificent manly specimen. You are intelligent, and, I believe, kind. I want you to be the first and only man to kiss my lips."

Jacob put an arm around Rosamund's shoulder and felt her body tense. With his free hand, he drew her face to his for a light, gentle kiss. Rosamund surprised him. Tension left her body, and she responded well.

Jacob kissed Rosamund's eyes, nose, cheeks, and the nape of her neck. Her breathing heavy, she pushed back. "Please, enough. I am aroused."

Alone with Rosamund, Jacob observed no evidence of any shrewish temperament. True, her staccato delivery annoyed him. He held both her hands. "And you, fair Rosamund, fill me with desire. I shall speak plainly. In so short a time, I cannot say I love you yet."

"Nor do I love you ...yet."

"Our Queen expects—nay, demands—we should wed."

"Then wed we must. We should select our wedding day."

"I suspect that has been decided by Queen Mary."

'Know this, Lord Rockmore. I have my expectations and demands, no less than Queen Mary. I want many sons so my Plantagenet dynasty will survive and thrive."

207

Part Three
Lord Rockmore
1692-1700

"Nobility stript of means makes no gentil figure.
It can't stand without golden supporters.'"

— *Pamphlet, The Gentleman Instructed*

"There's nothing done in all the world
From Monarch to the Mouse,
But every day or night 'tis hurled
Into the Coffee-House."

— *Pamphlet from 1672*

Chapter Thirty-Eight

Reunions

A message from King William informed Queen Mary of his plans to arrive in London the first week of November, before resuming his League of Augsburg war against Louis XIV in spring of 1693.

Mary loved card games and dance, and Rockmore was her favorite partner in both, and her only lover in bed. She summoned him one more time.

"If our husband brings with him his mistress, Betty Villiers, I shall further resent him."

Rockmore did not speak his mind. Given rumors he'd heard from Jacobites, she should worry more about those attractive young men amongst William's entourage.

Mary changed to another subject. "At first we thought you should wed Rosamund the last Sunday before Advent, the 30th of November."

"So soon? That would be the 23rd."

"Yes, but gossips would assume we would be rushing the wedding because Rosamund may be with child. Perhaps a day in June would be best. You shall by then be better acquainted. We pray she can bring you happiness."

*****

Rockmore's mentor and second father, Dirck Van Noordwijk, arrived in London ahead of King William. Jacob had not seen the Ambassador since he'd left for Barbados. Van Noordwijk, now in his late sixties, appeared frail and bent but still mentally alert.

They sat in Rockmore's library study sharing a bottle of claret. "I am so pleased you'll be able to attend my wedding in June."

"I would have swum the Channel to be present at your investiture in the Lords and to see you wed. A Plantagenet, at that. I didn't know any survived."

"I shall create new Plantagenets with my bride's help, God willing. Is your room at Lady Barbara's establishment comfortable? I'd prefer you reside with me."

"It is most comfortable, and suits me well, but I leave on the morrow to visit my daughters and lands in Gouda. You have a grand home. Have you visited Rosamund's manor at Basingstoke?"

"No, but I shall after we wed."

"Now, I want to know what happened in Barbados and how you became a Count."

Rockmore satisfied Van Noordwijk's curiosity. "I ask you to be my groomsman."

"I accept that great honor and look forward to meeting your bride."

"Rosamund should return from shopping in time for our midday repast."

*****

The following day, Henry Lambert returned to England with a surprise for Rockmore. King William had knighted him after his Huguenot cavalry turned the tide of battle against one of Louis XIV's armies.

After they lit pipes, Rockmore entertained Lambert in his library with a bottle of Port. Buccaneer settled at Rockmore's feet.

"I am pleased for you, Sir Henry. You have won a knighthead ahead of your father."

"I have yet to see him. Now that I am a colonel and knighted he may yet accept the career I have chosen. Now, tell me all that happened in Barbados."

Rockmore enthralled Lambert, omitting only Matty's and Sean's tragic murders. "And there's more." Rockmore related how he'd received his title, and how Queen Mary had introduced him to Rosamund and insisted they wed.

Lambert admired Jacob's portrait by Kneller. "'Lord Rockmore' now. How do you prefer I address you in public?"

"'Lord Rockmore,' 'Jack' in private conversation. "And you shall be my groomsman along with Ambassador Van Noordwijk."

"I congratulate you, Jack. I look forward to meeting your Rosamund. I, too, have a lady I have loved and hope to wed. Her father, Sir Edward Boyce, is an Alderman and disapproved of me because my family and I had no status. All that has since changed, and I ask you to be my groomsman as well."

"Now, surely, Alderman Boyce will give consent to your wedding his daughter."

"Pray, come with me now to Alderman Boyce. There I will introduce you as my best friend, and I shall ask for Elida's hand and wed her on St. Valentine's Day."

*****

Alderman Boyce, a short, paunchy man oozing self-importance, greeted Lambert coldly, but warmed when he heard of Henry's new rank and knighthood. He nearly groveled when introduced to Lord Rockmore. Boyce summoned his family. He announced Lambert's intention to wed Elida, and gave his blessing. The young couple embraced amidst family congratulations.

Rockmore worried for Henry Lambert. Although beautiful of face, Elida was thin of form, with blue veins showing on her exposed alabaster face and hands. Her hips were so narrow, Rockmore doubted she might survive childbirth, an opinion he dared not express to Lambert.

Chapter Thirty-Nine

Necessary Military Operation

Steady knocking on Rockmore's front door interrupted his evening meal with Lambert. Majordomo Tinker ushered a ship's captain to their table. The weathered sailor held a scroll.

"I am Captain Roberts. I've sailed and arrived this day from Barbados. I bring a message from Governor Kendall to be read only by Sir Jack Rockmore."

"I am Lord Rockmore." Jacob took the scroll sealed by Kendall's ring in red wax. "Does he expect a reply?"

"No, Milord. He said it concerns a matter only you can deal with. I have the governor's permission to tell you this. A sworn enemy of yours arrived today on my ship. He's mad with hatred toward you and has an obsessive desire to take vengeance upon you."

"Sir Arthur Greenway?"

"Aye."

"I thank you for that. Would you care to join us?"

"No, thank you, Lord Rockmore. I'm eager to go home to my wife and children."

"Before you leave, can you tell me if anyone was waiting for Greenway dockside?"

"Aye, a man in a plain two-horse hackney beckoned him."

Not an aristocrat. Must be a rental arranged by an ally.

"I thank you, Captain Roberts. Tinker, please show the captain out, and return here."

Rockmore unsealed the scroll and read its contents. "This is not good." He handed the scroll to Lambert.

Lambert read and returned the scroll to Rockmore. "What happened in Barbados that causes this Greenway to hate you so?"

"He coveted the plantation and home I won from Wilmot. Greenway's sister was Wilmot's mother and ran his plantation while he was away from Barbados."

Rockmore concluded with a description of Sean's and Mattie's murder and his slaying of Greenway's sons. "He has sold his plantation and slaves cheaply, at only fifteen thousand pounds sterling. I must alert Lady Barbara and the magistrate who signed Sean's freedom that Greenway seeks vengeance upon them as well."

"Why Lady Barbara?"

"She organized the game of Hazard and profited from my winnings. And now he wants to destroy me and all I possess and love."

Rockmore gestured for Tinker to sit at the table. "Obviously we must form a plan to thwart Greenway, but with 15,000 guineas from the sale of his plantation, he can purchase an army of criminals and bribe my enemies in Parliament to sully my reputation."

"Not if we strike first and quickly." Lambert leaned forward. "Have you a plan?"

"Yes. First you go to the hackney rental companies and learn where Greenway resides. Tinker, shed your livery and wear your least impressive clothes. Take our footmen with you and visit the most likely ale and bawdy houses to learn if Greenway is hiring ruffians to kill or capture me."

Rockmore rose from his table. He led Lambert and Tinker to his desk in the library. Rockmore used his key to unlock a drawer and removed a metal box. He opened it and handed Lambert coins of varying denominations. "For bribes to get information."

"More than enough, Lord Rockmore."

Rockmore did the same for Tinker. "For you and our footmen. I know your assignment may cause you great thirst."

Tinker weighed the bag of coins in his hand. "Most generous, Milord."

"Don't drink it all in one place."

"And what will you be doing, Lord Rockmore?"

"Making sure my weapons are ready. Henry, if you locate Greenway's residence, I may dispose of him tonight."

*****

Rockmore schemed and drank more Port during the hours after Lambert and Tinker left. He stroked Buccaneer, who kept him company, until loud noises outside caught his attention.

Rockmore opened his front door. A mob ran toward a great fire two houses away.

Lady Barbara! I didn't think Greenway would strike so quickly. Thank God Van Noordwijk is visiting his estate in Holland.

Rockmore armed himself, locked his front door, and ran to Lady Barbara's establishment. Too late. No one had dared risk a rescue through the flames. Outside, Lady Barbara's charred remains lay amongst those of other dead patrons and employees, including Magistrate Montrose who'd signed Sean's emancipation.

Rockmore mourned Lady Barbara. He'd developed a fondness for that clever woman. *My winning at Hazard led to her death. No, no guilt. Greenway murdered her, and his sons murdered Matty.*

Lambert joined Rockmore. "Such destruction. Did Lady Barbara survive?"

Rockmore named those dead he recognized. "Greenway is wasting no time. Did you locate where the hackney took him?"

"Your coins were most useful. The hackney driver described Greenway as a madman." Lambert handed Rockmore an address. "It is the London townhome of Sir Douglas Greenway, Third Baron Dumbrille. Do you know him?"

"A Tory swine and Jacobite in the House of Lords, who opposes everything I support."

"His home is on a busy street, and its front door is too public. But, a house next door has a 'for sale' sign and is empty."

"Most interesting. We must hasten back to my home before Greenway torches it."

Tinker and the footmen returned. They'd visited several ale and bawdy houses, but had not encountered Greenway or anyone suspicious hired by the madman. Rockmore stared at Dumbrille's address. "I am familiar with the area and architecture. It is one amidst a row of grey stone townhouses."

"Yes, and its front is too exposed for us to force an entry."

"True, Sir Henry, but there are separate steps outside leading to a basement door."

"Tinker, you men, tell all other male servants to be armed and alert to any trespassers here tonight. You're all military veterans, and I order you to shoot to kill. I do not fear anything happening to me in Parliament tomorrow, except that

Baron Dumbrille will start to destroy my reputation with lies."

"But you may be vulnerable traveling to and from Parliament and the palace. I will ride with you until we remove Greenway."

"I thank you for that, Henry."

"But how best can we thwart Greenway?"

"I have a plan."

Rockmore told Lambert what they must do.

"I approve."

"But we must carry it out within the next twenty-four hours."

The following day, Tinker rented a plain hackney. He and other servants absconded with a barrel of gunpowder and a long fuse.

"Perfect."

Lambert also tested the fuse. "What time do we strike?"

"Two in the morning. A thick fog will be our ally." Rockmore's expression hardened. "We take no prisoners. It's kill or be killed. I will not hold it against you if you are unwilling to follow me."

Lambert and Tinker swore they were in all the way.

As expected, a dense fog limited visibility to a few feet. Rockmore told his driver to park their rented hackney on the far side of the empty home adjacent to Greenway's temporary residence. His Tory host had no wife or children living with him.

Rockmore led his party to the basement steps. Two footmen were rolling the barrel of gunpowder, followed by Lambert and Tinker, who waited at the top. Rockmore descended to where a form huddled in a corner, either asleep or under a blanket for warmth. Swift and silent, he slit the retainer's throat, found his basement key, and beckoned for his team to join him.

With some difficulty they carried the barrel to the basement door. All drew their pistols. It was dark inside. Rockmore motioned for his footmen to roll the gunpowder in. Lambert attached the fuse, and Rockmore lit it. All hurried upstairs to the street and then ran to their hackney. Rockmore ordered his driver to head the horses homeward. When they were several blocks away they heard an explosion.

Enough time tomorrow to learn if the blast killed Greenway.

Chapter Forty

Politics

Greenway, Baron Dumbrille and most of his retainers died in the blast and subsequent fire, without collateral deaths or significant damage to the adjacent, unoccupied house.

Parliament was still in session, and Lord Rockmore had yet to take his seat in the House of Lords. Before his investiture, he further familiarized himself with Parliament's two political parties, the Whigs and the Tories.

Whigs advocated for the supremacy of Parliament and toleration for Protestant dissenters. They adamantly opposed any Catholic as king. They believed Catholicism was a threat to liberty, and that Catholics' blatant idolatry, along with their lack of reason and disbelief in human nature, constituted a subversion of all civil as well as religious liberty.

Whigs supported a constitutional monarchy answerable to Parliament. They invited William and Mary to reign over England, Scotland, and Ireland. They were permanent enemies of the Roman Catholic Stuart kings and future pretenders. Whigs tended to support toleration for nonconformist Protestants, and dissenters, such as Presbyterians.

Some Tories still favored a Catholic absolute monarchy and Papist dogma. They backed the exiled Stuart royal family's claims to the throne. All Tories supported the established Church of England and opposed Protestant dissenters and their rights to religious freedom of worship.

Whigs received backing from new industrial interests and wealthy merchants. Tories drew support from old landed interests.

After the Glorious Revolution of 1688, Queen Mary II and King William III governed with both Whig and Tory support, although many Tories still favored deposed Roman Catholic James II. Tories were generally friendlier to royal authority than Whigs, and William employed both groups in his government. His early ministry was largely Tory, but his government came to be dominated by the so-called Whig *Junto*, younger politicians who led a tightly organized political grouping.

An increasing dominance of the *Junto* led to a split with Country Whigs. Landed Whig gentry and nobles believed the *Junto* betrayed their principles, and they voted with the Tory opposition.

John Locke was a major influence on Whig political values, as expressed in manifestos such as *Political Aphorisms* and *True Maxims of Government Displayed*, an anonymous pamphlet supporting the liberal political stance of the Whig Party and its middle-class constituents.

At their inception, Tories advocated free trade. Whigs opposed the pro-French policies of Stuart kings Charles II and James II. Such an alliance with a Catholic absolute monarchy of France endangered liberty and Protestantism. Therefore, trade with France was bad for England and a deficit of trade with France was harmful because it would enrich France at England's expense.

The Whig party favored an extreme form of Protectionism and passed the Prohibition of 1678, which banned certain French goods from being imported into England. A Tory-dominated House of Commons repealed it upon the accession of James II. After William and Mary's accession, a new Act prohibited importation of French goods. Despite a political failure of their founding principles, Tories remained a powerful political party.

Rockmore worried about his spontaneous pledge to Queen Mary. One day, he might have to vote against her wishes if conscience demanded. The more he studied about government, the more he witnessed differences between gifts and bribery. Moreover, there was no uniformity of government. Each department operated in its own context. The bureaucracy was a mix of old and new, useless and efficient, corrupt and honest.

Rewarding friends and punishing enemies was normal politics. Bribery was a sensitive issue. A gift of venison was viewed as a normal tool of patronage, in contrast to more blatant corruption. London's commerce facilitated approaches to achieving goals. Shady deals had long existed, but the city's financial revolution created new ways to manipulate money.

Prior to Charles II's Restoration, cash favors were viewed as less than genteel. Currently, people assigned money values to more aspects of their lives, as cash became more accepted. Rockmore had more liquidity than most. If and when necessary, he had a willingness to use it.

Chapter Forty-One

House of Lords

I am but a minor player on the stage of Parliamentary pageantry.

In the House of Lords' cloakroom before his investiture, Rockmore donned his Parliamentary robe designed for a temporal peer. He'd purchased it and had it measured by London tailors Ede & Ravenscroft, founded in 1689.

Rockmore's garment was a full-length robe of scarlet wool with a collar of white ermine, closed at the front, with black silk satin ribbon ties down half its length; except for a short slit at the neck, it opened from the shoulder on the right-hand side. The opposite side was his robe.

White ermine bars edged with gold oak-leaf lace on the right-hand side of the robe indicated rank: four for a duke, three for a marquis or an earl, two and a half for a count and viscount, and two for a baron. To be inducted into the House of Lords, new peers required sponsors of the same rank. Dukes supported dukes; marquesses, marquesses; and so on.

Rockmore and his fellow count supporters next donned black tricorn hats. This costume was also worn at the opening of Parliament, when peers attended a church service, and other ceremonies.

Rockmore's procession entered the Chamber. Count peers led the way down the center aisle. Rockmore and his fellow counts stopped, removed their hats, and bowed three times toward the Cloth of Estate before reaching the Lord Chancellor. The Garter Principal King of Arms presented Rockmore's letters patent, issued from William — by proxy — and Mary, to create his new peerage.

Rockmore knelt before the Lord Chancellor, and presented a writ of summons issued by William and Mary to command attendance in Parliament. The Reading Clerk of the House of Lords read aloud Lord Rockmore's letters patent and the writ. Rockmore next took the Oath of Allegiance and the Solemn Affirmation, and signed the Test Roll, upon which the same Oath was written.

The Garter Principal King of Arms led Rockmore and his fellow Counts to a section of the Lords bench occupied by those of the new peer's rank. They put on their hats, rose, doffed them, and bowed to the Lord Chancellor, three times.

Rockmore shook hands with the Lord Chancellor as he left the Chamber with his supporters, escorted by the Garter Principal King of Arms and the Gentleman Usher of the Black Rod. He later returned and took his seat on a back bench amongst Whig Lords, now eligible to participate in a debate.

Rockmore glimpsed Queen Mary in attendance, sitting on a throne; Lambert and Van Noordwijk were in the small gallery above. Rosamund chose not to attend Rockmore's acceptance into the House of Lords. His great honor meant nothing to his future wife, who showed no interest in his activities, nor in his new portrait in Parliamentary robes by Sir Godfrey Kneller. Neither were his businesses, nor the time he spent in coffee houses or the evenings spent gambling and dining amongst friends of interest to her. Rosamund's sole concerns were to give birth to a healthy heir and for her Plantagenet line to survive.

*****

The following day, Queen Mary summoned Rockmore to Hampton Court Palace. They sat in her Dutch garden sipping tea.

"We are disappointed Rosamund did not attend your ceremony in the House of Lords."

"Yes, Ma'am."

"Is Rosamund unwell?"

"No, today she is fitting for her wedding gown."

"Have we made a mistake encouraging your marriage?"

"I shall wed Rosamund willingly."

"But we sense you are not happy."

Rockmore chose not to voice his belief that Rosamund had no love for him. "Rosamund is seventeen, young, and needs time to adjust."

"Be assured, Lord Rockmore, we wish great happiness for you. Perhaps becoming a wife and mother may soften Rosamund."

"Perhaps."

"As a member of the House of Lords, we expect you to be our partisan there. Lord Rockmore, are you still a committed Whig?"

Rockmore well understood that William and Mary added men to the House of Lords to sustain a majority of votes, "Ma'am, as you prefer, so shall I vote."

Forty-Two

Wedding Preparations

Several days later, Rockmore brought Rosamund, with her palace personal maid as chaperone, to his town home in Covent Garden. She inspected each room, calculating how many female servants were needed to run the household. Rockmore observed Rosamund blushing when she passed their marriage bed. He'd have to be tactful and gentle on their wedding night.

After her tour, Rosamund sat with him in his library. She made a list of servants who worked at de Clifford Manor, her family estate in Basingstoke.

"Before we wed, I shall send for them to staff this house. We must show my cook where to shop for the best quality food. Some furniture I wish to replace, and I want the finest porcelain and tableware."

"I am delighted to leave all household matters to you, except my majordomo and valet, the footmen, the groom, and the coachmen serve directly under my command. That frees me so I may attend to my business interests and politics in the House of Lords."

"We should consult with Queen Mary about our wedding date."

Marriages did not occur during Advent, Christmas, or Lent. Therefore, late November of 1692, before the First Sunday in Advent, was their choice for a wedding. After St. Hilary's Day, January 13th, marriages resumed. Rosamund did not want to wait that long. She considered eloping, but Rockmore told her that could be viewed as high treason because she was a ward of Their Majesties.

Some couples preferred Valentine's Day, but no marriages took place during Lent. From the Sunday after Easter they resumed. April was a popular month, but May marriages were regarded as unlucky. June was another favored month for weddings. Queen Mary selected June 6th, 1693, for their wedding date, at which time Rosamund would become not only Rockmore's wife but also his ward until her twenty-first birthday, on September 5th, 1696.

*****

William arrived in London during the first week of November. He brought with him his mistress Elizabeth "Betty" Villiers, which angered Mary. William, no less an avid collector than Charles I, also added new paintings to his collection.

Van Noordwijk told Rockmore everything he needed to know about Betty Villiers. Charles II had entrusted her parents with raising his Protestant nieces Mary and Anne. From the friendship that George, the Duke of Buckingham, had with James I to Charles's mistress Barbara Castlemaine, the Villiers family had close relations with the Stuart monarchy, and they supported William and Mary, as Protestants, over James II.

When Mary wed William, her Villiers childhood playmates traveled with her to The Hague. Although their marriage at first proved to be a happy one, Mary's miscarriages, false pregnancy, and inability to give birth to an heir led William to choose Betty for his mistress.

An odd choice, Rockmore concluded. She was no beauty, and courtiers called her "Squinting Betty" because of a cast in one eye. But she was intelligent, witty, and ambitious. Van Noordwijk believed William and Betty's relationship was not based on sexual attraction but mostly on friendship and intellectual compatibility, which further hurt Mary.

*****

Although both William and Mary were eager to rid themselves of their troublesome ward, William agreed with Mary's selection of Sunday, the 6th of June, 1693, for Rockmore's and Rosamund's wedding day in Kensington Palace chapel, to be performed according to the *Book of Common Prayer*. The Queen told Rockmore he must give his bride a wedding ring according to ritual and symbolism. Mary quoted Henry Swinburne: "The form of the wedding ring being circular, that is, round and without end, imparteth thus much that their mutual love and affection should roundly flow from one to the other as in a circle, and that continually and forever."

*****

During the months before their wedding, Rockmore altered his interior spaces to accommodate Rosamund and her servants. A kitchen, a pantry, and a dining room took up the ground floor. He added twenty feet of space to the rear of his house for each level, including rooms for his majordomo and valet. The second floor still included the parlor and Rockmore's library and bedroom, with new additions for Rosamund's bedroom suite and an adjacent nursery and withdrawal closet. The third floor was for female servants, and the top level for the male servants' dormitory.

Before their wedding, Rockmore discovered many of Rosamund's attributes. She demanded punctuality, manners, and cleanliness from her household servants.

Rockmore and Rosamund sat for their marriage portraits by Court painter Giodfrey Kneller. Queen Mary provided a trousseau for the bride suitable to her status, in addition to an extensive cash dowry from her fortune.

One morning when Parliament was not in session, Rockmore took Rosamund to John Lambert's warehouse on the Thames to select from his latest importation of porcelain.

"Oh, Jack, this set is the most elegant I have seen! After we wed and entertain Queen Mary, she will be envious when she sees it."

Rockmore took Lambert aside. "When Her Majesty visits, I shall mention your name. You may yet have that Royal Appointment."

Lambert's face reddened and his eyes teared whilst he thanked Rockmore.

*****

Rockmore's days and evenings left him little free time. Between staff meetings with King William and arguments and voting in the House of Lords, he also had to focus on his assorted businesses and investments.

Spring arrived. William, with Betty Villiers, left England for The Hague to resume battle with Louis XIV. Van Noordwijk and Henry Lambert accompanied their king.

*****

Queen Mary met with Rockmore in her blooming Dutch garden the day following William's departure. It was no romantic encounter. She discussed wedding details. "John Tillotson, Archbishop of Canterbury, will officiate your wedding ceremony, and we shall have subsequent festivities attended by the highest ranking members of our Court."

Rockmore doubted William would consent to Ambassador Dirck van Noordwijk and Sir Henry Lambert leaving his service.

Mary added, "We shall stand as Matron of Honor for Rosamund. Alas, she has made no friends amongst my ladies at Court. I shall select one of them to support her. If King William cannot attend, our Court Chamberlain shall give Rosamund away by proxy."

Queen Mary assured Rockmore that she and several of her ladies had discussed with Rosamund what to expect in their marriage bed. He was curious to know how his bride to be had reacted to those details, but thought it indelicate to ask.

Rockmore continued t have misgivings about agreeing to wed Rosamund. Mary believed he might be the only man in England able to cntrol her mod swings.

What other hidden flaws might Rosamund have?

CHAPTER FORTY-THREE

WEDDING

Horns sounded and Jeremiah Clarke, the organist for St. Paul's Church, and other musicians, played one of Clarke's Trumpet Voluntary Marches. Rosamund appeared in the chapel arrayed in silver satin and silk, a color symbolizing her virtue. A small number attended their wedding. Queen Mary, the Court Chamberlain as King William's proxy, Archbishop Tillotson, to conduct the ceremony, two court ladies as Rosamund's maids of honor, and two courtiers as Rockmore's groomsmen, instead of Van Noordwijk and Henry Lambert.

Rockmore tolerated the tedious *Book of Common Prayer* ceremony until he lifted Rosamund's veil, and they kissed to much applause. Rockmore could not have been more pleased with his bride's beauty and regal bearing.

He next placed a purse containing gold pieces atop the Archbishop's prayer book, according to custom. Rockmore chose not to give Rosamund the ruby ring his grandfather had received from the Infanta Doña María. He'd yet to love Rosamund as his *b'schert,* his soul mate.

Afterward, all retired to the palace banquet hall for a well-attended wedding feast that neither bride nor groom expected. Liveried attendants served wines and every known spirit with courses of meats and side dishes at festooned tables. A palace chef created a large bride-cake iced with egg white and sugar. The groom's plainer fruitcake had been cubed and was served to each guest in a small blue ribbon box as a lucky souvenir. Musicians played pavannes, sarabands, and other Court dances.

Rockmore sipped wines and spirits sparingly during the toasts for bride and groom, Rosamund not at all. He did not want to be inebriated on his wedding night. Rockmore observed Rosamund's tenseness, which did not bode well for their marriage bed.

*****

At home in Covent Garden, Rockmore finished bathing, dried himself, and put on a robe. He went to their candlelit bedroom and waited for Rosamund.

Rockmore shooed Buccaneer out of the room. How well had Mary and her court ladies prepared his bride? Rockmore sniffed pleasing fragrances from scented candles and a large porcelain basin on a stand filled with rose water.

Rosamund entered covered in a floral robe. Rockmore welcomed his wife with a gentle kiss and removed her robe. Rosamund wore a diaphanous shift beneath. His bride tensed as he guided her to their bed—no surprise.

Rockmore discarded his robe and positioned himself beside Rosamund. He thanked Lady Joan for teaching him how to please a woman. He kissed his bride's lips and the nape of her neck whilst lifting her shift. Rosamund's tenseness had yet to disappear. Rockmore next kissed with mouth and tongue Rosamund's shoulders, then lifted one arm, and concentrated on her smooth, baby-skinned inner arm. He lingered on the crook opposite her elbow.

Rosamund moaned. Her nipples hardened. No longer tense, she allowed Rockmore to caress and kiss her breasts.

Thank you again, Lady Joan.

He moved below to Rosamund's stomach and her inner thighs, and kissed her lower lips. Aware she was moist, well lubricated, Rockmore entered her.

After a brief cry of pain, Rosamund surprised Rockmore. She wrapped her legs around his back and participated with energy after the loss of her maidenhead.

Rosamund wanted more. Thrice, she demanded he penetrate her cunny. Rockmore expected Rosamund to utter endearing words of love. Instead, she repeated one demand over and over during their entire night of copulation:

"Give me a Plantagenet heir."

Chapter Forty-Four

To De Clifford Manor

Parliament was no longer in session. A week after their wedding, Rockmore and Rosamund closed their home in Covent Garden and left for her estate. It lay in Basingstoke, at the edge of Wessex Downs, fifty miles from London, a three-day journey. Rosamund rode with a personal maid in her comfortable well-upholstered coach to prevent bruising. Outside, two armed footmen sat behind, and an armed porter beside the driver.

Carrying a brace of pistols, carbine, and sabre, Rockmore preferred to sit upon his black Frisian Hannibal for a more comfortable ride. Armed male servants followed in his carriage and a covered wagon, all wary of gangs of the highwaymen who infested roads and byways. They often added murder to theft because hanging was the penalty for both crimes. *In for a penny, in for a pound.*

Tolls often slowed traffic when highways were busy. The turnpike system arose, by which the various local authorities received permission by Turnpike Acts to erect tollgates within their parish boundaries and exact contributions from travelers for the upkeep of roads. This was based on two principles. Each parish was responsible for maintenance of its roads, and those who contributed most to their wear and tear should pay for all repairs.

Increased traffic benefited innkeepers, and the 1600s experienced a steady growth of inns, with their black-paneled walls and square courtyards, along the highways. Fynes Moryson portrayed them as pleasant places in his three-volume *An Itinerary: Containing His Ten Years Travel Through the Twelve Dominions of Germany, Bohemia, Switzerland, Netherland, Denmark, Poland, Italy, Turkey, France, England, Scotland and Ireland.*

Moryson wrote:

> *The World affords not such Inns as England hath, either for good and cheap entertainments at the guest's own pleasure, or for humble attendance on passengers. For as soon as a passenger comes to an Inn, the servants run to him, and one takes his horse and walks him till he be cold, then rubs him and gives him meat. Another servant gives the passenger his private chamber and kindles his fire, the third pulls off his boots and makes them clean, and when he sits at table, the Host or Hostess will accompany him, while he eats, he shall be offered music, which he may freely take or refuse, and if he be solitary, the Musicians will give him the good day with music in the morning.*

*****

Rockmore's caravan approached a well-manicured lawn flanked by a wonderland topiary creation of bushes and trees trimmed as animals amidst the lush, rolling hills of the Wessex Woods. De Clifford Manor rose ahead at the crest of a hill. Its design surprised Rockmore. Rosamund had never described her home. Built by Inigo Jones, a follower of Italian architect Andrea Palladio, her neo-classic manor was neither gothic nor Tudor. Its domed, symmetrical, rectangular residence had a temple front pediment supported by Grecian columns and Venetian windows.

An army of servants, groundkeepers, and tenants awaited their masters with bows and curtsies. Rosamund introduced Rockmore to the throng, and she complimented Parish Bailiff Hugh Watson for maintaining her estate as seneschal whilst she resided in London. Grooms took care of their horses, and they entered the manor. Paintings of family members and ancestors covered walls in each room amidst tapestries, collectables, busts and statues.

Rosamund's family had been Tory and supported James II during the Monmouth Rebellion in 1685. When England's greatest general, John Churchill, switched sides in favor of William and Mary, so had Rosamund's father. Upon becoming King of England, William made Churchill Earl of Marlborough and Rosamund's father Duke of Basingstoke.

*****

A tall, austere woman, dressed to her neck in charcoal grey, awaited them in the grand foyer. Her face had been severely disfigured by smallpox, her mouth resembling a torn pocket. Rosamund introduced her to Rockmore as Mrs. Havers, chatelaine, responsible for ruling De Clifford Manor's household.

Mrs, Havers, her expression grim, stated when and where Rockmore's men would dine, sleep, and work. Beer, ale, and other "brews of the devil" were forbidden. She faced Rockmore's liveried retainers and declared, "You men, you are also not to have anything to do with our female servants."

Rockmore at first sight marked Mrs. Havers as an antagonist.

Let the battle begin!

"With all due respect for your position, Mrs. Havers, my men are answerable to me and no one else. I shall decide if their quarters are adequate and their meals nourishing. And they shall have their Devil's Brew if they so wish."

Manor servants snickered, and Mrs. Havers gave Rockmore a death glare. She turned to Rosamund for support.

"Lord Rockmore and I have agreed to the same in London" Rosamund said. "His manservants are answerable only to him. We've had a long journey. Have our servants show them their quarters and other parts of my manor. I will take Lord Rockmore to our suites."

Upstairs, Rosamund had separate chambers, a practice common amongst the aristocracy. No demands to make babies yet, she inspected her home with the bailiff, giving orders as needed to her servants. Whilst Rockmore's valet put away his clothes, he toured rooms and balconies. On the morrow, he intended to ride to the limits of the manor's grounds.

The journey from London and the first day at Clifford Manor left Rockmore exhausted. For once he enjoyed being alone in his bed, but it was not to be. Rosamund entered wearing a shift. "Let us make a Plantagenet baby."

Chapter Forty-Five

De Clifford Estate and Town

Rockmore spent the summer days familiarizing himself with Rosamund's estate. They inspected farms, grazing land for cattle and sheep, the woolery and the mills. Rockmore also spoke with tenant farmers and woodsmen. Evenings and nights, Rosamund demanded they make a Plantagenet heir without romance or love.

Rosamund's estate had many employees, and she ran her domain as a benign autocrat. Rockmore met her park keeper, head woodman, and steward. Skilled in bookkeeping, Rosamund went over their accounts to verify they were in order.

Ordinary folk, titled wealthy, and rich gentry mingled on the basis of neighborhood and shared interests. Kinship provided another variable given the centuries of intra marriage. Common local interests brought all classes together at church or on court benches. Yet, personal disputes and longheld grudges caused multi-generational feuds. Rockmore suspected venal kin resented Rosamund for marrying outside her family.

On Rosamund's lands, skilled craftsmen earned a shilling per day, unskilled laborers received eight pence, and women four pence for field work. A staff of fourteen house servants cost Rosamund £67 per annum, excluding her steward and the secretary. Rents might be high and discipline strict, but Rosamund took responsibility for her tenants' and parishioners' welfare, provided they obeyed her rules, enforced by her seneschal Watson,

Watson told Rockmore many wives and husbands came from different social backgrounds. "Our county squires are a cohesive body of 'natural rulers,' foremost amongst them being long-time property holders. Some have estates worth over £1,000 per annum, up to £10,000. Of course none approaches Lady Rosamund's estate, worth £3 million with an income of £50,000 or more, depending upon harvests and rents."

Watson ignored Rockmore's concerns about child labor and his desire to replace it with schooling. Rosamund sided with Watson. He showed Rockmore gentry mixing amongst common folk at assizes, elections, funerals, markets, fairs, and horse races. They also governed as magistrates, highway commissioners, militia leaders, tax assessors, and members of political caucuses.

Rockmore, given his liquid wealth, and his political, cultural and business interests, decided running a large country estate might not be worth the time, effort, expenses, and added responsibilities. Rosamund was bred and suited for that sort of life. He did appreciate the better air at Basingstoke as compared to London's summer stench.

Chapter Forty-Six

Venison Mythos

Rockmore earned respect from the local gentry for his shooting accuracy during quail and pheasant hunts to feed local estates and yeomen farmers. He did not participate in fox hunts, which he deemed to be cruel and too one-sided to be called a sport, and because foxes did not feed the local population as did venison and quail.

One aspect of country life fascinated Rockmore: the hunt for venison, a privileged food from aristocrat and royal deer parks. Under England's strict game laws, poaching venison was a hanging offence. For centuries, deer possessed significance beyond their importance as food. No other commodity or product was owned only by nobles and the Crown. Deer evoked traditional concepts of status and landed power.

Rockmore found a book in de Clifford Manor's library, *Thoughts on Hunting* by Peter Beckford, who wrote, "The chase is the soul of country life."

Other writings informed Rockmore that before England existed, deer had been considered to be miraculous creatures, gifted with magical powers. The ancients had believed deer lived up to one hundred years, and many contemporary hunters still asserted it to be true.

Pliny and Ovid wrote that deer bones, marrow, and antlers had medicinal value. Others praised venison's wit, cunning, and power over snakes.

Authors claimed hunting was a sport to be followed only by superior men. Poets, lyricists, authors, and painters glorified great stags in poems, songs, essays, and paintings.

Other manuals Rockmore found described the noble qualities of hunters, who made other men, as well as beasts, yield to their strength. They were not only wise and warlike, they were virtuous and protected by God. The focus required during the hunt led to training warriors.

Beckford concluded, "Thus, the hunt served as a metaphor for the patriarchal order and a locus for its values. King, nobles, neighboring gentry, foresters, masters of the hounds, huntsmen, servants, dogs, deer, and raven gathered together in a hierarchical display of the great chain of being."

*****

Rosamund surprised Rockmore when she and several other ladies participated in his first venison hunt. The stag they followed was a majestic beast, its noble head bearing wide antlers. Beaters and hounds surrounded their prey. Rockmore and other nobles and gentry riders moved in for the kill. Several men blew four *morts* on their hunting horns, signifying the stag was dead.

Huntsmen carried the stag to a glen. His death did not end the ceremonies of the hunt. Servants brought wine for participants and spectators, who joined in what seemed to Rockmore a religious mass. Whilst huntsmen gutted the stag, all present chanted liturgical songs and feasted on bread soaked in its blood. Rosamund and other ladies of quality who desired a white complexion also washed hands and faces in deer's blood.

A gentry neighbor described hunting rituals for Rockmore. "King James I daubed his courtiers' faces in deer blood and forbade them to wash it away."

Huntsmen carved the deer for distribution in a ceremony called the "Breaking of the Deer." This ritual revealed power relationships. Body parts were distributed according to rank or roles in the hunt. The best morsels—tongue, ears, and testicles—went to Rockmore and Rosamund as ranking personages. Huntsmen received haunches, sides, and innards. A shoulder each went for the keeper and carver. The Master of the Hounds received hides, and gristle bits were hung from a tree for ravens.

This allocation of the kill during its rites revealed basic values of the landed elite: paternalism, hospitality, privilege, pride, glorification of private property, masculinity, and authority. Over centuries, royalty, aristocrats, and landed gentry increased control over their land and its rights. Forest courts and the Crown no longer monopolized the hunt. Landowners in Parliament passed game laws with successively more severe penalties to affirm their privileges over lower classes. The prerogative of hunting, once monopolized by kings and nobles, now included wealthy private gentlemen.

During more drinking, tongues loosened. Reactionary landowners complained that London's rising middling sort was trespassing upon their social boundaries. One squire claimed, "Every gentleman with an income of £500 or £1,000 rent hath a park."

Another declared, "As non-landed professionals accumulate wealth, they intrude upon our social hierarchy. Our ordered ranks, so clearly revealed in the hunt, are blurred in London, where the breadth of occupations of those receiving venison now include drapers, merchants, doctors, lawyers, and officeholders."

Rockmore kept his opinions to himself. Power politics was shifting to London and to Parliament. Lords-Lieutenant and party managers now dispensed favors along with sinecures and pensions.

One knight asked £4.10s for a buck. Its haunch fetched between £3 and £5, and its offal commanded up to 16s. In years of scarcity, prices rose even more. It was no surprise that this illegal market was centered, like the Exchange and the marriage mart, in London.

Yet the economic impact of the deer was far greater than the money it brought. When gifts were sent to London, they stimulated a stream of shillings to park officials, keepers, carriers, and coachmen. As the venison made its way from hand to hand, cash came to those who touched it.

Rosamund's bookkeeper itemized a buck's delivery costs: fee to the keeper, 10s.; to the underkeeper, 2s.6d; shoulders and *umbles* (innards), 5s.; carriage, 7s.; and at least one shilling given to the person who brings the venison.

CHAPTER FORTY-SEVEN

HOUSE DIVIDED

By August 1693, Rockmore had had enough of deer and other game hunting, local fairs, and unstimulating rural conversations. He preferred London with its informed political discussions, theater, concerts, business, and access to literature. Parliament would be opening in September, and he needed to be in London by then. Rosamund, to the contrary, was in her element. She ruled her property and its inhabitants as a monarch, stern and just. She expressed no interest in returning to London any time soon.

Rockmore observed that his wife's extreme mood swings followed a pattern. In June, July, and now August, a week before her menstrual flow Rosamund became ill-tempered, shrewish, and even violent. During those irrational days and her period, she made no sexual demands. Rockmore wished his grandfather still lived. He believed Don Vicente Isaac de Rocamora could have diagnosed Rosamund's symptoms and suggested a cure.

After a week of Rosamund's headaches, morning nausea, and a missed period, a local physician confirmed she was pregnant. Then Rosamund agreed they must return to London where the best physicians resided before she was heavy with child and travel too dangerous along rutted roads. Her female servants and cook followed from Basingstoke, and Mrs. Havers took charge of them.

From the day her pregnancy was confirmed Rosamund refused to share Rockmore's bed, for fear, she said, of losing her anticipated son. A physician told Rosamund her due date would be in the first or second week of March 1694. Rosamund excluded Rockmore from her life. She refused Rockmore entry to her bedroom, where she took all meals. Yet her physician and midwife visited daily.

Rockmore chose not to assert his rights as husband until after their child's birth. Instead, he carried out his parliamentary duties, socialized with Whigs, and visited with Queen Mary at her maze-end pavilion. No one so far had discovered their trysts.

The following day, in her pavilion, Mary told Rockmore they must postpone their clandestine meetings. King William had landed at Dover and would be in England until spring of 1694.

Rosamund decided that nothing must interfere with the birth of her son and Plantagenet heir and went to bed for the final six-month duration of her pregnancy. She also refused to consider that her child might be a girl. Mrs. Havers moved into the adjacent nursery and barred all from Rosamund's suite. She ran a strict household.

Early in December, Rosamund made an exception. She invited Queen Mary and certain ladies of the Court for a dinner. Her chef outdid himself, musicians played well, and all the guests raved about her elegant porcelain plates and tureens.

"Lady Rosamund, your porcelain is superior to any in our palaces," Mary gushed. "Pray tell us where you obtained them."

Rosamund deferred to Rockmore, who said, "Your Majesty, John Lambert is our merchant importer. You might enjoy visiting his warehouse on the Thames. His Majesty knighted Lambert's son, Colonel Henry Lambert, who is on your husband's staff."

"Call for us tomorrow morning at ten, and you may bring us to this merchant Lambert."

After their guests departed, Rockmore dispatched a servant to Lambert's home with a note alerting him to Mary's visit in the morning. He sighed, facing another night without Rosamund sharing his bed.

*****

A crowd gathered outside Lambert's warehouse to see and cheer popular Queen Mary when she and Rockmore alighted from her royal carriage and Court ladies emerged from a second protected by a military escort. Lambert, his eldest son John Junior, and his employees oozed obsequies whilst greeting Mary. Inside, she behaved as a child amongst toys.

"Why had we not been made aware of your treasures before Lord and Lady Rockmore's dinner last evening, Mr. Lambert?"

"Your Majesty, it is most difficult to gain access to the palace."

"That restriction has ended for you. From where do you import these wonders?"

"I have a factory in Holland, and these sets on the table here come from China."

"A factory in Holland, you said? Why not build one here?"

"I have been considering it, Your Majesty, and I have been seeking a suitable site."

Mary gestured toward Lady Margaret Cecil, who handed her a parchment scroll. The Queen unrolled it. "This, Mr.

Lambert, is our royal arms. Can you produce your finest porcelain featuring it?"

"Absolutely, Your Majesty." Lambert clapped his hands, and several of his workers with great care carried wooden boxes to Queen Mary. They opened the crates, and Lambert removed protective cushions from one. He handed Mary a hand-painted porcelain plate featuring Queen Mary and King William in profile, with their royal arms emblazoned between them.

Mary held the plate, gazing at it in awe. "Never have we seen such fine craftsmanship. We must take this set with us for His Majesty to see. If he is pleased with the result, you may advertise 'as by Appointment to Their Majesties.'"

Rockmore prepared to catch Lambert, who seemed about to faint. The merchant almost did so when he offered to look for a convenient property site.

"The sooner, the better," Mary commanded. "We want English porcelain to be regarded as the best in the world."

Lambert struggled to calm himself until Mary and her entourage had departed. "Lord Rockmore, how can I ever repay you?"

"First, we shall visit a potential site at an appropriate time, although I'd prefer it be located on the Thames close to your warehouse."

Alone with Lambert, Rockmore shook the man;s hand. "Most clever of you, to have had your porcelain prepared."

"I did not want to wait for a long round trip to China and manufacture. By the time that was accomplished their favorable impression of me and my porcelain might have been forgotten."

Clever businessman.

*****

The following day, Rockmore met with Queen Mary at Hampton Court. Although she was delighted Rosamund was with child, she found it strange that Rockmore's wife had gone abed until she gave birth. Mary offered herself and King William to be godparents for Rockmore's firstborn. They walked alone through her gardens, her ladies a discrete distance away, out of hearing.

"Is Rosamund interested in politics?"

"We have never discussed such matters. My wife has only one interest, to produce a Plantagenet male heir."

"Are you more happily wed?"

"We're adjusting to each other."

Mary frowned. "Then Rosamund is being difficult?"

Jacob hesitated. "Not yet to any degree that concerns me."

"If serious problems arise, please consult with us before matters get out of hand."

Chapter Forty-Eight

Declaration of War

Early in January 1694, Rockmore arrived home midday and hung in his library famed Sir Godfrey Kneller's completed portrait of him in count's robes. He wanted Rosamund to view it but found her bedroom door locked. His key did not work. Someone had applied new locks to her door. After no response, he pounded harder.

"If no one answers, I'll force myself in."

Someone on the other side opened it a sliver. Mrs. Havers loomed at the entrance. "You know perfectly well that Lady Rosamund has gone abed until she delivers her son in March. This room is still closed to all except me, her midwife, and her physician."

Rockmore pushed the door open wide. "Know your place, woman. This is my house. I am her husband."

Mrs. Havers placed a hand against Rockmore's shoulder to prevent his entering. "That matters not."

Strong woman.

Rockmore cursed Mrs. Havers and swept her hand away. He seized her right arm, twisted it behind her back, and pushed her against a wall. "Woman, never touch me again. Never defy me. This is my house. All rooms are open to me."

Rockmore threw Mrs. Havers to the floor and looked beyond her to Rosamund, who was sitting upright in bed against several pillows, her eyes storm black. In a shrill voice she called out, "Leave her alone. Mrs. Havers is carrying out my orders. Do not come closer."

Mrs. Havers rose and rushed to Rosamund's side. "Your intrusion has aggravated my mistress. We have decided she needs to stay in bed until her son's birth in March. She must ensure a safe birthing for her child."

"Can you not speak directly to me, wife?"

"Go away, leave my rooms until next I summon you."

Chapter Forty-Nine

Without Rosamund

Rockmore spent evenings away from home, going weeks without seeing Rosamund, doing business at Canela's coffee house with his bankers and talking politics.

As a new Whig peer he hired Sir Godfrey Kneller to paint his portrait in Parliamentary robes. Between sittings they discussed politics and discovered they were like-minded.

The artist sponsored Jacob's membership in London's Kit-Cat Club, famed for its political and literary associations. Its members were committed to furtherance of Whig policies such as a strong Parliament and a limited Protestant monarchy. The Club included writers, politicians, artists, nobles, and magistrates.

A unique characteristic of the Kit-Kat was its toasting-glasses, used for drinking to the health of reigning beauties, on which were engraved verses praising them. This habit of toasting led Dr. Arbuthnot to produce an epigram repeated throughout London:

Whence deathless Kit-Kat took his name
Few critics can unriddle
 Some say from pastry cook it came
And some from Cat and Fiddle.
From no trim beaus its name it boasts
Grey statesmen or green wits
But from the pell-mell pack of toasts
Of old Cats and young Kits.

Jacob discovered the true origin of the club's name. The first meetings were held at a tavern in Shire Lane run by innkeeper Christopher Catt. He named his mutton pies *Kit Cats.*

Sir Godfrey Kneller created forty-eight portraits of Kit-Cat members in a standard format of 36 by 28 inches. He added Rockmore to the gallery,

*****

On St. Valentine's Day, 1694, Rockmore stood as groomsman for Henry Lambert when his friend wed Alderman Boyce's daughter Elida. It was no surprise that Rosamund declined to attend both nuptials and celebration. Henry's wedding came early in the year because in a month he would be leaving with King William to begin another spring offensive against Louis XIV.

Although Henry's bride was comely, Rockmore still worried about her health should she become pregnant. Delicate of form with narrow hips, Elida's pale skin still revealed blue veins at her temples, hands, and arms. In the end of March, 1694, Henry took his wife with him to the Dutch Republic when William returned to the Netherlands to launch his spring offensive and to cohabit with his mistress Betty Villiers.

*****

Queen Mary met Rockmore at her Dutch Garden. She questioned him about his marriage. Rockmore emphasized Rosamund's obsession with having a son. "She has no interest in my businesses or politics."

"Perhaps, after she has a son, all will be well."

Rockmore did not express his doubts about that to Mary. They next discussed King William's finances. Earlier in the year, Rockmore had invested the new Bank of England to finance William's wars and the building of a navy large enough to defeat France, whose navy was a dominant sea power. England had no choice but to build a powerful global navy. Alas, no public funds were available, and William III's government credit was so low in London it could not borrow the £1,200,000 at 8% per annum the government needed.

To induce subscription to a loan, subscribers were incorporated by the name of the Governor and Company of the Bank of England. The Bank received exclusive possession of the government's balances, and was the only limited-liability corporation allowed to issue bank notes. Lenders gave the government gold bullion and issued notes against government bonds, which could be lent again. The Bank raised £1.2 million in twelve days, half of which was earmarked for rebuilding the navy.

Parliament granted a Royal Charter on the 27th of July, 169 3, through passage of the Tonnage Act of 1694. Public finances were in such dire condition the loan had to be serviced at a rate of 8 per cent per annum, and a service charge of £4,000 per annum for management of the loan.

The first governor was Sir John Houblon, who was depicted in a £50 note issued in 1694. He also was director of the Whig-dominated New East India Company.

Back in the early 1660s, the East India Company discovered many unauthorized persons carrying on trade in precious stones with India, under cover of privileges granted in

1650 to owners and officers of East India ships. The Court of Directors allowed anyone who wished to participate in it, provided he paid certain duties to the Company. They gave permission for export to and import from India of precious stones and other goods of high value. Exporters had to pay two per cent of the goods' value to the Company and importers were to pay two per cent if they were stockholders of the Company, four per cent if they were not. That decision caused a rapid development of England's trade in uncut diamonds, which made London the foremost international center of trade in diamonds.

Rockmore took advantage of other opportunities for investment in factories manufacturing weapons of war, for which he obtained government contracts through political connections. He further expanded his varied business interests and purchased land along the Thames sufficient for Lambert to build a porcelain factory in which Rockmore was a significant investor.

Alert to other financial opportunities, Rockmore invested in new ironworks that made nails for the navy, factories producing bayonets for the Army, and £50.000 in the Bank of England. His investments brought him into more frequent contact with Sephardic merchants.

*****

For generations, Jewish economic life had been limited through Jews' inferior legal status and their jealousy of Christian merchants. All prevented Jews from making full use of the new economic opportunities England offered.

Banking expanded in both London and its provinces. Jewish absence from this field did not surprise Rockmore. These new profitable investments in deposits, unfamiliar to Jews, caused them at first to ignore any opportunity to invest, despite their familiarity with monetary affairs.

Yet, London's rise to be a major commercial center and the dominance it enjoyed in Lisbon enabled Jewish merchants to continue trading with Spain and Portugal and their New world colonies. Most major London Jewish merchants, or their fathers, had come from Amsterdam, Leghorn, or directly from Portugal.

Anglo-Jewish merchants established a virtual monopoly on European diamond and coral imports from India. Close mercantile and financial ties between London and Amsterdam and growing demand for international exchange services encouraged Jewish merchants to participate, including Rockmore's longtime Sephardic friends.

The houses of Salvador and Santcroos, leading Portuguese families pre-eminent in diamond and precious metal trades, advised Rockmore in investments and protecting his liquid wealth. Their sons and factors moved the diamond and bullion trade centers from Goa and Amsterdam to Madras and London.

Rockmore's friend, Francis Daniel Salvador, was acquainted with the Portuguese ambassador in London, Sebastian Carvalho, later Marquis de Pombal and Prime Minister, who held no prevalent hostility toward Jews.

Despite a hyper-aggressive Inquisition, the Portuguese Court turned blind eyes to crypto Jewish merchants who used several pseudonyms whilst exporting corn to Lisbon. They bought corn at Portsmouth or Falmouth through an agent who consigned shipments to Lisbon. These Jewish merchants who traded with Spain and Portugal also exported woolen goods and imported precious metals and Iberian wine.

Through Francis Salvador and his son Francis Jr. and other Sephardic merchants, Rockmore imported ingots and bars of gold from Portugal, which they consigned to Joseph Salvador in Amsterdam. They also sent goods to Jamaica and Spanish America. Jamaica's Jews also imported contraband bullion from Spanish colonies, whilst London's Jews were the main suppliers of manufactured goods to New World colonies through Jamaica.

During those months, Rockmore saw more of Queen Mary than Rosamund.

Chapter Fifty

Lamberts Rising

In November of 1693, Henry Lambert and Elida arrived in London with King William's entourage and sought Rockmore at Parliament as the day's session ended. "Pray, tell me, when may I be presented to your wife?"

Before relating the bizarre status quo of their marriage, Rockmore first described how Queen Mary had pressured him to wed Rosamund.

Lambert listened, horrified, without interrupting. After Rockmore concluded his tale of woe, he took Lambert to his home and led him to Rosamund's suite. Mrs. Havers barred their entry.

"This is my marriage," Rockmore remarked.

Back in the library, Lambert accepted a glass of claret. "Who is Mrs. Havers? She is a most intimidating woman. How did she come to wield so much power over your wife?"

"I have identical questions. I need someone discreet to make inquiries in Basingstoke."

"Pray, let me visit Basingstoke on your behalf. King William has given me leave until after the New Year. I'll take Elida with me."

Rockmore touched glasses with Lambert. "You are a loyal friend, Henry."

"It is the least I can do for you, Jack, given how much you promoted my career and my father's business with Queen Mary."

After two weeks, Rockmore met Henry Lambert at his father's warehouse. Henry read from copious notes.

"Mrs. Havers was born an only child to her titled father's second wife. She was seventeen when her parents died of smallpox and she was disfigured by that disease. Cheated out of her inheritance by older step brothers and forced into an unwanted marriage by them, she was left destitute when her husband died deep in debt. Mrs. Havers was taken in by Rosamund's family, her distant kin, and hired to be the girl's governess." He looked up. "Henry, I could almost pity that woman were she not so adversarial."

*****

At the end of January, 1694, John Lambert received two honors he'd long sought. His porcelain set displaying royal arms with the likenesses of Their Majesties delighted both William and Mary. They gave his business the right to use the phrase *"By Royal Appointment"* and added the long desired knighthood.

During celebrations at home, John Lambert told Rockmore he intended to improve his social status. "I have long observed an essential element of power is based upon personal connections."

In Rockmore's evaluation Lambert's sweet but plain wife Marie was a handicap for her family in advancing their social status. In London, women controlled manners. Politeness revealed one's status. Merchants like Lambert and as well as professionals acquired upward social mobility and thrived in

London's fluid, affluent environment if they made the necessary financial efforts and acquired manners.

The rise of a literate culture emphasized politeness. The easing of laws limiting religious and scientific speech led to hunger for information, which stimulated a thriving publishing industry and the spread of literacy for London women, who had fewer forms of self-expression than their male counterparts in business and the professions.

"As has been said often, Sir John, men and women have always lived for company. Tis hard for them to be confined, conversation being a great pleasure of this life. If you wish to rise socially, you must purchase or rent a coach."

"I have been admiring yours, Lord Rockmore."

"Calling upon one's friends in a carriage has become an important expression of London sociability. It is a fashionable way for individuals to gather and display their power and politeness. It surpasses gifts of venison as a symbol of elite culture."

"Aye, Lord Rockmore, 'tis no surprise London is where coaches have become a status symbol for those who wish to be seen with their superfluous, expensively garbed attendants. On carriages with gilded coronets in their corners, behind which stand two or three footmen attired in rich liveries."

"Similar to mine, Sir John. Are you willing to join in the game?"

"If I must. May I ask if it is cost effective?"

"That depends upon your goals. Currently, a coach requires more continuous expense than any other possession. One such vehicle may cost at least £50 plus another £50 for horses, and up to £100 for trimmings. Add £80 more for liveries, coachman, and coach maintenance. As an example, this year, I have paid £11 for the best silk and fringe alone."

Lambert gaped, horrified. "That much?"

"Some nobles and gentry save money by refurbishing old coaches and trading worn fabrics for new. Wages for a coachman, postilion, groom, porter, and three footmen can be modest. For a coachman, £6; and £3 for the others, though they also receive tips, bed, and board. So, even the most frugal families cannot avoid spending lavishly on their coaches so they may visit friends to give and receive hospitality à la mode, fit and proper."

Rockmore had a coach built to his specifications, separate from Rosamund's, with arms painted on each side derived from the de Rocamora crest: a tower on a rock above waves, against a sky-blue background with a mulberry leaf above and gold fleur de lys on either side, showing his family's French origins.

"Mentors are essential for merchants like you, Sir John, to rise in society. One titled dowager asserted in my presence, 'Not everyone shows the prick of good breeding.'"

Rockmore turned his head to include Lambert's wife in the conversation. "There are other expenses beyond the coach, Sir John. You and Lady Marie will require a finer wardrobe than your austere Huguenot garb. Whilst you toil in your warehouse and office, Lady Marie will be expected to make use of your carriage when making social calls."

Rockmore did not add that a woman's use of her family coach offered freedom, power, and independence as never before. Yet female control depended upon many other factors, including age, rank, wealth, and marital status. Unmarried females and spinsters borrowed carriages to take sacraments at church, appear at funerals, conduct marriage negotiations, and, most often, to visit. Wealthy widows also had their own carriages.

Alderman Boyce's wife rode with a black servant playing a trumpet and two liveried men on horseback, an imposing sight proclaiming her social position. Ladies shared news in their drawing rooms with liquid consumption and political gossip, just as men did.

Rockmore alerted Sir John to another reality. "Two powerful groups of women have created their own social codes beyond existing guidelines. They have modified rules and thus increased their influence over their husbands and other males."

"I cannot imagine my Marie behaving so outrageously."

"The rules have created a conflict between manners and morality. In continental models of gentility, politeness has led to artifice in personal relationships. *The Gentleman's Library* has warned 'the greatest part of mankind's conversation is little else but dissimulation. If gentlemen continually praise each other, one would never know their true sentiments.'"

"Alas, Lord Rockmore, I am a plain-speaking man. I cannot see myself flourishing in a world of artifice."

"Perhaps I have been exaggerating, Sir John. Excessive politeness goes against English customs and traditions consistent with England's new commercial and military power vis-à-vis France. They reflect a preference for more natural speech and regard those men aping French affectations in manners and extreme modes of dress as buffoons."

"Then those men are types with whom I could easily associate."

"Not their women, though. They pressure their men to observe French formalities instead of plain English speech, which one dismissed as 'the natural language of Buckinghamshire bumpkins.' Some believe politeness blurs gender boundaries with its emphasis on polite conversation, which might cause effeminacy in men, as exemplified by the fop. Sir John, city activities are replacing country rituals. We both know an ambitious, middling sort of lawyer, Dudley Ryder. He makes no secret of his desire to enter society, but declines to hunt. Influenced by *The Spectator* and experiences in coffee-houses, and abetted by his wealthy family, Ryder has risen to prominence. His main social activity is making endless rounds of visits. His social calls in a coach help Ryder and others like him to present themselves as polite gentlemen. Politeness means presenting a proper public figure, good breeding, and maintaining harmonious relationships. It requires intent to please and an ability to discriminate between different types of sociability."

Lambert beckoned for a servant to pour another round of Madeira. "I have been told an intimate connection exists between status and manners. You should know better than I. Is it that noble blood is less important these days?"

"Aye, it is. Instead, shared norms of public behavior identify members of polite society. Uses of restrained, but artful, compliments provide a language of courtesy, through which social relations are expressed. But polite conduct must appear natural, a complex, subtle art. The gentleman, not the courtier, has now become an ideal male. Yes, rules of proper behavior are needed here in London, where social hierarchies are fluid. Those with titles and the gentry share public spaces with a new urban propertied class."

"What am I to do, Lord Rockmore?"

"Periodicals such as *The Spectator* and *The Tatler* offer suggestions on how to shape a system of public morality. Virtue and commerce, they insist, can coexist with polished manners. Exchange of food is a key element of social relationships through dinner parties. It is kinder to dine than visit."

Despite Rosamund's absence from such events, Rockmore's acquaintances invited him to their homes where table seating ranged from twelve to twenty-four chairs. Hosts provided punch bowls and card games for guests. Also, wine and spirits flowed, releasing inhibitions.

"Sir John, the simple visit spiced with gossip has become a principal mode of town sociability and a school for manners. Like gifts of deer, visits are more than systems of exchange. They signify politeness, especially if done in a coach. One might spend more time paying and receiving calls than any other social activity. During a visit, one's speech, carriage, dress, wit, and manners are placed on public exhibition. Visits also may be read as barometers of power relationships. The right to call upon a patron is a public declaration of standing, whilst the status of one's visitors is another display of influence and proper self-presentation, to be seen in public as one's best. Your wife should read *The Lady's Preceptor*. It offers helpful hints for women on preparing for a visit such as 'it would not be at all amiss to consider, before-hand, what topics are suitable to the company, and to make yourself mistress of them.'"

"I shall find copies for Marie and my daughters."

"And thusly, Sir John, one must perform as an actor during any visit. But beware of women who modify visiting rules, for that is how they increase their control of social space and men. 'If there is a design to the visit,' advises *The Ladies Dictionary*, 'it is necessary to converse. But if it is made only to show ourselves, and let his Lordship know we are alive, we need do no more.' De Courtin's *Rules of Civility* includes sections on topics such as how to comport one's self when a noble person visits and when one is obliged to make returns."

Rockmore did not add that he'd purchased such reading material for Rosamund, who chose to ignore them.

John Lambert heaved a great sigh. "I fear I may never learn well such social graces."

"It may come easier than you anticipate. Adding '*By Appointment to Their Majesties King William III and Queen Mary II*' will send many nobles and gentry to your door. Invitations will follow. Be yourself. Remember, you may also hire experts to show your wife how to behave during visits."

Chapter Fifty-One

Firstborn

On March 6th, 1694, Rockmore returned home after a disappointing day in the House of Lords. His proposal to tax Barbados' Jews the same as Christians had failed by a wide margin, to much ridicule.

Rockmore faced a chaotic scene. Amidst cries for fresh towels, hot water, and servants scurrying to and fro, he heard Rosamund's screams coming from her upstairs bedroom.

Rockmore hurried to Rosamund, pushed aside Mrs. Havers, and arrived at his wife's bedside as she gave birth nine months from their wedding night to a girl, a beautiful fair child. Midwife and physician agreed, despite Rosamund's screams, that it had been a relatively easy birth, with no harm to mother and child.

Rockmore kissed Rosamund's forehead and cheeks. "Well done, my love. We have a beautiful, perfect daughter."

Rosamund turned her head away from Rockmore. "No, it is an imperfect child, a girl. I want a son. We shall have a boy next time. It must be a boy." Rosamund refused to hold her daughter. "Where is the wet nurse?"

*****

Rosamund wanted nothing to do with their daughter and left her in the care of a wet nurse. She decided on naming her Mary Elizabeth Maud Rosamund de Clifford Plantagenet, and Rockmore added his mother's name, Cordelia. He doted on his little Cordelia. She had the potential to become a great beauty. She had blonde hair, blue eyes, and was of a natural cheerful disposition. Everyone remarked how she looked less like a generic newborn and was blessed with perfect features.

So remarked Queen Mary, whilst she held Cordelia during her baptism. "A most beautiful child. When she is of suitable age, she will serve us at Court."

The Queen's eyes moistened, and Rockmore pitied her. After several miscarriages and a false pregnancy, Mary had been devastated when physicians told her she could never bear a child of her own.

At home, Rosamund failed to express love or *pro forma* interest in their daughter. Was she incapable of loving anyone? Yes, Rockmore concluded, except perhaps a son yet to be born. After Rosamond recovered from Cordelia's birth, she resumed her bedroom demands.

In mid-July of 1694 Rosamund announced she was with child and went to bed as before. She did not risk traveling to Basingstoke for the summer, fearing a miscarriage, which pleased Rockmore. He preferred never to visit Basingstoke again.

CHAPTER FIFTY-TWO

SEASON OF DEATH

In October of 1694, Henry Lambert returned from the Army in Europe after his wife's birthing. Elida, being frail and narrow in the hips, did not survive, as Rockmore had feared, and neither did their daughter. Henry brought them home for burial. Rockmore spent the following days assuaging his friend's grief with counseling and diversions at coffee houses.

In early December, at Kensington Palace, Queen Mary awakened with rashes on her arms. She'd never had smallpox, unlike most of her family. At first, palace physicians diagnosed she had contracted measles because she could eat and sit in bed. Still, her rashes spread,

Because Rockmore was immune to both measles and small pox, Mary allowed him to visit. "Lord Rockmore, pray be honest. Your grandfather taught you much about diseases."

"I wish I could be more optimistic, Ma'am, but I believe your physicians are wrong."

"I have smallpox?"

"Yes, it breaks my heart to say."

"I feared as much. I have other symptoms, headaches and nausea. That preventive treatment you suggested, is it too late to try it?"

"Yes, unfortunately, I regret to say."

"My physicians opposed it, and I must confess I was afraid to experiment."

"I pray you may have a mild case of the pox." Rockmore held Mary's hand. "There is much I want to say."

Mary squeezed his hand. "Your eyes have said all with much eloquence. I have sent for the King. Please, comfort my husband when he arrives."

"I shall do my utmost."

*****

Mary dismissed all ladies, pages, and courtiers who had not been exposed to smallpox. Rockmore helped his Queen burn letters and pages of her diary. Several entries surprised him, as did a few of the responses from a female named Frances Apsley when Mary was in her teens. He read each whilst Mary slept before burning them. The two women shared much affection for each other, but signed the letters with pseudonyms. Frances Apsley cooled and ended their correspondence after Mary became Queen. He read nothing confirming that they had sinned. He'd never learn if Miss Apsley burned Mary's letters.

Rockmore also read pages from Mary's diary in which she mentioned him, before burning them. She expressed her love for him, the memory of which would always offer much comfort, but posterity must never know.

Unfortunately, pustules on Mary's skin did not pop but sunk into her flesh, proof that she had fatal hemorrhagic smallpox and faced an inevitable horrible death, just as Lady Joan had. It was not surprising to Rockmore that Mary turned to her religion for comfort, often in delirium, seeking forgiveness for her sins.

After William arrived from Europe, Mary lay on her deathbed. He slept on an Army cot by his wife's side and seldom left her room.

During those last grim days and nights, Rockmore reflected upon Mary's complex persona. She could be merry and witty, with a zest for dancing and cards, and show much affection for him. She also could be cold, even ruthless, as demonstrated in her father's dethroning, her reaction to Betty Villiers' and William's betrayal—which led to replacing her entire household for not reporting to her what they knew about the affair—and her mistreatment of Anne for not ridding herself of Sarah Churchill.

*****

Rockmore received a surprising summons and unique request from Mary's sister, Princess Anne. Until now, he'd had no interaction with Anne. Everything he knew about her came from Court gossip.

Anne did not resemble the Stuarts. She was short and plump, unlike her tall, handsome, and beautiful kin. Anne's poor health included gout. Her education had been limited to languages and music; she had little knowledge of history and had had no instruction in civil law or military matters.

A sickly child with poor vision caused by watering eyes, Anne had survived a serious case of smallpox at age twelve. After she wed Prince George of Denmark, she suffered through many miscarriages and still births.

On May 12th, 1684, Anne Stuart gave birth to her first daughter, who was stillborn. Anne then had two live births: Mary and Anne Sophia. After Anne Sophia, Princess Anne found herself pregnant again, but, on January 21st, 1687, she suffered her first miscarriage. While that was devastating enough, two weeks later she lost her two living infant daughters to smallpox.

On October 22nd, 1687, Anne gave birth to a stillborn boy at seven 7 months. On the 16th of April, 1688, she suffered her second miscarriage.

In 1689, Anne and George had a son who survived, William, Duke of Gloucester. On March 23rd, 1693, Anne gave birth to a stillborn daughter, who was buried the following day at Westminster Abbey. The following year Anne had another miscarriage.

Mary had become estranged from her sister over Anne's dependent relationship with Sarah Jennings Churchill and her husband, whom Mary despised. In 1692, when Mary visited Anne, she demanded her sister remove Sarah from her household. Anne refused, and Mary vowed never to see her sister again.

Jacob now stood before Princess Anne, who was flanked by her ineffectual inebriated husband Prince George and Sara Jennings Churchill. Anne's gouty right foot rested on a cushioned stool.

"Lord Rockmore, how fares Queen Mary?"

"She will die soon from black smallpox."

Anne recovered from Rockmore's bluntness. "Did you inform our sister we wish to see her?"

"In the strongest possible way, I did, Your Highness, and I pleaded your case for reconciliation, as you requested. I regret to say, Her Majesty does not want to see you, and King William supports her."

"Has she no word for us?"

"None, Your Highness."

Anne dismissed Rockmore, who left for home. Rosamund, as usual, did not inquire about Mary's health.

*****

On the 28th of December, Rockmore stood amongst Mary's ladies and ranking Court officials outside her bed-

269

room when her physician announced the Queen had died too young, at age thirty-two. Her last request had been for her husband to rid himself of his mistress.

William was inconsolable. He lost self-control, sobbing before all and fainting. He continued to weep copious tears at any mention of Mary's name.

Many assumed William was going to die soon after, but he did not. He dismissed his mistress Betty Villiers and became a depressive, irritable drunkard, with worse health than before. Rockmore did not doubt William loved Mary as he had loved no one else. Life for His Majesty was not the same without her.

Henry Purcell wrote moving music for Mary's funeral at Westminster Abbey. Outside, snow fell. A robin flew inside to shelter from the cold during these last rites, and it perched for a while on the Queen's bier.

King William declared, "From being the happiest of men, I shall now be the miserablest creature on earth."

Rockmore grieved no less than His Majesty. Alone in his library, he wept for himself as well. Every woman who'd loved him had been taken away. His mother who'd died giving birth, his aunt Sarah Isaac de Rocamora who'd raised him from birth and died grieving after word arrived of her betrothed's death in the Philippines. His first cousin Sarah Salomon de Rocamora who had preferred her family above love for him. Lady Joan Fairfield who'd died from smallpox. And now, gone forever, Queen Mary, beautiful, affectionate, and intelligent, with a delicious sense of humor and zest for life.

And upstairs is a living wife who loves me not. Buccaneer rubbed against Rockmore and purred. *Yet even my cat feels enough to offer comfort.*

Chapter Fifty-Three

Golden Child and Rat

On the 15th of January, 1695, Rosamund went into labor and chaos reigned again in Rockmore's home. As before, during Cordelia's birth, servants ran in an out of her bedroom bringing fresh towels and buckets of hot water. A midwife, a physician, and a wet nurse also attended. So did mordant Mrs. Havers, who failed to prevent Rockmore from entering. Within a short while, Rosamund easily gave birth to a sturdy boy, blond and fair like Cordelia.

The midwife cut away the placenta and presented her newborn to Rosamund. "You have a son, Your Grace, perfectly formed."

Rosamund took her newborn. "My golden child and a Plantagenet heir at last." She waved away her wet nurse. "No, I shall suckle him myself until he is weaned."

Rockmore moved to Rosamund's side. She refused to let him hold their son. "He is mine, only mine. You ..." Suddenly Rosamund screamed, "The pain!"

Rockmore took his son, who was now crying. "My wife is bleeding."

The midwife thrust a hand into Rosamund's vagina. "It's a twin," she declared. "More towels. More hot water. May God help Her Grace. It's a breech birth. I can feel its legs and arse."

The physician frowned. "Too late for a Caesarian. You must turn its head."

The midwife rejected his clamps. "No, it is smaller than its brother. I can turn it with my hands."

Rockmore gave his crying newborn son to the wet nurse. He tried to calm and restrain Rosamund, who was still screaming and writhing in pain. The midwife used both hands to turn the twin. "Yes, it is smaller than the other. A good thing." Moments later, she delivered a twin soaked in blood.

Rosamund demanded the wet nurse return her firstborn son so she could suckle him. The midwife and physician applied salves. The second twin also was male and weighed five and a half pounds. Unlike his older brother, he was hirsute, and swart of complexion.

Rosamund took her first look at him and shrieked. "It resembles a rat, unlike my beautiful golden child. This is no child of mine." She beckoned her wet nurse. "Drown it. I never want to see that rat again. Drown it like the rat he is."

Rockmore peered at his second son and saw nothing repugnant. He resembled more the newborns of his de Rocamora and Touro kin. Rockmore gave his second son to the wet nurse to suckle.

*****

Rosamund's behavior further distressed Rockmore over the following weeks. At the christening of her first son, she named her golden child William Edward Henry Richard Stephan de Clifford Plantagenet Rockmore. In a separate ceremony that Rosamund did not attend, Rockmore named

William's fraternal twin Vincent James Moses Isaac Rock-more.

Rosamund kept William at her bosom during all waking hours. She ignored their daughter Cordelia and continued to reject baby Vincent. Mrs. Havers inserted herself between Rosamund and Rockmore.

"My mistress demands you rid yourself of that vile cat. Everyone knows they are familiars of Satan and smother newborns in bed. It must never come near her golden son."

"Woman, you have no authority to give me orders, and my cat stays."

Rockmore's home life now interfered with his obligations at the House of Lords and to King William. He had difficulty also concentrating on his business affairs. Rosamund had love only for her firstborn son and avoided Rockmore. Her fits of temper increased. Mrs. Havers and Rosamund bullied and harassed all the servants.

One morning Tinker took Rockmore into the kitchen. Buccaneer lay dead on the floor with foam on his mouth. "It looks a as if he's been poisoned, My Lord."

Mrs. Havers and Rosamund were locked in his wife's suite, their cook nowhere to be seen. Rockmore fumed, unable to prove who had poisoned his feline friend.

One morning, Rockmore caught Mrs. Havers slapping Cordelia's cheeks for disobeying her. He pulled his daughter away from Mrs. Havers. "Never lay hands on my Cordelia again." Rockmore repeatedly slapped Mrs. Havers, drawing blood from her mouth. He twisted the woman's right arm behind her back and pushed her into Rosamund's bedroom.

His wife lay in bed suckling and cooing to her golden son. Rosamund's eyes turned dark with anger when she faced Rockmore. "How dare you ..."

"I dare all in my house. I am informing you that this witch slapped Cordelia and made her cry, and I suspect her of poisoning Buccaneer. I am sending her home immediately."

Rosamund sat and swung her feet to the floor. "I shall leave with Mrs. Havers and take my son. Never to return."

"Do so, but I shall keep Cordelia—"

"And keep the rat. Better yet, drown it. Mrs. Havers, have the servants pack my things." Rosamund stood and faced Rockmore, her expression fierce. "Know that I never loved you. Queen Mary forced me to wed you. The rat has destroyed my ability to have more children."

She hurled a vase at Rockmore, which he avoided. "I curse you and the rat. Now get out so I can ready for my journey home. I never want to see you again."

"Then do so quickly."

Veins bulged on Rosalind's forehead, temples, and neck. Rockmore dodged a chamber pot before he left her room. Shaking with anger, he calmed when Cordelia came to him. He kissed and soothed his daughter, and took her to another bedroom.

"Come, let us see how fares your brother, Vincent."

Chapter Fifty-Four

To Dissolve a Marriage?

Estranged from Rosamund, Rockmore concentrated on his business and political interests. His liquid wealth grew exponentially, which placed him amongst the wealthiest men in England, and the most secretive.

Rockmore also faced his impending thirty-first birthday alone, not to celebrate but to evaluate his future. Rosamund was still his spouse, and his ward as well. She would be free of his mastery and the ruler of a vast, entailed ducal estate at age twenty-one, in September, 1696.

Soon he must find a governess and tutors for his children. Cordelia and Vincent must be introduced to the arts, languages, and sciences. His son had to master the sword, guns, and physical challenges in horsemanship, fisticuffs, wrestling, shooting, and trickery with swordplay as well.

For himself, Rockmore was secure in his wealth and mercantile connections. By good fortune, he also found a place in Princess Anne's court because of his connection with John Tillotson. The Archbishop of Canterbury with other Spiritual Lords persuaded King William to end his feud with Princess Anne, who was now heir to the throne.

After a session in the House of Lords, Rockmore met with Tillotson, asking about possibilities for divorcing Rosamund and obtaining sole custody of his firstborn and his other two children.

"As you must know, Lord Rockmore, traditional Church law places great emphasis on the sacrament of marriage and on its inseparability. Termination of a valid marriage with the possibility of remarrying is not recognized in England."

"My marriage is no longer valid. I am denied my wife's bed. She has said she never loved me."

"Why did she wed you?"

"As you may remember, she was a ward of William and Mary, and the Queen pressured us to wed."

"And so Lady Rosamund is both wife and your ward until she is twenty-one. Lord Rockmore, the accepted options for declaring a marriage invalid must be proven, such as infancy of the couple at the time of spousal, permanent impotence of the male or frigidity of the female, or discovery that the couple is in fact related. Declaring any marriage invalid would give both partners an opportunity to remarry."

"My wife is frigid, and I am convinced she is not well in the head."

"If proven and a divorce is granted, she will lose all inheritance rights and your children will be decreed illegitimate."

"She has her own entailed inheritance. But the latter is unacceptable."

"Another alternative of escape from an unhappy marriage is a legal separation from 'bed and table' as the phrase goes. This procedure is possible in cases of proven adultery or extreme cruelty. This separation does not affect the wife's inheritance rights, or legal status of the children. The disadvantage is the marriage bond remains intact and separated partners cannot marry again."

Tillotson squinted at Rockmore. "Is there a woman you wish to wed?"

"Not yet."

"Another option may be a procedure called *divortium a vinculo matrimonii*, granted only by an Act of Parliament, a protracted and expensive procedure."

Rockmore had been aware since 1690 that Parliament had come close to taking on a new role as a court of equity over matrimonial affairs. Men and women with a variety of marital grievances were allowed to petition Parliament for divorce with the right to wed another. The principles behind voting in both Houses were costly and lengthy. Decisions taken were erratic, inconsistent, and arbitrary.

"Surely an easier route to divorce must exist somewhere," Rockmore replied.

"Situated in the headquarters of civil lawyers at Doctors Commons in London, the Court of Arches is now an appeal court for cases before all ecclesiastical courts in the Province of Canterbury. Its jurisdiction lies south of a line running from the Mersey to the Humber containing three-quarters of the population of England and Wales."

Tillotson lamented a decline in morality over recent decades, as matrimonial and sexual morals cases coming before provincial courts declined. "Most cases now go to the Consistory Court of London, whose businesses have expanded along with the rapid growth of the city and the transfer of local legal business to the residences of the most skilled lawyers and judges. Suits brought by officials against offenders have disappeared as the laity's resentment against moral policing has intensified in our new rational age along with the hostility toward religious and moral enthusiasm. A second general reason is a growing secularization of society and officials of the courts, who formerly judged cases out of religious and moral conviction but now desire more to pocket fees."

Rockmore concluded his best option was a parliamentary route to divorce. He had access to the best lawyers and the wealth necessary to succeed. *If bribery is necessary, I shall be most shameless at that sport.*

But what terms might Rosamund demand?

Chapter Fifty-Five

Divorced

Rockmore greeted Henry Lambert in his library. "I'm pleased you could come on such short notice."

"Are you divorced?"

"Completely."

"She's keeping the boy?'

"It's the price I had to pay for her assent and signatures. I have Vincent and Cordelia. Rosamund is out of my life, no longer ward and wife."

Rockmore paused to pour Port for both himself and Henry. "We arrived separately at the Court of the Arches with our lawyers and clergy. Rosamund sat opposite from me, flanked by her lawyer, local bishop, and scribe. I sat between my lawyer and Archbishop John Tillotson, whose presence intimidated Rosamund's advisors. We laid documents on the table to be signed and witnessed. Rosamund refused to look at me. Mrs. Havers waited in another room with our first-born, William, whom I have not seen since Rosamund absconded with him and her belongings from our London home. She has not seen Cordelia or Vincent since that day and never inquired about them. Rosamund looked wizened, as if her true character has etched grim lines on her once beautiful face."

Rockmore paused to light his clay pipe. "Archbishop Tillotson read from a scroll our *divortium a vinculo matrimonii*, granted only by an act of Parliament, which dissolved our marriage. He added that we are free to wed others."

Lambert touched glasses with Rockmore. "My congratulations."

"I surrendered all parenting rights and contact with my son William, and all financial interest in Rosamund's Plantagenet estates, as well as forfeiting all claims on behalf of Vincent and Cordelia for any titles from Rosamund and her family. She agreed not to seek my title of Count for William. So, my title of Lord Rockmore will be inherited by Vincent or Cordelia's son should Vincent not survive.

"What about half your fortune, according to your marriage vows?"

"In that case, I would be entitled to half her income from Basingstoke, which she could never allow. I do confess I had some regret losing my son William to his mother, but it was a necessary price to pay. I've had no opportunity to father him. He is a stranger to me and shall be so the rest of our lives."

Henry raised his glass. "Then you have come out well."

"Better than Rosamund will ever know. She did reveal a plan for her son. Rosamund shocked everyone present when she announced her William will be groomed to be King of England after King William and Princess Anne die childless."

"Papa!'"

"Papa!"

Rockmore's children rushed into his library. He hugged and kissed four-year-old Cordelia and three-year-old Vincent. "Say hello to Uncle Sir Henry."

Cordelia curtsied and Vincent bowed. Then they sat at their father's feet.

A male servant knocked and entered. "My Lord, your midday meal is ready to be served."

Rockmore rose. "Sir Henry you will sup with us, and afterward I have a most important matter to discuss with you."

After the midday meal, Rockmore tucked his children in their beds for a post-prandial nap and resumed his conversation with Henry in his library over more wine. "I wish to discuss how best to educate my children. As we know, in well off families, boys and girls may first attend a petty school. While boys later go on to a grammar school, tutors sometimes teach both genders at home. Later, girls might attend a boarding school where they learn writing, music and needlework."

"Will you enroll them in schools or hire a governess?"

"I worry for Vincent because he is undersized for his age and may be bullied at any school. I have visited grammar schools. Boys start work at six in the morning and continue on until five-thirty, around sunset or dusk, with breaks for meals. Attendance at chapel is mandatory, corporal punishment and bullying by older boys the norm. I witnessed a teacher beating a boy with birch twigs on his bare buttocks whilst his classmates restrained him. Because of Vincent's size he would not fare well in any school until he acquired the skills necessary to defend himself."

Rockmore rose and ran a finger along some books filling the shelves in his library. "My collection is larger and more current than any school library. Medicine and knowledge of anatomy have improved over recent decades. I have here William Harvey's published discovery of how blood circulates through the body. Here is Robert Boyle's *The Skeptical Chemist*, published in 1661, Isaac Newton's *Principia Mathematica*, published in 1687, and John Milton's *Paradise Lost*."

"You are a far better reader than I."

"And than most physicians, too. Most of them are still handicapped by wrong ideas about the human body. They still believe four fluids or 'humors' determine health: blood, phlegm, yellow bile and black bile. Those doctors claim illness results when one has too much of one humor, and set out to bleed their patients. But a more scientific approach to medicine is emerging, and some enlightened physicians are questioning traditional ideas."

"And you want your children to read every book in your library?"

"Yes, eventually, read them all, and *understand* everything as well. They must learn Spanish, Portuguese, German, Dutch, French, Latin, Greek, and Hebrew, music and the sciences."

"You'll need more than a governess, and many tutors too."

"Then my children shall have them, if necessary. Henry, we live in wonderful times. A great revolution in science started with Sir Francis Bacon at the beginning of this century. He postulated that we can learn how the natural world works through careful observation and experimentation. The ancient Greeks believed that by using reason they could discover why the natural world behaves as it does. But they never tested their theories by carrying out practical experiments. As a result, many of their ideas about the natural world were wrong. Unfortunately, most scholars never questioned their conclusions until the late sixteenth century and early seventeenth century when Bacon and others conducted experiments to see if their theories held true. And now, Henry, a new scientific approach has appeared here in England and everywhere in Europe where scientists observe and experiment to discover how the world works."

Rockmore paused to sip his wine. "In 1645 a group of philosophers and mathematicians held meetings to discuss science and natural philosophy. Charles II was interested in science and in 1662 he made their club The Royal Society. In our new world of enlightenment, belief in witchcraft and magic has declined. The last hanging for witchcraft in England occurred thirteen years ago."

Rockmore invited Henry to stay for an evening meal. Whilst they were sharing a fine Port afterward, a package arrived from the Salvadors. It came with a note.

"Henry, another of my ships I financed has returned from China."

Rockmore opened the package and removed a cedar box. He showed Lambert its contents of fifty horse-hair bristled toothbrushes and assorted flavored powders. "I ordered these for myself, my children and my household servants. Henry, I have a longterm proposition for you. I need a tutor for my children in languages. You are fluent in French, which they can learn along with English, Spanish, and Portuguese."

"It would be my pleasure."

"Excellent, and there is more. As my son grows, he will need lessons in horsemanship, weapons, and manual self-defense, which both of us can teach him to master. My daughter must also learn to ride, shoot, and play a musical instrument, for which she might have some natural talent."

"I can teach both lute and guitar."

"Perfect. Of course, if you wish, you may reside here."

Rockmore led Lambert to a large unused room on the first floor. "Does this suit you?"

"It does."

"We will have it furnished to your taste. We can agree on your fee as well."

"You have saved my sanity. It is difficult living with my family."

They returned to the library. Rockmore told his housekeeper to bring the children. "Cordelia, Vincent, you know

Uncle Sir Henry. He will reside here and teach you many things." He paused whilst they yelled their pleasure and hugged Lambert. "You will have assistance, Sir Henry. I must also find a governess to teach other languages, music, and manners."

"Where will you find her?"

"I pray amongst Princess Anne's ladies, who might have a well-bred poor relation. I shall also advertise in local journals. You may participate in the interviews. Perhaps you may find one attractive enough to court and wed."

"No one can replace my fair Elida."

"True, but I believe you may yet find a suitable young woman."

Chapter Fifty-Six

Search for a Governess

In June of 1699, Rockmore added a toy spaniel and two cats to his family menagerie but failed to find an acceptable governess for Cordelia and Vincent. No Tory family offered any of their kin, and many Whig ladies at Anne's court disapproved of his divorce and did not suggest a poor relation. Those who answered his notices and interviewed lacked both the degree of intellect he desired in a governess and warmth toward children.

Rockmore was amongst several Whig philosemitic politicians invited to a wedding reception for a Santcroos groom and Salvador bride and groom. All gentiles invited supported equality for Jewish subjects of the Crown.

During the feasting, a tall young woman dressed in mourning black served food and drink. She sparked Rockmore's interest. Santcroos and Salvador daughters and nieces harassed her with petty and spiteful demands as if they were a swarm of Harpies. The young woman never changed expression and bore all annoyances with admirable stoicism. When she arrived at Rockmore's table to serve a meat course, her beauty further transfixed him.

She is at least as tall as Queen Mary, with excellent posture. Her features are symmetrical. Her skin is fair with pale golden freckles. And her eyes... unusual tawny pupils. Nay, golden they are.

At an instant, their eyes locked. For Rockmore, everyone else disappeared. She did not look away until *la Señora* Santcroos demanded her attention.

Rockmore had long ago decided that no future was possible with any woman from the rigid Orthodox Sephardic community. Still, she exuded an attraction he could not explain.

I must visit Santcroos on the morrow to learn more about her.

*****

At mid-morning of the following day, Henry Lambert entered Rockmore's study and informed him he had a visitor inquiring about a position as governess. "I think she is from the Jewish Spanish-Portuguese community."

Impossible that she could be the same attractive young woman I admired yesterday. Rockmore stood at his desk. "Bring her to me."

Not impossible.

Rockmore struggled to maintain his equanimity when he faced the same young woman all in black, more attractive than the day before. He guessed her height to be five feet ten inches. And her perfect posture enhanced her curves.

"I am Lord Rockmore. This gentleman is Sir Henry Lambert, my children's tutor in French, riding, and arms."

She moved closer. Her cinnamon scent pleased Rockmore.

"Your Grace, I am Fleur de Carvajal y Santcroos, daughter of the late Baruch de Carvajal y Herrera. I have come here to apply for the position of governess."

"Santcroos? You're related to Don Abraham?"

"He is my uncle. My mother, may she rest in peace, was his favorite sister."

Rockmore brought an armchair to his desk, motioned for Fleur to sit, and took his seat. "Henry, please stay."

Fleur pointed at Rockmore's library. "You have a most impressive collection of books, Lord Rockmore. Have you read them all?"

"Nearly all. Some are for reference. What have you been told about me and my requirements?"

"I know you were raised as a Jew by your grandfather, the esteemed physician Isaac de Rocamora, but later converted to the Church of England. Rocamora, Rockmore. A logical transition."

"Pray continue."

"You were able to divorce your wife, a most exceptional accomplishment, and have custody of your son and daughter."

Rockmore assumed Fleur also knew he was partners with Santcroos and Salvador. "What languages do you speak and read?"

"English, of course, Spanish, Portuguese, French, Italian, German and Dutch. I can also read and speak Hebrew, classical Latin and Greek. I have a natural skill with languages."

"What musical instruments can you play and teach?"

"Harpsichord, mandolin, and lute."

So far, Fleur met all of Rockmore's requirements for a governess. *Too perfect to be true?*

"How old are you?"

"Twenty-three."

"Why are you not wed?"

"I have yet to meet any man who attracts me. Also, I am a poor relation with no dowry. My mother died when I was still a child. My father, may he rest in peace, was a book binder in

Bayonne, more of an artist than a businessman. He passed away last year. My time of mourning ends tomorrow. I wrote to my Uncle Abraham who thought it best for me to move to England and live with him. I arrived last week. My uncle with his son was away inspecting his factories in Manchester. His wife accepted me, but only as a servant and personal maid for herself and her daughters. It has been the longest, most disagreeable week of my life."

A waste of Fleur's skills.

"*Doña* Fleur, I will now take you upstairs to meet my children."

*****

Rockmore led Fleur into his children's nursery. Henry followed. Fleur's features softened at first sight of Rockmore's children.

"Lord Rockmore, Cordelia is a most beautiful girl, and Vincent has a charming smile. His eyes are of an unusual color. I cannot say if they are blue or green."

Rockmore told Cordelia and Vincent that Fleur was applying to be their governess and would be teaching them new languages and skills. "But you must first approve of her. So, we shall leave you alone with Doña Fleur for a while."

Back in Rockmore's library, he and Lambert sat opposite each other.

"What do you think of Fleur?"

'She is good with your dog and cats. If your children approve, hire her. But..."

"You have reservations."

"She is a Jew. They have different diets and days of honoring their Sabbath. You would expect her to live here?"

"Of course."

"Will her family accept that?"

"That is a bridge to cross when the time comes."

"My friend, she is everything Rosamund was not. You may come to love her."

Rockmore forced a laugh but did not comment aloud.

Henry, you may be right.

*****

Upstairs, Fleur stayed with Rockmore's children until their midday meal. He invited her to join his family and Henry. Cordelia and Vincent liked Fleur and paid attention to everything she said.

After they supped, Cordelia turned to Rockmore before she and Vincent left for their siesta. "Papa, we want Doña Fleur to be our governess."

"I must discuss certain important matters with Doña Fleur, and I will let you know our decision."

Lambert took Cordelia and Vincent upstairs to their room. Rockmore led Fleur back to his library where he offered her a glass of Port, delighted that she accepted. They touched glasses, and she answered his unspoken question.

"I adore Cordelia and Vincent. They are intelligent and eager to learn."

"And they obviously approve of you. Now, as you have experienced, I do not observe *kashrut*, or the Jewish Sabbath. Most importantly of all, I expect my children's governess to reside here. That empty suite adjacent to their room will be yours. You may select new furniture and decorate the room as you will. But to be realistic, I cannot imagine your family will approve of such an arrangement."

"Of course they won't. They'll be scandalized and disown me if I move here. One thing you should know is that I have been conforming to avoid conflict. But my father, may he rest in peace, raised me to be a freethinker."

Fleur's confession pleased Rockmore. They next agreed on her wages and day off. "We shall plan a learning schedule for my children tomorrow." Rockmore rose from his desk. "Now, we shall go by carriage to your uncle, and collect your clothes and whatever else you need. Then we must settle matters with your kin."

*****

Don Abraham's wife and three daughters protested like squealing pigs when Rockmore and Fleur arrived. *Senhora* Raquel da Santcroos threatened to discipline Fleur with a scourging for disobeying her command to never leave her home without permission.

"What is all this commotion?" Don Abraham Santcroos, also known as Don Diego de Santa Cruz in Spain and Portugal, embraced Fleur and kissed her forehead. "My beloved niece, why did you disappear? Where have you been? Lord Rockmore, my friend, how did you find her? I thank you for bringing home my dear niece."

His wife started to speak, but Don Abraham shushed her. "I want to hear Fleur's explanation."

"*Tío*, the day before I arrived, you left for Manchester to visit your woolen factories,"

"Yes to be sure they were fulfilling an order to make uniforms for the Portuguese army."

"And after you returned, you did not observe how your wife reduced me to a servant and personal maid to her and to your daughters."

"I run my business, and my wife runs our home. I was not aware until now she had mistreated the daughter of my favorite sister, may she rest in peace."

"You always loved her more than me," Santcroos's wife interjected.

He glared at her and said, "Woman, be silent. Remember, our marriage was arranged as a business merger." Abraham turned to Rockmore. "What is your role in all this?"

"As you have heard, I was seeking a governess, and *Doña* Fleur applied for that position. I accepted her. She will reside in my home and earn a generous wage."

Abraham's wife screamed. "A scandal! An unmarried woman living in the same house with an unwed man? Husband, you must disown Fleur if she leaves. Ban her from all family contact! And you must end your partnership with Lord Rockmore."

"One last time, woman, be silent or get out of my sight. Is that your intention, Fleur, to reside with Lord Rockmore?"

"*Tío*, yes, as his governess, and I have come here only to collect my wardrobe and trunks."

Rockmore went to the front door and summoned two liveried footmen. They followed Fleur upstairs and returned with two large trunks, which they secured atop Rockmore's carriage.

Fleur came downstairs with a valise. She ignored her aunt by marriage and cousins, but kissed her uncle's cheek. "I shall never attempt to enter your home, but I do hope to see you whenever you visit Lord Rockmore."

Fleur went to Rockmore's carriage, but he stayed to speak in private with Santcroos. Afterward, he sat opposite Fleur.

"That went reasonably well. Santcroos and I are still partners."

"Now I am freed from their petty demands. Have you made a schedule for my teaching?"

"Yes, and we shall discuss it after you are settled in my home. First request, though ... my children must learn to speak and understand German."

"May I ask why?"

"It's complicated. I'll explain later."

Chapter Fifty-Seven

Domestic Bliss

Over the following weeks, Fleur refurnished her suite and followed Rockmore's teaching schedule for his children. After ensuring Cordelia and Vincent were asleep, she spent part of her evenings in Rockmore's library discussing politics, new scientific discoveries, music, art, and innovations. Fleur had a keen mind, which kept Rockmore home instead of drinking and gambling at his usual haunts.

Enjoying a new harmonious home life, Rockmore joined a committee in Parliament to deal with a serious problem: which Protestant Stuart was best qualified to succeed Princess Anne after she became Queen, should her eleven-year-old unhealthy son die ahead of her? Most eligible Stuarts were Jacobites, many were secret Catholics, which ruled them out of the royal succession.

The centennial year 1700 arrived, and with it a more urgent need for a Whig-controlled Parliament to decide on Anne's successor. On January 24th, she gave birth to a stillborn child after a seven and a half month pregnancy — her twelfth. Physicians said the child had been dead for a month in her womb. Even worse, six months later Anne's sickly son passed away.

The evening after his funeral, Fleur did not appear as usual in Rockmore's study. Concerned, Rockmore went upstairs to learn why. He found Fleur in her suite wearing a heavy robe and a towel wrapped around her head.

She faced Rockmore, concerned. "Is there something wrong?"

"*Doña* Fleur, you did not come to my study as you have done every evening."

'I was chilled, so I decided to enjoy a hot bath and wash my hair. Your servants were most accommodating. I shall be delighted to join you now."

"Good, because I wanted to explain why my children must be fluent in German."

A hour later, Rockmore and Fleur sat facing each other in comfortable armchairs by a warming fire and touched glasses of Port. "*Doña* Fleur, as you know, Princess Anne has no children who have survived."

"Why did she have so many miscarriages, children who did not survive, and stillbirths?"

"Her physicians have differing diagnoses. Anne has suffered from many ailments all her life, and some doctors have concluded she has weak blood. I agree with those doctors who blame it on Anne's rapid pace of pregnancies. They recommend waiting a month or two at least after suffering a miscarriage or still birth, but Anne has been anxious for a healthy child to preserve a Protestant Stuart dynasty."

"Are there no other candidates for the Crown?"

"Electress Sophia, whose Protestant parents fled into exile to the Dutch Republic after a Catholic military victory at White Mountain. Through her mother, she is the granddaughter of James VI and I, King of Scotland and England. At birth, Sophia was granted an annuity of 40 *thalers* by the

Estates of Friesland. Later, Sophia's first cousin, Charles II of England courted her, but she assumed he was using her in order to obtain money from her mother's wealthy supporter, Lord William Craven."

Fleur interrupted. "There are so many German states, and it can be most difficult to follow lineages."

Rockmore rose, complimented Fleur, and took out several sheets of paper from his desk. He refilled their glasses of Port, and again sat beside her. "Before her marriage, Sophia, as daughter of Frederick V, Elector Palatine of the Rhine, was referred to as Sophie, Princess Palatine of the Rhine, or as Sophia of the Palatinate. The Electors of the Palatinate were of the Calvinist senior branch of the House of Wittelsbach, whose Catholic branch rules the Electorate of Bavaria."

"I understand."

"On September 30th, 1658, Sophia wed Ernest Augustus, Duke of Brunswick-Lüneburg, at Heidelberg, who in 1692 was appointed First Elector of Hanover. Ernest August was a second cousin of Sophia's mother, Elizabeth Stuart, and they were both great-grandchildren of Christian III of Denmark. Sophia is said to be a woman of intellectual ability and curiosity. A friend of Liebnitz, she is well read in the works of René Descartes and Baruch Spinoza. Together with Ernest Augustus, she improved their Summer Palace of Herrenhausen." Rockmore paused to read from a second sheet. "Sophia has five children who reached adulthood, so her succession would be well-secured. Her eldest, George, born May 8th, 1660, has many titles: His Highness, Duke George Louis of Brunswick-Lüneburg, His Highness Hereditary Prince of Brunswick-Lüneburg, His Serene Highness, Electoral Prince of Hanover, and His Most Serene Highness George Louis, Arch banner bearer of the Holy Roman Empire and Prince-Elector, Duke of Brunswick-Lüneburg. George's siblings include Maximilian William of Brunswick-

Lüneburg born 1666, field marshal in the Imperial Army; Sophia Charlotte born 1668, Queen in Prussia; Christian Henry of Brunswick-Lüneburg, born in 1671; and Ernest Augustus of Brunswick-Lüneburg, Duke of York and Albany born 1674 and also Prince-Bishop of Osnabrück."

After Rockmore observed Fleur stifling a yawn, he stood and offered his hand. "I have kept you up too long. You need sleep to be fresh in the morning."

Fleur held Rockmore's hand longer than he anticipated. Her nearness aroused him. Tempted to kiss Fleur, Rockmore released her hand.

The time is not yet right.

CHAPTER FIFTY-EIGHT

MOMENTOUS DECISIONS

By the end of August, 1700, Rockmore's attraction to Fleur had grown exponentially. He no longer could feign indifference.

How will Fleur react to a declaration of love and offer of marriage? If she rejects me, she also may leave. What shall I do??

Minutes passed like hours until Fleur entered Rockmore's study and told him his children had fallen asleep. "And how was your day, Milord?"

"I did some business with your Uncle Abraham, and later met with an *ad hoc* committee of Whig parliamentarians, but I will not bore you with the details."

"I am never bored with politics."

"I know, but there is something of greater importance I must discuss with you."

Rockmore offered Fleur a glass of Port and poured another for himself. He stood over her armchair, and they touched glasses.

"*Doña* Fleur, over these past several months, I have appreciated your keen mind, and how well you teach and mother Cordelia and Vincent. I look forward to your precious companionship each evening. More to the point, I have come to love you as I have loved no one else." Rockmore kneeled before Fleur. "I ask you to be my wife."

Fleur is not reacting with surprise. Has she identical love for me, or indifference??

Fleur smiled. "And I have loved you no less since first sight."

Rockmore kissed Fleur's hands. She leaned forward and first kissed his forehead, and next his lips. Still on one knee, Rockmore reached into a pocket in his waistcoat and removed a small purple velvet box. He opened it to reveal a spectacular ruby stone attached to a golden ring.

"Querida mía, please accept this ring as a pledge of my eternal love for you, now and forever."

Fleur waited until Rockmore slid the ring onto her finger. "I have never seen a ruby so large and pure. How did you come to possess it?"

"When my grandfather was Dominican confessor and spiritual director for the *Infanta Doña* María, she gifted him with her ring. He secretly bequeathed it to me, and, no, I did not give it to my previous wife. From now, please address me as Jacob, or with any words of endearment, when we are alone or with the children."

"I do love you, and I want to be your wife, but how shall we wed? No rabbi will perform the ceremony."

"Nor do I want that."

"And I am loath to convert to any Christian sect."

"As a freethinker, you do not need to be sincere."

"But their idolatry and rituals repel me."

"There are many less formal sects than our established Church of England or the Calvinist offshoots such as Presbyterians and Huguenots."

"Perhaps we do not need to wed."

Rockmore reacted in a horrified manner. "But I want you to be known to all as Lady Rockmore, never my mistress."

"You converted to the Established Church of England. It is too much like Catholicism."

"So did our King William, who had been a Calvinist."

"You will be raising our children as Anglicans?"

"For conformity, but my plans for their education will lead them into freethinking. They must conform to protect their high place in English society. They can make their own choices after they come of age, including whom they may wed. I shall speak with Archbishop Tillotson. From what I know of him, he would be agreeable to marrying us in a private ceremony if you convert to the Church of England. All he would require is outward conformity."

"Please give me some time to think on how best we may wed."

*****

The following day, Rockmore met with John Tillotson, Archbishop of Canterbury, to seek his advice. "I have met a woman whom I wish to wed."

"Congratulations. Do you wish for me to perform the ceremony?"

"Yes, but I prefer to have a small, private wedding, nothing grand."

"Does your bride-to-be wish the same?"

"I believe she will."

"Pray, tell me about her."

Rockmore described how he'd met Fleur and hired her as his children's governess. "She is of the Spanish-Portuguese Jewish community, but a freethinker."

Tillotson frowned. "I will not and cannot perform any ceremony unless she converts. I must meet her, Lord Rock-

298

more. Born a Jew, but a female freethinker? Most exceptional."

"Fleur is well read in most religions, and all Christian sects. Unitarianism appeals most to her."

"Unitarianism would appeal to any Jew, because they reject the Trinity and believe God is one entity. Unfortunately for you, Unitarianism is not recognized as a legitimate Christian religion in England, Ireland, and Scotland. No Unitarian church has been allowed to be built anywhere in our British Isles."

"What if Fleur agrees to convert so we can wed, and not be a believer?"

"Who am I to read the mind of any congregant? Outward conformity is the only valid test of religious sincerity. Please bring your Fleur to me for an interview."

Chapter Fifty-Nine

Fleur's Theology

Rockmore and Fleur sat facing Tillotson across his desk in the Archbishop's office. "*Senorita* Santcroos, Lord Rockmore has informed me that you wish to wed and that you are no longer observant in your Jewish faith."

"That is true, Your Grace."

"Do you still believe in your God of Scripture?"

"I am neither an atheist nor an agnostic. I am a Deist, influenced by Bacon, Descartes, Spinoza, Newton, and Locke."

Tillotson raised his eyebrows, surprised. "You have read and understood them?"

"Yes, Your Grace. My father, may he rest in peace, was a bookbinder and also a bibliophile, who encouraged me to read."

Tillotson relaxed. "I am aware that two basic forms of Deism exist, with minor variations. Like Isaac Newton, some Deists regard God as a watchmaker; a distant Creator and Prime Mover who wound up the universe, set it in motion, and then stepped away. They assert it is pointless to pray to such a God who isn't listening. They reject revelation as a source of knowledge and accept only truths they established by reason alone."

"Yes, Your Grace."

"Other Deists believe in the immortality of the soul, posthumous punishment for the wicked, and rewards for the virtuous. They feel a closer connection to God and believe He hears and responds to their prayers. Those who believe in a watchmaker God reject the possibility of miracles. After having established natural laws and set the great cosmos in motion, God does not need to tinker with his creation. Others accept the possibility of miracles; God is omniscient and omnipotent, and He can alter His own natural laws. That dichotomy is similar to Christian thought from the time of Saint Thomas of Aquinas."

"Yes, Your Grace. I have read him and other writers of your early Church. They recognized two sources for knowledge of God: revelation and natural reason. The study of truths revealed by reason is called natural theology."

Tillotson smiled at Fleur. "You have a most impressive mind. Which form of Deism do you follow?"

"I hope I do not offend Your Grace. I am influenced most by many rational scientific discoveries. I dislike superstition and irrationality. I resent religions that use political power to prevent us from thinking freely and to censor, even punish, those who publish their beliefs."

"Specifically?"

"Your Grace, John Locke's *Essay Concerning Human Understanding* impressed me most. He attacked innate ideas, which forced other Deists to argue based on experience and nature. Following Locke's successful attack on innate ideas, other Deist writers appealed to reason, and evidence of the natural world made it intuitively obvious that God exists and created the universe, and that God gave humans the ability to reason."

Tillotson sighed. "But such assertions have led Deists to discard all books, even our Bible, which contain divine revelation. They also reject the Trinity and other religious mysteries, miracles, and prophecies."

Fleur did not reply, which caused Rockmore to be thankful she did not add what they often discussed: Fleur's belief that all organized religions were corruptions of an original religion that was pure, natural, simple, and rational. All had been debased by priests who manipulated them for personal gain and for class interests of the priesthood in general; religions became encrusted with superstitions, mysteries, and irrational theological doctrines known as *priestcraft*. Laymen were thus kept dependent on the priesthood for information about requirements for salvation. Baffled by these mysteries, they gave the priesthood positions of great power, which priests worked to maintain and increase. Deists believed it was their mission to strip away *priestcraft* and mysteries. Different Deists had different beliefs about the immortality of the soul, about the existence of Hell and damnation to punish the wicked, and the existence of Heaven to reward the virtuous.

Tillotson's expression hardened. "This has been a most interesting exchange of ideas, but now we come to several questions you must answer to my satisfaction if you wish to wed Lord Rockmore in the Anglican Church. First, you must affirm the Bible as divine revelation by God. You must acknowledge Jesus Christ is the Son of God and Savior. You must accept the Trinity. You must agree there is Heaven and Hell and that we humans all have souls. You must accept the realty that King William is head of our Anglican Church as shall be all subsequent kings or queens who succeed him."

Fleur held Jacob's hand. 'Your Grace, I will convert to your established Church of England and freely accept all its tenets and beliefs. I have read what you call the New Testament, King James's version, of course. "

"Even so, you will take instruction from me, and afterward, if satisfied, I shall marry the two of you."

"It will be an honor, Your Grace."

Alone in their carriage, Jacob asked Fleur why she had decided to convert to the established Church of England.

"Our Talmud has much wisdom. It says, 'the first question God asks is not "Did you follow ritual and attend synagogue twice a day?" The first question is, "Were you just to your fellow man?" Therefore, I decided conforming to any religion to wed the man I love is just, as either a practical or religious matter." Fleur added with a mischievous smile, "And I also accept Pascal's wager."

PART FOUR
LORD ROCKMORE'S APOGEE
1700 -1721

"He was the most pigheaded, stubborn boy who ever lived, who has round his brains such a thick crust that I defy any man or woman ever to discover what is in them."

Sophia, Electress of Hanover, about her eldest son, future King George I of Great Britain

Chapter Sixty

Swift-Moving Events

In the late morning of Saturday, the 20th of November, 1700, Tillotson performed Rockmore's and Fleur's marriage ceremony in a small Kensington Palace chapel, an hour after she had converted to the Anglican Church. King William attended the ceremony and gave away the bride. Henry Lambert stood as Rockmore's groomsman. Cordelia participated as flower girl and Vincent as ring bearer.

During a small repast afterward in an adjacent room, a Whig member of His Majesty's cabinet approached William. The king listened, turned to Rockmore's wedding party, and commanded silence.

"King Charles II of Spain has died at last. As expected, Louis XIV has announced he is the most legal heir to take the Spanish throne. We cannot let that happen. Our war against Louis XIV will expand into Portugal, Spain, and Italy."

Fleur tugged at Rockmore's sleeve. "By what right does Louis claim the Spanish throne?"

"His mother Ana, later called Anne, was sister to Philip IV. In 1615 she wed the future Louis XIII, and her brother wed Louis's sister Elizabeth, who took the Spanish name Isabella."

William coughed, wheezed, and recovered. "I shall call a meeting of my financial advisors, and military experts. We must make immediate plans to finance a wider war. Lady Rockmore, I require your husband's presence, and yours, too, Sir Henry."

Fleur left with Cordelia and Vincent. Rockmore, Tillotson, and Lambert accompanied William.

*****

William's cabinet agreed on three courses of action. First, the succession of Great Britain must be secured. Princess Anne's son had died earlier in the year, and no one believed she could give birth to a child who might survive. Parliament had already chosen Sophia, Elector of Hanover, to be Anne's heir, but a formal Act had yet to be passed. Many Scottish and English Jacobites preferred James II's son, who was living at Louis's Court in France and was known as "The Pretender." Rockmore also never forgot Rosamund's great hope to make their son King of England.

William called for quiet. "Parliament must pass an Act of Settlement before we meet with Sophia. Who amongst you is fluent in both Dutch and German?"

Rockmore and a few others raised their hands.

"Be prepared to accompany me when I meet next with Sophia. Lord Rockmore, I have confidence that Ambassador van Noordwijk taught you much about diplomacy."

"Indeed he did, Sire."

*****

Rockmore arrived home after sunset. Scented of cinnamon, Fleur had bathed, wore a robe, and helped him undress. Cordelia and Vincent slept well covered in their beds.

Alone in their bedroom suite, they consummated their marriage. Cognizant that Fleur was a twenty-three year old virgin, Rockmore prolonged gentle foreplay to arouse her. This time, he experienced true love and affection from Fleur, which had never happened with Rosamund.

Later, they relaxed in bed with glasses of Port. Fleur asked Rockmore what had happened at his meeting with William.

"*Querida*, Sophia of Hanover will be proclaimed the successor to King William and Anne shall be proclaimed Queen of England, Scotland, and Ireland by an Act of Parliament next year. Great sums of money must be raised to finance a wider war, with more men and weapons, against Louis XIV."

"That affects your factories."

"Yes, more arms and nails shall be produced, and uniforms, too. The third course of action will be to create a successful strategy in Iberia. We will send an army to aid our ally Portugal, and from there invade Spain."

"Who will England support to rule the Spanish Empire?"

A most intelligent question.

"The Austrians are enemies of France. Most likely he will be a Hapsburg Royal of Spanish blood, and William may send me to the Germanys on a diplomatic mission."

Fleur clung to Rockmore. "Not immediately?"

"More likely in late spring or mid-summer of next year. You and the children will accompany me, first to meet my family in Amsterdam, and then onward to Hanover."

Chapter Sixty-One

Act of Settlement

Rockmore received a message from Gouda: Dirck van Noordwijk had passed away in his sleep. The elderly diplomat had been frail for many months, unable to travel. Rockmore mourned his second father and mentor, and spent a long night reminiscing about their times together.

Parliament was in session, which prevented Rockmore from attending van Noordwijk's funeral. He sent condolences to the diplomat's daughters and family.

Rockmore told Fleur he supported Parliament's need to pass an Act of Settlement limiting the succession to the English and Irish crowns to Protestants only. Sophia of Hanover headed a junior line amongst the Stuarts, and she was a devout Protestant. During debates, a Tory majority in the House of Lords attempted to deny the line of succession to Sophia and her descendants, but their amendment failed in the Commons.

The Bill of Rights excluded Catholics from the throne, which ruled out James II and his descendants, but it did not provide for further succession after Anne. Parliament thus determined to settle the succession on Sophia and her descendants to guarantee continuity of the Crown with Protestant lineage.

The Act of Settlement provided the throne would pass to Electress Sophia of Hanover, granddaughter of James I of England and niece of Charles I, and to her descendants. It excluded "forever all and every Person and Persons who ... is, are or shall be reconciled to or shall hold Communion with the See or Church of Rome or shall profess the Popish Religion, or shall marry a Papist."

Those Stuarts who were Roman Catholics, and those who married Papists, were barred from ascending the throne. Eight additional provisions of the Act would only come into effect upon the deaths of both William and Anne.

Fleur pleased Rockmore with her opinion regarding the succession. "I could never live under Papist rule and an absolute monarch."

*****

On June 12th, 1701, Rockmore returned home and told Fleur that Parliament had passed an Act of Settlement declaring that in the event of no legitimate issue from Anne or William III, the crowns of England and Ireland were to settle upon "the most excellent princess Sophia, Electress and Duchess-dowager of Hanover" and "the heirs of her body, being Protestant." The key excerpt from the Act, naming Sophia as heir presumptive, read:

Therefore for a further Provision of the Succession of the Crown in the Protestant Line We Your Majesties most dutiful and Loyal Subjects the Lords Spiritual and Temporal and Commons in this present Parliament assembled do beseech Your Majesty that it may be enacted and declared by the King's most Excellent Majesty by and with the Advice and Consent of the Lords Spiritual and Temporal and Com-

mons in this present Parliament assembled and by the Authority of the same that the most Excellent Princess Sophia Electress and Duchess Dowager of Hannover, Daughter of the most Excellent Princess Elizabeth, late Queen of Bohemia, Daughter of our late Sovereign Lord King James the First of happy Memory, be and is hereby declared to be the next in Succession in the Protestant Line to the Imperial Crown and Dignity of the foresaid Realms of England, France and Ireland with the Dominions and Territories thereunto belonging after His Majesty and the Princess Anne of Denmark and in Default of Issue of the said Princess Anne and of His Majesty respectively.

Parliament decreed Sophia Heir Presumptive to preempt any claim by the Roman Catholic James Francis Edward Stuart, who would have become James III of England and VIII of Scotland, and also to deny the throne to many Stuart Roman Catholics and spouses of Roman Catholics who held a blood claim in the royal succession. The Act restricted the British throne to *Protestant heirs* of Sophia of Hanover who had never been Roman Catholic or married a Roman Catholic.

"*Querida,* I did more than vote for the Act of Settlement. I suggested Parliament should invite Sophia to reside in England. That would enable her to be crowned Queen immediately in the event of Anne's death. We argued such a course was necessary to ensure Sophia's succession, for Anne's Roman Catholic half-brother James resides in France, physically closer to London. Sophia agreed to a move from Hanover to London, but a majority of Parliament voted against it. They feared such action would offend Anne, who opposed any rival court in her future kingdom. Anne knows Sophia is more active and lively, despite her seventy-one years of age, and that she could cut a better figure than herself."

"That is understandable."

"Sophia has five children ages thirty-five to forty-one, and three legitimate grandchildren ages fourteen to eighteen, all of them Protestant. King William told me that sometime next year he will send me to Hanover, where I shall befriend Sophia's eldest, Prince George, and influence him to our way of thinking. As I mentioned before, I shall take you and our children with me."

"I look forward to that."

*****

Over several days Rockmore met with William and other wealthy lords. They discussed how best to raise money for an impending war against France and her allies regarding the Spanish succession. After one meeting, William told Rockmore they must confer alone in his antechamber. They drank brandy, and William surprised Rockmore with an unexpected question.

"Have you ever traveled to Devon?"

"Not since our landing there in 1688."

"As you know, it is slightly less than two hundred miles southwest of London. You are wealthy, but not yet a great land owner."

"I do have a large home in Covent Garden."

"But no country estate. Why is that, when you can afford it? Why stay in London during the summers, when the stench from the Thames and the unwashed streets is most disagreeable?"

I wish William would reveal what he wants.

"Lord Rockmore, there is a grand estate, well maintained, fully furnished and landscaped. It has been in our possession for three years, and with it comes an Earldom. The last Earl, Lord Clayton Ashbury, died suddenly without issue, and all

312

his wealth and property reverted to the Crown. We need more money immediately to prepare for war, and I am auctioning that Earldom with all its property. With it comes an annual income of £50,000 per annum."

"Where is it?"

"Sidmouth on the Channel coast in Devon." William laid out architectural renderings of a mixed Pallladian and neo-classical villa greater than that in Basingstoke.

"So many rooms."

"An adequate number of servants are staffing them. Here is a list of wages necessary to employ them."

"Are there any debts for which the next Earl must be responsible?"

"No, Lord Ashbury died solvent and left all to the Crown, which is why we can afford to keep it well managed." William handed Rockmore a scroll. "This will introduce you to our seneschal there, Sir Basil Worthington."

"I must discuss this with my wife."

"I advise you to accept. The Germans are punctilious about rank and lineage quarterings. No one less than a Prince, Marquess, Duke, or Earl will be accepted by Prince George."

"How high is the bidding?"

"Five hundred thousand guineas so far."

Rockmore had planned to donate one million for William's war. "How long do I have before I offer my bid?"

"Leave for Sidmouth on the morrow, and after your return you may submit your bid."

"I will take my family and Colonel Sir Henry Lambert with me."

"Lambert is a superb soldier with a keen mind. We approve." William drank more brandy and slurred. "I miss my beloved Queen Mary."

Rockmore listened to William praise Mary's virtues. "Yes, Her Majesty was a great and beloved queen during your absences, Sire."

"I was a fool to take Betty Villiers as mistress. I know it wounded my dear Mary, may she forgive me. But I know she remained chaste during my absences when she might have taken revenge for my lapses."

Rockmore considered William might be more sober than he appeared to be, to watch Rockmore's reaction.

Does he suspect Mary indeed took revenge for his philandering with Betty Villiers?

"Sire, Queen Mary, may she rest in peace, was beyond reproach."

"Yes, yes, so everyone has said."

Weeping, William poured another glass of brandy and dismissed Rockmore.

CHAPTER SIXTY-TWO

SIDMOUTH

The earldom lay at the mouth of the River Sid in a valley between Peak Hill to the west and red-rock Salcombe Hill to the east. Cliffs of red sandstone and white chalk rose up to four hundred feet above sea level along much of Devon's seacoast.

On the journey to Sidmouth, Rockmore rode Hannibal, Lambert his own mount, and they led two coaches. Fleur, Cordelia, and Vincent rode in the first carriage with an armed driver, Tinker at his side, and two footmen at the rear. Fleur's ladies occupied a second coach, protected by several armed retainers.

Word of their arrival preceded them, and King William's seneschal Sir Basil Worthington had a full staff awaiting Rockmore and his entourage in front of a grand Romanesque villa. It lay atop grassy Salcombe Hill between the hilly woods farther inland, and a red-rock cliff, a mile away, overlooking the Channel and fishing shacks several hundred feet below.

A chill wind and delicious fresh air also greeted them. All male servants wore livery of maroon and silver. Females had white starched aprons, collars, and cuffs attached to their gray dresses. Worthington, a lean, austere militarily formal type identified the estate staff.

Rockmore introduced his wife, children, Lambert and entourage. He further assured Worthington he had no plans to interfere with their daily routines unless he decided to purchase Sidmouth Villa or something egregious displeased him.

At a Palladian portico entrance, Worthington presented his wife, a plump, agreeable woman, and their two sons, close to Vincent's age. "Lady Agatha is chatelaine of this villa. Our sons Edward, age nine, and William, age seven, will accompany your children."

Lady Agatha gestured toward an open pair of doors. "Please come in, and we will show you to your rooms, after which we shall familiarize you with the interior and grounds, and share a meal."

Rockmore and Fleur found their bedroom commodious, with a convenient adjacent water closet, and their children's rooms no less comfortable. Agatha took Fleur to the kitchen. Worthington led his sons, Rockmore, Vincent, and Lambert to the stables. Cordelia explored the villa on her own.

The grooms' care of and the quality of the half dozen stallions and mares impressed Rockmore and Lambert. "Sir Henry, my steed Hannibal is getting along in years. This will be an ideal place to put him out to pasture and play stud with the mares."

Lambert whispered to Rockmore, "Speaking of such, who is that beauty approaching us?"

Worthington beckoned a young woman and her small young daughter to join them. "Alys is my younger sister, widowed since two years, who, with her three-year-old daughter Felicity is visiting. They reside in Sidford. Alys, meet Lord Rockmore, who may become the next Earl of Sidmouth, and Colonel Sir Henry Lambert."

Rockmore appraised Alys, a pretty straw-blonde young woman of much sturdier frame than Lambert's frail, ethereal deceased wife. He noted her positive reaction to Lambert.

Alys presented her daughter Felicity to Rockmore and Lambert, and Worthington gestured toward the villa. "Alys, take Felicity with you to the kitchen and there introduce yourselves to Lady Rockmore. My sons, show Master Vincent around the estate."

Vincent disappeared with Worthington's boys. Cordelia settled at a harpsicord in the music room, where she played her favorite melodies. Lambert escorted Alys and her daughter into the kitchen.

Can it be my good friend Henry is smitten with Alys?

Worthington and Rockmore walked a mile to a stone bench at Salcome Cliff's edge above several shacks and a pebble-strewn beach below.

"As you can see, Lord Rockmore, a lack of shelter in this bay prevents any construction of a port. Still, our last Earl hoped to build a resort up here and down there. Despite these chill winds, our air in summer is pure and refreshing compared with that of large cities."

"And what communities lie inland?"

"We can ride there tomorrow morning. Devon is renowned for its handmade lace and carpet-making industries in our interior market towns of Honiton and Axminster. High quality limestone has been quarried near the central coastal town of Beer for centuries and used for fine carvings and pillars in Devon's homes, churches, and administrative buildings."

Worthington led Rockmore back to the villa while describing the fruits and early-season vegetables grown in the fertile red soils of the lower Exer, Clyst, and Otter river valleys in the western areas of Devon.

"Dairying is also economically important. I will show you books of account to justify all the income generated for Sidmouth estate. I have invited our vicar, bailiff, Exeter garrison major, and the mayor of Sidford to dine with us at midday tomorrow. They will answer any questions you may have."

*****

That evening in their bedroom Rockmore conferred with Fleur and their children. All agreed that Sidmouth's air was healthier than what London offered. Fleur said, "Lady Agatha assured me summers here are mild and comfortable."

Excited, Vincent spoke of his adventures and a game Edward and William Worthington had taught him. "They call it Rugger, and I discovered I can run faster than any boy, even those who are older."

"And you, my wife?"

Fleur smiled at Rockmore. "I approve of this villa's accommodations and vistas."

Cordelia added, "I like its music room."

"Then it seems I shall be the next Earl of Sidmouth."

"Excellent, and how shall an Earl's wife be addressed? Surely neither as 'Earless,' or 'Earlette.'"

Rockmore shared a laugh with Fleur. "No, my love. You shall be addressed as 'Countess.'"

*****

Visits to adjacent communities, and introductions to local officials, clergy, and squires reinforced Rockmore's decision. Worthington promised to arrange a ball in the summer after Rockmore returned as Earl, to introduce him to prominent families in the area.

Before their return to London, Lambert proposed to Alys and received permission from Worthington to wed his sister in due time. Sir Basil and Lady Agatha were pleased to continue as seneschal and chatelaine until Rockmore arrived to take possession as Earl of the villa and adjacent lands. They owned a Jacobean manor on the other side of River Sid for their permanent residence.

Fleur surprised Rockmore when they were alone. "I do not completely trust the Worthingtons, nor should you."

"Have you observed something I missed?"

"Hugh Tinker learned from their staff that Sir Basil expected to be given the title to this villa and adjacent property as a baron or count."

"I have not observed the slightest sign of resentment or envy."

"Nor I, yet, but I shall watch Sir Basil and Lady Agatha carefully for any indication of malicious envy."

Chapter Sixty-Three

Family Reunion

Upon, their arrival in London, Rockmore paid William £650,000 sterling for Sidmouth's earldom. After his investiture, he and his family sat for a grand portrait by Sir Godfrey Kneller, to be hung at Sidmouth Villa.

They returned to Sidmouth in May. Fleur, a skilled bookkeeper, reviewed all accounts. Rockmore put Hannibal out to pasture and purchased another black Frisian he named Caesar.

*****

Back at The Hague, King William arranged a meeting with his cousin Sophia at the *Palais Het Loo,* forty-five miles east of Amsterdam. Given that William was ailing from asthma and frail, and his reluctance to remarry and sire an heir, and his choice of Sophia to be first in the line of succession were inevitable.

In July, Rockmore received an expected summons to join William's entourage with his family. They arrived in Amsterdam in early July of 1701. He brought Caesar, two armed coachmen, a valet, a porter, footmen, and Fleur's personal maid. Settled in William's palace in the great port city, he conferred with His Majesty, diplomats, and military officers on how best to deal with Sophia and her eldest son, Prince George.

Rockmore leased a comfortable coach for Fleur and his children, and with armed escort they toured Amsterdam. Wooden shoes fascinated Cordelia and Vincent.

Ready to proceed onward to Hanover with King William, Rockmore stopped first at his Uncle Salomon's home on St. Antonius Sluis across a bridge perpendicular to *Jodenbreestraat*, Jewsbroadstreet.

Rockmore told Fleur he had no idea how Salomon and his family would react to them. He had sent a message to his uncle when he arrived in Amsterdam, describing his intention to visit and introduce his wife and children.

"To them, I am still Jacob Moses de Rocamora, but an apostate. We shall arrive a half hour before their midday meal. I do not know if they will invite us to sup with them."

"I am prepared for rejection. I am certain word of my apostasy has reached your uncle, for he is my Santcroos kin's physician here in Amsterdam."

"Papa?"

"Yes, Vincent."

"Why are houses so narrow in Amsterdam?"

Rockmore explained how the Dutch reclaimed land from the sea and why living space was valuable.

Curious pedestrians slowed to watch Rockmore and his family alight from their carriage and approach his uncle's front door. In a maroon gold-trimmed plumed hat, coat, waistcoat, trousers, and boots, he projected high station and wealth. So did Fleur in a bronze ensemble, Cordelia in canary yellow silk, and Vincent in sky blue as a mini aristocrat.

Rockmore's fifty-one year-old uncle opened his front door and welcomed them into the vestibule. Salomon had become bald on the top of his head with long fine hair hanging to his shoulders A skull cap covered part of his bald pate.

Rockmore kissed Salomon's cheek. "My wife, Lady Rockmore, born Fleur de Carvajal y Santcroos."

Salomon's eyes widened when he focused on Cordelia. "I cannot believe it. Your daughter is a perfect image of your mother, may she rest in peace. I fear her appearance may distress your father."

"And my son, Vincent Moses Rockmore."

'The color of his eyes, his face and form, it is as if my own father has been reborn."

Salomon recovered his equanimity and brought Rockmore into his parlor. After more introductions, his wife-cousin Abigael offered a glacial greeting. More friendly, Salomon's second daughter Lea welcomed them with a warm smile, and introduced her husband Isaac da Costa Athais. She whispered to Rockmore that her older married sister Sara had left the previous day to visit relatives in Rotterdam.

Rockmore was not surprised. His uncle still feared their love for each other had never ended. "My wife, Doña Fleur de Santcroos y...."

"You were married by a rabbi?"

"No, Doña Abigael. We wed in the Church of England."

Abigael frowned and with her family backed away, as if fearing contamination.

"I've come here to visit my father and have him meet my family."

Salomon hesitated. "When Moses sees your daughter, her likeness to your mother may agitate him."

"I insist." Rockmore led his family up three levels to an attic, followed by Salomon and Lea. He hesitated at the top before entering and turned to Fleur. "This has been my father's bedroom and sitting area since his brain injury back in 1665."

Salomon stood by the entrance. Lea went to Moses who sat at a table by a window. Rockmore was pleased to see his father had trimmed hair and beard, and clean clothes, and lived in a well-ordered room.

Lea kissed her uncle's forehead. "*Tío* Moses, you have visitors."

Moses turned from the widow and saw Cordelia, who approached him and curtsied.

"*Abele.*"

Moses held Cordelia's hands and kissed her cheeks. "My Cordelia, tomorrow we sail to New Amsterdam and shall be wed by the ship's captain."

Rockmore led confused Cordelia away and beckoned Vincent. "Papa, here is your grandson, Vicente Moses Jacob de Rocamora."

Vincent bowed. "*Abuelo.*"

Moses stared at Rockmore's children, confused and weeping. Salomon intervened. "My brother is distressed, agitated by this visit and your daughter's strong resemblance to your mother. It is best you leave now."

"I'd hoped to take my father to the park, the same as on my previous visits."

"Next time come alone."

Lea soothed Moses. Salomon and Abigael did not invite Rockmore and his family to stay for a midday meal.

Outside, Fleur consoled Rockmore. "Their attitude was to be expected, but Doña Abigael's hostility toward you seemed unnatural."

"I should have told you this before." Rockmore described his aunt's and uncle's threat to disown their eldest daughter Sara if she eloped with him. "She was my first love, and they have worried Sara still loves me."

"I cannot imagine you confined to so narrow a communi-ty."

"Sara did me a great favor by choosing her family over me." Rockmore kissed Fleur. "You are the perfect wife for me."

"Your father surprised me. Despite the limitations of his mind, at age fifty-three he is stronger and healthier than your uncle Salomon."

"Yes, he may outlive his brother. Lea has always taken good care of him. So have her younger sisters. And now, we shall have a midday repast and later be on our way to Hanover with King William."

Chapter Sixty-Four

Electress Sophia and Prince George

Rockmore and his family arrived in Hanover as part of William's entourage. Raised in the Netherlands close to William's palace, Sophia was able to converse with her cousin in his Dutch native tongue. Rockmore thought Sophia must have been a great beauty decades earlier, based upon her portraits hanging throughout the palace. Now seventy-one, she still evinced vestiges of her youthful features.

Sophia welcomed Rockmore, Fleur, and the children. Their fluency in German impressed the Electress. Fleur praised Sophia's vast library. "You must have every work written by Descartes and Liebnitz."

Pleased that Fleur was an educated woman of like mind, Sophia offered free use of her library. "I look forward to discussing philosophy with you, Lady Rockmore. My Court is one of high culture. Both Descartes and Liebnitz are my guests as we speak, and you shall meet them this evening. We also will attend a concert featuring a sixteen-year-old prodigy we patronize, George Frederick Handel."

During the next several days, Rockmore watched older aristocrat boys jostling to meet eight-year-old Cordelia. Tall for her age and already a beauty, she reacted to their attentions with calm dignity or amusement. Vincent, meanwhile, enjoyed riding horses from Sophia's stables and earned respect from older noble boys because he ran fastest amongst them and handled swords well.

Before Rockmore had met Prince George, other diplomats had schooled him in the prince's background. George had been born ob May 28th, 1660, in Hanover City, in the Duchy of Brunswick-Lüneburg of the Holy Roman Empire. He was the eldest son of Ernst Augustus, Duke of Brunswick-Lüneburg.

George's brother, Frederick Augustus, was born in 1661, and the two boys, known as *Görgen* and *Gustchen* by the family, were brought up together. Sophia took a great interest in their upbringing, while also bearing Ernest Augustus another four sons and a daughter.

George was a responsible, conscientious child, raised to be a positive example to his younger brothers and sisters, but once he formed an opinion about individuals or policy no one could change his mind.

In 1675, Prince George's eldest uncle had died without issue, but his remaining two uncles had married, putting George's inheritance in jeopardy as their estates might pass lands and wealth to their own sons, should they have had any, instead of to George.

Ernst Augustus taught George hunting and riding, and took his fifteen-year-old on campaigns in the Franco-Dutch War to train and test him in battle.

In 1679, another uncle died without sons, and Ernst Augustus replaced him as reigning Duke of Calenberg-Göttingen, with his capital at Hanover. George's surviving uncle, George William of Celle, married his mistress to legitimize his only daughter, Sophia Dorothea.

A marriage was arranged between George and Sophia Dorothea as it ensured both a generous annual income and unification of Hanover and Celle.

At first, Sophia opposed this marriage because Sophia Dorothea's mother was not of royal birth, but she was won over by the money and land inherent in their marriage.

George's military prowess and courage impressed Rockmore. In 1683, George and his brother, Frederick Augustus, had participated in the Battle of Vienna where both German Protestant and Polish Catholic armies ended the Turkish siege and further Ottoman advances into Europe.

Also in 1683, Sophia Dorothea bore George a son, George Augustus. The following year, Prince George's brother Frederick Augustus was informed of the adoption of primogeniture, meaning he would no longer receive part of his father's territory as he expected. It led to a breach between father and son, and between the brothers, that lasted until Frederick Augustus's death in battle in 1690.

With the formation of a unified Hanoverian state, and the Hanoverians' continuing contributions to the Empire's wars, the emperor made Ernst Augustus an Elector of the Holy Roman Empire in 1692.

In 1687, Sophia Dorothea had a second child, a daughter named after herself, but no pregnancies followed because George preferred the company of his aristocratic mistress.

In August 1701, William invested George with the English Order of the Garter and within six weeks, the nearest Catholic claimant to the thrones, the former King James II, died. Sophia, older than Anne by thirty-five years but more fit and healthy, became heiress presumptive to Anne. Uncertain of what might happen after Anne's death, she later told Rockmore, "What Parliament does one day, it undoes the next."

Rockmore established mutual respect with Prince George based on their military adventures and his lessons in the complexities of English parliamentary politics.

George's future British subjects ridiculed him as unintelligent because he appeared stiff in public. Though he was unpopular in England due to a supposed inability to speak English, Rockmore knew George understood, spoke, and wrote in English. He also spoke fluent German and French, good Latin, and some Italian and Dutch.

George's mistreatment of his wife, Sophia Dorothea, became a scandal. The insular British assumed he had a succession of German mistresses and regarded him as too German.

To the contrary, Europeans viewed George as a progressive ruler, who permitted his critics to publish without risk of severe censorship. He also provided sanctuary to Voltaire when the philosopher was exiled from Paris.

Rockmore concluded George was reserved, temperate, and financially prudent. He disliked attending public social events. He avoided his royal box at the opera and often travelled incognito to a trusted friend's home to play cards.

Despite George's potential unpopularity, Rockmore reassured the prince that as a Protestant he would be accepted by most of his future subjects as a better alternative to the Roman Catholic Pretender James Edward Stuart, with Louis XIV's orders in his pocket and swarms of Jesuits at his court.

Electress Sophie assured Rockmore her son was genial and affectionate in private letters to his daughter, though dull, awkward, cold, and over-serious in public. Rockmore observed that George could be jolly, took things to heart, and was more sensitive than he cared to show. The fact that his mother was still in good health and Anne still vital ensured George would have several more years to eliminate or ameliorate his flaws before reigning in England.

CHAPTER SIXTY-FIVE

DELIGHTFUL AND DISTRESSING OCCURRENCES

After returning to England in October 1701, Fleur surprised Rockmore when she used his carriage daily to visit the salons of titled ladies and the wives of powerful parliamentarians, all of intellect. She received them at home as well. Fleur often included Cordelia and Vincent to improve their education in manners, as parents did on the Continent.

"All to help further your career," she explained to Rockmore. "And, there is something else you should know."

Rockmore listened, both amused and amazed, while Fleur described how many women she knew invested together, and attended lottery drawings in groups to earn more income. He'd been aware some, like Lady Barbara, ran Hazard and card games to earn money for luxuries. Fleur told Rockmore these women followed financial opportunities in newspapers and were able to discuss them intelligently, just as men did.

Fleur showed Rockmore a pamphlet titled *Advice to the Women and Maidens of London*. It advised ladies how to invest in the context of English property law, in which most women surrendered their assets at marriage. Widows, some clever wives, and spinsters developed financial plans even if they had to use males as brokers.

Fleur read Rockmore's expression. "Yes, I have invested, too, even though you are generous with me. Having the advantage of knowing how you invest, I was tempted to play the game." Fleur handed Rockmore a packet of banknotes. "I have made a profit of £875."

Rockmore kissed Fleur and returned the money. "Well done, *Querida*, I am proud of you."

*****

On Valentine's Day, 1702, Henry Lambert wed Worthington's sister Alys, who had a widow's income of £2,000 annually. Thus, Henry became a squire. Rockmore arranged a grand reception and feast at his villa for both families and the leading gentry. Alys had inherited a large Jacobean manor in Sidford, where bride and groom would reside. Thus, Lambert became a member of the Squirearchy and part-time neighbor.

*****

With others amongst King William's favorites, Rockmore hurried to Kensington Palace on March 8th, 1702. Previously, in the early morning of February 21st, William had gone riding on his favorite horse, Sorrel, confiscated from Sir John Fenwick, a Jacobite who had conspired against him. Sorrel stumbled into a mole's burrow and threw William, who suffered a broken collarbone. It was set twice, the second time after a twelve-mile jolting ride in a carriage from Hampton Court to Kensington Palace. He later walked through palace rooms and fell asleep in a chair by an open window.

William awakened feverish and still tried to hold meetings until his weakened lungs caught pneumonia. Complications followed, and on the 8th of March, 1702, fifty-one-year-old William was buried in Westminster Abbey alongside his wife Mary II. His sister-in-law and first cousin Anne became Queen Regnant until her coronation.

Rockmore grieved. Unfortunately, the English had preferred Mary and never warmed to the Dutchman. Rockmore followed what happened next in the Netherlands. William was the only Stuart member of the Dutch House of Orange to reign over England. His Dutch predecessors had served as Stadtholders of Holland and the majority of the other provinces of the Dutch Republic since the time of William the Silent. The five provinces of which William III had been Stadtholder—Holland, Zeeland, Utrecht, Gelderland, and Overijssel—suspended that office after his death. Thus, he was the last patrilineal descendant of William I to be named Stadtholder for the majority of Dutch provinces.

Under William III's will, John William Friso inherited the Principality of Orange and several lordships in the Netherlands. He was William's closest agnatic relative and the grandson of William's aunt Henriette Catherine.

With William's passing, Rockmore worried he'd be cast adrift at Court. He had been a favorite of both William and Mary and a participant in their inner circle and staff planning. He'd had little contact with Anne's court and only one assignment from the Princess to help reconcile her with Mary. He'd failed to achieve that.

Rockmore faced Queen Anne's accession with concern. Would he be allowed to continue his diplomatic position in Hanover?

*****

Rockmore hoped to spend more time at his estate with Fleur and their children, but Parliamentary duties called him to London and diplomatic assignments to Hanover, where on August 15th, 1702, Fleur gave birth with no complications to a healthy boy baptized Jacob George. Sophia and Prince

George served as godparents. Cordelia helped Fleur care for her newborn, and Vincent promised to protect his little half-brother.

Looming over everything else, the War of the Spanish Succession began. At issue was the right of Philip de Bourbon, grandson of Louis XIV, to succeed to the Spanish throne under the terms of King Charles' will.

In 1700 King Charles II, the last Spanish king of the House of Hapsburg, died with no direct heir to occupy the throne, but he had named his half-sister's grandson, who was first in line of succession to the French throne, as heir to the Spanish crown,

Thus Phillip of Bourbon, Duke of Anjou, became Spanish Felipe V. The Dutch and the English had planned to divide Spain and take her colonies; now who would be able to stop a united France and Spain?

England and the Dutch accepted Felipe as Spain's sovereign until the Bourbon family excluded them from the Spanish trade. By 1702 Europe was divided into two large factions. On one side an alliance amongst Louis XIV's France, Bourbon Spain, Bavaria and Cologne. Savoy also joined the Bourbons but later switched sides. These allies accepted Felipe V as the rightful king of Spain.

A coalition amongst Austria, England, the Dutch Republic and Portugal supported a contestant to the Spanish Crown. Archduke Charles Habsburg, brother of the Holy Roman Emperor, was crowned Carlos III in Vienna while Felipe V waged war in Italy. After Carlos' army took Barcelona, the regions of Aragon, Catalonia and Valencia gave their support to the Austrian.

In 1701, an Austrian army invaded Lombardy. Its goal was to take Milan. Savoy-Piedmont, a French ally, decided to switch sides, and Carlos III arrived in the peninsula with a claim to the Spanish Crown, which motivated Felipe V's return to Spain.

Rockmore had no difficulties convincing Sophia, Prince George of Hanover, and the heads of many other German states to oppose Felipe's claim to Spain's throne. They feared the French House of Bourbon would become too powerful if it also controlled Spain.

Prince George invaded his neighboring state, Brunswick-Wolfenbüttel, which was pro-French, writing out some of the battle orders himself. The invasion succeeded with few lives lost. As a reward, a prior Hanoverian annexation of the Duchy of Saxe-Lauenburg by George's uncle was recognized by the British and Dutch.

Rockmore returned to England satisfied with his diplomatic successes and delighted that Fleur had given him a son.

Chapter Sixty-Six

Queen Anne

Rockmore's friendship with John Taltson enabled him to learn much about Queen Anne, which corroborated his own observations and Court gossip. Aware her husband was troubled, Fleur told him she knew nothing about Queen Anne and asked why he worried one night after they went to bed.

"Anne is my age, thirty-seven. She has never enjoyed good health. Just before her coronation, as you witnessed, Anne suffered from a severe attack of gout and had to be carried to the ceremony in an open sedan chair with a low back, so her six-yard train could pass to her ladies walking behind. From birth, few expected her to survive to adulthood. Anne has poor vision, with watering eyes. She also suffers from polyarthritis and blotchy skin. Her constant pregnancies, many of which ended in miscarriages and stillbirths, have not helped. Only one child lived beyond a year or two, William, who became the Duke of Gloucester. Unfortunately he died two years ago, of hydrocephalus, at age eleven."

"The poor woman."

"Unlike her older sister Mary, Anne did not inherit her Stuart family's good looks, nor did she have a happy, stable childhood. By all accounts her husband, Prince George of Denmark, although handsome and of manly physique, is a drunk and a crashing bore. I have observed him to be a gross, ridiculous figure. Even King James II, Anne's father, was said to have complained 'I have tried him drunk and I've tried him sober, but there is nothing in him.'"

Rockmore described Anne's lonely early years. Four years old in 1669, she was sent to France for medical treatment, where she lived with her paternal grandmother, widowed Queen Henrietta Maria at a chateau outside Paris. Within a year, her grandmother died, and she went to live with her aunt, Henrietta, Duchess of Orleans, who was married for ten years to Louis XIV's younger brother Philippe.

"Henrietta also had health issues. For two years, she complained of intermittent, intense pain in her side and, shortly before Anne arrived, her pain progressed and she was having digestive problems as well. One morning late in June, she died. Anne returned to her family home in England. In two years, she had lost two close family members and resided in four different homes. Deaths of family members continued. Over a period of nine months, Anne's mother died of breast cancer, followed by her young brother Edgar and her youngest baby sister, Catherine. Of her seven brothers and sisters, only one sibling survived, her elder sister Queen Mary."

Rockmore pitied Anne, whose life must had been filled with confusion and death. "Next, her uncle Charles II sent Anne and Mary to live at Richmond in the care of Colonel Edward Villiers and his wife Frances. After their mother's death, they would be separated from their father, James, Duke of York . Private tutors instructed Anne and Mary in tenets of the Anglican faith. Anne's extreme piety, which emphasized distrust of Catholics, continued into adulthood and further complicated relations with her father after he converted to Catholicism."

"Why was James so foolish as to do that?"

"He had autocratic tendencies. In 1677, Anne was afflicted with smallpox and later she was too ill to attend Mary's wedding to Prince William of Orange. In 1683, she wed a suitable Protestant husband, Prince George, brother of King Christian V of Denmark. Despite the political nature of their marriage, Anne and George are devoted to one another, even though he drinks heavily. The only unsuccessful part of their marriage is continued childlessness. Anne has been pregnant an estimated seventeen times, with many miscarriages, stillbirths, and no children surviving past childhood."

"How terrible for her."

Fleur placed Rockmore's hand on her belly. "Our child is due in August. I pray it will be a successful birth."

"We shall ensure it will be."

Rockmore told Fleur he expected to be out of favor with Anne. He believed she resented him for not convincing her sister Mary II to reconcile. "My friendship with Taltson further lessens my standing. Although the Archbishop of Canterbury crowned Anne queen, he is in low favor with her. Anne is Tory inclined and believes Tillotson favors the Low Church. She has clashed with him over her sole right to appoint bishops. She ignored his preferences when she appointed Sir Jonathan Trelawny, 3rd Baronet, as Bishop of Winchester. When Tillotson protested, the queen interrupted and shouted, 'The matter is decided!' It was only with great difficulty Tillotson persuaded Anne to appoint his nominee William Wake as Bishop of Lincoln."

"What will you do?"

Rockmore kissed Fleur. "Perhaps I may withdraw from Court, tend to my businesses and Parliament, concentrate on raising our children, and give you all the attention you deserve."

Fleur snuggled against Rockmore. "Queen Anne would be foolish to dismiss you."

*****

Queen in her own right, Anne gave her husband high offices in the military and at Court. She also made John Churchill Duke of Marlborough and Captain General of the army waging war against Louis XIV.

Anne chose Kensington Palace as her residence. She hired Christopher Wren to complete the extensions William and Mary had begun, known as the Queen's Apartments and Entrance, with a shallow-stepped staircase so Anne could walk down gracefully. Anne used these extensions for easy access between her private apartments and the baroque parterre gardens with sections of clipped scrolling designs punctuated by trees formally clipped into cones, laid out by Henry Wise, the royal gardener.

Anne later summoned Rockmore for an audience. She allowed him to continue his diplomatic mission to befriend Prince George and acquaint Sophia and her eldest with English Parliamentary governance.

Anne, overweight and in obvious discomfort, rested her gouty foot on a soft ottoman. "Lord Rockmore, we know you tried your best to arrange reconciliation with our sister, who resented my friendship and dependence on Lady Sarah Churchill. We are coming to believe she may have been right about that lady."

Rockmore chose not to comment. Years before she'd became queen, Anne had met charismatic Sarah Jennings, who later wed John Churchill, a gifted soldier, courtier and brother of her father's former mistress Arabella.

Anne and Sarah Churchill were inseparably close friends for many years before Anne became queen, and when apart they corresponded using pseudonyms, Sarah as 'Mrs. Freeman' and Anne as 'Mrs. Morley.'

Rising from a lowly page at the court of the House of Stuart, Sarah's husband served James, Duke of York, through the 1670s and early 1680s. This gave him military and political advancement. John Churchill was one of England's greatest soldiers, a brilliant tactician who applied mobility and firepower in the field. Churchill secured James on his throne after he defeated and captured Monmouth in1685. Yet three years later he defected from James II for Protestant William of Orange, who at his coronation made him Earl of Marlborough.

Emotionally fragile because of so many failed pregnancies, Anne was dependent upon ambitious Sarah, who became her constant companion.

Is Anne questioning Sarah's ambition after so many years?

Rockmore welcomed a swift end to his audience with Anne.

CHAPTER SIXTY-SEVEN

TRIUMPHS AND TROUBLES

Despite his reluctance to be a courtier, Rockmore could not avoid honoring Queen Anne's summons for him to appear for an audience at Windsor Castle in late August of 1704, a few weeks after Fleur gave birth to a second boy, baptized Baruch, named for her father.

Before Rockmore discovered Anne's purpose, she bade him wait while she finished a game of dominoes with her new favorite, Abigail Hill.

Rockmore was not surprised Sarah Churchill was now often absent from Court. As her husband rose to new heights, Court gossip criticized the Duchess of Marlborough as becoming too full of herself. Many expected Sarah might be supplanted in Anne's affections by her cousin Abigail Hill, who caught the queen's attention during Sarah's frequent absences from Court.

Fleur had heard similar rumors during her visits and entertaining. According to reports, Abigail Hill was indeed a cousin of Sarah Churchill, Duchess of Marlborough. Her parents were Francis Hill, a London merchant, and Elizabeth Hill, née Jennings, who was Sarah's aunt. Reduced to poor circumstances through her father's speculations, Abigail had been forced to work as a servant in a squire's home.

Sarah Churchill, whilst Lady of the Bedchamber to Princess Anne, had befriended Abigail and brought her to her own household at St. Albans. After Anne's accession to the throne, in 1704 Sarah procured an appointment for her cousin in the queen's household.

A courtier colonel entered and interrupted Anne's game with a message from Sarah's husband written on the back of a tavern bill. He read it for all present to hear: "I have no time to say more, but I beg you will give my duty to the Queen and let her know that her army has had a glorious victory over the French at Blenheim."

Anne, with tears of joy running down her cheeks, gave the colonel a miniature of herself and a thousand guineas in reward.

*****

That same year, despite Marlborough's victory at Blenheim, Anne wearied of the duchess' frequent absences from her Court, and of her annoying political lectures when she was there. Anne continued to lean Tory, but Sarah was a devoted Whig, and she wanted Anne to appoint more Whig ministers who supported the Duke of Marlborough's wars.

The queen was unwilling to abandon the Church Party, as the Tories were known, religion being Anne's chief concern. Rockmore heard she confided to her Lord Treasurer, the Earl of Godolphin, that she and Sarah could never be true friends again.

Rockmore told Fleur he was doing his best to avoid taking sides as Abigail supplanted her powerful kinswoman as Queen Anne's favorite.

"It is well you do, but do you think she might be guilty of deliberate ingratitude toward the Duchess of Marlborough?"

"I believe her influence over Anne has less to do with subtle scheming. Abigail's genial and pleasing character contrasts with the overpowering personality of the duchess, which, after many years of undisputed sway, has now become intolerable to Anne."

"That is not the consensus amongst my lady acquaintances. Be wary of Abigail Hill, my love."

Chapter Sixty-Eight

Cordelia

Two days before Cordelia's twelfth birthday, in 1706, Fleur spoke with Rockmore about his eldest in his library. "Cordelia will soon be nubile and experience her first bleeding. I have tried to prepare her for it, but I think you should assist her, too, with your medical knowledge."

Rockmore snuffed his pipe and went to a locked section of his bookcase. He opened a double shelf with a key and removed several books and pamphlets. "I have saved these for Cordelia. Together we can disabuse her of superstitions and falsehoods."

"Yes, she enjoys science and is well-read, with understanding beyond her age. Cordelia has asked me questions whenever my time of the month arrives. I believed I convinced her there's no such thing as Eve's Curse and that it is a normal part of a woman's functioning, like Harvey's circulation of blood. I've given her several linen rags of the type I use when my bleeding arrives so she will be prepared."

"Well taught, *Querida*. I will speak with Cordelia and give her these books and pamphlets to read."

"Cordelia did tell me some girls she met at Court were not allowed to wash their hair during their bleeding for fear blood would rush to their brain and makes them mad."

"Yes, such beliefs are remnants of ideas from ancient texts such as Pliny the Elder's *Natural History*, which stated that the touch of a menstruating woman resulted in all sorts of chaos, such as causing wine to go sour, trees and crops to die, and that dogs went mad upon tasting menstrual blood. Send Cordelia to me now, and I will speak with her."

Cordelia entered Rockmore's library, and he regarded his daughter with love and pride. Tall for her age at five feet, eight inches and still growing, she was a voracious reader interested in science and new inventions. She was also gifted in music. She had a new favorite dog, Freya, a loyal German Shepherd and a gift from Prince George, which she'd raised from a puppy.

"Please sit, Delia. Your mother and I have been discussing your birthday and your concerns about the advent of your menarche, your first monthly bleeding."

Cordelia did not blush or fidget. "It is like a Sword of Damocles hanging over my head."

"You know I have medical knowledge taught by my grandfather, and your mother has kept current."

"I believe you are wiser than most physicians, Papa. You also, Mama."

Fleur squeezed Cordelia's hand. "Thank you, Delia. Some physicians believe menstrual blood is a build-up of excess blood during the month and discharged by the veins of the uterus. Bleeding during and after giving birth is seen as an equivalent of a larger menstrual period. So is blood sometimes lost on first intercourse. Each of these episodes of bleeding carries associations of a woman's growth to maturity. Menarche is the start of a girl's transition to womanhood, with defloration and subsequent postpartum bleeding all forming part of that process."

"Is it true a common expression for menstruation is 'the flowers'?"

"Yes, the flower image protects a woman's modesty, but also shows the absolute link between menstruation and fertility. You may have heard this adage: 'Where there are no flowers there can be no fruit.'"

"Yes, I have."

Rockmore offered Cordelia the books and pamphlets he'd saved for her. "Read these. They best explain how women manage their menstrual flow and pain. Some go to bed for several days. Others go about normal routines. Your mother and I will answer any new questions you may have."

*****

In 1706 Fleur gave birth to a girl she named Sarah for her mother. Rockmore educated his children when they were old enough to comprehend and reject the dominant medical practice of humoral medicine. This was an ancient system from the teachings of Hippocrates and Galen. The four main humors of the body were connected to the four elements of the earth and the seasons: blood was related to air and spring; yellow bile (*choler*) was related to fire and summer; black bile (*melancholy*) was related to the earth and autumn; and phlegm was related to water and winter. To maintain optimum health, it was held that these humors should be kept in perfect balance.

According to the teaching of Galen, men were able to cleanse the body of excess or unwanted humors by sweat produced from hard labor. Women were known to spend their days sitting and embroidering, which failed to use up these waste products as efficiently as men did. Instead, during the course of a month this excess built until it was discharged as a menstrual period.

Great importance was placed on evacuations in humoral medicine. Six factors affected bodily functions: the air one breathes, sleep, the intake of food and drink, bodily evacuations, including sexual emissions, movement, and emotions. The emphasis placed on regular evacuations was a reason a missed menstrual period wasn't necessarily taken as an indication of potential pregnancy and was way down the list of indicators of pregnancy. One example Rockmore cited to Cordelia and Fleur made them laugh. A midwife cited fourteen signs of pregnancy, and a missed period came sixth, after sour belching.

*****

Cordelia's menarche arrived two months before her thirteenth birthday. Her subsequent periods gave her manageable pain, and in the days before, her moods did not change. Fastidious about her person, Cordelia did bathe more often.

Both men and women bathed in flower-scented waters. Those who did not or could not afford such luxury might apply sponges soaked in perfume. For some, perfume replaced bathing altogether.

Wash balls made from soap blended with herbs, flowers, or scent became popular. Rockmore showed Fleur and his daughters *The English Housewife*, published in 1683 by Gervaise Markham, which offered a recipe for wash balls:

> *To make very good washing balls take storax of both kinds, benjamin, calamus aromaticus, labdanum of each alike; and bray them to powder with cloves and orris; then beat all with a sufficient quantity of soap till it be stiff, then with your hand you shall work it like paste, and make round balls thereof.*

345

Public baths remained open throughout the eighteenth century and were used socially or for medical concerns more than a means of bathing. These were often suspected of concealing brothels, so the most reputable bath houses advertised the respectability of their establishments and offered bloodletting as an extra feature.

Bathing at home was not an option for everyone. Although wash balls used for hands were popular, their composition suffered. Manufacturers cut them with fillers or lightening agents such as white lead. Perfumers continued to make quality wash balls for their wealthier patrons, but those sold to the middling and poor were significantly worse. In Lillie's *The British Perfumer*, the author described a process for making inferior, common wash balls, a significant difference from Markham's recipe:

One hundred-weight of tallow soap and fifty pounds of Spanish or common whitening, are mixed and beaten up with double the above quantity of water, and scented with oil of caraways or some other cheap essential oil. These wash balls are made large; and, to deceive the buyer, are made very round, by being skin-dried, or crusted, by laying in the stove for twelve hours; whereas good wash balls, dried in the air, generally lose their shape. Their roundness, with their large size at little expense, recommend such rubbish to the ignorant buyer; but as for washing, or any other use, it is well known that they will no more lather than a piece of clay, or a stone. There have been wash balls frequently made for this sort of trade, which are merely the shells of large French walnuts covered over with the above base composition.

For those with the means to afford quality cosmetics, the range of products available seemed endless. *Abdeker's Library of the Toilet* listed many products available for purchase at well-stocked chemists. Waters, spirits, essences, pomatums, oils, vinegars, pastes, wash balls, powders, and even gloves came in a variety of scents such as rose, lavender, wormwood, scurvy grass, and volatiles.

One could make wash balls at home, inspired by Markham's recipe. With a base of castile soap and rosewater, a person could make a wash ball in a kitchen.

In her *Artifice of Beauty*, Sally Pointer offered her recipe:

One bar bland white Castile soap grated, small cup rosewater, 1 tsp. lavender flower, 1 tsp. ores-root powder, 1 tsp. dried rose petals,1 tsp. powdered sweet flag root (or myrrh), chamomile, or marigold flowers.

Beat all the herbs being used to a powder, and sieve to get the larger particles out. Don't worry if the powder is a bit gritty. Warm the rosewater and dissolve the soap in it. When it has all melted, stir in the powders and remove from the heat. As soon as you can safely handle the mixture, divide it into several portions. Allow to harden for five minutes, then wet your hands in rosewater and shape them into nice, round balls.

Leave to set, then wrap in greaseproof paper and store in a dark place for a while to harden further. The longer they are left before use, within reason, the harder they will get and the more the scent will develop. It is a nice idea to store them in a paper bag in the underwear drawer or airing cupboard to scent everything. The slight grittiness of the powders makes the soap a good exfoliant in use. A small cheat to get an even deeper scent into your soap is to store your dry wash balls in a bag of dried herbs or pot-pourri. The scent will permeate the soaps very readily.

At his villa, Rockmore added large bathtubs for every suite. He demanded the kitchen always had several cauldrons of boiling water available.

Chapter Sixty-Nine

Acts of Union

Fear of an insurrection led by Catholic Stuart Jacobite loyalists with French aid to place Anne's half-brother James Edward on the throne required further Parliamentary Acts. In 1705 Parliament naturalized Sophia and her heirs as English subjects.

That was still not enough, and Parliament formalized a transfer of power through a Regency Council in case there should be a period between when Anne died and Sofia could be crowned. In the same year, George of Hanover's surviving uncle died, and he inherited another German dominion: the Principality of Lüneburg-Grubenhagen, centered at Celle.

Deeper political integration had been a key policy of Queen Anne's government from the time she ascended to the throne in 1702. Under the aegis of the queen and her ministers in both kingdoms, the Parliaments of England and Scotland agreed to participate in fresh negotiations for a union treaty in 1705.

The two countries had shared a monarch since the Union of the Crowns in 1603, when King James VI of Scotland inherited the English throne as James I from his double first cousin twice removed, Queen Elizabeth I. Although described as a Union of Crowns, until 1707 there were in fact two separate Crowns resting on the same head, as opposed to a single Crown and a single kingdom. There had been three attempts—in 1606, 1667, and 1689—to unite the two countries by Acts of Parliament.

Whigs supported union. Tories opposed.

Negotiations between English and Scottish commissioners took place between April 16th and July 22nd, 1706. Each side had its particular concerns. Within a few days, England received a promise that the Hanoverian dynasty would succeed Queen Anne to the Scottish crown, and Scotland received a guarantee of access to colonial markets, with equal footing in terms of trade.

After negotiations ended in July of 1706, England's Parliament passed a Union with Scotland Act, and in 1707 Scotland's Parliament passed a Union with England Act, *United into One Kingdom by the Name of Great Britain.*

The Acts took effect on May 1st, 1707. On that date, the Scottish Parliament and the English Parliament united to form the Parliament of Great Britain, based in the Palace of Westminster in London, home of the English Parliament.

In Germany, Rockmore assured Sofia and George that Scotland would honor a Hanoverian succession even though the Treaty led to popular unrest in Edinburgh and substantial riots in Glasgow. Scots feared the Kirk, their national Church, would be Anglicized and that Anglicization would remove democracy from the only democratic part of the Kingdom; and they feared higher taxes.

Not one petition in favor of an incorporating union was received by Parliament. On the day the treaty was signed, the carilloner in St Giles Cathedral, Edinburgh, rang the bells to the tune '*Why should I be so sad on my wedding day?*' Parliament imposed martial law to counter threats of widespread civil unrest.

*****

The Treaty of Union, agreed upon between representatives of the Parliament of England and the Parliament of Scotland in 1706, consisted of 25 articles, 15 of which were economic in nature. In Scotland, each article was voted on separately and several clauses in articles were delegated to specialized subcommittees. Article 1 of the treaty was based on the political principle of an incorporating union, and this was secured by a majority of 116 votes to 83 on November 4th, 1706. To minimize opposition from the Church of Scotland, an Act was also passed to secure the Presbyterian establishment, after which the Church ended its open opposition, although hostility remained at lower levels of the clergy. The treaty as a whole was finally ratified on January 16th, 1707, by a majority of 110 votes to 69.

The two Acts incorporated provisions for Scotland to send representative peers from the Peerage of Scotland to sit in the House of Lords. It guaranteed the Church of Scotland would remain the established church in Scotland, that the Court of Session would "remain in all time coming within Scotland", and that Scots law would "remain in the same force as before". Other provisions included the restatement of the Act of Settlement 1701 and the ban on Roman Catholics taking the throne. It also created a customs union and monetary union.

The Act provided that any "laws and statutes" that were "contrary to or inconsistent with the terms" of the Act would "cease and become void."

The Scottish Parliament also passed the Protestant Religion and Presbyterian Church Act 1707, guaranteeing the status of the Presbyterian Church of Scotland. The English Parliament passed a similar Act.

Soon after, the Union with Scotland Amendment united the Privy Councils and decentralized Scottish administration by appointing justices of the peace in each shire to carry out administration goals. In effect it took the day-to-day government of Scotland out of the hands of politicians and put it into those of the College of Justice.

In the year following the Union, the Treason Act of 1708 abolished the Scottish law of Treason and extended the corresponding English law across Great Britain.

Scotland benefited, gaining "freedom of trade with England and the colonies" as well as "a great expansion of markets," but recalcitrant Highlanders opposed the ending of trade with France. The agreement also guaranteed the permanent status of the Presbyterian Church in Scotland, and the separate system of laws and courts in Scotland. Scotland accepted the Hanoverian succession and gave up her power of threatening England's military security and complicating her commercial relations.

*****

Rockmore took advantage of an opportunity to expand his business before the Acts of Union passed both English and Scottish Parliaments. Using his connections at Court and in the House of Lords, he acquired new contracts with both Admiralty and Army to manufacture new flags and uniforms representing Great Britain.

Prior to 1707, colonels of regiments made their own arrangements for the manufacture of uniforms. This practice ended when a royal warrant of January 16th, 1707, established a Board of General Officers to regulate the clothing of the army. New uniforms supplied were to conform to a "sealed pattern" agreed by the board. Previous to the Acts of Union, red coats were lined with contrasting colors and turned out to provide distinctive regimental facings of lapels, cuffs and collars for the King's Regiment of Foot and buff for the 3rd Regiment of Foot. Now all regiments of Foot and naval Marines would henceforth wear scarlet tunics.

From the coronations of the Stuart King James VI of Scotland and James I of England in 1603, a variety of flags had been flown combining the Cross of St. George, England's patron, and the Cross of St. Andrew, Scotland's patron. Now they were combined in one uniform pattern. Rockmore signed a contract to provide flags for Colonial regiments, with the union crosses in the upper left section against a scarlet field. His bayonet and nail factories also had steady orders.

Tragedy struck Henry Lambert's family. Patriarch Sir John died of a heart attack, and his heir John Jr. failed to receive Anne's endorsement for their Porcelain. Henry never had any interest in their porcelain business, and Rockmore, a silent investor, agreed with the Lamberts to sell their factories and contacts to the highest bidders.

Rockmore earned a decent profit from his investment, while John Jr. received the largest portion of the sale, and all property and money from his father's will. Henry received a bequest of five hundred pounds sterling.

Rockmore offered Henry Lambert a position to oversee his factories and businesses, excluding his banking and monetary dealings. Lambert accepted his offer, which came with a generous income.

*****

Over the next several years, Parliamentary debates and votes, war on the Continent, and visits to Hanover interfered with Rockmore's desire to spend more time with Fleur and their children. In 1706, Churchill won another great military victory at Ramillies, and the Elector of Bavaria was deprived of his offices and titles for siding with Louis XIV against the Empire.

The following year, Prince George was invested as an Imperial Field Marshal with command of the army stationed along the Rhine. His tenure was not altogether successful, partly because he was deceived by his ally, the Duke of Marlborough, into a diversionary attack, and because Holy Roman Emperor Joseph I appropriated necessary funds for his own use.

Despite this, the German princes in 1708 confirmed George's position as a Prince-Elector. George did not hold Marlborough's actions against him, which he understood to be part of a wider plan to lure French forces away from the main attack.

Churchill won more victories at Oudenarde in 1708, and at Malplaquet in 1709. To show the country's appreciation, Parliament gave Marlborough land at Woodstock in Oxfordshire and built him a house called Blenheim Palace. Yet Churchill failed to win a decisive battle against the French to end the war.

Because of her absences from Court, Churchill's wife Sarah had been oblivious to Abigail Hill's growing favor with Queen Anne until summer of 1707, when she discovered her cousin had in private wed a gentleman of the queen's household, Samuel Masham, with Anne in attendance.

Rockmore complimented Fleur for her instincts regarding Abigail Masham. They proved correct after Prince George of Denmark died in 1708, leaving Anne grief-stricken. Despite his flaws, she had loved her husband and depended upon him to give her strength. Now alone, Anne relied more and more on Abigail's company and advice, which affected government policies.

CHAPTER SEVENTY

FAMILY

One evening in January 1710, in their London town home library, Rockmore served Fleur, Cordelia, and Vincent each a glass of Port. They sat in a crescent facing a roaring fire after a birthday feast for fifteen-year-old Vincent. The younger children, Baruch, Jacob, and Sarah, lay asleep upstairs.

Rockmore praised Vincent for his academic achievements at Eton and his athletic prowess as best swordsman, fastest runner, and undefeated wrestler. "By summer you will have finished your studies. Have you a preference for any career?"

"Yes, father. Like you and Uncle Henry, I want to serve in the Army until the war against France ends."

Rockmore calmed Fleur and Cordelia, who protested Vincent's decision. "My son, you are the primary heir to my Earldom, property, and businesses. There is much you have to learn. I will be forty-five later this year, and I've made a will. You should know the terms. Our younger children will learn all the details in due time, when they are older."

Rockmore removed papers from his desk. "I have discussed everything with Fleur, and she approves. Vincent, upon my death as Second Earl of Sidmouth, you will inherit all titles and properties, including income from this estate and from all businesses. Fleur, my love, you will have right of residence here in London and at our estate in Sidmouth, plus an unencumbered cash amount of £500,000. Our three younger children will each receive in trust £50,000, which will accrue interest over the years before each reaches majority."

Rockmore shuffled papers and smiled at Cordelia. "No, daughter, do not be distressed. I have not forgotten you. We must decide what to do about your future. You are an admired beauty, and many men, some young and some in their thirties and even forties, have asked my permission to court you."

"Who are they, Papa?"

"I will not reveal their names. Know that some are from old titled families, and at least two are German princes. Has anyone found favor with you?"

"No, Papa, but I am flattered by their attentions."

"So we have observed. That you are a great beauty and an heiress excites older men, young swains, and their families. You will be sixteen in two months and presented at Court here in London and at Hanover." Rockmore sipped his Port. "That will bring on an avalanche of new suitors."

Fleur intervened. "Jack, please tell Delia whether she is an heiress."

"Yes. Delia, first there is the matter of your dowry. You will receive annual income from £100,000 deposited with the Bank of London to share with your spouse, but another £250,000 in secret, to be solely yours, untouched by whomsoever you wed so you may maintain your independence."

"Thank you, Papa, but do you intend to select my husband, too?"

"Fleur and I prefer not to meddle. We want you to be happy and wed for love, but so should the man you choose, and not for your wealth."

Rockmore turned to Vincent. "By the summer, after you will have finished your studies, fighting in Europe will have ended and negotiations will have begun. If you join the Army, you most likely may see action against Jacobite rebels in Scotland or overseas in the colonies. I shall arrange you go in as a junior officer with the rank of Subaltern."

Chapter Seventy-One

Tory Ascendancy

During the debates over the Acts of Union, the War of Spanish Succession had continued. After Carlos III took Madrid and Zaragoza, he left Spain in 1706, believing it was secure, to pursue war in Italy. As a result, Valencia and Aragon fell back to the Bourbons, whilst the English took Minorca.

From 1706 onwards the Austrian army in Italy occupied Turin, Milan, Parma, and Naples. In 1708, Duke Ferdinand Gonzaga of Mantua died, and Austria annexed the duchy; the Spanish surrendered Sardinia.

By 1709, peace negotiations opened, although it took four and five years before all combatants signed a treaty.

In 1710, George of Hanover announced his hereditary right to succeed in Britain after Parliament removed Catholic succession from all Catholic Stuarts. He issued this declaration to convince Tories he was no usurper.

In Hanover, in mid-July of 1710 on the palace veranda, Rockmore maintained a calm exterior outside whilst Sophia and George ranted against Queen Anne. They cursed her in both German and English. Some pejorative German words and phrases he hadn't heard before, but others such as *"dummkopf"* and *"scheisskopf"* expressed a small part of their outrage.

Both mother and son paused to drink cool beer in the summer heat. Rockmore took advantage of their silence to describe how Abigail Masham had acquired power over Queen Anne. First he reminded Sophia and George of the continuing financial stresses from the War of Spanish Succession that had led most Tories to intensify their opposition, whilst Marlborough and Godolphin headed an administration still dominated by the group of Whigs known as the *Junto.*

Anne had grown uncomfortable with this dependence on the Whigs, whilst her personal relationship with the Duchess of Marlborough deteriorated, and Sarah Churchill spread rumors that the queen and Abigail were lovers. This situation also distressed many non-*Junto* Whigs, led by the Dukes of Somerset and Shrewsbury, who intrigued with Robert Harley's Tories.

"Lady Masham has used her increasing influence over Anne to promote familial and Tory aggrandizements. She also is a cousin of Robert Harley, Earl of Oxford, and after his dismissal from office in February 1708 by the Whigs, she assisted him in maintaining confidential relations with the queen. Abigail Masham's total influence over Anne manifested a few months ago when the Queen compelled Marlborough, much against his will, to give an important command to Colonel John Hill, Abigail's brother. She also influenced Anne to dismiss her Whig ministers from office, to be replaced by her cousin Oxford and other Tories."

Sophia interrupted, "But where was the Duchess of Marlborough in all this?"

"Lady Sarah Churchill sought an audience with the queen at Kensington Palace this past 6th of April and demanded she restore all Whig ministers. Queen Anne refused. She dismissed Sarah from her appointments at Court, and gave Baroness Abigail the Duchess of Marlborough's place as Keeper of the Privy Purse."

Rockmore paused to drink beer. "The new Tory ministry is dominated by Masham's cousin Robert Harley, Earl of Oxford, Chancellor of the Exchequer and Lord Treasurer, and Viscount Bolingbroke, Secretary of State."

Rockmore succeeded in calming Sophia and Prince George, assuring them that a Whig majority favorable to their succession would soon return to power. He continued to follow Prince George's career in Hanover. In 1710, at age fifty, he was appointed Arch-Treasurer of the Empire by the Emperor.

In 1711, Tory ministers, intent on bringing about the Duke of Marlborough's fall and seeking peace with France, secured a majority in the House of Lords by convincing Queen Anne to create twelve new Tory peers, including Abigail's husband as 1st Baron Masham.

Rockmore worried that The Holy Roman Emperor's death in 1711 threatened to destroy the balance of power in the opposite direction, and Marlborough failed to defeat France despite his many battlefield victories. Anne and her new Tory majority wanted peace.

Though both England and Scotland recognized Anne as their queen, so far only the English Parliament had settled on Sophia, Electress of Hanover, as heir presumptive. Scotland's Parliament had yet to decide upon a successor for the Scottish throne.

Chapter Seventy-Two

Inevitable Encounter

Cordelia turned sixteen in March of 2010, and later in the year made her debuts at both Anne's and Sophia's Courts, followed by appearances at many balls during the season before Christmas. As Rockmore expected, his daughter's beauty, grace, charm, and wealth attracted new suitors. He and Fleur chaperoned Cordelia everywhere and advised her against obvious fortune hunters.

Rockmore wished Mary II had lived. She'd promised to make Cordelia one of her ladies after his daughter came of age.

One evening after a ball which Fleur alone had chaperoned, Rockmore sat with Cordelia in his library by a warming fire drinking Port.

"Did anyone catch your interest?"

"No, Papa, they're all so shallow. Mother said no one yet is worthy of me. And I agreed. But, there was a young man who interested me, not for the potential of matrimony. Mother remarked he resembled both me and you as you might have looked when you were fifteen or sixteen. In truth, he did not stop staring at me."

"Did you learn his name?"

"William de Clifford, who, after he comes of age will be Duke of Basingstoke. He must be my brother, Vincent's twin."

Clever girl. "Yes, Delia, he is your brother. Were you able to discern what sort of person he is?"

"He did not dance with anyone and seemed awkward and diffident."

"If you see William again, you may invite him here without revealing you are his sister. If he wishes to reconcile, I shall welcome him into our family. But, we must be circumspect. His mother may have influenced him to hate me and his siblings."

*****

The following day, Vincent arrived on Christmas leave in full uniform as a subaltern in Her Majesty's Army. Rockmore and Fleur complimented him on his fitness and maturity.

Rockmore celebrated Vincent's visit with Claret for all except his three youngest children. "Where will you be posted next?"

"Not in Europe, Father. There are rumors of a Jacobite revolt planned in Scotland, aided by the French, to take place sometime after the First of the New Year. I am not yet privy to any plans."

"I'll find out what I can. In the meantime, we may have a visitor."

Rockmore described Cordelia's plans to bring their brother William to meet their family. "It will be a test of his character."

And why is he at Court?

*****

An answer to Rockmore's unspoken question came sooner than expected. Early in the morning a servant delivered a request from Abigail Masham for a meeting an hour before noon at Kensington Palace.

A maid opened a door to Lady Masham's parlor in her palace suite and announced, "Lord Rockmore, Ma'am." She closed the door and stood by another at the far end as if awaiting further instructions.

Wearing a beige and forest green dress with typical décolletage, Lady Masham sat on an upholstered cream and pink rosette divan of French manufacture. She beckoned Rockmore to sit in an upholstered armchair of the same design. Several silver and porcelain services lay on a gold-painted rococo table between them.

"Coffee, chocolate, or tea, Lord Rockmore?"

"Chocolate, Lady Masham.'"

She spoke while pouring for both. "A pity you were not at last night's ball. Your daughter outshone everyone. Did she speak to you about her triumph?"

"Cordelia was most interested in William de Clifford. She deduced he is her brother."

"And your son. I am aware of your acrimonious divorce. Rosamund was kin to me, distant kin, but kin nonetheless. Also kin to the Earl of Oxford. She passed away two months ago."

Rockmore, though surprised, did not react.

"Rosamund never remarried. And poor William was left alone to grieve at Basingstoke. Rosamund raised him believing his father died in battle. She never spoke of you."

Not surprised. "What about Mrs. Havers?"

"That wretched dragon died within days of Rosamund. She went mad and tried to burn Basingstoke. Servants restrained her and put out the flames before they spread."

Masham described William's cloistered life with private tutors and no attendance at any school. During her extreme temper tantrums, Rosamund had often beat William for peeing in bed and other childhood infractions. "She'd knock him down to the floor, and kick his head. That may explain his lack of coordination and slowness of wit. I brought William to Court to broaden his experiences and make friends."

"And to protect him from other grasping relations?"

"That, too. His death would create a war amongst distant kin claiming his title and wealth. Lord Rockmore, I know you will accept him into your family and protect him as your son."

"William must decide that."

Masham gestured toward her maid, who opened the door. William entered, escorted by his kinsman the Earl of Oxford. Rockmore saw a handsome boy about six feet tall, but gangly, not yet filled out, unlike his shorter twin Vincent.

He stood to face his son.

No doubting my paternity.

Masham spoke before Rockmore found his voice. "William, here is your father as I promised, Sir Jack Lord Rockmore, Earl of Sidmouth."

*****

During their carriage ride to his home, Rockmore found William to be polite but distant, as if tolerating his presence and questions. His son asked none of his own. At home, William accepted introductions to Fleur and their children with unexpressive nods. His aloofness continued throughout their midday meal.

After supping, Rockmore took William into his library and showed him documents detailing his divorce settlement with Rosamund. William evinced no curiosity or animosity.

"Now that you have met your family, know that you are most welcome and may reside here instead of Kensington Palace."

"I prefer residing with my maternal kin. Lady Masham and the Earl of Oxford are continuing the education my mother gave me."

Rockmore did not like William's arrogant tone. "And what education is that?"

"Why, to be King of Great Britain, of course. The Protestant Stuarts have no qualified heirs, and their Catholic branches are banned from the succession. We English will never accept a German king. Through my Plantagenet bloodline, I am the only true heir to the throne. Lady Masham and Oxford will arrange everything to ensure Queen Anne names me her heir before she dies."

Rockmore sat stunned, as if he'd heard Rosamund's voice. Recovering, he rose. "I've kept you here long enough. I'll take you back to the palace."

Rockmore did not make conversation in his carriage and said a formal goodbye outside Lady Masham's suite. From there, he went to Sir Robert Walpole's residence and told him and other prominent Whigs Masham's plans to use William as a cat's paw to seize absolute power.

Rockmore did not miss the irony. His father's brain damage was similar to his son William's, although the latter functioned better. And Masham and her coteries wanted to make William king.

Rockmore returned home and met with Fleur, Cordelia, and Vincent in his library. All shared similar opinions of William as an arrogant popinjay.

"He would not look at me," Vincent complained. "He's no brother of mine."

"When I asked him why he did not dance at the ball, he sneered and said it was beneath him," Cordelia added.

Fleur held Rockmore's hand. "I know how disappointed you are. He behaved as if we are inferiors."

"His mother had sixteen years to create him, and Lady Masham will reinforce those lessons. She and Oxford must be stopped, and William de Clifford rusticated to Basingstoke."

Chapter Seventy-Three

Changes

Rockmore shared the anger of the Whigs and their allies when Anne's Tory government negotiated the Treaty of Utrecht in 1713, which ended Great Britain's participation in the War of the Spanish Succession. The Treaty confirmed Felipe V as King of Spain, but at a price. He had to renounce his rights to the French throne.

The terms of the Treaty also partitioned Spain's European empire. Sicily and parts of the Duchy of Milan went to Savoy, Austria gained the Kingdom of Naples, Sardinia, and most of the Duchy of Milan. Spain ceded Gibraltar and Minorca to Great Britain, but Felipe V kept his overseas empire in the New World. He assented to the British right to trade non-Spanish slaves in the Spanish Americas for thirty years.

Hostilities between France and Austria would not end until a year later, when the Rastatt Treaty was signed in 1714. That same year, as Electress Sophia sought shelter during a sudden rainstorm, she collapsed in her gardens at Herrenhausen. She died on May 28th, 1714, at age 83.

Rockmore met with Prince George after attending Sophia's funeral with other Whig dignitaries. At a private audience with the prince he offered both condolences and congratulations on his becoming heir apparent to Great Britain's throne.

Rockmore next reported recent happenings at Anne's Court. "The queen is in physical decline. She is so obese she is mostly confined to a wheelchair. Her garments are soiled. Abigail Masham quarreled with Oxford over his vacillation between the Jacobites and adherents of your Hanoverian succession to the Crown. Abigail, a passionate Tory, argued against her cousin Oxford in Queen Anne's presence."

"*Ach,* that woman believes she is the real queen of England."

"It seemed so, Your Highness. After Queen Anne dismissed Oxford from his offices, Abigail schemed to have Queen Anne appoint the Tory Bolingbroke as her chief minister."

"Are the Tories intending to violate the Act of Succession?"

"Two messages arrived this morning before your mother's funeral." Rockmore handed George the first. "Queen Anne has suffered a stroke and lost her ability to speak."

"*Mein Gott.*"

"This second message is from the leading Whig Parliamentarian, Sir Robert Walpole. He assures us Bolingbroke has yet to make any coherent plan to thwart your succession. If he intends to proclaim the son of James II the Pretender king, he has made no moves to do so."

Rockmore did not show George a third message, from Walpole. Alerted to Lady Masham's plans to make William de Clifford Anne's heir, Prince George's Whig supporters, led by Sir Robert Walpole in the Commons and like-minded peers in the Lords, sought to change membership in the Regency Council to favor their party. As Anne's health worsened, the newly constituted Whig-dominated Council would take power and rule until and after George's crowning.

*****

Anne died on August 1ˢᵗ, 1714, aged 49. Having alienated her powerful Tory allies, Abigail Masham surprised all when she left Court and retired, enriched, to quiet private life at her country house in Exeter. Abandoned by all his former supporters, William de Clifford rusticated himself to Basingstoke without a word to his father.

A new list of Whig majority regents were sworn in, and they proclaimed George King of Great Britain and Ireland. Due to contrary winds, which kept George in The Hague awaiting passage, he did not arrive in Britain until September 18th. George was crowned at Westminster Abbey on October 20th, whilst Jacobite rioting broke out in over twenty towns throughout England. Many Scottish Jacobites still rejected the Act of Union because it destroyed their lucrative trade with France.

Rockmore took satisfaction in knowing he'd educated George well about the British system of government and had played a role in His Majesty's relatively peaceful accession. That same day, amongst other distributions of honors, King George raised Rockmore to Duke of Sidmouth. After Rockmore returned home, he took much pleasure in addressing Fleur as "Duchess."

Now I shall have more time to spend with my family and help educate my younger children.

*****

Within a year of George's accession the Whigs won an overwhelming victory in the general election of 1715. The new Whig-dominated Parliament passed the Septennial Act, which extended the maximum duration of Parliament to seven years, although it could be dissolved earlier by King

George. Thus Whigs already in power could remain in such a position for a greater period of time.

Several members of the defeated Tory Party sympathized with the Jacobites, who sought to replace George with Anne's Catholic half-brother, James Francis Edward Stuart, raised at Louis XIV's Court. His Jacobite supporters called him James III of England, and James VIII of Scotland. His Whig opponents referred to him as "the Pretender."

A clause in the Act of Settlement forbidding the British monarch from leaving the country without Parliament's permission was unanimously repealed in 1716. Anticipating George's trips to Hanover whilst King of Great Britain, they vested power in a Regency Council rather than in his son, George Augustus, Prince of Wales.

Several disgruntled Tories sided with a Jacobite rebellion. They became known as "The Fifteen" and were led by Lord Mar, an embittered Scottish nobleman. He had previously served as a Secretary of State, and he instigated rebellion in Scotland, where support for Jacobites was stronger than in England.

Rockmore's son Vincent fought against the rebels. He later reported to his father that The Fifteen were a dismal failure; Lord Mar's battle plans were ill-conceived, and James the Pretender arrived late, with insufficient money and fewer arms than needed.

In February of 1716, faced with impending defeat, The Pretender and Lord Mar fled to France. Although captured rebels faced executions and forfeitures, King George moderated the government's response. He offered leniency, spent income from confiscated rebel estates on schools in Scotland, and paid part of Scotland's national debt.

But George's relationship with his son worsened. George Augustus, Prince of Wales, encouraged opposition to his father's policies, including measures designed to increase religious freedom in Britain and expand Hanover's German territories at the expense of Sweden.

In 1717 the birth of a grandson led to a major quarrel between George and the Prince of Wales. The king, following custom, appointed his Lord Chamberlain Duke of Newcastle, as a baptismal sponsor of his grandchild. The Prince of Wales, who disliked Newcastle, angered his father when he verbally insulted the duke during the christening. Newcastle misunderstood it as a challenge to a duel. King George next banished his son from their royal residence at St. James's Palace. Father and son were never again on cordial terms.

The prince's new home, Leicester House, became a meeting place for the king's political opponents. George and his son were later reconciled at the insistence of Robert Walpole and the desire of the Princess of Wales. Although Caroline had moved out with her husband, she missed her children, who had been left in the care of the king.

King George directed British foreign policy during his early reign. In 1717 he contributed to the creation of the Triple Alliance, an anti-Spanish league composed of Great Britain, France, and the Dutch Republic; in 1718 the Holy Roman Empire joined them, and it became known as the Quadruple Alliance. The subsequent War of the Quadruple Alliance involved the same issues as the War of Spanish Succession.

Rockmore's weapons and uniform factories thrived.

Chapter Seventy-Four

Cupid's Accurate Arrows

Vincent resigned his commission as lieutenant and returned home in 1715 after four years of military service. Rockmore educated his son and heir in all facets of his many businesses and investments, gratified that Vincent had a natural aptitude for finance. He observed that Vincent often visited Henry and Alys Lambert in Sidford and guessed the reason why.

So did Fleur, and she told Rockmore her suspicions regarding Felicity and the Worthingtons. "I've made you aware of my suspicions regarding the Worthingtons' resentment of King William having chosen you instead of Sir Basil to be Earl of Sidmouth."

"Sir Basil could not afford the price."

"But I am convinced they are using Felicity to charm and wed Vincent, so not only will she become Duchess of Sidmouth upon your death, but also, should she give birth to a boy, her son will be, decades from now, Third Duke of Sidmouth."

"Vincent loves Felicity."

"I agree he is smitten, but does she love Vincent or the fact that he's heir to your title? Despite his charm and business acumen, he is not handsome, nor does he appear to be assertive or smooth with women."

Rockmore had not given voice to those same concerns. "I will speak with him."

*****

On a mild, sunny day in July 1716, Rockmore walked with Vincent from their villa to a stone bench overlooking the Channel.

"What is it you wish to discuss with me, son?"

"Father, as you know, I turned twenty-one this past January, and I believe I have performed to your expectations in our businesses."

"Nay, you have exceeded them."

"Thank you, Sir. I know you and mother have been curious why I have spent so much time visiting, when I can, Uncle Henry."

"Your mother and I have discussed it, and we believe we know why."

"After I left the Army and encountered Henry's adopted daughter Felicity for the first time in four years, her beauty and sweetness dazzled me. Felicity is now seventeen. We have declared our love for each other."

"And you wish to wed."

"Yes, Father."

"Are you certain she loves you, or the title you will inherit one day?"

"I know I am not tall and handsome, or glib of tongue, but I believe she loves me for myself and not for the title I may inherit."

"Have you spoken to Sir Henry and Lady Alys?"

"I wanted to know your opinion first. You and mother may prefer I wed a daughter from a titled family."

"No, we want you to be happy and wed for love, but I ask you to wait until after I speak to Sir Henry about your intentions toward Felicity."

"How soon?"

"This day... immediately."

*****

That afternoon, Rockmore discussed with Fleur his reaction to Henry Lambert and Alys regarding Vincent and Felicity. "Henry disappointed me."

"You have done so much for him. What happened?"

"He was not truthful with me regarding Felicity's true intentions. I can no longer trust him to be truthful with us regarding Felicity's motives. He defers to his wife and the Worthingtons in matters of matrimony. Of course, they are eager to welcome Vincent as a groom for Felicity."

"So we can no longer rely on Henry Lambert."

"Definitely not. He has become more Worthington than Lambert. Soon I shall sever my partnership with Henry, and all connections with the Worthingtons. Henry is smitten with Alys, just as Vincent is with Felicity."

"If it were not for Salic Law, Cordelia would inherit your title."

"Yes, that would be ideal, but we must face reality. Vincent shall inherit my title, and he shall wed Felicity."

Rockmore kissed Fleur and left to find Vincent grooming horses outside their stables. "Son, I suggest you ride to Sidford this day and ask Sir Henry and Lady Alys for Felicity's hand in marriage."

Vincent's smile almost pushed back his ears. "Yes, Father, as you command." He mounted his horse and spurred it toward Sidmouth.

*****

That evening, Rockmore reviewed his financial statements by candlelight whilst Fleur read a book by the fire. She glanced at Rockmore and walked to him.

"My love, you must stop rubbing your eyes. Your whites, they are completely red."

"I must concede, threes, fives, and eights have become indistinguishable."

Fleur kissed Rockmore's eyes. "Soon you will be fifty-one years old. It is time for you to be fitted with spectacles."

Rockmore sat Fleur on his lap, and kissed her. "As always, *Querida*, you are right. Tomorrow, I'll seek an oculist and have a fitting for several pairs."

*****

On another pleasant summer day in 1716, Rockmore sat with Fleur on that same bench away from their villa overlooking the Channel. "My love, I worry for Cordelia."

"Is there something I don't know? Cordelia seems happy and content."

"But she is now twenty-two and unwed."

"By her own choice."

"We cannot count the number of proposals she has rejected. No title, no charm, or good looks have caused her to fall in love. Do you think perhaps Cordelia may have a preference for her own gender?"

"Absolutely not. She still has time. As you know, I was twenty-three when we wed. I had no dowry, and young men in our Sephardic community did what their families demanded."

Rockmore kissed Fleur's cheek. "Fortunately for me."

"And for me when we first saw each other. I believe Cordelia will experience the same. She has confided in me that the young men she finds initially attractive are dull and shallow, unable to discuss philosophy, science, politics, and music intelligently. She enjoys more the company of philosophers and musicians like Handel. I foresee when Cordelia is settled with her own household, she will preside over the greatest salon in London."

"I so want to see her happily wed."

*****

Back in London, after summer, Rockmore met with Abraham Santcroos at his banker's office to discuss certain investments. His friend introduced him to a guest.

"Lord Rockmore, this is Don Aaron Furman from New York in the Americas. Don Aaron, Lord Rockmore is a grandson of Don Isaac de Rocamora, of whom we were speaking."

Rockmore made an instant positive evaluation of Aaron Furman: flaming red hair, hazel eyes, freckles, about five feet eight inches in height, stocky, muscular physique, and engaging personality.

"Lord Rockmore, I am honored to meet you. Were it not for your grandfather, I and my family would never have existed."

Rockmore listened, intrigued, to a story he'd not heard before. In 1648, his grandfather had encountered a twelve-year-old Polish refugee girl who'd fled a Cossack pogrom. He rescued Miriam bas Yaacov from pimps who tried to lure her into prostitution with false promises.

"Miriam was my grandmother," Aaron continued. "Your grandfather brought Miriam into his household as a servant to assist his wife, who was pregnant with her firstborn..."

My father.

"... and treated her more as a family member. Seven years later, she met my grandfather Lyzor, another refugee, but from Russia, and they fell in love. Your grandfather arranged for their marriage. Lyzor had been a furrier in Russia, but worked as a tailor in Amsterdam. In 1665..."

My year of birth.

"...your grandfather financed their voyage to New Amsterdam, as it was called then, with money enough to start a business. Lyzor became a furrier and took a new surname, Furman. He became sought after because of his skill with animal pelts, and my grandmother invested in property. They had six children who survived and became wealthy enough to build a grand house in New York City and a summer home up the Hudson River. My grandfather passed away two years ago, but my grandmother, who is eighty, still lives in vibrant good health."

"And what is the purpose of your visit?"

"I plan to meet with your family in Amsterdam, and from there go to Russia. I hope to bring back pairs of minks, martens, and white weasels to breed in New York."

Mink, sable, and ermine; a worthy ambition.

Aaron went on to tell stories of his interactions with Indian tribes, bargaining and hunting with them for beaver, fox, and other animal pelts.

"For how long will you be staying in London?"

"Another two days, Lord Rockmore."

"Will you join us for our evening meal? I am certain my wife and children will be enthralled by your stories of life in New York. I will send a carriage for you."

"I am honored to accept."

*****

Furman made an favorable impression amongst Rockmore's family and entertained all with tales of his hunting for pelts and trading with Indians.

"Yes, Vincent, they do scalp their dead victims in war. One chief in particular admired my flowing red hair, so at night I cut my hair short, sewed it to a piece of deerskin, and presented it to him in the morning as a gesture of good will. I made a friend for life, and he offered one of his daughters as a bride. I had to lie, saying I had a wife in New York."

Furman had degrees in philosophy and law from Harvard; he and Cordelia discussed Locke, Hobbes, Spinoza, and other great thinkers, politics too, and the values they shared in common.

After Furman left, Cordelia sought a conversation with Rockmore and Fleur in the library. "Father, mother, do you approve of Aaron Furman?"

As I observed, Cordelia is attracted to him.

Rockmore smiled at Fleur. "He is a most intelligent young man. But approve him for what?"

"I need to know more about Aaron, of course, but he is the most accomplished, intelligent, attractive man I have met. If my first impressions hold true, I would wed him if he asked."

Fleur gasped. "And leave us for America?"

"For Russia, too, if necessary."

Rockmore took Fleur's hand to calm her. "Furman leaves in two days for Amsterdam, and then he will go on to Russia. Cordelia, you may not see him for six months or a year, if ever."

"Father, mother, when I walked Aaron to your carriage, I invited him for our midday meal and for the afternoon tomorrow. I pray you approve."

*****

Rockmore trusted Cordelia to make an intelligent decision regarding Furman. He met with Santcroos and spent most of the day at Parliament. When he returned home, Furman had not left. He took Cordelia alone into his library.

"Well?"

"Oh, Father, he is the perfect man for me. He is a Deist, a freethinker, same as I. Politically, we do have some differences, but he is an abolitionist and a Whig. Some of his siblings, uncles, and aunts have wed Quakers and Protestants."

"Has he proposed marriage already?"

"Aaron is waiting to ask you and mother for my hand. I pray you shall accept."

"Get your mother, and send Aaron to us. Wait outside whilst we speak with him."

*****

Rockmore and Fleur faced Furman in their library after each took a glass of Port. Under amiable but serious questioning Furman explained why he'd fallen in love with Cordelia. Aside from her obvious beauty, he praised her mind, talents, and uniqueness.

Rockmore nodded. "All well and good, but we have two concerns. You say you are twenty-seven. Why have you never wed?"

"The young ladies I have met are alike, interchangeable, all making the same bland conversation. I never met that special woman to attract me until Cordelia."

"I discussed you with Santcroos. He told me your grandmother and family have banked with his firm since the 1680s, but he would not reveal certain details. Have you an independent account with his bank, or is it part of a larger account controlled by your grandmother?"

Furman passed a document to Rockmore. "Independent, My Lord, close to £50,000."

Rockmore handed the bank statement to Fleur. "All that from beaver and fox furs?"

"And my legal business."

Fleur returned the document to Furman. "Should you wish to wed, no rabbi will accept Cordelia, even if she converts, for she is not born of a Jewish woman."

"I know that, Lady Rockmore. We discussed it earlier, and we agreed to be wed by a Unitarian minister. Under your new king they are allowed to worship and build churches. Cordelia and I, we both are Deists. She told me you would not object on those grounds."

"We would not." Rockmore sipped his port. "We fear losing Cordelia forever if you take her to New York, a great ocean away. If you had enough land, could you raise your animals here in England?"

"You would have more access to wealthy clientele through our contacts amongst the nobility and at Court," Fleur added.

"Land is cheaper in the Americas."

Rockmore refilled Furman's glass. "Not if it became part of Cordelia's dowry and in her name as well as yours."

"That is something I must discuss with Cordelia."

"Of course." Rockmore turned to Fleur, who gave an affirmative nod, and raised his voice. "Cordelia, we know you have been listening at the door. Please enter."

Cordelia flung open the library door and rushed to Furman. "Father, Mother, you approve?"

Rockmore handed Cordelia a glass of Port. "Yes, but we will not announce an engagement until after Aaron returns from Russia."

All touched glasses. Rockmore added a caveat. "Aaron, if you ever lay a hand on Cordelia, your life will end."

"Your daughter, Cordelia, My Lord and Lady Rockmore, may be more likely to beat me. I have been told of her prowess in archery, swordplay, and wrestling. And Freya guards my love with her life. You have educated Cordelia well."

Chapter Seventy-Five

Letters

Rockmore wished King William had lived to see Louis XIV's death at last in 1715. Felipe V hoped to overturn the Treaty of Utrecht, but Spain did not support another Jacobite-led invasion of Scotland until 1719. Rockmore shared the news with Fleur and family when stormy seas allowed no more than three hundred Spanish troops to arrive in Scotland. A base was established at Eilean Donan Castle on the Scottish west coast in April, which British ships destroyed a month later.

Jacobites tried to recruit Scottish Highlander clansmen, but created a fighting force of a mere one thousand men. British artillery defeated the poorly equipped Jacobites at the Battle of Glen Shiel. Clansmen dispersed into the Highlands, and the Spaniards surrendered. The invasion never posed any serious threat to George's Whig government. As a result, the Spanish and French thrones remained separate.

Rockmore told Fleur he could not be more pleased with Great Britain's Whig government and the cleverness of George I. "*Querida*, in Hanover King George rules as an absolute monarch. All government expenditure above fifty *thalers*, worth between twelve and thirteen British pounds, and appointment of all army officers, ministers, and government officials above the level of copyist, are under his personal control. But in Great Britain, George governs through our Whig Parliament."

*****

In June of 1717, Vincent wed Henry Lambert's stepdaughter Felicity. Rockmore gave them as a wedding present a refurbished Jacobean home on the Sid River in an area known as The Byes between Sidmouth and Sidford.

The day following Vincent's wedding, two letters arrived, forwarded by Abraham Santcroos, one for Rockmore and another for Cordelia, both from Aaron Furman. Before he'd left Amsterdam, he'd written to his grandmother about his love for Cordelia.

After Aron returned from Russia and arrived in Amsterdam, an angry letter from his grandmother awaited him. She commanded him to bypass England because their fur business was a family business. She added that an arranged marriage awaited him.

Aaron described his success smuggling valuable pairs of minks, martins, and white weasels out from Russia. He promised Cordelia that, after settling his family business, he would sail directly to England, marry her, and practice law in England. Aaron wrote Rockmore a similar letter and implored him to be his ally in convincing Cordelia he loved her more than his family and that his £50,000 was more than enough to support her without financial aid whilst he earned his license to practice law in England.

Rockmore and Fleur consoled Cordelia in their library. His daughter had yet to cry or react with anger. They compared letters, and Rockmore was surprised that Aaron had included his grandmother's missive as well.

"Did Aaron ever mention to you his grandmother had arranged a marriage?"

"No."

"Do you believe Aaron?"

"I want to. We should know if he is sincere in a short time. It is June. I shall expect his arrival by June of next year, and a letter before then."

*****

At the end of September, Cordelia received another letter from Aaron through Santcroos. He detailed bitter arguments with his grandmother and parents over his decision not to wed the bride they had chosen for him and his intent to move to England. Cordelia gasped after reading further. "Oh, how terrible for Aaron." Her eyes teared. "His grandmother, his father, they threatened to recite for him *kaddish*, a Hebrew traditional prayer for the dead, to disown him if he disobeyed."

Rockmore took Cordelia's letter and put on his spectacles. "Do not panic, Cordelia. Look here. Aaron added that he told them you are the granddaughter of Moses de Rocamora, whom his grandmother helped raise from birth. That changed everything, and they gave their blessing to you and Aaron marrying."

Excited, Cordelia snatched her letter from Rockmore and continued reading. "Aaron promises to visit, propose marriage, take me to New York, and introduce me to his family after we wed. Oh, how wonderful! He added he'd packed his belongings and was to set sail for Bristol in two weeks. According to the date of his letter, he must already be at sea."

Fleur embraced Cordelia. "Aaron has chosen you over his family. You may be sure of his love."

Rockmore kissed Cordelia's forehead. "I shall create a family compound in London, a house larger than ours in

Covent Garden, an adjacent home for you and Aaron, and another for Vincent and Felicity."

*****

Aaron arrived in early November. Rockmore had never seen Cordelia happier; neither had Fleur. Both women made plans for an immediate wedding, before Advent. A Unitarian minister wed Cordelia and Aaron, and Rockmore carried out his promise regarding her dowry.

In December, Vincent and Felicity announced that she was expecting a baby due in June. Rockmore embraced Fleur. "At last, we are to be grandparents."

He also reflected upon his three children with Fleur. They exhibited different personalities and interests. Eldest and most studious was Jacob, age fifteen, who excelled in science and medicine. He aspired to be a forward-thinking physician, the same as his great-grandfather, Vicente-Isaac de Rocamora, whom he admired.

Baruch, age thirteen, tall and athletic beyond his age, was a mystery to Rockmore. An image of his father, Baruch had yet to focus on a choice of career. Eleven-year-old Sarah Georgianna, resembling Fleur, and physically fearless like Cordelia, admired and emulated her half-sister in music and sport.

A surge of satisfaction overwhelmed Rockmore. He and Fleur had created a loving, harmonious family, their gatherings filled with love and laughter. They had music, too, when Cordelia played her piano, a recently created instrument invented by Bartolomeo Cristofori of Italy in 1700; Rockmore had purchased one for her in 1706. Whilst in Hanover, Cordelia had mastered the instrument thanks to lessons from Handel. To everyone's delight Aaron accompanied her on his violin, and Sara added her mandolin to each family concert.

Chapter Seventy-Six

Father and Son

Rockmore advised George's Hanover government at the end of the Great Northern War between Sweden and Russia for control of the Baltic. Sweden ceded Bremen and Verden to Hanover in 1719, and George paid Sweden monetary compensation for its loss of territory.

In early summer of 1720, sixteen-year-old Baruch completed his studies at Eton with decent marks, but not the exceptional grades his brothers and sisters had accomplished. Rockmore did not doubt his son's exceptional intelligence, gift for mimicry, which aided his skill in learning languages, and his innate situational awareness.

After a celebratory party at Sidmouth welcoming Baruch home, Rockmore walked with his son to a bench overlooking the Channel and flocks of noisy seabirds. Baruch was tall as he, a younger, more handsome and muscular replica of himself, Rockmore conceded, but the most difficult of all their children for him and Fleur to understand.

Baruch's mature appearance and how he carried himself made him seem to be a young man in his twenties. His blond mustache and goatee added to that impression. He also preferred to be addressed as "Barry."

Baruch spoke first after they sat. "Father, I know you and mother expect me to choose a career, a business, find some purpose, and perhaps even enlist in the Army or Navy."

"That is true."

"But I'm not like my brothers. Running a business like you and Vincent, choosing medicine or the sciences like Jacob or even the arts like my sisters ... nothing appeals to me."

Rockmore heard pain in his son's voice. "You have my undying love, and your mother's too. We want only the best for you. We will not cast you out with no means of support. Be assured of that. Perhaps, if we financed a Grand Tour of Europe, even as far as Russia, you might discover some purpose."

"I do appreciate your offer, Father, but I want more than that."

Rockmore listened to his son's true ambition. Baruch wanted to explore distant lands, including islands in the Pacific, Japan, China, India, Africa and South America.

"Yes, the entire world, Father. I'd be away for years, which I know would upset Mother, and which you would never finance."

"Do not be so sure of that. As we have provided homes for your brothers and dowries for your sisters, I am willing to finance your adventure."

"But what will Mother say?"

"She will resist your leaving but eventually agree. We have always believed our children must be free to choose their own paths in life, regardless of consequences, a family belief established by my grandfather. When do you propose to leave, and where will you go?"

"I have given it much thought, Father. I might be of value to your import businesses. I wish to leave as soon as possible for East Africa and India. I'll meet your factors there and see what else I might import from there and export as well, whilst traveling and learning about different cultures."

"An admirable undertaking, of which I approve."

*****

Two months later at Bristol Harbor, Rockmore and Fleur with their children said goodbyes to Baruch before he boarded a ship bound for East Africa and India. His mother and sisters hugged and kissed him, weeping as they waved farewells.

Fleur wiped away tears. "I fear we may never see him again."

Rockmore comforted Fleur. "Baruch might have joined the military instead. He will be living a life of free choice. I have arranged an account of £10,000 sterling with letters to my factors in East Africa and India to lend him more should he need it."

"He may not write us, or, if he does, his letters may be lost. I shall be imagining terrible things that might happen to our son."

Rockmore never voiced his concerns to Fleur as he did to his son. Baruch's itinerary included perils of foul and loathsome diseases, poisonous reptile and insect bites, hostile tribes, wild animals, treacherous false friends, and fatal women. True, Baruch had physical strength, skill with weapons, and common sense as shields against danger. Rockmore's final advice to his son could not have been more emphasized:

"Baruch, beware of men who would befriend you too soon and easily, and women working in concert with cutpurses, pimps, and other criminals. Rely more on my factors' introductions, their counsel, and your instincts, but do not reveal too much to them. They may view you as a business rival."

"I understand, Father."

Rockmore had also done what he could do practically to safeguard his son. "Your ship will be well armed, and most of the crew will be experienced Sephardim privateers from the Caribbean, plus some seamen who can teach you Urdu and Hindi, the main languages of India."

CHAPTER SEVENTY-SEVEN

FINANCIAL WISDOM

One evening in May of 1621 during a family gathering at their villa in Sidmouth, Rockmore read aloud the first letter he'd received from Baruch, sent from the Portuguese colony of Mozambique. His voyage had been uneventful; he'd learned conversational Urdu and Hindi from Indian crew members. Rockmore's factor, a Sephardic Portuguese, and his family had welcomed him in Mozambique and were most helpful. Baruch's next port was somewhere in India. He ended with expressions of love for his parents and siblings.

Whilst Fleur took possession of Baruch's letter and read it several times, Vincent asked Rockmore what he thought about investing in the South Sea Company.

"Son, I strongly advise against it. The South Sea Company is a joint-stock company. It was created as a public and private partnership to consolidate and reduce the cost of our national debt. To generate income, in 1713, Parliament granted the Company a monopoly to supply African slaves to islands in the South Seas and South America. As abolitionists we must never invest in that abomination known as the slave trade."

"I didn't know, Father."

"Vincent, always research thoroughly before you invest."

"I'll remember that. I have another question. Why did you remove all your currency and gold from the Wisselbank in Amsterdam?"

Rockmore took Vincent into his study for a private conversation. "As heir to my title and businesses, it is time for you to know everything. I should have told you this sooner."

Rockmore paused to light his pipe and smiled when Vincent did the same.

"Son, after William and Mary became king and queen, having England as an ally at first improved the military situation of the Dutch Republic. William III became uncompromising towards France. Dutch funds paid for his expensive military campaigns. By 1712 the Republic was so financially exhausted it withdrew from international politics and was forced to let its one great fleet deteriorate, allowing Great Britain to be the world's dominant maritime power. At the same time, my banking advisors convinced me the Dutch economy, burdened by a high national debt and high taxation, suffered from other European states' protectionist policies. To make matters worse, the main Dutch trading and banking houses moved much of their activity from Amsterdam to London, shifting world trade dominance from the Republic to Great Britain."

"I understand, Father. I must become better acquainted with your bankers."

"Our bankers, Vincent, and I shall henceforth include you in all my meetings with them. "

*****

Rockmore and his family followed new problems arising over South Sea's financial speculations and management of the national debt. Certain government bonds had been issued when interest rates were high. They could not be redeemed without the consent of the bondholder. As a result each bond represented a long-term drain on public finances because investors seldom redeemed them.

In 1719, the South Sea Company proposed to take over £31 million, three fifths, of the British national debt, by exchanging government securities for stock in the Company. The Company bribed Lord Sunderland, King George's mistress Melusine von der Schulenburg, and Lord Stanhope's cousin, Charles Stanhope, Secretary of the Treasury, to support their scheme.

The Company also enticed bondholders to convert their high-interest, irredeemable bonds to low-interest, easily tradeable stocks by offering preferential financial gains. Shares costing £128 on January 1st,1720, became valued at £500 when the conversion scheme opened on May 24th. In June the price peaked at £1,050. The Company's success led to speculative flotation of other companies, some of a bogus nature, and the government, in an attempt to suppress these schemes and with support of the Company, passed a Bubble Act.

The market rise ended, and uncontrolled selling exploded in August. Stock value dropped to £150 by the end of September. Many individuals, including aristocrats, lost vast sums, and some were ruined.

King George, in Hanover since June, returned to London in November, sooner than usual, at the request of his advisors. This economic crisis, known as The South Sea Bubble, made George I and his ministers unpopular.

Not involved, Rockmore followed subsequent disastrous results regarding The South Seas Bubble. In 1721, Lord Stanhope, though personally innocent, collapsed and died after a stressful debate in the House of Lords, and Lord Sunderland resigned from public office.

Sunderland, however, retained a degree of personal influence with King George until his sudden death in 1722, which allowed Sir Robert Walpole to become *de facto* Prime Minister, although the title was not formally applied to him. Officially, he was First Lord of the Treasury and Chancellor of the Exchequer.

Walpole managed the South Sea crisis by rescheduling debts and arranging compensation, which led to financial stability. Through Walpole's skillful management of Parliament, King George managed to avoid direct implication in the Company's fraudulent actions. Accusations that George I received free stock as a bribe proved to be false, supported by the evidence of receipts in the Royal Archives, which demonstrated that he'd paid for his subscriptions and lost money in the crash.

Chapter Seventy-Eight

Farewell to Amsterdam

Whilst panic ensued during the South Seas bubble crisis and investors faced financial ruin, Rockmore suffered a personal loss. His uncle Salomon Isaac de Rocamora passed away in 1719 age sixty-nine. Word from his cousin Lea Salomon Athais arrived too late for him to attend his uncle's funeral. She added that though Rockmore's father, Moses Isaac de Rocamora, was still physically strong, he was unaware his younger brother had passed.

Rockmore sent a letter of condolence to Lea, but chose not to visit during his family's year of mourning. He did not allow Salomon's death to interfere with the celebration of Aaron's having earned his license to practice law in Great Britain. As a gifted eloquent barrister, he'd soon be a King's Counsel.

In 1621, two years after Salomon's death, Rockmore's instincts alerted him that something might be wrong with his seventy-three-year-old father, Moses. He left for Amsterdam without giving advance notice to Salomon's family. Cousins Lea and Ester greeted Rockmore with affection at their family home in the St. Anthoniesbreestraat and told him his arrival was well timed. Moses lay dying.

Rockmore's entire de Rocamora and Touro family gathered in the parlor and dining room, praying for his father, but all avoided eye contact except their curious younger children. For the first time in thirty-three years Rockmore saw Sara Salomon Gaon, his cousin and first love. She did not dare acknowledge him. Her appearance disappointed and saddened Rockmore. Wizened at fifty-one years, Sara was identical to other older women present, all in mourning black, her youthful beauty gone forever.

Rockmore followed Lea and Ester to the attic where his father lay in bed, hovered over by Salomon's two sons, and a rabbi praying. He brushed past them and kissed Moses' forehead.

"*Padre mío*, I am your son, Jacob Moses de Rocamora. I am here to honor you and bid you farewell."

Moses died moments later. Excepting Lea and Ester, no one offered Rockmore condolences. No one asked him to be a pall bearer, nor invited him to Moses' burial at Ouderkirk Cemetery the following day. Rockmore went anyway. During his father's burial ceremony, he kept his distance and laid stones on the graves of his grandparents, uncles, and aunt. He waited until after all left Moses' grave to place more stones there and recite *kaddish*, the traditional prayer for the dead.

Rockmore allowed himself to grieve his old fantasy. *What might have been had my father and mother sailed as planned to New Amsterdam and wed? How many siblings might I have had? What adventures might we have shared?*

Rockmore returned to his grandfather's grave and held a long, one-sided conversation with the man who'd adopted, raised, and educated him. His self-pity and grieving ended.

Rockmore's grandfather once told him he was denied free choices to seek his own life. He wanted to soldier for the Crown but was tricked into swearing an oath to help his family advance politically and socially. They chose the clergy for him.

Many years earlier, Vicente-Isaac had promised his grandson he would be free to choose his own path, as he had promised Moses, whom he'd encouraged to wed Cordelia Schiffer and sail to New Amsterdam.

Those first years in England Rockmore had worried what his place might be. Now, he reflected with pride, he was one of the wealthiest and most blessed of men in Great Britain, his life further enriched beyond material wealth.

He and Fleur loved each other and celebrated their twentieth wedding anniversary. They'd raised accomplished children who gave them grandchildren, with more to come. Through good fortune, Rockmore was a Peer of the Realm in the House of Lords, and had served William and Mary, Queen Anne, and George I, rising to the rank of Duke of Sidmouth and making Fleur a Duchess.

Rockmore turned from his grandfather's grave and did not look back. No regrets—he was done with Amsterdam and all it represented. Tomorrow he'd sail to England, to Fleur and their children, where he belonged.

Chapter Seventy-Nine

Baruch Rockmore Returns

A week after Rockmore arrived from Amsterdam, his son Baruch returned with luxury goods from India that he sequestered at his family's warehouse on the Thames. Everyone remarked on how much Baruch had filled out physically and matured.

Rockmore complimented Baruch for his fluency in Hindi and Urdu, which he'd learned from Indian sailors during his voyage to Africa and India. With the aid and advice of Rockmore's Portuguese and Dutch factors in Goa, Bombay, and Madras, he'd made valuable contacts with Sephardic investors and exporters from diamond mines, coral beds, herb and spice plantations and with village headmen whose female relatives wove colorful bolts of silk. On his own he'd invested in herb and spice plantations.

Baruch's older brother Jacob, Fleur and Rockmore's firstborn, offered to purchase stocks of several herbs, spices, and teas he knew to be efficacious for healing his patients. Fleur, his sisters and his female in-laws gushed over bolts of woven silks with gold and silver threads.

Baruch had a keen eye for objects of art: statues, hand-knotted rugs of silk, cotton, and wool, and illustrated books. He'd also gained skills in haggling worthy of the predominant Muslim natives of the places he'd visited.

Baruch disappointed Fleur when he revealed his intent to return to India and Asia and do more business. He did not reveal to his mother his main reasons for doing so. That revelation took place during a private meeting with his father, Vincent, and Henry Lambert when he showed them the contents of a trunk worth a fortune, filled with diamonds, precious gems, and coral.

Rockmore squinted at Baruch. "Why is the *Nizam* of Hyderabad so generous?"

"I put those weapons I took with me to good use. This largess is both payment for them and an advance for another larger purchase from your factories. I arrived in Hyderabad at a most opportune time. Asaf Jah has been Viceroy of the Deccan under the Mughal Empire since 1713."

Rockmore interrupted Baruch "What is the meaning of *Nizam?*"

"*Nizām-ul-mulk* was a title first used in Urdu by the Mughals to mean "Administrator of the Realm.""

"And what sort of man is he?"

"Asaf Jah has much pride in his family origins, claiming descent from the first Caliph, Abu Bakr, successor of Muhammed. His family of *Nizams* in India also claim descent from Turkoman Khans of Samarkand who were favorites of the Mughal emperors. Asaf Jah will celebrate his fiftieth birthday in August. He is a trusted nobleman, and achieved the rank of General of Mughal Emperor Aurangzeb's army in 1707. In 1714 the new emperor Farrukhsiyar installed him as Mughal Viceroy of the Deccan—administrator of six governorates in South India, which includes Hyderabad."

Rockmore frowned at Baruch. "Are you sure it is wise for you to be involved in foreign conspiracies and internecine war?"

"I had no choice. From 1719 to 1721, Asaf Jah expanded his control over different Mughal princedoms and ended rebellions led by sons of former Emperor Aurangzeb."

Baruch paused to drink more wine. "By then, without informing your Portuguese factors, I offered Asaf Jah the arms I'd brought with me and trained his soldiers in platoon fire. At his final military victory, I served as Asaf Jah's commander of platoon musketeers. In gratitude, he offered me trading concessions."

Vincent held a diamond large enough to be a paperweight that he'd removed from Baruch's trunk. "And what is this lavish payment for?"

"I told Asaf Jah our factories manufactured those flintlock muskets, bayonets, and musket balls." Baruch produced a signed document. "Here is the *Nizam's* order for 1,000 each of our most advanced muskets and bayonets, plus many more musket balls. Asaf Jah has access to enough black gunpowder. He has added that if the weapons arrive in time, we will have exclusive trading rights in Hyderabad, and I will be appointed one of his advisors. He wants me to return as soon as possible with more weapons to use against further rebellions and likely encroachment by either the Dutch or British East India Companies supported by Portuguese merchants."

Rockmore placed his hand on Baruch's shoulder. "Well done, son. You have made me proud. Although I dislike your leaving so soon, we must fulfill the *Nizam's* order."

Vincent and Lambert agreed and also congratulated Baruch. They did not tell Fleur or anyone else about Baruch's secret cargo. Rockmore intended to provide Baruch with an armed ship and another trustworthy Sephardic pirate crew from the Caribbean.

Vincent said, "Tell me, brother, did the *Nizam* offer you a delicacy from his harem?"

"Vincent, I am not interested in his harem. I am going to wed a young woman from a Mizraim family."

"Mizraim?" Vincent repeated.

"Jews whose families never left the Near East or Asia."

Chapter Eighty

60th Birthday

The year 1725 was one of further Whig ascendancy, which Rockmore supported. As requested by Walpole, King George revived *The Order of the Bath*, which enabled him to reward and gain political supporters by offering that honor. Walpole became more powerful, gaining authority to appoint ministers of his own choosing. Rockmore approved Walpole's choices.

Unlike his predecessor Queen Anne, King George seldom attended meetings of Great Britain's cabinet. Most of his communications took place in private, and he did significantly influence British foreign policy.

With the aid of Lord Townshend and Rockmore, King George arranged ratification by Great Britain, France and Prussia of the Treaty of Hanover, designed to counterbalance the Austro-Spanish Treaty of Vienna, and thus protect British trade.

George I, although reliant on Walpole, could still have replaced his ministers at will. Walpole worried more about being removed from office by the Prince of Wales, the heir to the throne. Meanwhile, he continued to command a substantial majority in Parliament. Thus, the office of a powerful Prime Minister became a *de facto* fixture of Great Britain's politics.

"Great policy," Rockmore told Fleur, who agreed.

*****

One week before the Jewish Holy Days of Rosh Ha Shana and Yom Kippur in the Christian year of 1725, late at night in his study with Fleur, Rockmore drank his best Port and smoked a clay pipe. Earlier, his entire family had gathered at his home in their London compound to celebrate his sixtieth birthday. Still sturdy and in good health, Rockmore was aware of aging's inevitable results as he adjusted his spectacles and read wishes of gratitude, long life, and good health from his children and grandchildren, and letters sent by friends and colleagues, including King George I.

Rockmore recalled his concerns of decades earlier concerning whether he could make a life in England. *Dame Fortuna* had favored him beyond his wildest speculations. Thanks to his grandfather's bequest of five thousand gold florins, he'd inherited a foundation with which to build great wealth from wise investments. Also, Rockmore's conscience had never bothered him for keeping gold for himself from the derelict Spanish galleon because he'd given the Crown a significant portion.

Despite disappointments and false starts in romance, in Fleur Rockmore had found lasting true love and a perfect mother for his children, ensuring a personal dynasty of accomplished progeny.

Cordelia, Rockmore's daughter with Rosamund, so beautiful, intelligent, and talented, had made a successful marriage with Aaron Furman, a brilliant barrister, and had given birth to a boy and a girl.

Added to her accomplishments, Cordelia had a natural talent for law. She researched well for many of Aaron's cases, and in a just world she could have been a female Solicitor. That was why she and Aaron had moved permanently to New York. If she could not practice law in England or in the colonies, one day perhaps her daughter might have an opportunity to be a lawyer if that was her goal.

Rockmore appreciated Cordelia and Aaron making their journey across the Atlantic to attend his birthday celebration with their children. Their firstborn, Jacob, aspired to be a physician, and their daughter Abigael, a talented musician, resembled her mother in appearance.

Jacob, his and Fleur's firstborn, was already a successful London physician-surgeon. Jacob had wed the daughter of a prominent Sephardic physician. They had a daughter and another child due in a month.

Nineteen-year-old Sarah Georgianna, named after Fleur's mother, and no less a talented beauty, had in June of 1724 wed Prince Sebastian von Pfalz-Teuffelreich. They'd been playmates from early childhood, and the couple now resided at *Schloss* Teuffelreich near Dürkheim with their newborn son. They'd also come to London for Rockmore's birthday. Much of the prince's land had been ravaged by French troops, but his vineyards and wine cellars had survived. Rockmore had given Sarah Georgianna a generous dowry to help her husband afford the rebuilding his princedom.

Baruch, called Barry, Rockmore's second son with Fleur, had provided the greatest surprise amongst their children. He'd left home for Hyderabad a second time at age eighteen in 1722. Not all the letters he'd sent had arrived, and Fleur had suffered much anxiety during his extended absence until a message arrived in March of 1725 dated months earlier, with word that he expected to be home by summer in time for his father's 60th birthday.

Twenty-one year-old Baruch arrived in June with a mini-flotilla of three ships filled with goods from Hyderabad, and a wife. On his first evening home, he enthralled all with his adventures, and his wife Tamar impressed his family with her beauty and charm, which Rockmore and Fleur praised. Baruch's wife was sloe-eyed and of perfect form, and her flawless skin suggested polished mahogany.

Baruch described for his parents how he'd courted Tamar and wed her before they'd sailed from Hyderabad. He'd taught his bride English during their journey to Bristol. In addition to her exotic beauty and charm, Tamar impressed the Rockmores with her unusual dress of banana fiber dyed in alternating vertical one-inch stripes of sky blue and fuchsia with gold thread trim between and along the edges.

Baruch next described how he, with his cargo of weapons, arrived in time to aid Asif and his army to defeat all rivals by 1722, with the support of the new emperor.

Because of his ambitions, Asaf Jah resigned from all imperial offices, moved to the Deccan and established himself as first Nizam of Hyderabad, which also included the Deccan provinces of Bidar, Berar, Bijapur, Adilabad, Golkonda, and Hyderabad. With later annexations of Khuldapur and Burhanpur and access to the Bay of Bengal through Masulipatam, Hyderabad became the largest and wealthiest province in India.

In his study, Rockmore shared wine with Baruch. "Pray tell me Asaf is no tyrant."

"He is not. Asaf Jah I rules through common sense, pragmatism, balance, and restraint in his personal conduct. He wisely did not declare independence from the empire. He flies the Mughal flag and has not been crowned, while still ruling independent of the Mughal Empire."

Baruch described how the *Nizam* rewarded him with exclusive trading rights in Hyderabad and placed an order for more muskets from Rockmore's factory. "Asaf Jah antici-pates potential encroachment on his lands by either the Dutch or English East India companies. But now, Father, I have chosen another business. I met David Ben-Ezra, who has a successful business with spices and herbs gathered from India and Asia. He has no sons, and he was willing to take me into the family business if I married one of his daughters. I already was smitten by his eldest, Tamar, whom I wed in a Jewish ceremony."

"Baruch, you have done well in all you have attempted. Your mother and I could not be more proud of you." *I wish we could say the same about Vincent.*

*****

Later, when Rockmore was alone with Fleur in their li-brary, she interrupted his musings. "Our Baruch is, amongst all our children, most like you physically and in strength of character and purpose. But, I fear we have lost him to India."

Rockmore left his chair, went to Fleur, and kissed her, expressing gratitude for a life they shared better in reality than any imagined alternatives. "You are more beautiful than my first sight of you, and may we live long enough to see Baruch succeed in all his endeavors, and those of all our children and grandchildren as well."

"But I worry Vincent is a lost cause."

Rockmore sighed. "I regret I must agree with you. I am now convinced the Worthingtons have used Felicity as a will-ing cat's paw to gain control of Sidmouth through her mar-riage to Vincent. Something must be done about Vincent and the Worthingtons."

PART FIVE
FAMILY SCHISM
1737-1738

CHAPTER EIGHTY-ONE

BETRAYAL 1737

Seventy-two-year-old Lord Rockmore and his wife, sixty-year-old Duchess Fleur faced his eldest son in the study of their Sidmouth estate, the first time Rockmore had seen Vincent in almost a year. His son's appearance dismayed him. Vincent had lost weight and dark shadows surrounded his red eyes. His hand trembled whilst holding a glass of Port. Vincent appeared older than his forty years of age.

"My son, have you been ill?

"Sick of heart is what I feel. I am experiencing the worst year of my life."

Fleur encouraged Vincent to sit. "Is it your wife, Felicity?"

"I no longer recognize Felicity. It is as if the ghost of Rosamund, who gave birth to me and rejected me, has taken possession of Felicity. Her mother Alys and the Worthingtons have supported her behavior. Felicity and everyone in her family ignore me as if I no longer exist. I should have come to you sooner. We had a terrible row almost a year ago, and Felicity said she married me not for love but instead for the title I shall be inheriting and the status of Rosamund's royal lineage. Felicity behaves as if she already is Duchess of

Sidmouth and confessed her resentment of me for giving her daughters and no son."

Rockmore softened his voice. "Has Henry Lambert played any part in the Worthington's estrangement?"

"No, same as I, he has concentrated on our businesses. Father, the best thing you can do is to disown me and make one of your sons from Lady Fleur to be your titled heir, or Jacob, Delia's eldest son."

Rockmore accepted a refill from Fleur. "I would do what you said, but that cannot be done because England follows Salic laws of male primogeniture. Otherwise your older sister Delia would inherit my dukedom for herself, and after her, her son. You shall be the Second Duke of Sidmouth upon my death. If you have no sons, then Fleur's and my son Jacob will inherit the title."

"That will not happen. I have not had any opportunity to inform you. Last month Felicity gave birth to a boy whilst I was doing business in Manchester, and she had him baptized as Plantagenet Rockmore."

Fleur gasped, and Rockmore held her hand. They cried out together, "She never informed us!"

"Nor did she inform me, until the baptism," Vincent lamented.

"Can you prove Plantagenet is not your son?"

"I cannot. I have Felicity's oath that he is mine, and my name is on Plantagenet's baptismal certificate as his father."

Rockmore and Fleur chose not to challenge Vincent. "Have you spoken with your sister Cordelia?"

"No, because Felicity has severed all ties with my family, abetted by her family. What can we do, Father?"

"I cannot prevent you from becoming Second Duke of Sidmouth upon my death. Vincent you do not look well. We must isolate Felicity and her family."

"She has already accomplished that, Father. I shall go to Manchester and take care of our businesses."

And I shall consult with Cordelia and Aaron.

Chapter Eighty-Two

Rockmore's Decisions, 1738

Rockmore and Fleur summoned their children and older grandchildren to their Sidmouth Estate. He offered them copies of his new will, created by Aaron and Cordelia, based on his decisions where possible. They excluded Vincent, Felicity, Alys, Henry Lambert, and the Worthingtons.

Weeks earlier, Rockmore had bought out Sir Henry Lambert with a fair lump sum and ended their friendship because of Alys's support for her daughter Felicity's betrayal.

Rockmore obtained silence. "Be aware Vincent's Worthington family is dead to Fleur and to me. Because of English laws of primogeniture, Vincent and his son Plantagenet are heirs to my titles, but to nothing else according to my new will and current decisions. And, not one of you will appeal or attempt to change my decisions, which Fleur also accepts."

After Rockmore's attending children and grandchildren assented, he added, "I will supervise my factories until total liquidation, after which Cordelia, Aaron, and my grandsons, physicians and surgeons Jacob Furman and Jacob Rockmore, will inherit their shares. Our daughter Princess Sarah has already received an ample dowry to ensure her husband's castle is repaired and vineyards restored. Duchess Fleur will reside here in Sidmouth whenever she chooses until death. Only then may Vincent and accursed Felicity take possession."

Rockmore shuffled papers, poured some Port, and raised his glass to Fleur. "I am pleased to confirm several of the girls who were educated in our factory schools have returned home to teach. We have had success with others who've become musicians and nurses, and some boys who've become lawyers and physicians, also thanks to our schools. Now, to Duchess Fleur's and my children. Our eldest, Jacob, will inherit our account at Bank Santcroos-Salvador. Our second son, Baruch, will receive a significant sum of money, also at Bank Santcroos so he may expand his worldwide spice business."

Rockmore paused and opened a door to his study. He welcomed two men. "My family, meet your bankers, Don Joseph Santcroos and Don Moses Salvador."

Rockmore and Fleur supervised the introductions, and the bankers distributed and explained account books to their children and grandchildren.

That evening, Rockmore and Fleur raised glasses of Port.

"*Querida*, I believe we have protected our family from any possible attempts by Felicity and the Worthingtons to legally challenge our wills."

Fleur touched glasses with Rockmore. "They are dead to us."

"I wish we could live long enough to see our descendants survive and thrive over many generations."

"We have done our best to ensure that will happen."

"Yes, we have, *Querida*, and we can take comfort in that."

Fleur was quiet a long moment, then said, *"Mi amor,* I foresee after several generations of separation, our two Rockmore branches shall unite as one."

"I cannot foresee how, but I also believe they shall."

THE END

Author's Notes

I found no evidence in my research that Mary II broke her marriage vows. So why did I choose to write of a **fictional** affair with my **fictional** protagonist? I decided to apply the logic of human nature. Mary's father, James II, her Uncle Charles II, as well as many of her Stuart kin, male and female, were promiscuous. Why not Mary?

Historians have written that Mary II liked the company of attractive men and enjoyed dancing. Some documented her long and seemingly loyal marriage first cousin and husband, William III, as a Stuart anomaly. Unlike his predecessors, took only one mistress. Of all possible choices, he selected Mary's best friend from childhood, Elizabeth "Betty" Villiers. Some historians suggest that William, who also preferred the company of attractive young men, may have been romantically attached to them as well. I found no evidence he bedded any male. Those rumors seem to have been spread by William's Jacobite enemies.

Logically, Mary should have reacted in kind to William's philandering, given her hot Stuart blood, her appreciation of handsome young men, and her husband's long absences from England. Also, historians have written that William was abusive toward Mary because of his heavy drinking, his envy that she was more popular than he amongst an English population distrustful of foreigners, and over his frustration that she failed to give him heirs.

I have used sources from the Internet over many years. The two most important and useful sites are no longer extant: *The Scholars' Bookshelf* and *Questia*.

*****

For Raphael Sabatini fans, you may find the story of the historical Henry Pitman reminiscent of the author's superb swashbuckler *Captain Blood*. Surgeon Henry Pitman published his misadventures as an indentured slave in *A Relation of the Great Sufferings and Strange Adventures of Henry Pitman* in 1689. To find Sabatini's extensive, well-documented inspiration on the Internet, please Google "Henry Pitman Surgeon" or *Captain Blood, the History Behind the Novel* by Cindy Vallar.

For the Reader

Rocamora Rising was completed for publication after I celebrated my 91st birthday on June 24, 2023. I have three more novels in mind for the Rocamora-Rockmore saga. It will need at least two years to research and write each of those novels, with no guarantee I will live long enough to complete and see all three novels published. So, I now summaries each of those three books because I do not know how much time I have left to research and write them.

Projected Fourth Rocamora-Rockmore Novel

Baruch Rockmore's Mizraim wife Tamar bas Ezra gives birth to six boys and three girls. Baruch's sons, sons-in-law, and grandsons follow him in the spice trade, settling in Basra, Madras, Manila, Hong Kong, Shanghai, Rangoon, Jakarta, and Singapore. **Ezra Rockmore**, descended from Baruch Rockmore, is the Protagonist of my fourth projected novel. By the early 1800s, Rockmore Spices becomes a brand name.

During the colonies' War of Independence, a titled English Rockmore officer battles against Furman Rockmore. After independence and the War of 1812, Ezra's family sends him to Oxford University in England where, after graduation, he is expected to open a warehouse on the Thames River for his family's spices. British classmates and professors at Oxford label Ezra a WOG, "Worthy Oriental Gentleman," because he resembles men from the Near East by complexion and features. In London, he is rejected by the Rockmore descendants of Vincent and Felicity, who deny they have Jewish origins.

Angered by the prejudice he experiences in Great Britain, Ezra moves to New York, where his Furman cousins welcome him. Ezra goes to law school and weds a Furman daughter. She gives birth to a son named Morris, Hebrew name Moses, and two daughters. A scarlet fever epidemic kills Ezra's wife and daughters. Ezra and Morris survive.

In 1846, the Furmans and Ezra support the creation of America's first Reform Jewish Synagogue in New York City.

Ezra plans to travel westward to California, open a warehouse for his family's spices, and import and sell them throughout the West.

Ezra and sixteen-year-old Morris leave for California in 1848 and move faster than they would if attaching themselves to a wagon train. Farther West, they are captured by Lakota Sioux Indians. Ezra and Morris are the first Jews encountered by these Native Americans.

Morris' riding and wrestling skills impress the tribal leaders, and he is talked into participating in their Sundance Ritual to become a member of their tribe. Morris attracts one of the chief's daughters, but he and Ezra attach themselves to a wagon train of Scandinavian farmer immigrants. Morris has a romance with Christina, a girl his age, but religious differences end it.

A cavalry company on the way to California, because gold has been discovered, protects the wagon train. The officers want Morris to apply to West Point because of his physical skills.

In San Francisco, Ezra establishes his warehouse in San Francisco, practices law, and weds a daughter of German Jews who have a thriving department store. Morris goes to West Point and returns four years later as a lieutenant. He rescues the daughter of a Spanish land grant family threatened by land grabbers. They wed and have several children. So do Ezra and his wife.

The Civil War begins. Morris returns to the army and leads a regiment of California volunteers, including many Vaqueros. Morris is promoted to colonel at Gettysburg, and his success on the battlefield impresses General Grant. However, Morris' wife and children in California die from malaria. After the war, Ezra's family grows, but Morris is lonely and restless.

Grant becomes President and asks Morris to be Ambassador at Large with the rank of Brigadier General, visiting the armies of England, France, Prussia, Russia and Austria-Hungary. Morris has a typically unpleasant encounter with the noble Rockmores of Sidmouth, who deny any relationship. Back in California, he weds a relative of Ezra's wife and joins his father in importing and selling spices.

Fifth Projected Rocamora-Rockmore Novel
1906-1936

The Rockmores prosper and are part of the wealthy elite population of San Francisco in the last decades of the nineteenth and early twentieth centuries. An amateur pilot, **Nathaniel "Rocky" Rockmore,** grandson of Morris Rockmore, is the protagonist for this fifth novel. He graduates from the University of California at Berkeley at age twenty-one in June of 1916, and that evening he is expected to announce his engagement to debutante heiress Mitzi Rhinelander, whose father owns much property and stocks.

After Nathaniel announces instead his intention to leave for France and fly with the Lafayette Escadrille, he burns bridges with Mitzi and her family.

In France, Rocky achieves acedom. Subsequently, he receives in the mail a section of a San Francisco newspaper sent by his parents. The society page is about Mitzi's marriage to a rival Rocky disliked as a twit.

Rocky meets and falls in love with Gabrielle, the daughter of a French noble. After the United States enters the war, Rocky switches to the U.S. Army Air Corps and is given command of a fighter group. He and Gabrielle wed, and in 1918 Gabrielle gives birth to their son.

The great postwar influenza kills his wife and her family. Rocky's son Roland survives, and he brings him home to America after the war.

Nathaniel introduces Rocky to an international secret society, G.O.D., Guardians of Democracy, which is anti-Fascist, anti-Communist, anti-absolute monarchy, and anti-authoritarian dictators. Based on news from his family members in the spice trade, Nathaniel and Rocky are convinced that war with Japan is inevitable.

In the 1930s G.O.D. believes the Prince of Wales has fascist leanings and do what can be done to disqualify him as the future King of England.

Roland loves flying, same as his father Rocky. Nathaniel's former fiancé Mitzi is a divorced alcoholic and wants him, but he rejects her. Age eighteen, Roland arrives in Spain in 1936 and flies for the Republicans. He shoots down two Italian planes, as well as one German plane that crashes behind Republic lines. Roland lands beside it. He inspects the cockpit and finds documents and correspondence belonging to the dead pilot, who is a fascist Rockmore from England, Plantagenet Rockmore III. End of the fifth Rockmore-Rocamora novel.

red rag and pink flag
black shirt and brown
strut mince and stink brag
have all come to town
some like them shot
some like them hung
some like them in the twat
nine months young

— e.e. cummings

Sixth and final novel in the Rocamora-Rockmore Saga,1936-1946

Roland Rockmore is the protagonist of this sixth novel. The Spanish Republicans lose. Aid from Germany and Italy ensures Francisco Franco becomes dictator of Spain. Roland escapes both fascists and Stalinists and returns home in 1937.

But not for long. In 1938 Roland is in England as George VI becomes King. After England and France declare war against Germany in 1939, Roland joins the Eagle Squadron of the R.A.F., which welcomes American pilots. During the Battle of Britain he scores many kills in his Spitfire and becomes an ace. Meanwhile, Japanese soldiers murder Rockmore Spice merchants in conquered cities.

Roland meets Cecilie, a captain in Great Britain's WAAF, the Women's Auxiliary Air Force, and a Rockmore. Roland tells her he shot down her brother in Spain and gives her the documents he saved. Cecilie concedes that Plantagenet III was a fascist, shunned by his parents and relations.

When Roland explains the origin of their surnames, Cecilie is skeptical. She emphasizes her family has no evidence of the First Duke and Duchess of Sidmouth and their children in her family's records.

Roland switches from the Eagle Squadron to the American 8th Air Force after the USA enters the war. His father, Nathaniel, is attached to the 8th Air Force Intelligence.

Germany unleashes V-2 rockets as terror weapons against English civilian targets, and debris from one hits part of the Rockmore London estate. A hidden trap door is exposed. Below, a portrait of the real First Duke and Duchess of Sidmouth is exposed. More suppressed documents prove Roland is right about the dukedom's origins.

London Furmans add more proof. Cecilie ensures Roland is declared the male heir to the dukedom. They wed after the war, and the Rockmore family division ends.

ABBREVIATED DE ROCAMORA GENEALOGY

**fictional*

Vicente-Isaac (1601-1684)
  m (1647) Abigail Moses Touro y Delgado (1621-1663)

—Moses Isaac (b 1648) **m *Cordelia Schiffer*
  —** Jacob Moses (b 1665)*

— Salomon (b 1650) m (1669) Abigail Abraham Touro
  —Sara
  —Lea
  —Isaac
  —Ester
  —Hanna
  —Debora
  —Abraham

April 5, 1712. Publication of the banns of Isaac Salomon de Rocamora from Amsterdam, Doctor of Medicines, 36 years old, living in the St. Anthoniesbreestraat, assisted by his father Salomon Isaac Rocamora and Rachel Mendes da Costa from Bayonne, 20 years old, parents deceased, assisted by her uncle and guardian Samuel Henries Medina, living on the Zwanenburgwal. Isaac de Rocamora and Rachel Mendes da Costa were the parents of Daniel circumcised February 17, 1729 and Salomon circumcised March 18, 1713). --Note, the date for Daniel is suspect and may be in error —JR

And in a letter from the same dated May 13, 1987, Dr. Pieterse adds further:

June 24, 1712. Publication of the banns of Abraham de Rocamora from Amsterdam, medical doctor, 30 years old, living in the St. Antoniesbreestraat, assisted by his father Salomon de Rocamora and Rachel da Costa Athias (from Amsterdam, 14 years old, living as above, assisted by her father Isaac da Costa Athias). According to this deed and *ketuba/dowry* registration, Abraham was the son of Salomon Isaac de Rocamora and Venetian Abigail Touro.

Fictional Characters As They Appear

Jacob Moses de Rocamora, aka Jack Rockmore, fictional grandson of historical Vicente-Isaac de Rocamora and son of historical Moses Isaac de Rocamora and his subsequent children from fictional wives.

Lady Joan Fairfield, lady-in-waiting to Mary Stuart

Dirck Van Noordwijk, Dutch Ambassador and Jacob's mentor

Colonel Sir Randall MacFarlane, regimental commander

Henry Lambert, Huguenot cavalry officer, Jacob's loyal friend

Edmund Wilmot, Lord Lyndby, cavalry officer, slave owner

Ramses, aka Sean Wilmot, Lyndby's mulatto half-brother and slave

Hugh Tinker, Rocamora's valet and bodyguard

Lady Barbara Corning,
    owner of a hotel, gambling club and bordello

Sir Simon Montrose, magistrate

John Lambert, Henry's father

Douglas Greenway, Baron Dumbrille, Rockmore's inveterate political opponent

Admiral Pierce, commander of a flotilla

Barbados Planter Sir Arthur Greenway and sons

Lady Mary Wilmot, Greenway's sister and Edmund's mother

John Hobart, Wilmot Plantation overseer

Mattie, mulatta slave

Agamemnon, mulatto slave

Abraham Mendes, Sephardic bookkeeper for the Wilmots

Joseph Salvador, Jacob's classmate at their *Yesibót*, religious school, in Amsterdam

Don Samuel Abarbanel, Barbados merchant banker

Caleb Fletcher, ship's captain

Hugh Tinker, Rockmore's valet/majordomo

Lady Rosamund de Clifford, heiress of Basingstoke, Rockmore's first wife.

Bailiff Hugh Watson, De Clifford Manor seneschal

Mrs. Havers, Rosamund's chatelaine

Abraham Santcroos and family, one of Rockmore's bankers

Sir Basil Worthington, seneschal of the Sidmouth Estate

Lady Agatha, Sir Basil's wife

Lady Alys, Worthington's widowed sister

Felicity, Alys's daughter

Aaron Furman, a furrier and attorney from New York

ACKNOWLEDGMENTS

Publishers

Publisher-Artist Pam Marin Kingsley "discovered" me and published my first four novels.

Publisher Michael James, of Penmore Press, republished my first four novels and three subsequent novels.

Agents

Al Kingston, my first Hollywood agent, set in motion my sale of a teleplay for the TV series MR. NOVAK.

Bernie Sindell, my second Hollywood agent, completed the sale of my teleplay to MR. NOVAK, directed by IDA LUPINO.

Both passed away shortly after.

Muriel Nellis, literary agent, tried to sell ROCAMORA in the 1990s when conventional trade "wisdom" lacked enthusiasm for historical fiction.

Those Who Hired Me to Write Without an Agent

Paul Stader, Sr., stuntman, fight choreographer, fencing master, 2nd Unit Director, stunt double for Cary Grant and others, asked me to co-author a film script about Hare and Hounds motorcycle racing.

My uncle Louis Krieger who arranged for me to meet Paul Stader, mentioned above.

Dan Dale Alexander, "Health food Guru," author of *Arthritis and Common Sense*, hired me to ghost for him *Your Hair and Your Diet*.

Producer Sig Schlager hired me to write a film about the Native American Ghost Dance, the massacre at Wounded Knee, a fictionalized meeting between Sitting Bull and artist Frederic Remington, and the murder of Sitting Bull.

Carl DeSantis hired me to write as a "with" his creation of Rexall Sundown Vitamins, Vitamin En*riched*, and to write as a "with" for Dr. Lawrence Hakim's *The Couple's Disease* about causes, cures, and prevention of sexual dysfunction.

Bill DeClemente, real life "Karate Kid," hired me to help write his autobiography as a "with."

Those Who Encouraged and/or Promoted My Writing

Louis and Ruth Platt, TIP, my parents, who bought every book I wanted and allowed me to read novels they read when I was as young as eight.

Seamon Glass, RIP, Marine, actor in films, TV, and commercials, journalist, author, high school counselor and Santa Monica Harbor Patrol.

Gary Brown, RIP, Marine, best friend of 31 years in Florida, whose introductions led to my meeting the above-mentioned Carl DeSantis.

Barnaby Conrad, RIP, famed author, diplomat, restaurateur, matador, and writers' workshop creator who encouraged my writing and approved his positive "Blurb" on the front cover of ROCAMORA.

Famed Author Anita Shreve praised my writing, predicted I would sell ROCAMORA, and introduced me to her editor at Little Brown.

Others are mentioned in Acknowledgments in each of my published novels.

Deceased Educators Who Influenced Me

Having been a high school teacher and Social Studies Department Chairman, I wish to credit specific educators who made positive contributions to my academic and social development.

Miss Valis, Vine Street Elementary School in Hollywood, rescued me from a boring second semester of kindergarten and placed me in the First Grade, January 1938.

The teachers and student teachers of Frederick Burke Elementary attached to San Francisco State Teachers College, who placed me another semester ahead in the Second and Third Grades and allowed me to develop my potential ahead of my school grade age, fall 1938-April 1940

Miss Green, my Fifth Grade teacher at Cabrillo Elementary in San Francisco, crusty on the outside but kind of heart, who expanded my vocabulary, 1941-1942.

Miss Tennessee Kent, my Sixth Grade and all-time best teacher, 1942-1943, who at Cabrillo encouraged my love of history and ability to mimic film cartoon characters and movie stars, and taught our class how to dance foxtrot, waltz, rhumba and samba to prepare us for Junior High, along with folk dances and so much more.

Mr. Briggs, my biology teacher at Presidio Jr. High in San Francisco, 1944-1945, the best science teacher I had, including in high school and college.

Mrs. Bowman, drama teacher at Presidio, 1944-1945, who encouraged my acting and introduced us to Shakespeare, teaching "The Taming of the Shrew" and arranged for our class to see the greatest Othello production with Paul Robeson, Jose Ferrer, and Uta Hagen.

Miss Beardsley and Mrs. Kallberg whose English teaching at Lowell High School in San Francisco, 1945-1948, improved my writing and introduced me to great American and English authors.

Mr. Tucker, my Latin teacher at Lowell, 1945-1946, who kept his classes interesting and wore great sports jackets as examples of sartorial splendor.

Mr. Fast, social studies teacher at Lowell, 1948, who made his classes interesting and had us subscribe to Time Magazine.

Dr. Fred Stripp, my Speech professor at U.C. Berkeley, 1949, who improved my public speaking.

Dr. Jelevich, my Eastern European professor at Cal, 1952-1953, who allowed us to think for ourselves in his interesting classes.

Dr. Fischl, who taught Islamic Studies and Jewish Studies well at Cal, 1953-1954.

Dr. Roland Lea, creative writing professor at San Jose State (SJS), 1957-1958, who helped me polish my writing style.

Dr. Josephine Chandler, English Professor at SJS, 1958-1959, who improved my formal essay writing.

Dr. Jack Fisher at SJS, who encouraged my creative writing, 1959

Dr. Hans Guth at SJS, who introduced me to atheistic and religious Existentialism, 1959.

SJS Faculty judges who in the annual Senator Phelan Literary Awards May 1959 Contest awarded me a First and Second in Plays; First and Second in Essays; First and Third in Free Verse.

In Hollywood, Donald sold his writing to the TV series, Mr. Novak, and worked for and with diverse producers. After moving to Jupiter, Florida, Donald co-wrote Vitamin Enriched, 1999, for Carl DeSantis, founder of Rexall Sundown Vitamins; and The Couple's Disease, 2002, for Lawrence S. Hakim, MD, FACS, Head of Sexual Dysfunction Unit at the Cleveland Clinic.

Born and raised in San Francisco and a graduate of Lowell High school and U.C. Berkeley, Donald also has taught History, English, and Creative Writing and has been an Adjunct Professor of Writing at Polk Community College. He currently resides in Winter Haven, Florida with his wife, Ellen,

Donald is also currently being house trained by his new cat, Bodo, a loquacious tyrant.

Photograph of Donald Michael Platt, courtesy of:
Richard V. Pezzimenti, Pezzimenti Photography
356 3rd St. NW
Winter Haven, FL 33881
Web site: http://pezzimenti.com/

ROCAMORA

DONALD MICHAEL PLATT

No man is closer to a woman than her confessor, not her father, not her brother, not her husband.

-Spanish saying

Vicente de Rocamora, the epitome of a young renaissance man in 17th century Spain, questions the goals of the Inquisition and the brutal means used by King Philip IV and the Roman Church to achieve them. Spain vows to eliminate the heretical influences attributed to Jews, Moors, and others who would taint the limpieza de sangre, purity of Spanish blood. At the insistence of his family, the handsome and charismatic Vicente enters the Dominican Order and is soon thrust into the scheming political hierarchy that rules Spain. As confessor to the king's sister, the Infanta Doña María, and assistant to Philip's chief minister, Olivares, Vicente ascends through the ranks and before long finds himself poised to attain not only the ambitious dreams of the Rocamora family but also—named Spain's Inquisitor General

PENMORE PRESS
www.penmorepress.com

HOUSE OF ROCAMORA

DONALD MICHAEL PLATT

A new life and a new name ...

House of Rocamora, a novel of the 17th century, continues the exceptional life of roguish Vicente de Rocamora, a former Dominican friar, confessor to the Infanta of Spain, and almost Inquisitor General. After Rocamora arrives in Amsterdam at age forty-two, asserts he is a Jew, and takes the name, "Isaac," he revels in the freedom to become whatever he chooses for the first time in his life. Rocamora makes new friends, both Christian and Jew, including scholars, men of power and, typically, the disreputable. He also acquires enemies in the Sephardic community who believe he is a spy for the Inquisition or resent him for having been a Dominican.

Praise for Rocamora, 2012 Finalist International Book Awards:

PENMORE PRESS
www.penmorepress.com

QUEEN OF BLOOD

BY

SARAH KENNEDY

The Year 1553

Queen of Blood, Book Four of the Cross and the Crown series, continues the story of Catherine Havens, a former nun in Tudor England. It is now 1553, and Mary Tudor has just been crowned queen of England. Still a Roman Catholic, Mary seeks to return England to its former religion, and Catherine hopes that the country will be at peace under the daughter of Henry VIII. But rebellion is brewing around Thomas Wyatt, the son of a Tudor courtier, and when Catherine's estranged son suddenly returns from Wittenberg amid circulating rumours about overthrowing the new monarch, Catherine finds herself having to choose between the queue she has always loved and the son who seems determined to join the Protestants who seek to usurp her throne.

Between Two Kings

By

Olivia Longueville

Anne Boleyn is imprisoned in the Tower of London on false charges of adultery, high treason, and incest on the orders of her husband, King Henry VIII of England. Providence intervenes – she escapes her destined tragedy and leaves England. Unexpectedly, she saves King François I of France, who offers her a foolhardy deal, and Anne secretly marries the French monarch.

With François' aid, she seeks vengeance against the English king and all those who betrayed her and designed her downfall in England. Henry must face the deadly intrigues of his invisible enemies, while his marital happiness with his third queen, Jane Seymour, is lost and a dreadful tragedy also strikes the king. The course of English and French history hangs in the balance.

From the gloomy Tower of London to the opulent courts of England, France, and Italy, brimming with intrigue and danger – Anne Boleyn survives, becoming stronger and wiser, and fights to prove her innocence. Her hatred of Henry is inextricably woven into her existence.

Penmore Press

Challenging, Intriguing, Adventurous, Historical and Imaginative

www.penmorepress.com